Patricia Reynolds

Keeper
of the
Souls
SERIES

A SCATTERING OF LEAVES
BOOK TWO

Copyright page

KEEPER OF THE SOULS SERIES
A SCATTERING OF LEAVES
BOOK TWO
Published by Old Crow Publishing
WASHINGTON

Copyright © by Patricia Reynolds 2019
ISBN: 978-0-9998348-2-4
LCCN:
Cover design by Damonza.com
Edited by: Roberta Edgar

January -1869, General Philip Sheridan quoted:
The only good Indians I ever saw were dead.

Later the remark became, "The only
good Indian is a dead Indian."

After the Civil War, General William Tecumseh Sherman, (a hero of the civil war)

was sent to be in charge of the U.S. Army's full-out assault to "quell the savages." He

said, "All the Indians have to be killed or maintained as a species of paupers."

ACKNOWLEDGEMENTS

As always… to the wonderfully, unique Timothy. A thousand blessings to you, and many more.

William Jenner - Thank you for your tremendous insight that has helped me along the way.

I think my sister's ears must be burning, listening to my endless calls, while reading to her. Thank you, Nancy Williams.

FIRE IN THE SKY

A METEORIC EXPLOSION OF light barrels down from the sky on this otherwise serene and peaceful night turning the darkness into light. Magnificent and frightening, the light blazes and flashes — pulsing like a heartbeat. Hidden Spirit lies unmoving. Curled into a ball, he feels a tingling sensation run up his spine. A jagged bolt of lightning riveted through the universe like pounding waves, setting off an earth-shattering phenomenon. The sky turns red, blood red. Then a huge fire bursts forth on the horizon. Flames licking, burning furiously, set the sky ablaze with a crackle of energy. Children scream.

Hidden Spirit stirs. Perplexing thoughts filter through his brain. He is able to move his limbs with his thoughts as his body flutters upward. From somewhere far off he hears the familiar whinny of a horse. He pauses. The screams reverberate in his ears. His thoughts are jumbled, confused, as he floats along, as if on wings, through the clouds of mystery.

Then he hears whispers in the currents. "Please help... don't leave us here. We are dying." But he keeps floating along as the clouds gather, propelling him along on the ethereal winds. He can feel the softness of feathered wings tickle his face as they whizz on past — the caw... caw... caw echoing through the winds and misty vapor. But the persistent whispers continue to haunt him.

"A warrior you have been and still are, even as you lie high in the clouds and walk between two worlds. If you choose to go with our Great Spirit, and follow the path into the otherworld, I will understand. But if you choose to remain on the ground of our mother earth, all will celebrate... the four-legged as well as the two. The universe hummed with joy and celebrated your birth, and now she awaits your decision... for that alone is yours to make. I will be with you, Mi-thakoza, whatever path you choose." His golden sheen shifts with the light.

Hidden Spirit feels light and free as the light and the airy dance of his forbearers chants, "Awaken my son, awaken!" Then he hears another call that stirs somewhere in his being — a desperate call. "Help us, help us," the voice echoes. "Despair is all around." He can feel tears dripping, stinging like hundreds of knives, penetrating deep into his wounds, and he can feel the suffering. "I need help. We all need help." He stirs a little more. "Where are you, Hidden Spirit? Have you forgotten us? Have you forgotten Morning Star?" A voice whispers. "Little Moon has lost all hope." All is still — deathly still.

Hidden Spirit drifts on, more slowly now, and hesitates at the entrance of the tranquil tunnel of light. Its illuminating colors beckon to him, calling, "Come inside. Be free." He is wrapped in a cocoon of warmth unable to move. He feels stuck between two worlds, and he sees life as he once knew, slowly slipping away. He reaches out his arms to the light, ready to enter the deep chasm, but something pulls him back—something mystical and powerful.

Then he looks down and can see the outline of hands and a beautiful face — images of raw, red, bleeding hands and trailing tears of blood... he can taste the salty mixture that flows like rivers. Then a startling image floats in front of him. He can see the outline of a noose dangling from a rope. He gasps, "Little Moon. What are you doing?" Then he feels a familiar presence surround him — Chasing Rabbit. Her arms encircle his body. He feels chills and the rise of goose bumps.

Then he hears, "My brother — the one that lifts my heart and gives us hope. I beg you not to go into the light... not yet. You have much to do. I love you, my brother. Let your soul live." Hidden Spirit moves on, in his cocoon of warmth, waiting in limbo. The light at the end of the tunnel is powerful, capable of whisking you away in a flash.

A deepening hum permeates throughout the lands, getting louder now.

"Awaken my boy, awaken.

The world is awaiting.

Do not take the red road.

Do not listen to the call.

Do not surrender.

Come back to the light.

See the ones watching you, praying for you.

Awaken, my boy, awaken."

A deep vibration rumbles. Other spirits begin to sing and chant mysteriously. The sounds permeate his soul. Hidden Spirit blinks. He feels himself falling, falling at the speed of light. His breath catches in his throat as he zooms down, landing on the ground with a whoosh. Back inside his body, he jolts awake, and looks around in a daze.

In the next moment, he hears someone on horseback thundering near, as dust-devils rise high in the air. Amidst the foggy debris and dust, he hears a man holler out, "Whoa," as the horse comes to a grinding halt, sending clouds of dust billowing.

Amidst the foggy debris and through glazed eyes, Hidden Spirit sees a soldier hurrying over, then hunkering down next to him, where he spits hard on the ground. "Another stinking Indian. You alive, boy?" he asks as he shoves him over.

Hidden Spirit's eyes flicker open and he stares into rabid eyes, cold as frost. The soldier smirks. "Looks to me like you're half-dead. Maybe I could do you a favor and finish you off." He laughs at his own remark.

Hidden Spirit sees a glint of metal at the hip of the soldier, who stands, feet widespread in a pool of light, fingering his pistol and rubbing his chin, as if deciding what to do. Easing the pistol out of his holster, the soldier suddenly whirls around as he hears a horse trot over and paw the ground. Hidden Spirit smiles. The soldier cusses as he notices the boys grin. He pulls the pistol and aims threateningly. "You think that's funny, Injun… ?" Before he can finish his sentence, Ghost Dancer races over in a flash, and, with flailing hooves, knocks the soldier off his feet—the gun sliding from his hand. The soldier hobbles up and stumbles over to his horse, boots crunching hard on the ground. "Hope you rot in Hell." He kicks his spurs into the animal's side, and gallops off down the road.

Hidden Spirit exhales slowly and feels a wet nose touch his cheek—a shrill whinny sounds. Deep blue eyes stare into his, and the horse whinnies again. Ghost Dancer briskly clops in circles, legs and hooves shoot high in the air—like he is dancing upon a cloud of dust. The horse bends down and nudges him, as if telling him, "it's time to get up."

Hidden Spirit lifts himself off the ground, little by little, until he can stand without falling. He grabs onto Ghost Dancer for balance, hugs him tightly around his neck, and leans back against him, enjoying the feel of his loyal mount. As the blood returns to his limbs he hops gingerly atop Ghost Dancer, and whispers. "Let's go." Just as they are ready to gallop off, a sultry haze with unusual colors appears before him.

"Mi-thakoza, I see you are back among the living. It makes my heart sing with joy. There are many trials yet to come, as you have

MOONBEAMS AND UNUSUAL DREAMS

L ITTLE MOON AWAKENS in a daze and almost falls out of bed as an earsplitting sound shatters the silence. She holds her pillow to her ears to stifle the noise.

Mrs. Burns marches through the room blasting a trumpet, like an army corporal summoning the cavalry. The children are scared and don't know what to think, as they look at her, eyes wide in disbelief.

Maybe all the teachers are going mad or maybe we are losing our minds here, she thinks as she scrambles out of bed and joins the other girls, all of whom are covering their ears while slipping quickly into their clothing.

Little Moon's eyes are so swollen, she can barely see as she glances slowly toward Chasing Rabbit's bed. Her mind reels as dark thoughts come flooding back. She can't believe it… both of her friends are gone. *What will I do now?* She wonders. Her hopes of leaving this place have vanished with them. A sudden burst of tears cascades down her face and a loud sob erupts. She squeezes her hands so tightly together that she feels a stinging jab. She had forgotten she was still clutching the bear claw when she fell asleep. Racked with guilt, she puts it to her lips and whispers, "I'm sorry, Chasing Rabbit, I took your totem. It was supposed to protect just witnessed with that white man. You will be rewarded in ways that are not yet known. All will be revealed in time. Let peace and our knowledge seep inward—they shall be your guide. Toksa ache, Broken Feather says softly. He smiles with deep satisfaction, proud of his grandson, as he fades back into the sultry haze.

Hidden Spirit watches the mist vanish, as Broken Feather disappears. *It's as if he's light as a feather, gliding into the ethers.* He waves at the faint and lingering mist that blows away. He waits another moment, then, rides off in search of the children at the boarding school.

you. Maybe you would still be alive if you kept it. I know I'm not as brave as you. I wish I were… I'm sorry for being weak."

Little Moon sits back down on her bed, sniffling, paying no attention to the silence that descends upon the room. Her grief is overwhelming as she continues to talk to her departed friend.

Mrs. Trimble comes striding into the room and finds Little Moon still sitting on her bed, with her head hung low, rocking back and forth. She flings her arms wide in exasperation. "Miss Moon, there will be no lollygagging in bed today, or any other day," she proclaims, and whacks the girl on the side of her head. "Up and at 'em, missy. Today is a new day."

Little Moon sniffles, rubs her head, quickly hides the bear claw, and wipes her bleary eyes.

"Hurry up, and get dressed, young lady! Everyone has already left," says an irritable Mrs. Trimble, walking away, and then turning back. "I suppose you're bereaved about your friend. It was a tragedy she died, of course. But think about our beloved preacher, who was trying to help save the child, only to be viciously attacked by her. She could have killed the poor man. Now that would have been a tragedy."

Little Moon glares at Mrs. Trimble, and mutters under her breath. "I wish she had. Maybe then we could go home."

Mrs. Trimble is horrified. "What vile words did you utter? You must have picked up that Rabbit girl's bad behavior," she barks. "And her wicked ways to boot. You'd best pray she doesn't meet up with the Devil in the pits of Hell," she sputters. "I suggest you pray for your own salvation. Now, get moving. Opal's class starts shortly."

Little Moon rises to her feet slowly, grasping the bear claw even tighter. In her young life, she had never felt hatred… until now. She feels a surge of anger course through her body as she stares at the cold woman, causing her face to burn brightly. These new feelings of hostility confuse and frighten her.

"The good Lord says there is no better cure than a good day of hard work and prayer," Mrs. Trimble emphasizes, a little more kindly.

Little Moon's hands tremble as she reluctantly finishes dressing. Her mind is numb. She doesn't feel like going to class or anywhere else, but she has no choice. What little happiness she had known in this place, vanished in a blink with the death of her friends. She squeezes her eyes tightly shut to keep the tears from falling.

In Opal's room, Little Moon sits in the back row and stares at the man on the cross. It is obvious that the white man doesn't care about her or her people, and she can't understand why they are expected to pray to someone who threatens to send them to a scary dark place when they died. Opal's lecture is tedious, and Little Moon pays little heed to what the woman is saying as she stares dully off into space thinking of a plan.

*

In the dining room, Morning Star spots Little Moon, and runs over to her. She grabs her sister, hugs her tightly, and pulls her face up to hers. Seeing her eyes red and swollen, she looks at her little sister with sadness. "I feel like this is a bad dream. I pray to wake up one day soon, and find us all home—and we survived this place. I wish it were true for Chasing Rabbit. I can't believe she's gone." A tear slips down her lovely face," and whispers. "I don't know how we'll manage here much longer." Morning Star hugs her sister again, this time even more tightly, and says sadly. "There is pain everywhere I look. The eyes of the girls are filled with confusion and sadness. We must plead for the Great Spirit to guide Hidden Spirit to us. He's the only one who can help us get out of here. Let's make a promise. Every night before we go to sleep we must ask the Great Spirit to send him... before another one of us dies. We must believe he will come, Little Moon... we must," says Morning Star resolutely.

Little Moon looks blankly at her sister. She doesn't believe help will come, so she just nods her head in agreement as Morning Star pulls her close and smothers her with kisses. "I must go," says Morning Star, and hurries back to the kitchen where Mrs. Barlapp has been waiting impatiently for the girls return, while dishing up a steaming platter of fried eggs and potatoes. "You'll be the death of me yet with your tardiness. If only they could teach you how to be more diligent. Now get moving. You know serving my food cold fetters my hackles... it's an abomination. Those loyal, hard working, women deserve better. Now skedaddle before I wallop you."

Little Moon watches as Morning Star hurriedly places the large platters of food on the teachers' table. But this time she doesn't care what they are eating, and pays no mind to the mouthwatering aromas that drift her way. All she can think of is her friend who isn't there. She feels a growing emptiness inside her as gloom fills the void. She can barely think straight. All the girls are quiet as they stare at Little Moon, who sits staring at the wall, still too sad to speak.

Miss Snodberry comes to the table and whispers in Little Moon's ear. "Try and eat something, my dear. I am truly sorry for what happened to Chasing Rabbit. I know she was your dear friend. You must be devastated." She bends a little closer. "I don't believe she's in Hell. I believe with all my heart that she's with your Great Spirit." She pats the forlorn girl on her shoulder, and squeezes her hand. "Let me know if I can help. I could pray with you, if you like."

Little Moon's eyes blink in surprise at the woman's words, but she shakes her head no.

Later that day, after staring out the window in Mrs. Trimble's room, Little Moon is told to stand in the corner. Because she can't concentrate, she receives a whack on her legs with a strap to help her pay better attention. Red welts surface, but Little Moon barely feels them. Her mind is too numb, and she is oblivious to her surroundings.

After class, Mrs. Trimble stops Little Moon with a warning." You best get ahold of yourself, and soon. You will be taking over the laundry after today. This will be your last day in the barn. It's time you do your fair share around here and put in a little more effort instead of lazing your day away, playing with the cow. I hear you talking to that animal, instead of working… as if that beast understands what you're saying and can talk back." Mrs. Trimble snorts her disdain. "That just goes to show how backwards you people still are," she says smugly. "And that's exactly why you're here. To learn to be civilized…learn to be a young lady. Not talking to animals and such."

Little Moon's spirits sink even lower. After lunch, as she trudges down the gravelly path heading toward the barn, she can hardly bear the thought of giving up her cherished job. Once inside, she runs over to Bessie to tell her the sad news. "I won't be able to see you anymore, Bessie," she says, her voice quivering. "Mrs. Trimble says I have to do laundry now. She thinks I'm lazy, but I'm not, and she makes fun of me for talking to you. But I want you to know, I think you're the best thing about this place." She gives Bessie a big squeeze around her neck. Bessie stops chewing, and looks at the girl curiously as she twitches her ears. Little Moon pulls her arms away and pats the cow's stomach. "It looks like your belly is full. I'd better start milking you before you burst." She pulls the pail over, sits on the stool, and lets off a dejected sigh. "I have very bad news, Bessie. My friend died yesterday. Her name was Chasing Rabbit. You would have liked her. She sneaked into the barn once to see you and said that you were the most beautiful cow she had ever seen." Little Moon leans her head against Bessie. "She was so smart and brave. But now, she's gone. I'm sad about everything. I'm sad that I can't be with you anymore. I'm sad I can't go home. I'm *really* sad my two friends, Chasing Rabbit and Otter died here... I don't think we will ever leave this place. I have no reason any longer to live, Bessie. I feel like dying, too."

Bessie chews contentedly, glancing occasionally at Little Moon as she swishes her tail rhythmically, as if to soothe the girl.

Little Moon pats the cow and starts milking. The sound of the milk hitting the bucket has a calming effect on her. Once she finishes the task, she lifts the bucket of milk, leans over, and kisses the cow's ear. "Thank you, Bessie, for the milk. It's sweet, like you." Then she begins her next chore — cleaning the stall. She runs to get a shovel and rake and removes the droppings. When that is finished, she puts out fresh hay. Next she drags a bucket of fresh water and sloshes it into the trough. When she is finished, she walks back to Bessie and hugs her tightly while whispering in her ear. "Bye, Bessie. I love you and will miss you very much. You're a real good listener too. I don't care what Mrs. Trimble says about me talking to you. I know you understand. I think you're wonderful."

Bessie responds by letting off a soft moo, while she continues swishing her tail.

Bedtime seems to take forever tonight, as bed check is extra thorough. Mrs. Trimble rambles on to Mrs. Burns about the children and their lack of discipline and how much work is yet to be done.

Relieved that this long and miserable day is over, Little Moon starts to undress, and simply mouths the Lord's Prayer, not bothering to kneel, then climbs into bed, pulling the covers over her head. She hears Mrs. Burns talking to the girls. "Make sure you say your prayers correctly, and be sure to ask the good Lord's forgiveness for all your sins. Can't be negligent in that area. I'd say there's a lot of sin in here that needs forgiving. Now, make it snappy. It's getting late."

Once Mrs. Burns leaves, Little Moon hears whispers about Chasing Rabbit. "Do you think Chasing Rabbit tried to kill Preacher Jim?" one girl asks. A low buzz filters through the room, as the girls speculate about what happened. Not wanting to talk to anyone, Little Moon pretends to be asleep, and ignores the questions. Finally, the last of the whispers and sniffles is heard, and all turns quiet. A few of the girls start to snore lightly, and soon everyone is drifting off to sleep.

Little Moon waits for what seems like an eternity, then slowly eases her way out of bed, cautiously tiptoeing down the long dark room, hoping not to awaken anyone. When she arrives at the door she listens for any sounds of movement before fumbling for the handle. With sweaty palms, she turns the cold knob ever so slowly and pushes on the door... it makes a loud creak. Hands clasped over her mouth, she freezes, hoping everyone is still asleep. A couple of grunts are all she heard. Relieved, she sprints down the hall, slides around the corner past Mrs. Trimble's room, and heads toward an old storage closet — grateful for no more mishaps. Shivering in her thin nightgown, she slides past a window and skids to a stop. Her breath catches at the sight of a big, full silvery moon. A nostalgic feeling overtakes her, as she stands, looking at the wonder in the sky. She reluctantly pulls her eyes from the beautiful sight and then hurries on to the broom closet. Fall is fast approaching, and the nights are getting colder. Shivering, she blows on her fingers to warm them. She slips her hands around the doorknob to open it, but it doesn't budge. The heavy door feels as thick as a tree. After jiggling it for a few moments, she pushes hard, and it finally gives way as she stumbles into the smelly room. The strong odor of lye soap bursts out, assaulting her eyes and nostrils, causing her eyes to burn as she starts to cough. *There's no shortage of that smelly soap around this place*, Little Moon thinks, covering her nose. *They should replace that smelly stuff with food.*

The sizeable closet is full to the brim of every cleaning tool imaginable. It's crammed with buckets, mops, brooms, rags, soap, brushes, and odds-and-ends of every sort. Adjusting her eyes to the darkness, Little Moon makes her way over to a large window and flings open the shutters, grateful for the fresh air. Standing by the window, Little Moon stares once again at the silvery moon that is now rising above the treetops. She lingers, unable to pull her eyes away as she leans out the window, soaking in the cool fall evening and takes a deep breath. For a moment, Little Moon forgets where she is — mesmerized by the brilliance of the moon. She thinks of better times, of being with her family. The wind starts to rise and she blinks back to reality. With a sigh she turns slowly away from the window, then remembers why she is here. Determined not to falter or change her mind she walks through the stinky room looking for the wooden barrels she saw earlier in the day. In the hazy light, she spots them, and hurries over. But, in her haste, she trips and stumbles over a large metal bucket with a rusty washboard inside, and knocks it over. She cringes as it clangs noisily across the floor and goes crashing into a pile of brooms. Little Moon can't believe her luck, and gasps at the commotion she caused. Her mind races frantically. *What am I going to do?* she panics, almost in tears. She's ready to flee out the door, but stops at the sound of footsteps running down the hall — wooden floorboards rattling beneath. Without thinking, she races to hide behind a stack of boxes where she ducks down just in time as the door flies open, with a bang.

Mrs. Trimble emerges, flustered, with lantern in hand. "I know someone is in here," she says panting from her exertion, swinging her lantern high in the air. "You'd better show yourself before I catch you." She inspects the room with lifted brows and rising anger. "Who's in here? I demand to know. I assure you there's going to be big trouble if I find you, you hooligan. Stealing, no doubt."

Trembling, Little Moon bites down hard on her lips and slaps her hand over her mouth to keep her teeth from chattering. She chokes back a cry.

The floorboard creaks as Mrs. Trimble walks around the room, muttering under her breath and coming within inches of Little Moon. She is so close now that Little Moon can smell the woman's usual fragrance of lilies. She sees her angry face in the flickering light with her brows creased together in consternation as her eyes search the room.

Suddenly, a large gust of wind bursts through the window and, blowing with it, a pile of leaves and dust. The shutters bang noisily against the frame as the breeze extinguishes her lantern. She hurries to close the window, but is unable, as a strong rush of wind whips up fiercely, and blows more leaves and twigs through the opening. They swirl and scatter throughout the room.

"Damn and tarnation," she says, pursing her thin lips into a grimace as she smacks away the annoying leaves fluttering against her face.

"Yoo-hoo. Mrs. Trimble. Is that you?" Mrs. Burns sweeps into the closet wearing a floppy nightcap and a voluminous nightgown of tattered cotton. She peers around the dimly lit room.

"Yes, Mrs. Burns, it's me."

"What on earth are you doing here in the middle of the night? Counting soaps?"

"Oh, for pity's sake, no." Annoyed by the woman's remark,

she says, "I heard someone making a racket in here. I came to investigate. My duty, you know."

"Well… yes, of course. I know you are most vigilant," Mrs. Burns replies, dubiously.

"My lantern has gone out and I could use your help to close this blasted window. The room is full of leaves and such."

Holding her lantern high, Mrs. Burns rushes over to help Mrs. Trimble. Just then, another big gust of wind howls through the room. Mrs. Burn's nightdress billows up and around her stout legs, sending her gown flapping over her head. Screeching, she fights to pull the bulky nightdress down. "Land sakes, almighty," she says in a fluster. "It's blowing something fierce outside. Could blow us down if this keeps up. Let's hope it doesn't get any worse."

"Well, long as this darned window stays shut, I don't care what the weather is out there. The Lord will protect us and keep us safe inside," says Mrs. Trimble, as the ladies struggle to close the window and finally snaps the latch shut.

"Whew!" Mrs. Burns, breathes out. "That was a dickens to shut," she says in relief, straightening her nightdress. "Hope it holds."

"Thank you, Mrs. Burns. You have been most helpful. I'm grateful you came along when you did."

Mrs. Burns holds her lantern high, and they both take one last look around the room before leaving.

"Looks like everything's in order," Mrs. Trimble says with a discernible grunt.

"Well, I suppose we can go back to bed now," says Mrs. Burns. "I certainly hope there won't be any more commotion with the window tonight. I'm as tired as a hen that just laid a passel of eggs."

Mrs. Trimble sniffs. "Yes, but, as you know, the work of the Lord is never done, especially around here, Mrs. Burns. I shall inspect this room tomorrow and see if the latches are loose."

Little Moon exhales with relief as the ladies leave. "That was a close call," she says to herself, and hurries to the corner where the wooden barrels stand. The moonlight shines through the cracks in the shutters, providing her with enough light to see. She drags the heavy barrel under the beam and stacks a couple of wooden boxes, one on top of the other — making certain they will not topple. Standing on her tiptoes, she reaches for the twine hanging on a nail near the door, wraps the prickly rope around her shoulder, and climbs up the barrel. Undoing the rope, she makes a knot at one end and attempts to toss the other end of the rope over a large beam. It takes several tries, but it finally goes over. Then, she ties another knot, like the one she used for Bessie on one of those rare occasions she was lucky enough to take her to the pasture. Taking the bear claw from her pocket, she holds it against her heart, looks upwards, and speaks quietly to the Great Spirit, "Please guide me to the otherworld where I might find Chasing Rabbit and Otter. Please. And please don't be mad at me." Her words are barely audible now. "Life is horrible here. Everyone I love is gone, except Morning Star. Tell her, I'm sorry."

Sniffling, Little Moon slips the rope around her neck. "I love you, Mama. I love you Papa. Please understand my sorrow." Standing on her tiptoes, her legs wobbling, she tightens the scratchy rope around her neck. Taking a deep breath now, she squeezes the bear claw hard, ready to kick the barrel away, but stops when she hears a noise. Her heart pounds at the thought of Mrs. Trimble barging through the door again, so she tilts her head, and listens carefully. She hears a rustling sound at the door. It seems as if the wind has made its way inside the closet, as sounds of leaves whirl and whoosh about — while frightening images dance throughout the room. In a corner, a silhouette of Hidden Spirit illuminates from the shadows, and, for a brief second, he calls to her with outstretched hands — as if he's helping her. Just as she's ready to call out and take his hands, his grasp slips away, and he disappears back into the darkness. She wonders if the shutters came unlatched again. *The moonlight must be playing tricks... I must be seeing thing. I could swear it was Hidden Spirit.* She feels a cool burst of air sweep into the room surrounding her. *It feels velvety with its icy glaze touching my face,* she thinks. It seems to be caressing her face and she shivers nervously, not knowing what to think or do. Maybe she should hurry and kick the barrel out from under herself, or maybe she should hop down and run. Then, before she can contemplate any further, a chilly wind whips furiously around her legs, rocking her back and forth on the barrel. She struggles to keep upright, and smothers a scream as she loses her balance and tumbles backwards. Her scream is abruptly silenced as the rope cuts deeply into her neck, tearing the delicate flesh. She gasps and chokes as the rope tightens, cutting off her air supply. Sucking in a trickle of air, she kicks her feet wildly as she struggles in vain to regain her footing. Through glazed eyes, she sees a spurt of light appear from beneath the door, careening toward the girl — blinding her. She panics. *I'm going to die,* she thinks, in alarm. She suddenly regrets her decision to hang herself — but now it seems too late. A tiny spark whispers in her brain. *I'm sorry, Hidden Spirit. I'm sorry I didn't wait for you to come.* Suddenly, something balmy and peaceful fills the room. Its light and airy tendrils circle her cradles her with its obscure presence — picking her up and gently guiding her to the ground. Little Moon's head falls sideways — her eyes roll back in her head. She lies on the ground, unmoving.

A wisp of rose-colored light touches Little Moon's lips and breathes air into the lifeless girl. After what seems like an eternity, her chest begins to rise. Slightly at first, and then she gasps, sucking in huge gulps of air. Stunned, she eases her way to her elbows, and looks around the dingy closet in amazement, trying to understand what has been happening and who it was that helped her. *Maybe it was the Great Spirit,* she thinks, *or maybe it was Hidden Spirit.* She struggles to sit, holding her throat, still confused. Feeling a slight breeze brush across her face, she hears a faint voice, barely a whisper.

"Little Moon." The voice drips with sympathy. "I have come to help."

Little Moon's eyes widen. She is entranced by the silky voice. It's mesmerizing. Who is it that's calling her? She wonders, rubbing her bruised and raw neck.

"It is not your time, little one," the voice says.

Little Moon wonders if she is slowly, surely, losing her mind. First, she was seeing things, now she's hearing voices. She pinches her arm to make sure she isn't in the afterlife. Then the cool, comforting breeze grows stronger, sweeping across her entire body, causing her to tense and shiver. *Maybe the Great Spirit is angry at me for trying to take my life,* she thinks. Then she hears the silky voice call out. "You are loved more than you know, and missed."

She gasps at the words and struggles to stand, but she is too weak. *I must see who is talking so kindly to me.* She tries once more to stand, but falls back hard against the barrels, sending them rumbling across the floor. She watches in horror as they smash into the door, sending splinters of wood flying into the air.

Slumping to the ground, she is frantic with fear. *Oh, no! I'm going to get caught this time. Mrs. Trimble will kill me, or worse.* Then she sees a hazy glow — opaque and fuzzy — appear in the corner, standing alone. She squints to get a better look and begins to cry. *It must be a hallucination. Or, maybe, I'm going crazy.* Through her tears she sees the hazy image come closer — so close that she can feel the vibration and taste the cool mist flowing gently in the translucent breeze. A sliver of hope fills her trembling body, and she feels her tears dissipate.

Through the glowing mist, a face appears.

Little Moon's eyes grow wide with wonder the longer she stares. She whispers in disbelief. "Is that you, Chasing Rabbit? Have you returned, or am I imaging things? Am I alive, or am I going mad?" Her words tumble out in shock. "I think I saw Hidden Spirit too," she breathes softly, feeling a slight movement across her mouth and covering her lips. Before she can ask another question, she hears the sound of bulky shoes clatter down the hallway… in a run. As Mrs. Trimble's voice ricochets against the walls, the sounds are getting closer and closer. Little Moon panics, searching for a place to hide. She hears a voice whisper to her, urgently. "Stay calm." She is so confused she starts to shake — not sure where to go or what to do, she simply crumbles to the floor. Outside the door, Mrs. Trimble is yelling indignantly, "Open this door."

Little Moon's heart jolts in her chest as the woman jiggles the handle. It doesn't open. To her amazement the door is stuck.

Mrs. Trimble curses as she shakes the door again, violently.

"Mrs. Trimble," another voice shrieks. "What on earth are you doing out here, again?"

"I don't know what in tarnation is going on around here tonight, Mrs. Burns. More than likely there are spirits lurking about… evil ones." Shaking the door with even more force this time, it still doesn't budge. Mrs. Trimble is so angry she kicks the wooden door with her foot. "Blast it, and damn it. I've just about had it with this place — and these Indians. Being awakened twice in one night is unsettling enough without having strange goings-on, to boot. It's just too much, to be constantly on guard at all hours. I'm going to bed. Come along, Mrs. Burns. I don't give a rat's behind who's in that closet. They can steal all the lye soap they want… and the buckets and brooms, as well."

To Little Moon's relief, Mrs. Trimble gives up, and goes off in a huff. All the way down the hall, she complains to Mrs. Burns about this horrible night. After a while, their voices fade in the distance.

The drifting light floats overhead. Sitting in shock and amazement, Little Moon stares at the wavering shape. "Is that really you, Chasing Rabbit? I miss you so much. I prayed every night that I might see you again. I know you must think I did a terrible thing, but… I was miserable here without you. I didn't want to live anymore… not with these people. I hate them. I wanted to be with you in the afterlife, but then I changed my mind when I thought I was going to die. I thought it was too late, but someone… I'm not sure who… helped me. Was it you, Chasing Rabbit, or was it Hidden Spirit?"

She can see her friend's face a little more clearly now, as the form hovers nearby. "Oh, my," she says in a whisper, completely intrigued. "I can't believe this is happening. It really *is* you, Chasing Rabbit!" Desperately wanting to hug her, she puts her arms around her, and clasps icy cold droplets. A rush of cool air fills her from head to toe. She shivers. "The Great Spirit has answered my prayer," Little Moon says, filled with joy and bewilderment. Her pent-up emotions let loose and she starts to cry.

Chasing Rabbit glides closer to Little Moon, touching her face… sending out glittering sparks that light up the room. Little Moon instantly feels the force of love sweep over her. She wipes her eyes, staring at the bedazzling form in awe, and hears Chasing Rabbit say, "The Great Spirit sees your suffering, and it pains him greatly. He is with you always. You must remain strong."

"I will, I promise."

"I must go soon, my friend. I feel the strings of the otherworld pulling me, Little Moon… to the place of wonder and mystery."

The words sound like music to her ears and she feels a wave of joy spread throughout her body as the glowing light crackles with electricity surrounding her ethereal friend. "I wish you could stay," Little Moon says, wistfully. "Can I go with you for a while, to see your place of wonder and mystery?"

Chasing Rabbit blows away a tear from her cheek. "I'm afraid that is not possible, Little Moon. You must be brave now, like a warrior. Your life will change, I promise. Now, let me take you to your room. I have little time before I must go."

"Can you tell me... you didn't go to that awful afterlife like Opal said you would, did you? Mrs. Trimble said you were going to burn in Hell."

"No," Chasing Rabbit smiles tenderly, "I didn't go there. I'm not sure how to put it into words, where I was. I'm not even sure how I got there, but it's... well, it's... magical... like the stories we used to hear when we were little. I can tell you, I have seen crystal forests and talked to the dancing flowers, and listened to the rivers that sing... it's like nothing I've ever seen before. Broken Feather says I will soon go to the otherworld. I don't know what that means or how I will get there, but he says 'soon I will discover all.' I think of you often, Little Moon. Just remember,... even though you don't see me in the light, know I am near. You must stay and fight for our people, for the children at this school. Help is coming."

A bolt of silver stardust bursts into the darkened room, zipping throughout the room as if on wings. Then, in a blink, the glittering stardust zooms out the window, disappearing into the night sky amongst the stars.

Little Moon pinches herself to make sure she is not dreaming, and runs to the window to see if Chasing Rabbit has disappeared with the silvery dust. She no longer sees her friend, but blows her an imaginary kiss out the window and then makes her way to the door, ready to go back to her room. "Oh no. It's locked." Swooning from fright, she whispers, "I'm afraid I'll be trapped here until morning, and then I'll be caught." Her moment of wonder has vanished, and a sickening feeling of terror returns. For a fleeting moment she is unable to move. "I wish I could fly away with the stardust," she says in a panic. A dry sob burns in her throat. Suddenly something flutters against her cheek. She sees a faint glow flickering by the door handle and reaches up to turn the knob. It clicks. Her heart thuds as she feels the door swing open. She bounds up and jumps for joy, and hurries outside before it closes. Once in the hallway, she takes in a deep breath, hardly believing what has occurred on this incredible night. She walks down the hallway feeling light and giddy. Then she feels a silky cool arm drape over her shoulder, sending chills up her spine. She looks up in surprise to see the shimmering face of Chasing Rabbit smiling, gliding silently by her side. Little Moon is ecstatic as she walks back to her room, while basking in Chasing Rabbit's presence, asking a thousand questions. Once inside, Little Moon quietly walks to her bed, and whispers, "Thank you for coming back."

Little Moon is so excited about her friend's return that she isn't certain she will be able to fall asleep. She pulls up the covers, smiling, and asks her friend, "can you stay with me for awhile, Chasing Rabbit?"

Sensing Little Moon's excitement, Chasing Rabbit removes a stray lock of hair from her face and says, "I'm sorry, my friend, I cannot." She brushes her fingertips over Little Moon's eyes. Soon, they grow heavy and she falls into a deep languid sleep. Lingering a moment longer, Chasing Rabbit gently caresses Little Moon's bruised neck, and whispers, "Toksa akhe wanchiyankin kte. I will see you again."

LITTLE MOON'S SURPRISE

LITTLE MOON DRAGS the cumbersome bucket down the hill near the stream, ready to begin the day's chores. It's cold this morning, and her fingers turn numb in the icy water. She places the washboard into the tub, and begins to scrub. As she looks at the huge stack of clothes in front of her, she sighs, wondering how many dresses are in this heap. Some church ladies had brought some dresses over the other day for the teachers, and Mrs. Trimble must have decided all of them should be laundered today. "I'll be scrubbing until it's dark," she moans, "and my hands will be so raw, they'll probably fall off."

When Chasing Rabbit was around, this place had at least been bearable. Little Moon misses everything about her friend, especially her funny antics. Then her thoughts turn to the other night and she beams — thinking about her friends' mysterious appearance. She sits back for a moment reflecting on what she witnessed. She hugs herself to keep from shaking. She could still see her friend's opaque face glistening in the dark and could still hear her comforting words to be brave. "I wish help would hurry," she murmurs, looking up, hoping Chasing Rabbit is near.

"I don't have Bessie to talk to anymore, Chasing Rabbit, and she was a real good listener. I could tell Bessie I saw you and she would believe me. She wouldn't think I was seeing things. She understands everything, but mostly when I am sad. I pinch myself every day, remembering you and my night of despair and magic."

Little Moon looks at her huge pile of clothes. "Now, all I have is dirty clothes for company and I barely get to see Morning Star," she grumbles miserably, and she plops another dress into the water.

Mrs. Barlapp and Mrs. Trimble keep Morning Star busy all the time with their unreasonable demands. She hears them telling her to hurry up... move your feet... and on and on. *She always looks sad, and tired, and lonely... just like the rest of us.* Little Moon thinks and takes a deep breath. "I'd better hurry if I want to finish these clothes before supper." She picks up another dress and sloshes the gargantuan thing around the bucket, then shoves it up-and-down, up-and-down on the scrub-board. *My arms are already tired and I haven't even made a dent in this huge pile.* She stands up, stretches her back, and blows on her burning fingers, which sting from the noxious lye soap. She kicks the bar of soap that had fallen on the ground, and feels a brief moment of satisfaction. She smiles remembering what Chasing Rabbit once did with the laundry. *She got into real big trouble, too,* Little Moon thinks with a giggle.

Chasing Rabbit was running late and didn't want to get into any more trouble, so she gave the clothes a quick douse in the water, and added lots of lye soap... especially to the undergarments, and hung them on the line to dry. The women itched like crazy for a week from the soap. It was worth the spanking she got from Mrs. Trimble, she told her.

Little Moon brightens, remembering the story, but she doesn't have enough nerve to do anything like that. So she entertains herself as she starts to work by imagining the teachers scratching like a swarm of pesky mosquitoes had bitten them and that Mrs. Burns gets a big red rash. The amusing thoughts make the time pass, but only for a while. The water weighs down the clothes so much that it takes all her strength to lift the dresses from the bucket to the line. She can't understand how Chasing Rabbit did this, day after day—she is exhausted. Her arms feel like rubber, and the smell of lye soap nauseates her. The lingering odor seems to hang in the air and sting her nose. She flops on the ground to rest once again and dreams about the other night… when Chasing Rabbit appeared and saved her life. Death had come so close. Little Moon couldn't believe she was going to take her own life. She felt there was nothing to live for. She was wrong. The night turned from tragic to miraculous. She put her hand to her heart, and murmurs, "Thank you, Chasing Rabbit." She just wishes she would have asked more questions — like, when is help coming? She knows she must be patient and she's trying, but just how patient does she have to be — and for how long? She brushes a loose strand of hair from her eyes. "If you see the Great Spirit, tell Him to hurry… and we're sick of it here," she says softly. Getting back to work, she lifts a bulky dress that had been soaking — causing water to drip down her arms and onto her clothes, drenching her. As she pulls the humungous garment from the bucket, it slips from her grasp, and falls onto the dirt. "Oh, darn! It's so heavy. It must weigh as much as Mrs. Burns," she groans. She drags the sopping dress and heaves it into the bucket. Out of the corner of her eye, Little Moon catches a flicker of movement behind the dense grove of trees. Her breath catches, and she glances over to see who is there. Startled, she sees the gangly figure of Preacher Jim hiding behind the tree, peering at her between the branches. She quickly looks down, pretending she doesn't see him, and begins scrubbing furiously — wanting to leave, but knowing she can't. A queer feeling rises inside. Her belly thumps, and her heart races. She can feel him staring at her. "Oh, Chasing Rabbit. I wish you could come back now and help me. Preacher Jim is staring at me from the trees. I'll try to be brave, like you said, but..." Goose bumps rise up her spine, and she is unable to stop her hands from shaking. She keeps her head lowered, hoping he will go away — hoping it's just a bad dream.

A shrill voice chirps in the distance, disrupting her frantic thoughts and causing her to jump. The voice belongs to Mrs. Trimble, who is all worked up, flying across the yard, waving a black embroidered dress. "Lazy Moon! You forgot my dress. You just can't go dashing out the door, down to the stream like you're having a Sunday picnic. This is my nicest dress — the one I wear for the Lord's day. I do like to look my best for Him in church." Mrs. Trimble eyes the girl warily. "Are you sitting and brooding the afternoon away? And just look at these clothes yet to be washed." Irritated, she shakes the black dress in her face. "Let us not be slovenly in our duties. You must take pride in your work if you are to succeed. Laziness is not tolerated here."

Mrs. Trimble contemplates walloping the girl's backside when she hears a noise in the bushes. She shrieks as Preacher Jim steps out from behind the tree and gives a wave. Walking casually toward her, he swishes a willow branch and calls out. "Blessed day, Mrs. Trimble."

"Oh, my heavens! You gave me a start," she says, all atwitter. "What on earth are you doing?" Realizing she shouldn't question the preacher, she stops. "I... I... um... I didn't mean to pry, or question what you were doing."

"My apologies for frightening you, Mrs. Trimble, but I've been keeping an eye on this one. I see we have another wayward child in our midst," he says, pointing the branch at Little Moon. "Bad to the bone, I fear. I have been watching. The Lord says, 'Be watchful, the Devil prowls around like a roaring lion, seeking someone to devour.' I fear evil has seeped in and tainted her soul. Overheard your admonishments, Mrs. Trimble. Very good! Got to save as many heathens as we can. We don't want her to end up like her cunning friend. Bad behavior will not do around here," he admonishes, sending his Adam's apple bobbing, up and down. Little Moon's eyes are glued to his throat.

"We know what happens to girls who misbehave... who still believe in their wicked ways." Preacher Jim's eyes narrow, assessing Little Moon, giving her chills.

In a panic, she nicks her hand on the washboard. A trickle of blood oozes out, and onto the clothes.

Mrs. Trimble furrows her brow, and looks at the preacher. She agrees the child is negligent, but is curious why the preacher was hiding behind a tree to observe her. *Maybe I should ask him*, she thinks. Appalled at her thoughts, she just as quickly puts them out of her mind. *He's just dedicated to his work, that's all.* Gathering her composure, she says, "The girl left my dress behind, my Sunday best. Can't be attending your service looking disheveled, after all."

"The good Lord loves your devotion, Mrs. Trimble. You know that we cannot send these children out into the world untrained or unlearned. We don't want to coddle them either, and have them think we are soft. It might entice cunning behavior... cause rebellion... that sort of thing. We stand by the rod and the Bible and the Almighty. So, like I said, I've been watching for signs of evil entering these quarters, and possessing them... snatching their souls." Preacher Jim holds his hand to his heart, and closes his eyes, as if in contemplation. "The good Lord shows me all I need. That's why we must be strict, to help them learn better... give them discipline, where it has been lacking. We don't want to encourage slothfulness, either... lead them to believe they'll get handouts for the rest of their lives."

"Why, yes," Mrs. Trimble says, agreeing wholeheartedly. "They should most assuredly earn their keep and be grateful. That's what's important."

Preacher Jim continues to talk as Little Moon, feeling dazed, barely listens. She wishes she could run away, as the words she hears wash over her. "Permanent wards of the government... a burden, for certain..."

Preacher Jim straightens, and says, "Why don't you send this girl to my office. There I will educate her on the words of the Lord and read passages to her from the Bible."

Mrs. Trimble says, "Oh, my goodness. I hate to bother you with..."

Preacher Jim holds out his hands, and interrupts. "No need to fret over my heavy load. The Lord gives me the strength of Samson, even though my hair is shorn."

Little Moon listens with rising dismay, and fights back her tears. *Oh, no! That's where Chasing Rabbit died. Maybe I'll die there, too. I can't sit in his office, night after night,* she thinks, as her mind whirls. She has to tell someone about her fate — but who? Certainly not Mrs. Burns. She would be glad to see her go. Maybe she could tell Miss Snodberry. *No, she would be too afraid to help.* She could tell Morning Star, but what could *she* do? Her hands shake so badly that she accidently splashes water on Preacher Jim's trousers.

He jumps back in surprise. "Don't be so careless," he scolds, attempting to wipe his pants dry. "Be mindful of what you do, even if it's washing clothes. Let me show you how to do it properly," he says gruffly. Maneuvering his way toward her, he bends down on his knees, takes the lye soap in his hands, lathers up the clothes, and scrubs until beads of sweat surface on his forehead.

Little Moon cringes at his closeness.

Mrs. Trimble looks perplexed, watching the preacher.

After scrubbing the dress vigorously, he shakes it out. "This is how it's done." Then he plops it into the water to rinse. Without looking up, he addresses Mrs. Trimble. "You may leave now.

I'm sure you have other duties to attend to. I will continue here. Remember what Jesus did when he forgave that prostitute, Mary. So this is the least I can do." Patting the girl's head, he says, "Teach her the fundamentals. Soon she'll make a fine wife... if instructed properly." His large boney hands clench hers, soaping up another dress for washing.

Little Moon flinches as he rubs the soap into her hands, which turns her already raw fingers into gaping red sores.

Collecting her thoughts, Mrs. Trimble stumbles for words. "Well... all right, if you insist."

Preacher Jim, preoccupied with the girl, shoos the woman away.

She turns to leave, then looks back, thinking Preacher Jim is acting a bit strangely of late. But she promptly chastises herself for having such wicked thoughts. "How ungodly of me," Mrs. Trimble says to herself. "He is a good man... a dedicated man... showing that child how to launder properly. Well, maybe I'll get some clean dresses from now on. Wouldn't that be nice for a change?!" She walks up the hill to the school, clacking her strap against the palm of her hand.

Preacher Jim turns to Little Moon. "When you are in my office I will show you the way of the righteous. We will learn verses together and sing the praises of the Lord. You must not think of this as punishment, but a blessing. I will teach you many things. The first rule... you must not be late," he says brusquely. "The good Lord frowns on tardiness, as do I."

Little Moon squeezes her eyes shut, praying for help. She opens them a crack when she hears a whisper of wind seeping through the branches. Cracking them open a little further she sees a beautiful white feather floating around in circles, sailing gracefully through the tall evergreens and back down, like a ballerina — spinning lightly, freely. *It looks like the feather is dancing,* she thinks. Her hand flies to her mouth in astonishment as she sees a stick rise from the thicket, seeming to drift near the feather, twirling. Mesmerized, her eyes fix on the dancing feather and stick.

From seemingly out of nowhere a boy slips out of the bushes and in a blink he dashes over, dumping the bucket full of clothes and soapy water on top of Preacher Jim. Just as quickly as he appeared, the boy disappears, like a phantom.

Little Moon is stunned. Not knowing what to think, or know who it was, she flies off the ground and away from the soapy water, watching the spectacle. She wants to laugh, but is too afraid. The preacher roars back in indignation, gangly legs floundering in the air, trying to regain his balance. He knocks the bucket off his head, sputtering and thrashing about, as his arms get entangled in the garments. Pushing the cumbersome bucket aside, he looks around the yard, and curses. "What the devil is going on?"

Little Moon is too afraid to answer and stands unmoving, eyes glued to the havoc that just ensued.

Through hazy eyes Preacher Jim sees a cluster of crow feathers heading toward him, twirling in circles — and then stopping, inches from his face. A lone white feather with its soft wispy quill hangs in the air, flutters, then without warning zooms down and pecks his nose, leaving a bright red mark. Furious, Preacher Jim lunges at the feather, just missing it by a hair. He snatches at the air wildly and finally has the white feather in his grasp. "You vile, evil thing," he snarls. He is ready to snap it in half, when the feather twirls, slips out of his hands, and floats back up into the trees amongst the crow feathers circling above, gathering in an odd shape. Preacher Jim pauses momentarily, cursing at the devious things. *Looks like a war bonnet,* he thinks in alarm, *with all those bird feathers.* Disconcerted by the sight, he shakes his fist and stomps off. In his haste, he slips on the bar of soap and nearly trips over his feet. Righting himself, he glares at Little Moon. "These wretched heathens are playing tricks on me, on my mind... that's what they're doing."

Completely mesmerized by the sight of the feathers, Little Moon shuts her mouth, grateful to be out of the preacher's clutches. "Thank you!" is all she can say, as she looks around the grounds. "I know I asked for help, but... " at a loss for words, she looks around and sees that Mrs. Trimble is gone and the grounds are empty. An exciting notion occurs to her. *Could it be Hidden Spirit?* She looks intently at the thick scrub and trees where the feathers had disappeared. She gasps! She swears she sees a face hiding in the shadows. She prays it is Hidden Spirit. Little Moon clutches her chest. It's pounding so hard she can feel it vibrate up her back and into her neck. "Hidden Spirit!" she whispers. "Is that you?" Ready to run, she turns around when she hears a sharp voice. "What in the world is going on?"

It's Mrs. Burns! Her puffed up face is full of astonishment as she approaches, huffing. "Land's sake, Almighty. Have you lost your mind, throwing the clothes all over the place?" Her face swells like a roosting hen and reddens even more as she looks around in dismay. "I should whip you for a month of Sundays, but that is not my job. I'll leave that to Mrs. Trimble."

Little Moon frantically begins picking the clothes off the ground and hurries to get more water. While looking out of the corner of her eyes to see if it really was Hidden Spirit, she drops the water and feels a whack across her head.

"I need an answer, missy."

"I... I... Preacher Jim... he, um... he knocked the bucket over... and slipped... uh... and I'm not sure what happened."

"Oh, for the life of me, stop babbling and clean up this mess," Mrs. Burns wails. "I shall report this to Mrs. Trimble." She huffs back up the hill. *I'm going to need more than ham hocks and biscuits tonight to settle my nerves around this place,* she thinks, completely rattled. *If anyone asks for my two cents, I'd tell them I'd send every last one of these hooligans packing.*

Shaking, Little Moon begins picking up the scattered dresses, and rinses them off, all the while looking over her shoulder at the bushes. *I know it was Hidden Spirit. It had to be. Who else?*

She is so excited she wants to scream out his name, but refrains from the outburst. As she hangs the dripping clothes on the line, she pays no mind to the water running down her arms, or that her clothes are getting drenched. She just keeps her eyes glued to the bushes, hoping Hidden Spirit will appear. Deep in thought, she practically jumps out of her skin when she feels someone poke her on the shoulder.

"Little Moon. What happened? I was coming over to help you when I heard my father hollering. He sounded real mad, so I hid behind the barn to see what was going on. I couldn't believe it. I almost fell over laughing as he got himself tangled up in the ladies' garments. Did you do it, Little Moon?" Ellie asks incredulously and looks at the girl in amusement.

Smiling brightly, Little Moon shakes her head. "Nooooo…"

"Well, I waited until my father left, and I was ready to hurry over when I saw Mrs. Burns flying down the hill, looking all flustered. Who do you think did this?" Ellie asks again.

"I think it was Hidden Spirit," Little Moon says proudly. "Chasing Rabbit's brother."

"How daring!"

"He must be here, somewhere. I'm sure he is. He just seemed to come out of nowhere and disappear. I swear I caught a glimpse of him in the bushes." The girl looks over at the trees, hoping he will magically appear. Little Moon edges closer to Ellie, lowering her voice. "Everything happened so fast, and I was so surprised. Before I knew it, Preacher Jim had clothes and water all over him."

"I wish I had seen your Hidden Spirit," Ellie says, enviously. "He sounds wonderful."

"Well, he is and it was... like... magic. Hidden Spirit can do mysterious things you know. He's our hero," she says, proudly. Little Moon is so excited that she stands up, hops on one foot, grabs a wet dress, and twirls in circles. "He must be near, Ellie. He must be. I have prayed to the Great Spirit every night to guide him to us so that he will take us home."

"Home?" Ellie repeated, grabbing the girl's wrists. "That's marvelous news, Little Moon... to leave this god-awful place."

"You know," she says, beaming, "The elders knew he was going to be special, the day he was born. They said he is destined for real big things and that Hidden Spirit's, grandfather, was going to teach him big secrets from another place... so he could be a really good medicine man. His grandfather is dead, but still has the power. The crows became his friends when he was little, and, when he shot one of them, they taught him a big lesson. Now they protect and guide him. Hidden Spirit is brave," Little Moon says with her newfound confidence. "He's a warrior, too. Our people have lots of powers, you know. They wouldn't scalp you or anything like that, like the white people say."

"I wish I could meet Hidden Spirit someday. Maybe he could make my parents, vanish. Wouldn't that be something?" They both burst out laughing. "We'd better get these clothes hung on the line, before you get into even more trouble."

"Chasing Rabbit was always in trouble," Little Moon says, matter-of-factly. "Now, it seems *I* am. I heard Mrs. Trimble tell Mrs. Burns that we are vile, and calls us other names when she gets mad. I'm not sure what vile means, but I think it's not good. It's been hard getting used to this new life... a life we didn't want. Preacher Jim is scary and he's so..." Little Moon stops. "I'm sorry. I know he's your father and..."

"Don't apologize for my father. I am not close to him, at all. I know I'm not supposed to say this, but mostly I despise him, and Opal, my mother, is… well, she's just as bad."

"Opal says our parents brought us up evil… that our skin color has tainted us. I don't know what that means, but she says our parents are wicked and they passed it down. That's why we have to work so hard… to get rid of our sins."

"I'd like to get rid of *them*," says Ellie, fuming. "Let's hope Hidden… um… what did you say his name was?"

"Hidden Spirit," Little Moon says, proudly.

"I like that name. It sounds mysterious."

"I wish you could go with us," Little Moon says with a hint of sadness.

"I try to think every night to find a way out of here," Ellie says. "I don't mean to complain about my life, Little Moon, especially when you girls have it so much worse, but it's difficult to live with my family. We see everything differently. I know my father thinks he's helping, but I can't get him to understand or even consider that what he's doing isn't right. I hate what you girls have endured at this place. It's horrible. I often wonder why they brought you here in the first place. I suppose my father thinks he is helping to save your souls. But, if you turned out like them, that would be the tragedy."

Little Moon is resolute. "I never want to be like them."

Ellie holds Little Moon's hands and notices her bloodied fingers — nails cracked and skin covered with blisters. "You're very special, Little Moon. I'm sorry that this has happened to you," she says kindly and kisses her hands.

Little Moon is grateful for the girl's friendship, and says tentatively. "I wish you could meet my father, Ellie. His name is Long Braid. He is very kind, and he loves me very much. He would never hit me or say bad things to me, like they do here. Papa and

Mama must worry a lot about us being gone. I saw them cry when the soldiers made us leave on the wagons. I waved to them, but the dust was so thick I don't think they saw me. Everyone was crying. It was a very sad day. I can remember it real clear, because it stays in my mind. I try not to cry when I think of them, but it's hard. I wonder if they know Otter and Chasing Rabbit are gone to the otherworld?" Little Moon's face fills with pain at the memory.

"Gosh. I'm sad just hearing about it, Little Moon. That must have been awful. If they came and took me away I would jump for joy, and sing at the top of my lungs. But I know for you it's different, and I'm sorry for all your pain. I wish I could do something to help..." Ellie's eyes brighten. "Maybe we could escape together," she says, excitedly. "I'll need to get some money first... then we could run away to New York. I would figure out a way to get you back home once we get there. I know it's not the same as being with your Mama and Papa, but they could come there if they want to. You know what my dream is?" Ellie continues on and now bubbles with enthusiasm. "I want to design dresses... pretty ones made of lace and silk... with daring necklines and big bustles. I have pictures that I stare at for hours, passing away time in my room... daydreaming about my creations. Sewing is what I love most of all, and it keeps me somewhat sane, living at my house. I know I could make a living selling my dresses... I know I could. I am not a zealot like my parents, but I do pray every day for my dreams to come true. I know one day they will. They just have to."

"I believe your dreams will come true, Ellie, and I'm glad you're my friend. I would run away with you, but I think Hidden Spirit is here." A shiver of excitement fills Little Moon as she looks hopefully across the grounds.

"Oh, I hope so."

The girls hug each other tightly.

"You are the sweetest thing, Little Moon. I'm not the bravest person, but if Hidden Spirit isn't here, remember… I will really try to help you run away."

"Don't forget about Morning Star, too."

"I won't. I've seen her in the kitchen working so hard. She's very beautiful." Looking up, Ellie wrinkles her brow and says, "Let's hurry, before the clothes get drenched again. The sky is beginning to fill with rain clouds."

The girls talk and giggle as they hurriedly gather the spilt clothes from the ground and struggle to hang them on the line. Ellie finds some sticks to bang away at the clothes, trying to remove the mud that coated some of the dresses. They talk as they work and Ellie asks more questions of Little Moon's earlier life. "Did you ever eat buffalo? How did it taste? Did you live in a tepee?" Little Moon happily complies, and answers all the questions, filled with pride.

The clothes are still damp, and even a little dirty, when the girls pull them from the line. Ellie walks with Little Moon up the hill and stops. "I don't dare take the clothes inside. Mrs. Trimble would have a fit, and then she'd tell my father. I'd better go now before someone catches me here." Ellie hugs the young girl, noticing how pretty she is when she smiles. *Not that there is much to smile about here, but, it seems to light up her face,* she thinks sadly.

She hurries off, waving goodbye.

Dragging the clothes down the long hallway, Little Moon hangs the dresses on a wooden rack in Mrs. Trimble's room, and then runs down the hall. In her haste she bumps into Mrs. Burns, who gives her a scathing look.

"Slow down there, miss. Not a fire in here. You're lucky Mrs. Trimble is busy right now because I'd bet she'd tan your backside, but good, after your prank today. I hope you got your mess cleaned up."

"Y-yes, I did. There were so many clothes, but I finished. Mrs. Trimble would be proud of my work," Little Moon says, hiding a grin.

"Well," Mrs. Burns says, fumbling for words. "I'm not sure, after that kerfuffle you had. Now, be on your way and don't forget about choir practice after dinner."

Little Moon smiles, thinking she is getting to be like the whites, speaking with two tongues.

THE WINDOW

WORK DONE, AND clothes put away, Little Moon sails into the dining hall, where she sees Morning Star, and tries to get her attention. But her sister is too busy running in circles, catering to Mrs. Barlapp's demands and complaints. "Hurry up, and get the roast... it's starting to burn. Set the table, and add some flowers... it's so dull in here..."

Morning Star dutifully obeys the woman, but she seems more flustered than usual this evening as everyone is out of sorts and grumpy... but that was nothing new at this place. Mrs. Trimble waves her hands to get Morning Star's attention. "Good Lord, child, the teachers are starving and Mrs. Burns is fretting about her wretched day. Where on earth is supper? The flowers might be a nice touch, but, really... You put a lot of strain on Mrs. Barlapp's shoulders with the amount work she has to get done. Serving three meals a day, plus tending to your food and, on top of it, keeping track of you girls, as well... please try to ease her load and not make her life any more difficult than it already is."

Morning Star covers her glare with a nod of the head, and hurries back to the kitchen to retrieve the scrumptious dinner, setting mouthwatering dishes on the table.

Little Moon looks at the frazzled Morning Star, still hoping to get her attention, and having no luck as she hears a demanding

Mrs. Barlapp call out, "Morning Star, hurry back and take the rest of the food before it gets cold and ruin all my work." Unable to resist the temptation, she stops momentarily at the table, and takes a big sniff. *Oh, to be able to devour the mouthwatering dishes, just once… that would be wonderful.* As she inhales even more deeply, her body goes limp with hunger. She strains to see what they are having, and spots fried potatoes, ham hocks, rutabaga, and cabbage along with piping hot biscuits and a huge cherry pie. It smells so good she is tempted to grab a ham hock on her way to the table, and inches her hand along the side. But she quickly dismisses that idea as Mrs. Trimble stands and stares at the girl… shooing her away.

Little Moon sits at her table and eats the tasteless food brought over by Miss Snodberry. The food is just something to fill her belly, a little. She is always hungry after their meals, which are never enough for growing girls. Well, at least her belly has stopped rumbling — for a while.

When dinner is over, the girls are quickly ushered into Opal's room, where the woman sits at the piano, warming up. In one grand gesture, she flings her fingers high in the air and pounds the keys like a concert pianist awaiting the applause of a large, appreciative audience. Little Moon stifles a giggle and thinks she looks ridiculous. Anxious for Morning Star to arrive, she looks toward the door, and taps her toes in anticipation. *Mrs. Barlapp is probably keeping her in the kitchen to finish the pile of dishes and sweep the floor before she can leave.* She moans… her excitement is about to bubble over as she keeps an eye on the door. "Hurry," she says, barely able to sit still, squirming in her seat… bursting at the seams to tell Morning Star what happened.

Once everyone has arrived, Opal raps the piano to get everyone's attention. "Girls, settle down. Now, let's look smart and sing with enthusiasm tonight because I have wonderful news. We will be singing the Lord's praises this Sunday in front of the congregation. Let's impress the townsfolk. Show them the fruits of my labor… show them that you feel joy in rejoicing the Lord. The song we shall start with is something I wrote myself," she cooed. "It's called 'Archangels, Flying High.' Now, listen carefully. I will sing it through once, then you will follow along. We may have to do it several times, which is why I am giving you a head start… to prepare you for the special day." Opal leans back, opens her mouth wide and belts out the song in a high-pitched voice:

"Oh sweet angels, come to me tonight,
Gather us close in your wings, Oh, Lord, and
Keep us from sin,
Hold us into your folds,
Deliver us from evil…"

The girls stare at the woman in disbelief, and then look at one another.

Little Moon's eyes bulge out and she smothers a laugh. She can't believe they will have to sing that awful song in front of the white people on Sunday. *They already stare at us enough,* she thinks. *Now we will look foolish, and they'll laugh openly at us instead of behind our backs.* She rolls her eyes, and refuses to sing — unconcerned about being caught. Finally, her attention is drawn to the doorway where Morning Star, thankfully, enters the room. Little Moon waves enthusiastically to her sister, and motions her over.

Opal looks up, as she enters and stops singing. Exasperated, she calls out, "Morning Star, would you please come up front and help me. For the life of me, I can't get these girls to understand the words to my song. They sing like an annoying kettle of fish, and off-key, as well. It doesn't matter how many times I try repeating the words… over and over. I wanted this to be a surprise for the parishioners. I wanted to impress them with my verse. But instead, they will be dismayed by these dreadful sounds. I will be a laughingstock in town."

Morning Star, sighs, and does as she is told.

Little Moon can't believe it. Her news will have to wait. "Darn," she mutters and stomps her foot in frustration. *I can't wait until this silly practice is over.* She glances around the small, musty room, thinking how different it looks in the evening. The lanterns flicker... making the pictures hanging on the wall appear even more sinister than usual. An unexpected chill wafts down her spine. Little Moon is jittery — unable to concentrate on anything but Hidden Spirit. She glances toward the window, when a slight movement catches her eye. She blinks hard at the sight of the wafting object that just blew into the room — a silky white feather. Her breath catches. This is the second time today she has seen feathers floating in the air. She whispers aloud: "Hidden Spirit." To get a better look, she stands on her tiptoes and squints. The clanging of the piano stops abruptly. Opal shouts out at her. "Little Moon! Why aren't you singing... and what in God's name are you staring at?"

Little Moon freezes.

Opal follows her gaze, then abruptly stands and hurries to the window, where she looks out. Seeing nothing unusual, she slams the window shut, and frowns at Little Moon. "Because of you, we will be staying a little longer tonight. Goodness knows everyone needs the practice. Especially you!"

Morning Star gives Little Moon an annoyed look.

Once again, all settles down, and the singing starts up. Opal bangs furiously on the piano keys now, as she waits for the girls to keep up with her. She wails out her song, loud and jarring, trying to get the girls to follow along.

The silky white feather is now floating across the room, high up in the ceiling, occasionally dipping down. One by one, the girls look up and stare in amazement. Finally, Morning Star looks, and gasps at the sight of the feather, clutching her heart. This looks like the same feather she saw at Grandfather's tepee. "Could it really be?" she murmurs, praying that Hidden Spirit is near, and steadies herself, as she looks around the room, desperate to see some sign of him. Her eyes focus on the open window. When she sees a shadow flicker across the pane, she jumps in anticipation. Without a second thought she bolts out of the room, banging the door behind her. Opal stops playing, completely stunned by the outburst, and even more shocked by Morning Star, who has never given her a moment of trouble.

Morning Star looks around outside, and calls out softly, "Hidden Spirit... is that you? Oh, let it be you," she pleads desperately. She waits and listens — looking into the night sky. The air is still — not a single leaf is stirring around her. An unexpected shiver runs down her spine and, out of the quiet, she hears a voice, swirling in the stillness, whispering her name. "Morning Star."

Her heart skips a beat as she turns her head upward — listening, hoping to see who is calling her. The door bangs open, revealing a furious Opal. "What on heaven's earth are you doing out here?" she says, snapping her fingers in the girl's face.

A disappointed Morning Star ignores the woman, and continues to stare off into the night, searching feverishly for Hidden Spirit — eyes wide with wonder.

"You look like you've seen the Devil himself," Opal says sarcastically. She looks at the wide-eyed girl and scans the area, as if the evil spirit might jump out any moment. Shivering, she rubs her arms.

Morning Star remains silent.

"You girls are incorrigible," Opal says, crossly. "We have work to do, and you, of all people, are the last one I thought would cause trouble." Opal snaps her fingers with a bit more force this time. "Get inside immediately!"

"S-s... sorry, Opal... ah, Mrs. Crumm," says Morning Star,

pulling her eyes back to the woman. "I… I was feeling a little sick to my stomach. I thought a breath of fresh air might help."

"What a bunch of hooey," Opal says, with marked disapproval and hurries Morning Star inside the door. "We have plenty of fresh air inside, you know. Sounds to me like a made up story."

Sitting back at the piano, Opal regards the girls sternly. "That will be enough interruptions for the night. You girls need to sing this song correctly," she declares. "It's not 'Gather wings in flight…'" It's 'Gather us close in your wings, Oh, Lord…' I don't know how many times I have to repeat this verse. You girls act like you're dense *and* that you couldn't carry a tune if it hit you in the head. Maybe that's what I should do… knock you girls in the head. It just might work. Something has to." She raises her arm to signal she's ready and vigorously pounds on the keys to get her point across. After an hour or so of trying to get the girls to sing in harmony, she snaps. "I've had enough of this wretched singing for the evening. We will try again tomorrow." Opal seethes, barely able to contain her fury. "I will pray heartily that you sing with a little more enthusiasm. Goodnight."

Opal shoos the yawning girls out of the room — except for Morning Star, whom she detains.

As Little Moon stumbles out the door, annoyed that she still can't speak to Morning Star, she overhears Opal fuming at her. "They will never be ready on Sunday," she says, irritably. "Tell all the girls we will stay here, every night if necessary, and practice until it's perfect." Ushering Morning Star out the door, she walks her down the hallway, complaining as they go.

The next morning is cold and damp. Morning Star hardly notices as she jumps out of bed before anyone is up, and dresses quickly. *I have to see if Hidden Spirit is here*, she thinks, hoping that she was not imagining things last night. "I'm sure I heard him talking to me in my sleep. I can feel him," she declares, nervously. "I know he is near."

Running headlong into the kitchen, she startles a busy Mrs. Barlapp, who is heating a pot of water over the fire. "Land's sake, girl, you scared the daylights out of me. Don't be sneaking in here like that," she says, banging the pot in preparation for breakfast. "Never know what can happen… heard stories about you people scalping innocent ones and such…" She looks at the girl accusingly, "Not saying you would, mind you, but still… " Her words trail off. "Well since you're here, you may as well get to work. You can start with the potatoes."

"I'm sorry, to frighten you, Mrs. Barlapp. I didn't have time to gather the eggs last night. Had to hurry to choir practice. That's why I got up early this morning."

Mrs. Barlapp is surprised by the girl's frankness. *It's a damp morning. It might be nice not to have to go to the chicken coop, hunting around in the dark for eggs.*

"Well, that's very thoughtful of you. You may go. Just don't come tearing in here, scaring me again."

After Morning Star assures her she wouldn't, Mrs. Barlapp reminds her, "Choir practice is important to Opal. Heard you girls can't sing for a hill o' beans. I'll say a prayer for the virtuous woman. Can't believe the patience she has with the lot of you."

Morning Star rolls her eyes at the woman, and hurries outside. She can hardly believe it. Her dream of seeing Hidden Spirit is finally here… she hopes, crossing her fingers. She takes off in a run down the path to the barn, hoping he might be inside. As she swings open the barn door, she hears Bessie moo — nervous at the sudden intrusion. "Sorry to startle you, Bessie," she says biting her lip. Her eyes scan the darkness as she whispers, "Hidden Spirit, are you here?" Standing motionless, holding her breath, she listens for a response. Only silence fills the barn, except for Bessie shifting in her stall. Morning Star feels her heart drop. "Please be here," she says in a desperate plea. A slight rustle from the loft gives her a start, and she stifles a cry as someone drops down beside her, landing lightly on the hay-strewn ground. Her skin prickles and she gasps at the outline of the masculine figure with long flowing hair, twined with feathers. *It has to be him*, she thinks hopefully. She could never forget him or his scent. It's what has kept her sane living at this place.

Before she can think what to do, or say, Hidden Spirit grabs her by her shoulders in one swift motion, and wraps his arms around her. He squeezes her so tightly she can barely breathe as he brushes his lips against hers. Morning Star feels transported to another time and place. Her knees are so wobbly she can barely stand as she clings to the young man who fills her thoughts, night and day. He holds her closely now, and his touch sends ripples of joy throughout her tense body. She wants to tell him a thousand things — about how desperate the girls are — and about their anguish — and also about her feelings for him. But the words stick in her throat, making it impossible for her to utter a word.

Hidden Spirit looks at her silhouette in the shadows as raw emotions flood through him. Struggling to keep his anger at bay, he whispers in her ear. "You and Little Moon will come with me soon. You will no longer stay here among the white eyes. I need a few days to let Ghost Dancer rest and hunt for food. We've had a... long journey."

Morning Star presses her cheek against his, and wraps her arms around his neck. Her pulse quickens and her voice can barely lift above a whisper. "You're here? I can hardly believe my eyes. Every night I prayed you would come. I would look at the stars and imagine you were up there looking down. I believed you would come to help. I held that thought close so I could fall asleep before the tears came and stained my pillow."

Hidden Spirit lifts her hand, puts it to his face, and speaks in a hushed tone. "I know it's been hard, but only a little longer… and you'll be free."

She nods her head. Forcing herself to calm her jitters, she wipes her eyes. His words — his closeness — his touch sends her spirit soaring. If she could hold onto this moment forever, she would. She would go to the spirit world content, her heart bursting with joy.

A jarring bark startles Morning Star out of her hypnotic moment.

"For Pete's sake, girl… what's taking you so long? Mrs. Barlapp hollers from the doorway. "Are you laying the eggs, or collecting them? Hurry up! I'm running late this morning. I could have been there and back by now."

Morning Star begins to panic and fights the urge to run, as her knees threaten to give way.

Hidden Spirit nudges her. "Answer her, Morning Star."

Morning Star, unable to speak, stands frozen.

"My batter will be ruined. Don't make me come down there."

Her voice cracks with fright. "Be right there, Mrs. Barlapp. The chickens are giving me a hard time. They… um… I'm trying to get them off their roost."

Frantic thoughts whirl in her head as she hears Mrs. Barlapp's threat of coming to get her. "Oh no! The eggs!"

Morning Star bolts over to the chicken coop along with Hidden Spirit. Side by side they fly inside the pen, as the chickens squawk at the intrusion. Hidden Spirit quickly pushes them off their roosts and plucks the eggs from under the hens. Morning Star's hands tremble as she reaches for an egg, barely able to concentrate. With Hidden Spirit's help, she quickly fills the pan, then he hurries Morning Star out of the chicken coop. He lingers by her side and pulls her to him, saying, "I have missed you more than you can image. Believe me, you will not be here for long." He brushes the tip of her nose with his and follows the outline her face. He pulls her close and kisses her deeply. She feels transported by his touch and marvels at how soft his hair feels flowing against her skin.

Morning Star thought she might melt with happiness. After gathering her senses she feels renewed — alive… like a dormant force inside her has awakened, sending sparks of electricity surging throughout her body.

"Go now," says Hidden Spirit, breathlessly.

Morning Star hesitates, not wanting to leave, the air thick with unspoken emotions. She takes a long look at him, memorizing his presence, his face, before taking off in a run — before Mrs. Barlapp comes out looking for her. Holding the eggs carefully, she dashes off to the kitchen, her face flushed and turning into a pale red hue. Mrs. Barlapp gives her a suspicious scowl and snatches the eggs, while simultaneously barking orders to start chopping.

Morning Star's hand trembles so much she can barely hold the knife, yet she somehow manages to slice the potatoes trying her best to remain calm. She feels as though she is in a dream, and smiles to herself in recollection of her enchanting encounter with Hidden Spirit.

PLIGHT OF THE PREACHER

ELLIE RACES DOWN the road to Frae Beadle's butcher shop. She was supposed to have been there an hour ago, but got sidetracked on her way and wandered toward the river. "Ugh. It makes me sick just to think about him." She spits her distaste knowing she'll have to see the man this evening as she cuts through the fields and skims past wooded areas filled with large oaks, plump with acorns and leafy maple trees, where buckets are set out to capture the delectable syrup. She just can't believe Beadle is coming for Sunday dinner. Another long, boring Sunday that seems to come far too soon. But this time, what's even worse, is that ogling Beadle will be joining them. He reminds her of a huge June bug, with bulging eyes that unnerve her and that never smile. She dreads every time she has to see him.

As she glances through the thick foliage Ellie detects a slight movement. She stops and scans the area, wondering if someone is following her. Her heart pounds in her chest as she picks up the pace. Hurrying through the area that is filled with thick grasses and twigs, she sweeps past a sharp branch that snags her dress. She stops again, and looks around. Ellie sees no one, but senses that something or someone is lurking nearby. Before she can react, a pair of hands grabs her from behind and drags her under the cover of giant oaks.

Ellie stifles a scream as she is thrown to the ground, leaving her frozen and breathless. *Is it Beadle?* She wonders, fearfully. Brushing away a strand of hair that had tumbled across her face, she blinks hard and gasps at the sight of the most breathtaking and terrifying face she has ever seen. Looking at this wildly savage young Indian makes her feel strangely excited, like a giddy young school girl.

A long knife is thrust at her throat and a threatening voice commands, "Make a sound, and it will be your last." Her pulse escalates as she stares at the wild creature and marvels at those extraordinary eyes flashing with danger. Crow feathers line his raven black hair that complements his bronze skin and high cheekbones. Ellie is spellbound. *Looking at this person is…it's like an aphrodisiac.* Incapable of pulling her eyes from his intense gaze is disarming—and being so close to him, is so exhilarating. She can feel the thundering beat of his heart and see beads of sweat glisten on his chest. She wants to say something, to tell him she has heard of him and that she knows Little Moon. Desperately wanting to speak, but only a slip of air drifts out from her lips.

Sounds of an approaching rider on horseback snap her out of her reverie. To her horror, she sees Frae Beadle riding down the field.

"Don't make a sound," threatens Hidden Spirit as he grips Ellie's arm so hard it goes numb. She studies the fine lines that trace the side of his jaw and sees a wicked scar on his cheek — and the deadly resolve in his fierce expression. More than frightened, she is curious. *This has to be Hidden Spirit… it has to be, the one Little Moon speaks of with such affection.* Unable to overcome her jitters, she manages to get out a few words. "H-H-idden Sp-spirit… Y-you must be Hidden Spirit."

His eyes narrow with distrust as he stares at the girl with the golden hair. "How do you know my name?" He demands, and squeezes his hands around her throat.

"Little Moon and Chasing Rabbit, they... they spoke of you often," she chokes. Hidden Spirit's hands lighten their grip. "They told me stories... fascinating stories about you and... I feel like I know you." Ellie swallows hard.

He puts his knife at her throat. "You white people are full of lies and deceit. How can I know you speak words of truth?"

Ellie tries to sit up, and cries out. "I do speak the truth. How can I make you believe me?" she says, with tear-filled eyes. "The girls are my friends. I'm sorry they were forced to come here. I want to help them get away... I was going to help them escape... take them to New York."

Hidden Spirit snorts in disdain, his eyes leveling hers.

"Please... I tell you the truth. I'll help you get them out of here."

"If you lie, I will cut your throat," he says as he pulls her hair back viciously. "Understand?"

Ellie trembles, as much from his closeness as from his words. She doesn't doubt he would do that. "I tell you the truth. I swear."

"Is it your father who keeps our children captive?"

"Yes." Ellie says, alarm filling her voice. "Chasing Rabbit is... that is, my father, was..."

Hidden Spirit raised his hand to silence her. "Do not speak to me of my sister," he threatens. "I have seen her death."

Ellie sees a flicker of pain cross his handsome face and feels the sadness rise in his eyes as he quickly glances away. "My father thinks he is helping, keeping the children here... but I think it's awful, what he's doing."

Hidden Spirit looks at her coldly, almost ready to strike, but he lets her continue on. "I wish someone would speak up and tell him how miserable they are. I know he wouldn't listen. The teachers at the school don't understand, either. They think they are helping a noble cause."

Hidden Spirit relaxes his grip slightly and scrutinizes the girl with golden curls, ready to hear more.

"My name is Ellie," she says, her face turning a pale crimson. "Tell me how I can help... anything at all... and I will do my best. And if..." She pauses to assess the handsome boy, and a spurt of courage fills her. She is determined to ask him a crucial question that could change her life, forever. So, before she loses her courage, she blurts out. "Would you... would you consider, um... consider taking me with you and the girls... please?" Without waiting for an answer, she continues on so fast, she stumbles over her words. "I beg you. If you could take me anywhere, just as far as you can, I could catch a train or walk the rest of the way, I don't care. Please..." She wrings her hands nervously. "I will die if I stay here," she blurts out, almost in tears.

Hidden Spirit watches the girl, suspiciously and waits for what seems like an eternity before speaking. "It would be dangerous to take you along. The white people would hunt us down... kill us. I will not risk the lives of Morning Star and Little Moon for you. If you want to help... I could use some food and a horse."

Ellie says, "The rider that just passed... he is a wretched man, but he has a fine horse. I will try to get him for you." She pauses a moment and averts her glance. "I understand that you can't take me along. I'm sorry for asking. I was being selfish."

He watches her with his eyes in silence. "I will ponder your words."

A bit of hope stirs in Ellie. *A way out*, she thinks, crossing her fingers. *Oh, please let him say yes*. Her heart races at the thought of leaving this place and the danger that it would poses.

Interrupting her thoughts, Hidden Spirit demands, "Tell me where my sister is buried."

Ellie sits up and quickly describes the site the best she can, drawing a map in the dirt while describing the burial mounds' locations.

*

Hidden Spirit weaves silently through the trees, making his way to the top of the hill. It is still daylight, and he needs to be careful... needs eyes in the back of his head. The thought of Chasing Rabbit tossed inside a hole in the ground sends fury burning in the pit of his stomach. *I will avenge her death*, he thinks, bitterly. *They will pay.*

As he rides through the brambling brush, he passes a small creek and winds his way to the top. Tormented thoughts filter in, as visions of his sister appear. *I should have taken her with me to the hills. She would still be alive today instead of lying in a pile of dirt.* Wiping away the mist that settles over his eyes, he rides on, thinking about the bear claw he had given her before she left. He had pondered a long time to choose the right amulet for his sister — praying day and night that it would come to him. One misty morning he awoke to discover a huge bear claw lying outside his cave... like it was waiting for him. He picked it up and ran his hands over the sharp edge and thought, *this is it... this is for Chasing Rabbit.* He bent on his knees and gave thanks to the Great Spirit, praying its strength would protect her. To purify the claw, he rubbed it with the sacred herbs of sage and flat cedar, sat facing east, and said a prayer each morning to ensure her safety. Once he deemed it ready, he prayed again to the Great Spirit to make it full of power, to keep her safe. *Something must have happened.*

Cautiously stepping out from the cover of trees, Hidden Spirit looks in all directions and sees no one about. From a distance he spots several mounds of freshly dug dirt. *That has to be the children's burial site.* He takes off in a run toward the graves — struck by the number of them. The taste of death lingers on his tongue... he can hear their cries... calling for help. He falls to the ground and covers his ears to blot out the noise... his body trembles... his eyes harden — glued to the mounds of dirt in disbelief. Searching the sky, he questions the Great Spirit. "Why? How could you let this happen? We are your people, who love and pray to you daily." He picks up a handful of dirt and throws it into the air. The wind picks up the dirt and scatters it over the mounds, swirling beneath his feet. "To let our children go like this is… is wrong."

His cries echo in the fleeting wind that hold no answer. Only a sprinkle of dirt and dust fall in response. Hidden Spirit is overcome with grief, his heart bursts with sorrow, and he openly weeps as he clings to the soft mounds beneath him.

In the breeze, a silver feather flutters above. Hidden Spirit does not notice as a crow flies overhead cawing. It hovers briefly before it dips down and brushes against his face. He sits upright, and wipes his eyes, surprised by the crow's uncanny arrival. He brushes away a strand of hair that had fallen in his eyes, and looks in amazement, at the silver winged crow who flies to the furthest mound and drops a twig from the cottonwood tree. Tufts of cotton alight and begin to swirl around the grave. Then the silver-winged crow lands on the dirt. His sharp beady eyes focus on Hidden Spirit, who watches with interest.

The small crow caws noisily. "I see anger still follows you, clever one. Your judgment will be clouded, dear boy if you don't let it go." The crow begins to hop around in circles, scratching the dirt with his sharp talons. "Be wary, my fierce friend. Revenge is bittersweet." The crow ruffles his plumage, flaps his silvery wings, and flies off before Hidden Spirit can thank him, once again."

Once the crow is out of sight, Hidden Spirit pulls himself together. He hops up from the ground and walks over to the burial site where the crow had dropped the twig. He begins to dig with his bare hands, praying all the while as dirt is flying around him. Soon, he feels something hard against his fingertips, and he digs even faster, beads of sweat glistening across his face. He can feel his sister calling to him. He feels something rough. It's a body. He tenses. "Chasing Rabbit," he calls out, "I'm sorry I didn't come sooner." His mind races in turmoil. Ready to pull her tiny body from the grave— oblivious to anything else. He is so wrapped up in his grief that he pays no mind to the squawking crow, telling him, *Trouble is coming,* but it's too late. He is completely caught off-guard as three boys approach, with guns drawn.

Get your hands up," Ezekiel says, as he hops off his mount. "High as you can reach Injun boy." He prances over to the young Indian. "Whatcha doing digging in the dirt? Looking for roots and shit? Turn around, boy, now... real slow-like." Zeke isn't prepared for the stoical face and bold demeanor, almost daring Zeke to come near. His mouth about pops open when he sees Hidden Spirit's cool gaze appraise him with malice — eyes seething with hatred. He is powerless to pull his gaze away, and stands frozen, unable to move — until Abe comes rushing over to Zeke's side. Abe looks at the Indian and then back at Zeke, wondering what's gotten into him. He shakes him. Catching the boy's fierce gaze, he casts an admiring glance at the tall and proud Indian boy, who stares back, unblinking. An uncomfortable thought filters through Abe's mind. This boy has a wild streak — the likes of which he has never encountered before. A chill slices through him. *I've been in my share of fights, and could lick the best of them, but this one is something different,* he thinks, looking out of the corner of his eyes, noticing the boy's fierce stance and calm demeanor. *We'd better watch it. Doesn't seem to matter to the kid that he's outnumbered by three of us with guns.*

"Best take it easy, Zeke," Abe says with a warning nod of his head. "He looks to be a tough bugger to fight. Maybe he ran off a reservation."

"Probably a reward out for him, too," Zeke says, tearing his gaze from the boy and brushing Abe aside. "What's with Indians, nowadays?" Ezekiel says, trying to regain some composure. He puffs up his chest, feigning a swagger. "Think they can wander anywhere they want? Well, I'll set the Injun straight," he says, swerving close to Hidden Spirit, poking him with his gun. "The school is full, dirt-digger. If you're looking for a handout, go back where you came from." He did his best to sound brave, but the quaver in his voice gave him away.

Hidden Spirit's angry stare silenced Zeke. Hidden Spirit doesn't move a muscle.

Abe is wary, and stands back, watching. Not that Abe minds a fight, but why provoke one when he feels the odds are not in his favor. "Let's just take this Indian to your pa, Zeke, and be done with it. He can deal with him." Lowering his voice, he continues. "Besides, like I said, you'll need to be careful of this one." He scrutinizes the boy a little closer this time, impressed by his self-control and his well-formed body. He concludes the kid would be fast as lightening.

"What's he gonna do, Abe? Got my Winchester pointed squarely at his noggin'." Zeke cocks the rifle, aims it high, then shifts nervously as Hidden Spirit steps forward. Zeke quickly backs up, catching the Indian's glower.

"Do what you want," says Abe. "But I still think your pa should decide what to do with him."

"Well maybe, first, we ought to strut him through town. Show Janice I... uh... we caught us a dangerous renegade." Zeke says, puffing his chest again. "A runaway. Once she sees who we captured, maybe she'll want some fine company, like, me." Zeke hooks his thumb on his pants pocket, and hollers importantly. "Homer, get the rope." While trying his best to keep his gun steady.

Fixated on Hidden Spirit, Homer is simply too astounded to move and can only stand in place, staring. "A real live Indian... wild as they come," he says, breathlessly. *Just like the ones I read about in my books.* His stomach knots in anticipation of what might happen, but still... to be this close is exhilarating. The Indian is even more formidable than he had seen in the pictures, plus, he's really handsome. Homer admires every detail of his appearance — from his hair to his clothes to the moccasins on his feet. He senses, or rather feels, that this Indian is special. He agrees with Abe, *he's not the kind of Indian you rile.* But golly-dang — he'd love to draw his picture.

Zeke hollers in exasperation. "What's wrong with you, Homer? Are you scared looking at an Injun? Think he might scalp you, or something? I need the rope from Abe's horse, fast. So hurry. Never know with Injuns. Might be more coming."

Homer reluctantly moves to get the rope. *I really wish I could tell Zeke to do it himself,* he thinks, but he knows it's a bad idea. Still looking sideways at the Indian boy, he does what he is told — he gets the rope and hands it to Zeke.

His face deceptively calm, Hidden Spirit slowly calculates his chances with these three. His jaw muscle works furtively as he takes in the boys' every twitch and tone and move. Then a movement in the tree catches the boys' attention and gives Hidden Spirit the opportunity he needs. Before Zeke can blink, he plunges his fist into his face and knocks him backwards. The gun drops to the ground and a dazed Zeke grapples to stay upright, as Hidden Spirit let loose another stunning blow — this time to Zeke's nose. A loud crunch is followed by a gush of blood spurting across his face and ran in ribbons down his shirt. Zeke staggers in circles, lifts his fists for a fleeting second, then collapses on the ground, howling in pain.

Momentarily stunned, Abe raises his gun. He cocks his pistol ready to shoot, but not in time to avert the blow that grazes his temple and spins him around. Hidden Spirit kicks the gun from his grasp, and launches it into the air. As it lands in the scrubs, it lets off a thunderous blast.

Hidden Spirit's extraordinary face is alive with fury. He tilts his head back and echoes a deep war cry that sends chills down the boys' backs. His muscles taunt, ready for battle — he is now the warrior, brave and fearless and pounds his chest. His thirst for vengeance is unwavering, and he is ready to kill.

As the bloodied and battered Zeke lies in the dirt, moaning in pain, he spots his gun near the bushes and looks out of the corner of his eye to make sure the Indian isn't looking. He slithers over, and grabs it.

Homer stayed put, hiding behind the trees, watching. He is so amazed by the turn of events, he doesn't know whether to stay, run, or help the boys. Increasingly impressed with the Indian boy, he opts for the former, and stays put.

The fight is impressive. Abe's eye is swollen, almost shut. Each powerful punch he throws, Abe seems to only graze Hidden Spirit, who is more than adept, and sidesteps his blows, and throws a solid counterpunch. He now has Abe on the ground, straddles the boy, threatening to slice his throat.

Zeke manages to pull himself up, and staggers over to Hidden Spirit who's back is turned to him. With the swift butt of his gun, Zeke throttles him on the back of his head, and knocks him out cold.

Abe pushes Hidden Spirit off him. His knees wobble as he fights to regain his balance and stand. It's just as he had thought — that Indian is dangerous. He stumbles to his horse to get a coil of rope, and shouts out to Homer, who he eases his way from behind the tree. Abe is furious. "Where the blazes were you? Hiding behind a tree? I don't believe this." Not waiting for his reply, he hurries back to tie up Hidden Spirit before he regains consciousness. An expert with the lasso, Abe can tie a knot quick as any grown man, and he jerks hard on the rope to make it's tight enough to cut into his wrist.

Abe is muscular… a good fighter, and he's had his share of brawls… but nothing like this. This Indian kid is amazing. Rather than being upset over his ass-whooping, Abe is impressed. The ease with which this boy fought seemed like it hardly took any effort on his part. He almost hates to turn him over to Zeke's pa, but there is no other choice, especially with Zeke so furious about the whooping he took and the broken nose that is now spread flat across his face. Abe catches himself smiling at the damage done to Zeke's face. Abe hides his grin as he smacks the dusts off his pants, but there is little he can do about his grimy shirt, his stiff shoulder, and his aching jaw — which feels like a sledgehammer hit it. His swollen eye has gotten worse. It will be quite a shiner by tomorrow. Abe looks over at Zeke, who appears dazed, with blood spurting from his nose and a deep one-inch gash to his lip.

"Say, that was quite a fight," Abe says, with a grin. "Bet your nose is real sore."

Zeke isn't in a grinning mood. His pale face quivers like a tick, as he shoves his sore shoulder back, and grimaces. "Pa says Injuns got the Devil in them… that's why they're so wicked and evil." He narrows his gaze as he studies the Indian, who is now awake — and he turns him over roughly, with palpable disdain. "Had enough of this sons-a-bitch? I ought to kill him outright — save Pa the trouble of trying to help him."

Homer's spell is now broken. He looks at the furious Zeke as he approaches and Zeke shoves him backwards in disgust. "You're nothing but a chicken shit. I saw you hiding in the bushes, while Abe and I took care of this mess. Run home to Mama, you lousy turd. I don't know why we bother with you." Homer let Zeke's words blow over him like a windstorm…they rustle and bluster for a while, then settle down.

He searches for words to explain what he was feeling when he looked at the Indian boy. It wouldn't be worth the bother or make any sense to Zeke. What is he supposed to do, tell them he's fond of the Indians… that he feels bad for them? So Homer does his best and tries to explain, as his face colors fiercely. He can only stumble over his words and hope for the best. "I, uh, well, I saw n-no point in interfering without a g-gun… so I… uh… stayed out of the way."

"Horse shit, that's what it is… and a coward's lie. You couldn't fight a rooster, if it were lame and blind."

"Hey, Zeke. Leave him alone. We all know he's not much of a fighter. Let's get going."

A snap from the bushes startles the boys. Zeke's bloodied face blanches. "More damn Indians, I bet. Just shoot 'em, Abe. Don't even ask a question. Shoot every last one of 'em."

Abe raises his rifle in preparation of what may come, when he sees a wild mustang trot out from the bushes, shaking his head back and forth. His mane, the color of burnished sunshine, flutters in the air like a gusty wind. The horse holds his head high… regal, as if surveying the boys with his bright blue eyes. Then the horse starts clacking his teeth as if speaking something only the boy can understand. He trots over to Hidden Spirit, nudges his arm, and whinnies softly.

Surprised by the horse's arrival, Abe lets out a low whistle. He knows something about the breed, and boasts. "It's a mustang. I've heard about those horses. They're smart as a whip and strong… able to run for miles on end without tiring. I've even heard rumors that they can read your mind."

"Horseshit. I know a thing or two about horses, as well. Kick 'em hard and show 'em the whip. I bet they'll read minds then. That'll be quicker than your way, Abe. Besides, who cares about mind-reading crap?" Zeke eyes the horse, determined it should be his and makes a move toward Ghost Dancer. He waves his arms in the air, shouting, "come here, come here." The horse snorts and backs up.

"See? All you have to do is show 'em who's boss." Zeke doesn't notice that Ghost Dancer's blue eyes have darkened, or that his ears are drawn back, menacingly, as he paws the ground. Catching Zeke off-guard and without warning he lowers his head, charges at the boy and butts him in the seat of his pants, sending him skidding across the ground.

Abe and Homer run for cover.

Zeke scrambles to his feet and takes off in a run to get away from the wild horse, and trips over a root in his rush and falls face-first onto the ground, hitting his nose. Screaming in pain, he crawls on his belly, slithering like a snake away from the horse, and hides behind an enormous oak. Hands trembling, and nose bleeding, Zeke instructs Abe between huge gulps of air. "Shoot that lousy horse, Abe. Shoot him… now! That horse is a killer."

Abe peers around the tree and sees the horse pacing nervously beside the young Indian, who is struggling to free himself. He motions for Zeke and Homer to be quiet, grabs his rope and walks behind the grove of trees, where he waits and watches the horse. Ghost Dancer appears to be tugging at the Indian's rope. Abe deftly swirls his rope in small circular motions above his head, then lets it fly into the air and slide around the horse's neck, like butter on bread. "Whoa there, boy. Calm down."

The mustang stands rigid, as puffs of steam rise from his flared nostrils, looking dangerous. Ghost Dancer looks at the boy then thrashes about with fury with sides heaving, tossing his golden mane.

With a strong grip on the rope, Abe pulls slowly, wrapping it around his arm — inch by inch. Uncertain he can hold onto this wild creature, he winds the rope around a sturdy branch — drawing the horse ever closer.

Holding onto the tree, Zeke takes a cautious peek and sees Abe with the horse. He picks up his gun and thinks angrily, *that crazy bag-o-bones is good for one thing… glue.* He shouts out. "Stand back while I shoot the damn thing."

"Shut up, you fool. I've got him."

Unbelievably, the horse suddenly calms down, and stops thrashing.

Zeke cocks his gun, still uncertain about the horse. Ghost Dancer, looking all the while like a stately steed, begins to paw the ground and prance — first forward, and then back. His feet clop around in circles, sending dust scattering in the faint breeze. Then he moves back and forth, back and forth, lightly, like a ballerina. As the breeze picks up, the dust swirls around the horse like a giant cloud. All you can see is the startling blue eyes peering out from the mist.

Homer is beside himself, and jumps out from behind the tree. "That horse is dancing," he says, staring wide-eyed at the creature. He thinks that it has to be the strangest and most amazing thing he has ever seen.

Zeke's eyes are practically bugging out at the sight. He quickly shuts them, lowers his gun, then opens them a crack, and watches through narrow slits, trying to determine if he is seeing things. *That horse must be crazy.* Then he ducks back behind the tree, watching the mustang. It seems to look straight at him, with its startling blue eyes. Zeke trembles still watching.

As the whispering winds pick up, unusual sounds are heard as the unusual horse with the flowing mane starts to move gracefully, swaying with the singing winds.

Homer can hear the music, ever so slightly, and feels like dancing, but he hums to the mysterious sounds instead. The sound moves him to tears.

Abe and Zeke look up, perplexed, as lines crease their brows. They fear their eyes must be deceiving them. *Horses don't dance.*

Ghost Dancer tosses his head, nickers, and then kicks up a huge cluster of dirt with his hind legs. A whirling of clouds gathers once again around the horse, dark and dangerous. And in the whisper of winds, the horse seems to vanish into the clouds of dust and mystery. A moment later an eerie yowl accompanies on the night air, sending hackles up the boy's back.

*

Preacher Jim is seated at his desk in contemplation when the door slams open. He jumps halfway out of his seat, looking at the sorry sight of Zeke and Abe walking in the door, dragging an Indian boy along with them into his office. Eyes bulging with curiosity, he hollers, "What the devil just happened? Where in the dickens did you find this boy?" He scrutinizes Zeke's bloodied and obviously broken nose, and notices Abe's black and bruised eye. And then there's Homer, lagging behind. Preacher Jim rubs his chin wondering, why on earth do they hang out with this scrawny kid? *Not even a single scratch on him*, he notes with a grimace. His eyes dart back to Abe and asks, "You boys get into some kind of tangle with this Indian boy?" Then he fixes his gaze on the boy, and pauses. "I see you boys brought me the elusive creature that's been in my dreams." Excitement courses through him as he jerks his hands in the air. "The Lord works in mysterious ways. He has sent another sinner… This one is different from the others, though. He doesn't appear to be afraid of the white man," he ponders, looking him up and down, "or subservient I might add." He directs his question to Hidden Spirit. "You run off a reservation, boy?"

The boy stands stoic and silent, looking past him.

"Say, I'm talking to you, boy. You speak the heathen tongue or our English language?"

Hidden Spirit ignores the preacher.

"I bet you understand me," Preacher Jim fumes, hating to be ignored. "This one's stubborn. He's going to need a lesson or two," he surmises as he walks around the boy, scrutinizing him like a prized gelding ready to break. He observes the resolute set of his jaw and the fury burning within. "Yes, indeed. I'll need the hand of God and the wrath of the Devil himself to tame him." *But, soon enough, he'll see the error of his ways, and come around,* he thinks with a slow grin. *I'll have him docile and praising our sweet Jesus, if it's the last thing I do.* "The Lord has spoken and will guide me in my mission," he says, still assessing the boy. "I've got a place for you." He pokes the boy in the ribs, and is practically hopping up and down with excitement, reflecting on his plan. "I will work with you at my leisure; ensuring you are filled with the gospel and the light." Leaning in close to Hidden Spirit, he lowers his voice, almost a purr. "Until I can trust you have seen the errors of your ways, and that you won't run away, you will spend your days and nights thinking only of Him, the Lord Almighty. He'll be watching from on high." He claps his hands and raises them upwards. "Hallelujah!" He pronounces with a wink and a wicked smile.

As he looks over at Zeke, he says, "Now you skedaddle on out. I've got this under control. You did good work, boys."

"Pa," Zeke says, hesitating, "Look at those feathers in his hair. I'll run and get the scissors so you can cut his mangy mop."

Preacher Jim studies the boy hard. "No, I won't cut his hair," he says slowly, holding the thick locks in his hands. "Like I said, this Indian boy is different. He shows no fear. Look into his eyes. They're filled with the utmost defiance."

Zeke opens his mouth to reply, but can't figure what to say. He would've shot him, and now his father wants to tame him. Zeke is livid and thinks his dad is wrong.

Abe stares in amusement at the situation, thinking he couldn't care less about the Indian. He wants that mustang of his, and he is eager to find him... even though there is some sort of strangeness in that horse. Whatever it is, he doesn't care. That wild mustang is a prize.

The boys start to leave. Homer looks back from the door, thinking the preacher is… well, he can't figure it out, but something is off. He's just glad he isn't going to kill the Indian kid.

Preacher Jim has never been so elated in his life. *This is my test. I must surely be His chosen one.* Grinning ear to ear, he virtually dances around the room, his hands raised upwards and his eyes swivel sideways in a bizarre motion.

"I know that the Lord sent you," Preacher Jim says, beaming widely, "because I am to be your teacher of all good tidings. I will guide you in the ways of His kingdom and His words, *true* words… not words filled with blatant falsehoods. I know the good Lord wants you to believe and trust in Him, as do I. The world can be a cruel and harsh place, but it is brought upon your people by their ignorance. Non-believers. Trust in me and in my teachings and you shall walk upon this earth in peace. Disobey me and you shall pay mightily. I will seek His vengeance if you do not obey His words." The preacher runs his long fingers through Hidden Spirit's hair and brushes his locks across his face, inhaling the wild fragrance. *Oh sweet Jesus. This boy has the hair of Samson. I can feel the great power in those locks and I shall transfer that power unto me so that I may tame the terrible beast that surely lies within.*

Preacher Jim is ecstatic, thinking that this is his chance to redeem himself in the eyes of the Lord… especially after the recent catastrophes. Two squaws are dead as well as a slew of Indian boys — most likely on their way to Hell. It does not bode well for a preacher who was sent here to save these children from that very fate. He will contemplate this new mission ahead of him. *I will win this wild one over, snatch his power.* Preacher Jim grunts with satisfaction at his plan. "Come along, boy. We have much to do."

Hidden Spirit pulls his arms away, and glares, as Preacher Jim takes a firmer hold to usher him out the door.

"Now you can come easy or come fighting. Up to you, but I wouldn't recommend the latter. Won't do around here."

At the furthest end of the grounds stands a small, isolated building of crumbled brick and rotted wood. It measures about twenty feet by twelve feet in diameter... with a flat slanted roof. A tiny sliver of an opening in the wall allows the only light in the room. Inside there is a dirt floor and a bucket full of water in the corner. "I'll bring along some food and drink for you later in the day," he says triumphantly, taking Hidden Spirit inside. "I'm going to leave you tied up so you won't be tempted to try anything foolish. Take time to reflect on your ways, boy, and on the sins of your people. Repent, sayeth the Lord. Repent, and the light of God will be your salvation. Got rules to abide by now, boy. Enjoy your stay. See you later." The thick wooden door closes with a thump and the preacher bolts it with a long heavy board, and padlocks it.

ELLIE, WHERE ART THOU

ELLIE IS SO elated that she has to steady her nerves. *The one with the unusual name might have just saved my life,* she thinks happily, skipping down the road. She hopes he will be careful at the gravesites.

When she enters the house, she hurries into the kitchen and discovers her mother is nowhere to be seen. She calls out, "Mother, are you home?" Then listens. No reply. Ellie finds it strange that the house is so quiet and that the roast is left out on the table. Ezekiel is out with his friends, but, as for her mother, well, something must have come up. She sees a squirrel running across the yard and glances out the back window as it hops onto the shed. An idea flashes through her mind. *Oohh… I wonder if I dare,* she thinks, giddy with excitement. *I've been dying to see what's in there.* In her delight, she twirls about the kitchen. *This must be my lucky day,* she thinks, humming merrily.

Her father's shed is off limits. It is his private room, her mother has always reminded her. Curious to discover why, Ellie impulsively slips out the back door and runs down the yard. A nervous tremor fills her as she stands on tiptoes and peers through the grimy window. Unable to see a thing, she mutters to herself. "Darn." The door is always kept locked, but curiosity gets the better of her, and she decides to try it, just in case. Her heart does a somersault when she finds it slightly ajar. She pushes it open, pokes her head inside, and stands there, staring. "This is my father's special place," she says, aghast. At first glance, it looks like a storeroom full of junk. She hesitates before entering. "I made it this far, and I can't turn back now just because of spiders or whatever else is lurking in there." Braving herself to go forward, she runs face-first into a low-hanging cobweb. Stifling a scream, she pulls the sticky web from her hair, hoping the spider isn't lurking in her locks. Determined to go further inside, she shrugs off her trepidation, keeping a wary lookout. The boards creak beneath her feet as she walks through the damp room, her eyes adjusting slowly to the dim light. There is nothing much but a lantern sitting on a table with an open Bible and a pair of muddy boots underneath. A bulky cabinet leans against the wall containing numerous jars of canned goods. She sees moldy peaches, from the hazy light filtering in the window, with brownish colored pickles, corn, and rotten tomatoes. She blows the dust off another jar, and screams as a bluish-tinged, pig-snout floats up in the brine. Backing up in disgust, she hurries away.

What can possibly be so secretive in this place, she wonders, as she looks across the murky room — deeply disappointed after all the anticipation. She had felt certain there was some great secret out here, and now she has come up empty-handed. Her mother's explanation is that "he likes to pray for all the sinners of his flock. His worry keeps him up at night." Ellie finds that hard to believe. It has to be something else. Her eyes roam slowly around the room, thinking *there is nothing of interest in here*; and turns to leave. But when she does, a floorboard beneath her feet bows. So, she kneels down and searches for the loose board. Shuffling her hands across the wooden floor she stops when she finds the wobbly plank, and gives it a tug. Her heart skips a beat and she exhales in relief as it comes up easily. Sliding the board to the side, she peers down into the hole, wiping away a few cobwebs. As she inches closer to the hole she sees a small chest bound with a thick leather strap. Adjusting her eyes to the dim light, she forgets her fear of spiders and other crawly insects, and quickly shoves her hands inside the opening before she changes her mind — pulling up a heavy box and tugging at the lid. Finally it opens and she gasps at what lies inside — a huge pile of sparkling coins. She straightens up, and lets out a huge sigh. "There's a fortune in here!" She runs her hands through the glittery contents again — just to make sure it's real. She can hardly believing her good luck, and wonders, *where did all this money come from?* Her father is quite frugal. He buys nothing that isn't an absolute necessity. Maybe that's why her mother asks for free hams and roasts from Beadle. "Humm," she says, pondering the riches inside this old weather-beaten shed. *Maybe it's because God loves a generous soul,* she thinks, hearing that quote from her father every Sunday in church. She surmises a fair amount came from them — but the people really don't have much to give. Then in a flash, she recalls her Grandmother Opal, who died before she was born, and left her father an inheritance. Her parents never mention the money. Now, she is furious. *My father has been hiding all this for years! I can't believe it. He's a miser. A stingy miser! I've always been denied a new dress or a trinket or anything else… while hoarding all this.*

A screeching sound causes Ellie to jump and she drops the lid, smashing her fingers. "Oh, no! Mother's back." She quickly pushes the box back into the hole, scrambles to her feet, and throws the loose board back in place. Frantic that she might get caught snooping, she takes off in a run. Along the way, she slips over a tree branch that had fallen from the storm, rips her dress on a spikey limb, and stains the bodice with dirt. Sailing around the side of the house, she slides into the kitchen, just as Opal comes walking in.

Opal's mouth tightens into a grimace. "Good gracious! What on earth have you been doing? Look at your dress."

"I… uh…I forgot to take something to Mrs. Trimble," she says, fidgeting with her hands.

"I do declare. You're beginning to act like those wild hooligans that you like so much. I just bet you went to see one of them. For the life of me, I don't understand why you won't associate with your own kind. You have been brought up better than that. How many times have I told you to surround yourself with Christians? Your life would be so much better." Suddenly her mood brightens. "You can't imagine what your brother and his friends discovered lurking near the school grounds." Not waiting for a reply, Opal hurries on. "They caught a wild heathen in the woods, that's what. He was skulking around the graves. He must have run away from a reservation. Your brother says he looked like a bloodthirsty barbarian, out for revenge. Be thankful they found him. Your father has locked him up in the stockade… where he won't be bothering any of us."

Ellie drops her apron, and freezes.

"What's the matter with you?"

Ellie's voice fails to respond.

"Cat got your tongue? Well, in that case, I certainly hope he keeps it… with all your sass and nonsense. Land's sake, Almighty, what are you staring at? The way you're behaving, looks like you've seen Lucifer in the flesh."

Ellie feels a little life flow out of her and is beside herself with worry. She has to do something, so she forces out a slow breath, trying to act calm. "Nothing's the matter, Mother. I'm just surprised, that's all."

"I would think so. Now get some wood for the stove, and start cleaning the house. Then, I need help fixing the curtains. One of them has slipped down. We have lots to do, young lady, and I don't want to see you moping around the house. We have a big day coming up for tomorrow's special supper. I must finish the shopping. And, I expect you to dress properly for our guest."

Zeke comes barreling through the door, whining, "I'm hungry, Ma. What's for lunch?" Opal gives him a warm smile. "Oh, my big growing boy," she declares proudly, and prepares him a nice big ham sandwich.

Ellie rolls her eyes. This is turning into a horrible day. *It's Hidden Spirit they've captured, I know it.* Her mind whirls as she stares blindly out the window, trying to figure what to do. Her dreams of leaving home have come crashing down around her — and her future looks grim. She has to do something to help Hidden Spirit — but what? She feels lost. She must let this awful news sink in first… then maybe something will come to mind.

The next morning, Ellie comes downstairs feeling glum, is already late for service. Opal shoos her out of the house. "Good gracious, we're late. Hurry, hurry," she screeches, hustling out the door, leaving Ellie behind. Ellie, dreading church today, drags her feet down the road.

It is crowded this morning with people wedged tightly into the pews and some lining the walls. As Ellie enters, the congregation is already on its feet, singing a hymn. She is grateful to have slipped in unnoticed without suffering her father's disapproving glare. She pushes her way inside and squeezes past the fat Mrs. Coons, who, in turn, gives her a nasty jab to the ribs and a hateful stare. "You're disrupting the service," she says, haughtily.

The woman is an intolerant gossip and a bigot, and her mother's best friend. Ellie can't stand the woman, so she ignores her as she inches her way forward. Anxious as she is to tell Little Moon about what happened, she sees that will be impossible with the girls squeezed so tightly together, leaving no room for her. *It will have to wait,* she thinks, and stands near the wall.

The singing comes to an end and Ellie sighs, preparing herself for a long and boring sermon.

"Now, we have a surprise for you," Preacher Jim proudly announces. "A wonderful way to start the service and the blessed day. My wife, Opal, has written a song for the children to sing. Everyone, please give a round of applause for Mrs. Crumm, and be sure to thank her after services. For some time, she has wanted to do something to thank you and reward you for your dedication to our place of worship each and every Sunday."

Opal bows and ushers the girls toward her piano, where she starts to play. Her hands fly through the air, pounding the keys like a seasoned pianist as she wails out, "Oh, sweet savior…" The song is abysmal and the girls are mortified as they nervously follow along and sing off-key. Most are trying hard to remember the lyrics to Opal's song. Ellie feels sorry for them, being subjected to this humiliation. She looks at the parishioners as some are rolling their eyes and others hiding their mirth. Finally, when the song comes to an end, the parishioners applaud politely — mostly with a sense of relief.

Opal takes a bow and ushers the children back to their seats as everyone is now silent.

"Redemption!" Preacher Jim shouts as he bounds up to the pulpit, making the parishioners jump in their seats. He nods his head and scans the room, saying, "Those who are looking for salvation shall find it in the Lord's house today," his voice rising excitedly. "That will be today's topic." His eyes carefully search each row as he speaks solemnly. "This will be an important day for these children in need of a Savior. I speak of the wayward ones who attend our school. We must forgive them their ignorance. They have been raised in sin, oblivious to the Word of God. Some of the children will follow me to the river after service, to be purged of their sins, and thus be reborn. It will indeed be a glorious day. Praise be to God."

The parishioners follow with, "Amen. Praise be to God."

The girls look puzzled, whispering among each other, wondering what will happen after service.

"I shall have Mrs. Trimble select the chosen ones on this fine day."

Little Moon stares at the preacher defiantly. She doesn't care about a baptism, today or any other day — whatever "baptism" means. She is going home with Hidden Spirit.

The preacher's voice rings out as he steps down from the pulpit, and stands before the girls. "Even though your ways are sinful, and your blood is tainted, and your skin is red, God is merciful."

The crowd responds with an applause and an, "Amen."

Preacher Jim paces back and forth, his voice booms out, "Praise the Lord almighty for these lost souls." A few parishioners wave their arms in the air, praising the Lord. He prattles on, and feels the room temperature rise and the need to loosen his necktie. He continues to drone on and on. After a while a few parishioners begin to nod off. "Anyone who strays from our flock or prays to false gods will be forever condemned to the fiery pits of Hell." Some parishioners nod their heads in agreement. "And those who are unwilling to give," he says, eyeing the crowd, "shall be looked upon as weak." He is quoting his favorite verse from Proverbs when he gasps out. *Something strange just flew past my head.* He stops preaching a moment as he looks around the pulpit. Seeing nothing, he assumes it must have been a bat or some other creature that brushed the top of his head. In fact, it was probably nothing at all, he surmises with relief. *Just my wild imagination,* he thinks. Dismissing the incident, he straightens his back, clears his throat and once again feels reenergized over his sermon, talking about the temptress. All set for his fiery tirade, Preacher Jim's voice suddenly constricts, as something else strange floats past. "What the…"out of nowhere, he sees a small translucent image with a greenish tinge appear right in front of him, seeming to hover in mid-air. The preacher pants. *My eyes must be playing tricks on me.* He gropes inside his pocket for a handkerchief, wipes his face to clear his vision, and scrunches his eyes. *It's gone*, he thinks with confusion and relief. Then he pauses a moment, looks throughout the room, and warily begins his sermon — though with far less gusto this time. After a while, with no interruptions, he dismisses the disturbance as his favorite topic spurs him on. "The sins of women!" he thunders. "Tempting men with their feminine guile — not to mention their brazen smiles — while wearing indecent dresses… to entice an innocent man." He smacks the pulpit with his Bible for reinforcement, while letting his words sink in. Then says slowly, emphasizing each word. "So women can show off their ankles." On a roll now with hands waving, he clutches his chest to demonstrate their wickedness when, out of the blue and to his dismay, the strange form reappears. This time, it takes on a vivid shape. The preacher shouts out, while swatting wildly at the apparition. "Get away from me, you vile thing…" and he plunges to the floor, frightened. Then, just as quickly as the form had appeared, it disappears. He waits on the floor a moment longer, panting in fear. He hears nothing, and carefully peers around the pulpit on hands and knees. *Make sure the coast is clear,* he thinks in a panic. The only image he sees is the astonished faces of parishioners staring back at him, bewildered by his action.

He jumps to his feet, brushes off his pants and feigns a nervous laugh. "I… I was so carried away by the Lord's words, I fell to my knees, rejoicing," Preacher Jim tries to smile, but couldn't quite manage one, and stammers. "A… a sign from the heavenly Father."

Several parishioners laugh politely, while others squirm in their seats. Some wonder if he is overcome by the Holy Spirit's presence. It has been known to happen, especially after a vigorous sermon.

To Preacher Jim's relief a sense of calm is restored. He looks around seeing nothing, and starts to relax. "Must be seeing things… glasses might be in order," he says under his breath before clearing his throat. Raising his hands to the sky, he plows onward, passionately reciting his favorite passage from the Bible. "The wicked lie in wait for the righteous, and seek to put them to death and…" Then, without warning, a balled fist emerges out of a milky haze and heads straight for Preacher Jim's nose. Wham! A spurt of blood trickles down his face. He almost faints at the abomination as he sees a whitish film start to spread over the exact passage from which he was reading — now blurring the words. "Blast it," he says fearfully, glancing around the pulpit. Beads of sweat pop on his forehead, and he begins to sway. He tries his best to regain his composure, while his heart is pulsing with a fiery, numbing pain.

The room begins to buzz with speculation as Preacher Jim stands at the podium, shaking. Seemingly at a loss for words, he struggles to speak, but he can only whisper out. "This can't be happening… Oh dear God, what torment is this?"

He smacks the pulpit in frustration as it rocks crazily back and forth, then slams the Bible shut. "I am being persecuted," he utters through gritted teeth.

He can feel the chilling air circle around his head, and then stop. The image is now so vivid he stumbles back in fright, and cries out. "It's that damn heathen who almost killed me," he says, in shock. The sight of the girl hovering right in front of him frightens him. She is staring boldly into his eyes. "I'm losing my mind," he whines, and without thinking, he clenches his fist and barrels it into the apparition. The buoyant image soars above his head, and begins circling around him again. A silvery whisper makes his neck prickle. "Take heed, Preacher Man when you speak of the Devil. He may soon pay you a visit…" Before finishing the words, the hazy form emits a burst of white light and in a flash, disappears.

Preacher Jim is mortified. He looks at the parishioners who are staring back, perplexed as they shuffle uncomfortably in their seats.

"Service is over," he cries out, ripping the passages from the Bible and slamming the book shut. Then he hustles out the side door, banging it closed behind him.

Mrs. Trimble runs after Preacher Jim to find out if he is still doing baptisms today. "Preacher Jim!" He turns around to face her, and looks pale and frightened. She has never seen him like this, and she wants to ask what happened, but she knows this isn't the time. "Still doing baptisms today?" she asks nervously, thinking he looks to be on edge.

"I will be at the river shortly," he says, and quickly strides off — leaving the woman wondering what will happen next.

The congregation is stupefied by the preacher's strange outburst. It's the oddest service they have ever attended. They rise from their seats and walk outside, where they mill beside the church and talk amongst themselves about the peculiar service they had just witnessed. Usually, Preacher Jim is at the door waiting to greet everyone and shake their hands, but not today.

"I think he's overtasked," Mrs. Coons says with a sniff. "And I'll bet his outburst comes from those vile heathens at that school. Never should have brought them here... *never*," she says to her daughter with indignation. "And his daughter, Ellie... she's a wicked one, as well. Consorts with them as though they are one of us. Imagine!"

"I heard Mrs. Beach tell Mrs. Baker that the Indians practice witchcraft," her daughter says, lowering her voice, and hisses. "They communicate with the Devil."

"No doubt, indeed," Mrs. Coons says with a snivel and a handkerchief to her nose. "Poor Opal. She certainly has her hands full."

The last of the parishioners had gone, except one. Stephanie

Burgess. An outcast in Mrs. Coons mind as she watches her walk down the steps.

Stephanie sees the two ladies and tries to pretend she doesn't notice them, but is unable as the eagle-eyed Mrs. Coons spots her and comes hurrying over asking, "So, Miss Burgess. Did you enjoy today's service?" Without waiting for an answer she continues on in one long breath. "Can you imagine, a baptism for the heathens? I have never heard of…" and abruptly stops. "The preacher is doing his best and I suppose we will have to get used to these barbarians in our midst."

Stephanie wants to tell the lady to mind her own business, but instead she forces out a smile and says, "yes, I will attend the service. I look forward to it."

Mrs. Coons can't help herself and sniffs with disdain, looking at Miss Burgess and her attire, then huffs off, giving her a frown.

Stephanie once had a taste of her vile tongue and that was enough, so she does her best to avoid Mrs. Crumm whenever possible.

TALES OF THE BUFFALO

Chasing Rabbit dips her toes in the opalescent water, bubbling with shifting colors. The effect is mesmerizing, as are the tales of Broken Feather's youth, which hold her spellbound.

"I was nine years old when my powers came," Broken Feather says. "It was a hot, sunny day in the season of the popping cherries. I was off by myself, wandering through the prairies... tall sweet grasses and wildflowers. I walked for a very long time and became tired, so I crawled under a crab tree and was lulled into contented peace and fell asleep. Suddenly my eyes flew open. In the distance I saw thousands of buffalo lining the vast plains, as far as I could see. There were so many, they looked like brown dots covering the hillside... grazing on lush sweet grass. I stood up and rubbed my eyes to make sure I was not dreaming. I'm not sure how this happened, but, suddenly, I found myself standing amongst the great herd. I watched for a long while, mesmerized by the animals' intense eyes staring at me. Bewildered, I tried to understand how I had gotten into the middle of this huge herd. As I looked around in awe I saw an enormous buffalo amble over to me and shake his head... his shaggy beard almost touching the ground. The black curling horns that crowned his head looked like lethal weapons, and his intense eyes reached into my depth, daring me to sit atop his massive back. When he snorted, he sent plumes of steam upwards. I hesitated for a moment, and then, without another thought, I hopped onto his back, took hold of his rich, shaggy hair… and clung tightly. A flock of crows screeched overhead, flapping their wings in alarm, startling the complacent herd. The buffalo took off in a flurry of hooves and dust, and roared across the plains… thundering at breakneck speed. I clung to the beast, wrapping my arms around his neck. Then, without warning, a lightning bolt shot out of the blue sky. Its jolt coursed through my body, standing my hair on end, and singeing my arms, which seemed to be on fire. My heart raced faster than the roaring herd as I felt the power of the buffalo surge through me. After a time, the great herd slowed its pace and came to a stop beside a wide river… all the buffalo panting heavily. My legs were unsteady as I jumped down from the enormous bull and my body quivered, pulsing with the buffalo's energy. I wiped the dust from my eyes, and saw the enormous creature look back at me, and snort. In the next moment, I found myself sitting under the same tree, as the musty scent still lingered. Was it a dream, I wondered, or was it real? My face was flushed with heat, my heart was pounding, and my arms were scorched. I took a deep breath, raised my arms to the sky, and heard the call of the buffalo. I knew then that my powers were great."

Chasing Rabbit was enthralled by the story. "Please tell me more, Grandfather."

"Now it seems, our beloved buffalo have gone the way of the winds. The roaring boxes cut through our pristine lands, covering our hunting grounds with their wooden tracks. The white eyes came and killed our brothers by the thousands, leaving their carcasses to rot on the plains." Broken Feather sat silent a moment, remembering.

"So one day as the leaves were turning golden, I wandered into the white man's town. I was unprepared for the vision that stung my eyes. Our beloved buffalo had their massive heads cut off and nailed to the walls and posts. Soldiers and sharpshooters lined the street, bragging about the slaughter of our brothers, auctioning them off to the highest bidder for greenbacks or whiskey. Didn't matter which.

"I walked on in pain, dazed at the sight, barely breathing. Then at the end of the street I saw the stunning head of the buffalo I had ridden in my youth. I could never forget its massive face and golden horns. I hurried over, touched his soft curly hair and shaggy beard. Pain ripped through my heart like an arrow. I looked into his eyes, that revealed our past was fading. I knew then that my years on earth were nearing an end, and I let my emotions consume me. Agony and despair struck me like a thunderbolt, and, as tears rushed down my face, I fell to my knees. I heard an intake of breath. I looked at the buffalo's head, which had begun to move. I stood in awe of the powerful beast, and wrapped my arms around his head. I told him I didn't understand such mindless cruelty, and was sorry to see him end up like this. We are not much better off, my friend. Soon there would be more white men on our lands than stars that fill the sky. It would only be a matter of time before we would have to move to one of their reservations, living in fenced cages, with no means to hunt and roam freely… like we once did." Then, the buffalo let off a slow rise of steam. As I stood next to the buffalo, talking to him for a long time, a white man came up and laughed at me. 'How do you like the buffalo now, Injun?' he said, and shoved me backwards, slamming me into the wall. 'All 'bout dead now, 'cept for a few cows. Stupid as hell, too. I'd say 'bout as stupid as you, old man.' He continued to taunt me, but I paid him no mind. My heart was still saddened by the sight of my old friend. Then he pushed me to the ground. I still didn't respond. He became angered at my silence and came at me, his gun pointed at my head… threatening to shoot if I didn't get out of town.

The buffalo's eyes shifted, and a light plume of mist erupted from its nostrils. The man with the gun looked at the buffalo and thought he had seen the head move. I could see his hands shake. He hesitated for a moment before he spoke. 'Gonna shoot the both of you dead,' he said, and aimed for my head. 'Put a bullet right in...' That's when he lost his words as the sharp horns of the buffalo arched to the right and gouged the man's stomach. He dropped his gun and slipped to the ground, fright filling him as he held his belly. That buffalo still had his power. I pulled the massive head off the hook and carried him with me to the hills to pray. I fed him water and comforted him the best I could. I held him in my arms, and told him of our lives, and how empty the plains were now, without the buffalo. I held him until I felt his final breath. His glassy eyes stared at me with sadness... then went blank. I saw a single tear slip down his craggy face. My heart ached for this powerful beast I so admired."

Broken Feather was silent for a moment before continuing. "We have gone the way of the buffalo, my child. But there is hope, if the young can remember the ways of our past... our traditions. They will need it for the times that lie ahead."

Chasing Rabbit listens, riveted to the story. Splashing her feet, she wrinkles her brow in contemplation — feeling a tremendous sadness surround her. Then she hears a mournful song, coming from a long way off, as if from a hollow tube. She recognizes it as the death song. It fills her heart with even greater sorrow. She bends down on her hands and knees and peers through the clouds to find out who is singing. As she strains to see better, she loses her balance, topples over the precipice, and begins to tumble through the air — down, down, and down through a narrow portal, whooshing at a tremendous speed. She is going so fast now that her body scrunches into a ball of mist.

Feathery hands surround her, and an admonishing voice

speaks. "You must be more careful, dear, of where you look," Broken Feather says, as he eases her lightly onto her father's lap.

Chasing Rabbit can't believe it is her father. *It's him singing the death song.* She reaches out to comfort him, but her hand is only a misty vapor and cannot touch his face. Determined, she pulls herself upright, gaining strength. She wants to tell her father not to mourn — that she is safe. As she floats close to his brow she carefully observes each detail of his face and traces his outline with a brush of air. She yearns to kiss his cheek, which appears so much older than what she remembers. And she tries to whisper, to tell him she is with Broken Feather — but only a slight wisp of air comes out.

When he feels something soft caress his cheek, White Cloud stops singing his mournful song, and slowly opens his eyes.

Chasing Rabbit hovers over him as a wide smile spreads across his face, and he wipes his tears. The form of his beloved daughter has taken shape. He stares into her depthless eyes, which seem to drift into forever and waver before him like a flowery mist. He inhales her beauty. Beside himself with happiness, he says, "Oh, my dear. My heart swells with joy to see you. You have been in my thoughts every day since you left for that school. Your arrival into this world was so welcome that even the rabbits danced in delight. Now I am heartbroken that your life was taken without cause... and too soon." He chokes back a sob. "You were so far from home. To have you leave this world and never see your face again is unbearable..."

"Sshhhh. Please father, do not mourn so. I'm with Broken Feather. I'm in the afterlife now, and will soon go to the other-world. I will see the buffalo, and meet my ancestors at the place of the unknown. Grandfather says that all my ancestors will be waiting to greet me, and there will be a big celebration."

Chasing Rabbit lands lightly on his shoulder, and kisses his cheek. "I will tuck your heart into mine, and savor its love," she says in a whisper. "Forever. Tell Mother I love her, and give her this." A glittering orange flower, the size of a walnut, zooms down and floats softly around White Cloud. Its soft petals open, revealing its full beauty, and let loose a puff of pollen that hangs in the air like golden sunshine.

White Cloud inhales the delectable odor and smiles — then he tucks the unusual flower into his shirt.

Chasing Rabbit feels a strong tug. "I must go now. Goodbye, my father," Chasing Rabbit whispers, and disappears in a whirling orb that draws her back to the ethers.

"My child," Broken Feather says, awaiting her arrival, "It is time for you to go now, before you get into any more mischief down there. I know you are brave like your brother, but you must not take so many chances. It could turn dangerous for you, being amongst the living. You are not ready for that just yet."

He takes Chasing Rabbit's hand as she walks by his side. "Can you tell me more about the otherworld, Grandfather?"

"That will be yours alone to discover," he says.

"Will I see Mama or Papa there?" she asks solemnly.

Broken Feather smiles at his granddaughter. "Not at this time, but I do have one more surprise for you."

A lightness fills Chasing Rabbit. As she skips along beside her Grandfather, she wonders what it can be.

They suddenly turn onto an amethyst path filled with dazzling gemstones, milky quartz bursting with hues, and marvelous rubies — so rich, the colors fill your senses with their opulence and beauty. There is every shape and color imaginable, and chimes tinkling all around. It's as if a sprinkling of love is sent from the hereafter and envelops the young girl. Broken Feather smiles at the surprised girl and snaps his fingers, sending a sharp crack throughout the vastness of the illuminated space. A moment later a clopping of hooves echoes and a magnificent white stallion appears, looking like a dreamlike vision. The horse's wild eyes flash like glittering diamonds — accentuated by long curly lashes and a silver mane that touches the ground. The horse prances over and bows down next to Broken Feather. Broken Feather pats the animal's nose and then lifts Chasing Rabbit onto its powerful back. Then a sparkling violet hue shimmers in the distance, and a blue-eyed mustang, with a flowing mane the color of burnished sunshine, emerges and trots over to the white stallion. When they touch noses the mustang whinnies and the stallion whinnies back. To Chasing Rabbit's amazement, the mustang begins to lift its hooves, like a warrior dancing before a hunt and starts to dance, its rear legs kick high into the air, moves sideways, and is swept away —on a bed of polished coral. The white stallion follows, prancing delicately, lifting its forelegs high until they find themselves in a field of shimmering rainbows, surrounded by an intricate maze of colors.

Chasing Rabbit giggles, feeling as light and free as the wind, while she sways gracefully on top of the steed. Further on, flutes and drums throb while other strange music is heard in the faraway fields.

In the distance she notices a wavering light flickering at the far end of the path. *It's the same light that beckoned to me when I first arrived at this magical place,"* she thinks, with elation. The mustang abruptly comes to a stop, whinnies, and shakes its huge flowing mane. The horse with its blue eyes, looks back at the girl and the stallion, as if communicating a secret plan. The white stallion rears on his hind legs, paws the air, and then gallops off down the enchanting path. The whirling light comes closer and closer until they are surrounded by sounds and colors and chiming bells that urge the horse to follow. As the girl and stallion enter into the labyrinth of rainbows, wisps of color trail behind, and Chasing Rabbit's memories slowly begin to fade, until they are no more.

But if you look closely, one could see the silhouette of the horse and girl soaring into the illuminating light and beyond.

Then, a scattering of leaves, whoosh throughout the sky and drift down, ever so lightly, until there is nothing left but silence and hope filling the air.

GATHER AT THE RIVER, LITTLE SINNERS

THE DAY IS frigid and overcast. *It is far too cold to be doing baptisms in the river at this time of year.* Ellie worries about the girls, but is certain that old puss, Mrs. Coons, and her daughter could use a good douse in the icy water. *Maybe it would relieve them of some of their nastiness.* She smiles at that notion, as she sits on a stretch of gravelly dirt across the river, while ardently watching Mrs. Trimble instruct the girls on the virtues of being saved.

Ellie has always been perplexed by the words written in the Bible, filled as they are with hypocrisy. *The age-old writings could easily be misinterpreted by the many as extremely violent, especially for the ones who espouse goodwill and love.* The book is big and difficult to understand. Despite its size and complexity, Ellie has read the Bible all the way through. It was always a nightly occurrence in her home after supper. Her father liked to focus on those passages that he felt most effective in keeping the parishioners in line — and coming back for more.

When no one was looking and after she tired of reading the Bible, she would quietly sneak her favorite magazine between the pages — to admire the high fashions of the day. The magazine was worn and tattered, but that never mattered to her. She could still see the images of the stylish lace-trimmed dresses and their puffy shoulders. She especially liked the dresses with the ruffles at the wrist, and the big bows set atop the bustles on the beautiful gowns. Ellie dreamed of wearing dresses like those one day, and hoped that day was not far off. *But now, all hope seems lost.* Hidden Spirit has been captured. Of all people, it had to be her stupid brother with Abe and Homer. Now he's locked up and unable to help her, or anyone else. *Without him, my life is doomed.* She didn't know the boy, only what the Little Moon and Chasing Rabbit told her… but still, she has to hold on to a shred of hope, even though he is locked up. Ellie is restless. She knows that she needs to be careful and not arouse suspicion, especially around her mother. *And yet, I have to do something or I fear I will go mad.* Ellie tries to concentrate on a plan to help him escape, but her mind is too jumbled. Thoughts of marrying Beadle kept creeping in, and she shivers, imagining all the horrible things he would do to her. Her life would be ruined. To think that her own mother would force her to marry against her will. It is the most despicable thing a mother could do. It sent her mind reeling and feels nauseated. Forcing herself not to panic, she jolts back to the present, and sits up, and watches the spectacle take place across the river. Ellie cringes, as Mrs. Trimble calls out to the girls in her shrill voice.

"Girls! Remove all of your clothing, except your undergarments, and hand them over to Miss Snodberry," she commands. "You will retrieve them after your baptism."

The girls hesitate. They are out in the open, where the church people can see them. Little Moon refuses to undress and runs over to a nearby tree, where she hides.

Miss Snodberry takes notice, and rushes over to her side, coaxing Little Moon to undress. "Come, my dear. I know you don't want to do this, but it will be over quickly. You can undress behind me and go into the water when you are called. Then you will be saved."

"Saved from what?" Little Moon spat, biting her lip. "This place? I'm not going in there. The river is cold, and looks very dangerous."

"Well, I'm sure it's a little cold, but I'm not sure about it being dangerous. It will only take a moment before your baptism is over, then everyone is happy. You won't have to go in very far."

"They want us to forget our Great Spirit," Little Moon says miserably, "and our families. I won't be happy either."

"Preacher Jim wants the best for you children," Miss Snodberry says, urging her to comply with the rules. "They all want the best for you girls."

"I don't think they care about us. Mrs. Trimble is cold and mean. I never want to be like any of them. Besides, going into the freezing water to get saved sounds stupid." Little Moon surprises herself, sounding so much braver than she feels. Inside, her stomach tumbles in knots.

White Doe timidly walks over with Raven. "Mrs. Trimble says that once we are dunked in the water we'll be saved from the Devil, and we'll go with the white man on the boards. I *want* to go with Him," she says proudly.

"I would rather go with the pitchfork man," Little Moon says, stubbornly, slowly removing her dress.

Miss Snodberry gasps at her words, hoping Mrs. Trimble hasn't heard. "Why would you say such a thing?"

"Opal says there is suffering down there, wherever "down there" is. But it can't be worse than this place," Little Moon states adamantly, crossing her small arms.

Miss Snodberry starts to say, *that's not true. God loves you,* but she can't quite manage to get the words out. She has no words of comfort to offer, or words to convince them that God truly loves them. She secretly wonders if the girl is right and, before she can think any further, she quickly ushers the children behind the trees.

The girls undress and try their best to cover themselves as they stand waiting — dreading what is to come.

"Are they going to drown us," Raven asks, lips quivering in the damp air.

Miss Snodberry takes her hand, and squeezes it. "No, no. Preacher Jim will be gentle. It's just a quick douse... and..." Unable to finish her words, her eyes light up at the sight of Miss Burgess, standing quietly by herself to the side of the congregation. As their eyes slowly meet, her hands begin to tremble.

A few more girls come over by the tree, nervous. "I don't want to forget our Great Spirit," Raven says sadly. "Me neither," another girl replies. "They are cruel to make us do this," Little Moon adds. Raven walks up to Miss Snodberry and timidly pulls on her sleeve. "Will this make our skin turn white?" She waits for her to answer.

"Wha... what did you say?" Miss Snodberry asks weakly. Her cheeks are stained scarlet as she draws her attention back to the questioning girl.

"I heard Opal talk about the purity of being white. I wonder if we will turn white after we are saved... then we will be pure," one of the older girls says. "I think it must be true," Raven says. "I would like my skin to be white."

"That's a lie! They are not pure," Little Moon screams, horrified by Raven's remarks. "Don't believe Opal or any of them. I would rather die than be white. We must be proud of who we are. We can never forget our blood."

Miss Snodberry does her best to hide her shock. *Did Opal really tell the girls they would turn white?* She wonders. *Why would she say such a thing?* She tries to comfort the girls, assuring them they will still be Indian girls after the baptism. But her heart is troubled, not only by what the girls say, but by another matter. Then, her eyes stray once again to the handsome Miss Burgess. She forgets about praying to God. *I have searched my heart and found peace with my feelings. I know He understands.* Miss Snodberry is overcome with adoration for Miss Burgess. Her feelings are so strong they could knock her over. She has never felt like this before, and can hardly breathe. Her mind is reeling with desire and confusion.

Mrs. Trimble walks by the girls and is delighted, albeit a little surprised, by the large turnout. She had been concerned not many would show up after the unusual morning service. As a feeling of relief courses through her, she thinks, *why not make the best of this while they wait for the preacher to arrive.* Mrs. Trimble moves to the center of the group and raises her hands like a conductor, inviting the parishioners to join her in song. Her high-pitched voice is scratchy and a trifle off-key, but that doesn't deter her. She closes her eyes and warbles out, "We shall gather at the river, the beautiful, beautiful river…" The parishioners sing along tepidly as the wind picks up and rain clouds gather overhead. Mrs. Trimble starts to sway, and lifts her hands toward the sky. She seems oblivious to the weather, so engrossed in this moment and song. It is as though she is waiting for the coming of Jesus as she stands there, staring upward — her dress billowing in the wind.

The girls huddle together in their underclothes, watching, as Preacher Jim walks down the path, a smile on his face, and welcomes the parishioners, thanking them for coming to "this wondrous event."

Mrs. Trimble stops singing and heartily applauds, grateful for his arrival.

To everyone's surprise, Preacher Jim seems composed — as if nothing out of the ordinary happened earlier. He speaks out with great enthusiasm. "This is a glorious day for the lost souls in our presence. These children, who have walked a path of wickedness and worshipped false Gods, will be born again. Let's all rejoice and say, 'Hallelujah!'"

The group repeats: "Hallelujah!"

"The Devil came to visit today," he says with a serious expression. "Into the house of the Lord, he came. I had to rid the evil presence at our holy place." Lowering his voice, he embellishes his words. "I believe Satan has followed the heathens, who have infiltrated the sanctity of our church."

The preacher nods to one of his devout parishioners, who is awed by his words, and listens intently.

"Had a dickens of a time getting rid of the Devil, but the Lord always prevails," he says, gushing proudly as he clasps his holy book to his heart, and clears his throat. That's why you might have seen me act... well... a bit different today. Had to go off and pray... pray mightily to save us all from the evil lurking in the shadows... waiting to snatch the innocents and lure them into a life of sin and debauchery."

The parishioners gasp in response. A few clutch their hearts, but most are heartened by the explanation — relieved to know that the preacher is of sound mind. But a few among them wonder why he bothers with the Indians and why he brought them into their church. Thoughts of demons spook a few and some worry about what other evils these nasty heathens have brought with them. Miss Burgess has her doubts and remains skeptical of the preacher and his odd behavior. However, she keeps her opinions to herself.

Stephanie Burgess, new in town, was ostracized from Newburg, Pennsylvania, for her masculine behavior. So she tries to keep a low profile as she goes about her business. She comes to town infrequently, only to buy supplies. On most Sundays, she makes the long drive from her farm to attend church services. She had heard about the school and is sympathetic toward the Indian children. She considers it a crime that they were forcibly taken from their families and brought to this place, where disdain and narrow mindedness prevails. On her first trip into town, Stephanie was unfortunate enough to run into Mrs. Coons. She knew right away that the lady was trouble… a gossip and relished telling tales, tall or otherwise. The woman practically pounced on her the moment she saw her and questioned her beliefs. First, Mrs. Coons asked if she attended church. Then she wanted to know where she came from, why she left there, and why in the world was she wearing men's trousers. Scrutinizing her a little more closely, Mrs. Coons asked, "Why is it you, a younger woman, have never married? You're a might unattractive, but still, there had to be someone who would court you."

"Why, Mrs. Coons. I'm not meaning to be rude, but that is none of your business why I am not wed. I am very content with my life." Stephanie felt like slugging the woman, but instead, forced a smile. She thought, *this town's not much different from the one I left behind. Who knows? It might be worse. I would certainly not expect anyone here to try to understand my views or my lifestyle.*

Mrs. Coons sniffed and walked away thinking she had every right to ask a simple question of a new person in town. *You just never know with whom you're dealing. The woman might carry wicked and impure thoughts. I've heard about women like that. You know the type… they look like a boy, dress like a boy, and wear their hair like a boy. And yet they have bosoms. It's possible she's hoping to snare one of our purest of innocents from this community and taint her with her wanton desires.*

"My Rebecca, will not be associated with the likes of that vile woman," she fumes, strutting down the road. "This is a righteous and God-fearing town. Besides people like her, we have those Indians amongst us, bringing with them their barbaric ways. I hold my nose and cringe as they walk past, but I tolerate them for the preacher's sake. Still, I shiver at night with thoughts that they may escape and scalp me in my bed when I sleep. A frightful nightmare I have to live with. And now I have to worry about women with… unnatural inclinations." She snorts.

Standing by herself under a lone maple tree, Stephanie surmises that Miss Snodberry is the only one in town who has shown her kindness, even interest. Stephanie's face burns bright pink at the thought of seeing the woman today at the baptism, and eagerly scans the group of parishioners — waiting.

*

Little Moon watches the river nervously, as small waves crash along the edge. She can't believe that Preacher Jim is sending them into that watery mass. "I can't swim," she says to Mrs. Trimble. "None of us can. We'll drown. I'm not going in there!"

Mrs. Trimble is appalled at the girl's remarks and is ready to shush her, but before she can comment, Little Moon continues, ignoring the sharp look. "Besides, we're going to be with our ancestors when we die."

The girls gasp at Little Moon's bravery, and look at Mrs. Trimble nervously.

"It looks so cold," Raven says worriedly. "I don't want to do it, either."

Mrs. Trimble glares at the girls. "What utter nonsense. You children are most ungrateful. You have come here so we can save you from an eternity of suffering after you leave this world… and this is what we get for our troubles?!"

"We suffer here… at this place," Little Moon says under her breath.

Mrs. Trimble responds with a smart slap across her face. "This is for your impudence."

The girls stare at Mrs. Trimble, uncertain of what to do or say.

Resolved not to cry, Little Moon stands and stares at the woman, squeezing her fists defiantly. "We didn't want to come here, but were forced to. My friends, Chasing Rabbit and Otter, are dead because of..." She can't finish her sentence and starts choking up at the mention of her friends. "We just want to go home."

"Little Moon," Mrs. Trimble says sharply, "if this wasn't such a special day, I would tan your backside good. But, today, and only today, I will be forgiving and ignore your rudeness."

Raven is shaken and starts to cry.

"Everyone... settle down," Mrs. Trimble says, irritably. "You are testing my patience. You know Opal explained this to you in class, so... unless you girls are not paying attention, or maybe some of you are a bit..." Biting her words, she glares at Little Moon. "This is a matter of grave consequence when you die. You'll be sorry you didn't heed my words, but by then, it will be too late. You have sinned since the moment you were born!" She smacks her hands in exasperation. "That's why we're doing this for you... so you will see Jesus after you die. You should be thanking us for trying to save you."

Just then, a breathless Mrs. Burns hustles over. "I wanted to come to witness the baptism... and imagine... holding it in the river, is..." She glances at the rippling water. "Oh, goodness! It looks frightening."

White Doe starts to whimper.

"Now see what you have done, Mrs. Burns? There is no need to carry on so. They're already nervous enough, and I've got my hands full." Mrs. Trimble is so agitated she feels like whacking Mrs. Burns up the side of her head. "It's just a little douse in the water, for Heaven's sake. So, it might be a little chilly, but the girls will be in and out in no time."

But, Miss Snodberry has misgivings about the baptism, and starts to say something to Mrs. Trimble — but she catches herself, knowing it would only cause more trouble and her wrath. *I wish*

I could tell her my feelings on this matter… how the girls feel, she thinks, annoyed at herself for not speaking up, and looks around for Miss Burgess.

"I wish Preacher Jim would hurry and get started," Mrs. Trimble mutters to Mrs. Burns. Annoyed at the delay, she lowers her voice. "It would be rude to interrupt him while he's talking… but, really… keeping us waiting like this?"

Finally, Mrs. Trimble catches Preacher Jim's eye, and waves. He excuses himself from the group and hurries over. "I see you have everything in order, as usual, Mrs. Trimble. Forgive my delay, but everyone seems to have so much to chat about."

"The girls are getting restless," Mrs. Trimble says, clearing her throat. "Are you ready to begin?"

He nods. "Indeed I am." Not bothering to remove his shoes, Preacher Jim walks down the steep banks and enters the murky water. Oblivious to the cold, he walks without faltering toward the middle, where the water rises past his waist. He waves at Mrs. Trimble. "Send the first girl in."

Mrs. Trimble clicks her fingers excitedly at Little Moon, and gives her a shove. "You will be the first to sample the bliss… now, go. Make Preacher Jim proud. And smile for pity's sake… smile. This is a glorious day! You're getting baptized."

Little Moon can't believe this. She looks at the steep bank wondering how to get down, and decides the safest way is to slide. So she sits at the edge, gives herself a push, and sails down the side. At the bottom, she pulls herself up, her underclothes thick with mud. But she doesn't care in the least how she looks, and walks over to the water's edge. Little Moon tentatively sticks her toe into the water, and quickly pulls it out. *This is freezing,* she thinks, and stands staring at the river, shivering. "How am I going to get to Preacher Jim without drowning?" she wonders. "He's so far out."

Annoyed and impatient, Mrs. Trimble rushes to the side of

the bank and scolds her. "Hurry up and get in that water… and don't embarrass the preacher."

Little Moon forces herself to comply. The water feels like ice shards against her skin and she grits her teeth. Feeling desperate, she turns to look back, hoping someone will see her plight and offer to help. But there is only the vexed Mrs. Trimble, staring down, anxiously waving her on. She forces one foot to move and then another, and, before she knows it, the water surrounds her, rises up, and swirls around her legs. The currents are strong and threaten to whisk her downstream, if she isn't careful. She wonders if she will die trying to get to the preacher, who stands in the water like a statue, apparently unaware of the freezing water and of her plight. After what seems like an eternity and with much struggle, she finally reaches him… dazed and out of breath, she can't believe she didn't drown. Little Moon is so cold by now she can scarcely feel her legs or any other part of her limbs, and she wobbles from the exertion.

Preacher Jim jerks his eyes at the girl, as if coming out of a trance, and pulls her close. His voice booms out with pride as he calls to the parishioners. "Congratulations, to this blessed child. Let us rejoice in the name of the Lord." He looks solemnly at the girl. "I will now immerse you in the water to baptize you and cleanse you of your sins… and…" he lowers his voice so only Little Moon can hear — "the Lord will now remove the evil that has followed you here."

Before Little Moon can take a breath of air, he plunges her deep into the murky depths.

Mrs. Trimble stands on her toes and squints to see the girl being baptized. She hopes this will tame that girl's willfulness and maybe even help her to see the light. *A blessed relief that would be*, she thinks, grimly.

Mrs. Burns follows Mrs. Trimble's lead and rises on her toes.

"I suppose he wants to make certain he washes all her sins away," she says to Mrs. Trimble, seeing the girl's feet flail in the water. A wrinkle creases her brow. She wonders how long it takes to baptize a person. She's just glad it isn't her in that frigid water and wonders if the preacher might be taking the dousing too far.

Little Moon's legs are now kicking frantically, but Preacher Jim seems oblivious. With water almost to his neck now and praying with all his might, he cries out to the Lord, as the wind picks up. "Please help me remove the demons that are lurking nearby. I have seen the demons in church. They taunt me... harass me. They even tried to kill me. Slay the demons, oh Lord." He lowers his voice to a whisper. "Please Lord, for my sake and sanity, help me in my hour of need."

Miss Snodberry keeps her eyes peeled on the preacher, concerned how long he's keeping the child under water. She decides that if he doesn't bring her up soon, she will run in there herself and bring the child out... if she isn't drowned by then. She is beginning to question herself, as she paces back and forth. *Why am I here? I hate how the girls are treated. They are so sad, I could cry watching them. I feel so ashamed... and yet there is nothing I can do to help. I wish I were stronger. I would box Mrs. Trimble right in the ears.* Feeling someone is watching her, she looks up. Then her eyes are drawn to Stephanie, who is watching her intently. She quickly looks down at her feet, feels her hands tremble, and looks away. *I must do something,* she thinks, *or I will go mad. I have been such a coward.* Gathering up her nerve, she walks over to Mrs. Trimble. "It's been too long to leave the girl under water. Maybe you should say something."

"Yes, yes. I'm sure Preacher Jim knows what he is doing, for heaven's sake."

Just then, Preacher Jim pulls the sputtering girl out of the water, and claims, "This girl is now saved in the name of the Lord."

Mrs. Trimble responds in kind. "Praise the Lord."

Breathing a sigh of relief, Miss Snodberry impulsively hurries down the incline toward the river, to wait for the girl.

Gasping for air, Little Moon spits out the murky water, her head spinning. *I thought he was going to drown me*, she thinks in a panic, and looks to the shore. Without waiting a second longer, she struggles to make her way back to the river's edge. By this time her fingers and legs are so numb, she can barely move them, but she pushes forward with her last bit of strength. She prays to the Great Spirit she won't get swept downstream, as she fights the currents. Finally, Little Moon makes it to shore. She falls to the ground in a heap, and kisses the muddy banks, grateful to be alive.

Miss Snodberry hurries to the girl's side, shaken to the core. To her mind, the baptism was cruel, and she doesn't care what Mrs. Trimble or anyone else thinks. "Here, take my hand, Little Moon," she says kindly. As the quivering girl reaches up, Miss Snodberry loses her footing and falls backwards onto the soggy ground, landing in the mud, next to Little Moon. She knows she must look a sight as she looks up at the gaping crowd. Then, without a care, they both giggle and then burst into laughter. She hugs Little Moon relieved she didn't drown. Miss Snodberry feels a sense of freedom for the first time in her life… she's lying in the mud not caring what anyone else thinks.

Mrs. Trimble leans over the side of the bank, and screeches. "Good gracious, Miss Snodberry, what on earth are you doing down there? Get a hold of your senses and get back up here. Little Moon! Get up! You're making a fool of yourself and a mockery of this event." She is so frustrated and angry she barks orders to Mrs. Burns. "Get down there and help. They are covered in mud, lying there laughing like this is some kind of joke. Preacher Jim will be mortified. It's enough to expect it from the Indian girl, but certainly not Miss Snodberry. I'm so embarrassed, I don't know what people will think, watching this behavior."

"Yes, yes, I quite agree, but wha… what do you expect me to do?" the woman asks, completely unnerved. "The banks are steep and…"

"Oh, just hurry up, and do as I say." Mrs. Trimble takes the woman's arm, and walks her to the side of the bank. "Now, get down there. I will give you a hand and the Lord will guide you the rest of the way."

Mrs. Burns is utterly astonished at the demanding woman. She stares at the slippery bank and cries out. "I can't go down there. I will surely slip and fall."

"Oh nonsense," Mrs. Trimble says with annoyance. "Just be quick about it and you'll do just fine."

Mrs. Burns takes a tentative step on the bank, testing her footing. Mrs. Trimble, anxious for this nonsense to be over, helps her… with a little nudge to her back, Mrs. Burns go sliding down the hill, dress flying over her head, petticoats flapping — looking like a goose ready for take off, and lands at the bottom with a splash into a puddle of mud.

Squawking and blustering, the woman flails about, trying to get up. The parishioners gasp, not knowing what to think about this outrageous behavior.

The girls cover their mouths and start to giggle at the sight of Miss Snodberry and Mrs. Burns covered in mud. Unable to contain their laughter, it becomes contagious as the girls hold their bellies, laughing in delight. This is the first time the girls have dared to laugh out loud in front of the teachers. A few snickers are heard from the nearby group of younger parishioners, while the others huff off in disbelief.

Quite a dismal beginning for the baptisms, Mrs. Trimble thinks, and she shouts out to Miss Snodberry, wishing she could throttle the woman. "Look what you have started, with your unsightly behavior. You have made a mockery of this wondrous occasion. I shall see to it that you are properly reprimanded."

Miss Snodberry pulls herself up out of the mud and glares at the angry woman. Unleashing her pent-up fury... the likes of which she has never known, consumes her. Ever since she can remember, she has repressed every one of her feelings. She was never allowed to speak up or voice an opinion without a whipping or a warning or a slap to her face. On this day, all of her pent-up feelings unleashes until she finally snaps. Impulsively, she picks up a soggy pile of mud, packs it tightly, and hurls it at Mrs. Trimble, hitting her squarely on the side of her face.

For once, Mrs. Trimble is at a loss for words, and stumbles backwards. Dumbstruck by Miss Snodberry's actions, she feels the blood drain from her face.

Just then, Miss Burgess flies down the steep bank and runs to Miss Snodberry's aide. She wipes the mud off her face and clothes... then without a moment's hesitation, twirls her around, saying, "You were most kind to help the little girl, Miss Snodberry. I think it's time we leave now." Miss Snodberry smiles at Miss Burgess and nods her head. "Yes, I believe it is time." The two women walk together down the rivers edge, holding hands, talking excitedly to each other about their plans.

The few parishioners that remain look at each other, appalled by what they had just witnessed... "that teacher's behavior is unforgiveable," some grumble. They can't believe that this is happening on baptism day. It was supposed to be a victory over the Devil, but it has turned into a travesty. Some even fret about the outcome as they watch the preacher leaving the water in long strides.

"Baptisms are now over," says Preacher Jim hurling his angry words at the women as he walks toward shore, glaring at the mud-strewn Mrs. Burns, then eyes Miss Snodberry, who is traipsing down the path with a woman. He stomps off, without looking back or speaking another word, shaking his head.

Holding hands in unity, the girls continue to giggle as they walk down the road, grateful they didn't have to go into the dangerous water and that Little Moon didn't drown. The best part of the day was seeing Miss Snodberry throw mud at Mrs. Trimble, something they all would like to have done. And then she left with that lady.

Mrs. Trimble, too livid to speak, picks the dried mud from her face as she leads the way back to the school, her feet stomping furiously as she walks.

Miss Snodberry failed to show up at the school the next morning, much to Mrs. Trimble's chagrin. She was itching to give her a piece of her mind. Word in town was that she was spotted riding away in a wagon with Miss Burgess. "Can you imagine," Mrs. Trimble says, thoroughly vexed, "that woman never bothered to leave a note for me or to apologize for her sinful actions. The Devil with her and Miss Burgess."

Tongues waggled around town about the baptism and about Miss Snodberry leaving so abruptly — Mrs. Coons' tongue, more precisely. She intimated they should have tarred and feathered that Burgess girl the moment she arrived in town. *Sent her packing is what they should have done. Thrown her out by the seat of her man-pants.*

"Look at the mess that hussy has caused in our quiet little town," Mrs. Coons intimated to the still fuming Mrs. Trimble. "Devil in disguise… that's what she is," Mrs. Coons continues to rant. "I knew she was no good the moment I laid eyes on her. I'm a good judge of character, you know. Got a quick eye for women of questionable moral character… not to mention your Miss Snodberry. Did you not have even an inkling about her? Well," Mrs. Coons prattles on, "I say, you can't really blame the woman with the likes of that Burgess character around, eyeing our delicate ladies in town, whilst throwing temptation and sin in the face of the Lord. One day, she will pay dearly. She will end up suffering in Hell with all the other reprobates down there. Under the circumstances, I doubt Miss Snodberry will be returning to the school. In fact, I would rally the town folk to tar the girl, should she ever show up again. Must show her that we will not put up with such flagrant behavior. As for our devoted preacher, this must put a terrible strain on him, witnessing such wickedness right under his nose."

THE CROWS TAKE FLIGHT

IN THE EARLY morning hours, Opal sees a flock of crows circling above. Her breath catches in her throat at the sight of those ugly black devils. She has heard stories about those creatures, and how they bring bad luck — even death. She frantically waves her hands to shoo them away, and looks at them in fear and disgust. "I can't stand those birds, with their sharp beaks and beady eyes. They look like they are doing something deeply sinister… like the Devil's bidding. The good Lord must have made a mistake when he created those ghastly things," she sputters. As she hurries toward the school, one of the crows with a silver wing swoops down and, with a loud squawk, pecks her sleeve. Opal shrieks, tripping over her feet in alarm, and flapping her arms like a madwoman. She swats at the crow, screeching, "Get away from me, you vicious fiend." She flails her hands in the air, and brushes the tip of the bird's wing with her fingertips. She scurries down the road and looks up in alarm to see the cawing birds still following her. One fat crow, the size of a cat and with eyes blazing yellow orbs, flies beside her and clacks its beak near her face. "Run, Opal, run," it squawks. "Time is going to catch you."

Opal flies inside the building, and hastily shuts the door with a bang. Clutching her chest, she cries out in terror, while trying to catch her breath. "Mrs. Trimble, Mrs. Trimble. There is something terrible going on outside. I was attacked by a flock of crows. They tried to murder me!"

A sound of steely shoes clatter on the floor as the curious Mrs. Trimble opens the kitchen door with a look of surprise. "Yes, Opal, what is it?" she asks in consternation. "Has something happened to the preacher? Are you ill?" Mrs. Trimble regards the harried woman in alarm, as she looks at her pallid face.

"There are a bunch of vicious birds out there," Opal says, breathlessly. "And one of those foul things attacked me. I had to run for my life as another one tried to peck my eyes out. We need to set some traps or call Mr. Banks to come and shoot them. I just know they followed the heathens here."

Mrs. Trimble tries to hide her irritation at the mention of crows. She thinks it's a bunch of silly hogwash. "Yes, yes. I'll see what I can do about that. I am glad you are not ill. See to your morning class and don't fret about the birds."

Mrs. Trimble is irritated at the woman for complaining about a few birds. *Yes, the crows can be a nuisance at times, but, really, carrying on like this is, well… I really should mind my thoughts. I have more important matters to attend to.* She walks back to the kitchen, and continues her discussion of this week's menu with Mrs. Barlapp.

Opal is on edge and jittery, and snaps at the girls in her classroom over a trivial matter. The encounter with the crows this morning left her at her wit's end. Fielding a barrage of questions from the girls didn't help, either. They are still upset over the disastrous baptism from the previous day. She did her best to defend the ritual, even though she privately thought it a disaster. Moreover, she is miffed about *that wretched Miss Snodberry.* She had sensed something wasn't quite right about her from the beginning, and now she has left the school without giving notice. But, far worse, she left town with that odd, Stephanie Burgess. Rumors had been rampant about that woman and her lurid ways, but Opal can barely think about it now. And all this combined with that flock of birds attacking her... which is a sure sign of the Devil. *No doubt about it... evil is lurking around this place. It gives me the cold chills.* She could strangle her husband for having taken in another heathen. *It's most likely his fault that all this is happening. I'll have a talk with him later and insist that he send that heathen back to where he came from.*

*

Hidden Spirit struggles to sit up. The rope that binds his hands cuts deep, leaving imprints. His skin is raw, his arms are numb, and his wrists are throbbing. After a sleepless night of troubling dreams, his thoughts race like thunder. Preacher Jim has threatened to keep him locked up, "till Hell freezes over." Those words ring clearly in his head from last night, and he frowns remembering. He knows the preacher is determined to convert him, at whatever cost.

"The road of the wicked you walked, boy, and it took you in the wrong direction. And now, you have been brought to me. You best come quick-like to the white man's way of thinking. Your people worship a heathen God and they're akin to the Devil. That's why you heathens have been defeated. Can't you see that? It is written as plain as daylight for all to see, and it's as sure as the sun sets in the west."

Hidden Spirit wants to rip his head off as he recalls each mind-numbing word. His stomach knots as he thrashes about in the damp, dark room from which he vows to find a way out. *I have come to free the girls,* he thinks, seething through clenched teeth. "Morning Star, hear my words. You are the one who lights my heart... who makes my world soar. I will set you free... I will. No matter what they do, I will find a way." Thoughts of her keep him rational, as he paces back and forth in the tiny room. Each step fills him with a steely determination.

Then he stops pacing. *Maybe that white girl could help*, he thinks cautiously. He doesn't trust the white eyes much, but he needs to do something. *She might be of use.* He shuts his eyes, slows his breathing and prays. He talks to her in his prayer, and asks her to come. He can only focus on his prayer for a few minutes, as other thoughts come tumbling in. Anger and frustration take over, and he is unable to concentrate. He kicks his feet in frustration, thinking of the many ways he would like to kill the preacher — all of which gives him momentary satisfaction. *I could slice his neck and leave him for the badgers to eat, or take his scalp and throw it to the scavengers.* As thoughts of torturing the preacher subsides, and his satisfaction diminishes, he sits back against the wall, closes his eyes, and begins to pray, harder. "Great Spirit, I have been foolish with my thoughts I know… my anger, my pain, hold me captive. My life, I fear, is waning inside this hole. I need your help."

Inexplicably he starts to weep — something he has not done for a long time. His body convulses with deep, painful sobs as he prays with all the force he can muster. A feeling of warmth fills his body. With eyes clenched tight, he begins to concentrate on the spirit beings of his past. He feels them start to gather and hears a far-off cry. The sound comes closer, but still so faint he has to lift his head to hear. "Hey, hey, hoka, hey…" The intensity of the song strikes a chord deep in his heart… so deep he doubles over and clutches his chest to ease the pain. It makes his mind whirl. Once the singing subsides, he hears a low buzzing sound — like a swarm of angry bees zooming around his head, faster and faster, until he thinks he might faint. Then, abruptly, the sound stops. Hidden Spirit breathes out a slow, uneasy breath. A deep silence engulfs him and he begins to feel the earth shudder beneath him — filling him, and then he falls into a spellbinding dream.

The only sound is the beat of his heart, thumping as though it were outside his body. It now beats with the sound of drums — pulsing, pounding, throbbing — louder and louder. He holds his heart. A surreal vision appears in the distance. He sees his ancestors, dressed in hunting regalia. Hundreds of the ancients line up around a campfire, whirling, singing, and chanting as they moved rhythmically — to the mesmerizing sounds of beating drums.

Out of the periphery and smoke he sees his grandmother, Leaves Dancing, and his pulse skips a beat. She smiles at him so brightly that his heart leaps with joy. Feathery lines crinkle around her eyes and a halo of light surrounds her petite silhouette. Broken Feather is beside her, his eagle headdress descending regally to the ground. As the two dance around the fire, Leaves Dancing beams. She twirls about, shaking a rattle, and her face is filled with pleasure. She looks as though she is floating on air, dancing as graceful as an eagle, soaring high, and gliding on the wind — yet, all the while, her feet never miss a beat. When the drums stop beating, Broken Feather takes her arm and pulls her aside to talk. They look solemnly at each other and then at Hidden Spirit — and they nod their heads while continuing to talk. Hidden Spirit strains to hear, but the words sound hollow, like a distant echo. He tries to get closer, but a force holds him back.

Hidden Spirit's eyes cloud with visions of the past. He does not weep for his captivity, but for the loss of a way of life. He weeps for his grandmother, for his sister, and for all his people. As tears flood his eyes like a mournful river, his body convulses in pain. Then, his thoughts float back to the time of his grandmother's meaningless death.

*

He remembers that cold winter day like it was yesterday. He can still see the soldier's pale eyes harden and smile wickedly as he shoots Leaves Dancing in the chest and then laughs when she falls to the ground — his eyes glinting with smug satisfaction. Then the soldier rides off looking for his next victim to slaughter without cause.

Hidden Spirit wanted to kill every last white man on that cold December day. His thirst for revenge raged deep within him, as his heart ripped open in sorrow — while holding his lifeless grandmother in his arms.

"I miss you, Grandmother," he whispers. "I should have killed that soldier. I should have avenged your death." In that instant, his tears slow. He feels a warm, electrifying presence surrounding him, comforting him. Then his thoughts float to a time when she held him as a young boy, and comforted him. Memories of her beautiful life fill him with joy, like a soothing balm. He smiles in remembrance of her love of life and her love of dance. *That's why she wanted to go to Wounded Knee... to dance.*

A rustling noise distracts him. The sound is coming from the small window. He opens his tear-streaked eyes at the sight of hundreds of shimmering yellow and orange leaves floating inside, whirling brightly throughout the room — swaying and fluttering, up and down and around. He sits up. *It's like the leaves are dancing.* He marvels at the enchanting scene that is filling the dark room with melodic sounds and tinkling bells.

A few raucous crows fly into the room, cawing and flapping their wings, swooping and darting among the golden leaves. They clack their beaks, and move in tempo to the whirling leaves, floating, soaring. After a while, a mixture of coos, clicks, and rattles brings the dance of the leaves to an end. When the noise finally settles and everything calms, a soothing voice speaks through the stillness.

"Mi-thakoza, I have heard your cries from afar, calling out to the otherworld. The ethers shudder with your sorrow, and it fills my soul with pain. Do not blame yourself for my days ending. I thank you for trying to save me. Running through the gunfire was very brave, Mi-thakoza. I am most grateful the bullets did not kill you. The Great Spirit has put you on our sacred earth for a very important reason. You must find it."

Hidden Spirit feels a windswept kiss brush his cheek, light as a summer breeze. A ray of sunlight filters through the tiny window. He watches the dappled leaves rustle and gather and then disappear out the window. The crows fly behind, sounding their raucous caws as they say goodbye.

Suddenly a noise is heard at the door as the slat is removed. Hidden Spirit stirs, shaking his head — his reverie broken. He sits upright and squints as Preacher Jim pokes his head inside. "Good day to you, my boy," he says, smiling — carrying a large basket under his arm. "Did you sleep well? Thought I'd check to see how you managed through the night." His craggy brows arch high as he looks around the cramped room. "A blessed new day awaits. Did you contemplate my words while you sat alone? Pray to the good Lord, to thank Him for all His blessings bestowed upon you? Did you ask for forgiveness for your wicked, immoral ways? Did you pray to our Lord Almighty that he might 'take ye into His folds so that ye shall be born again'?" Not waiting for answers, he continues on as he holds the basket close to his chest, and boasts proudly. "Smell the delectable food inside. Opal fixed us a fine lunch… fit for a king. You will need your strength, I dare say, as will I, with all the work that lies ahead."

Preacher Jim moves closer and begins to run his hands through Hidden Spirit's long hair. "I brought scissors with me to cut thy locks." He puts the boy's thick strands to his face, smelling the faint traces of smoke and herbs. "But I have changed my mind. I know the Lord sent you, heathen, unto me." He smiles a huge toothy smile, looking at the boy, nodding his head and rummages through the basket excitedly. "This is cause for celebration, my heathen warrior," he says, extracting two slices of bread between which he stuffs a half-cooked piece of liver. "From the loins of the beast to thy mouth. First, let us pray before we partake in His good tidings." Preacher Jim bends to his knee on the dirt floor, closing one eye, while the other stays latched on Hidden Spirit.

"Dear Lord. Help me impart your words to guide this fine species of savagery. I give thanks for your blessings and know that this boy has the hair of Samson. In that I shall find strength... strength I shall use as the power for my teachings. I shall be known the world over. I will impart my wisdom to all, and especially, to this wild one. He will learn and rejoice. Then he will go to his people and pronounce to them they have lived a sinner's life and must repent."

Hidden Spirit glowers at the preacher's words.

Preacher Jim continues on and on, reveling in his rapture.

Hidden Spirit refrains from lashing out. He is restless and annoyed by the endless preaching. It was just a moment ago his grandmother's soothing voice filled the room with beautiful images, and now... to listen to this is jarring. He stares longingly out the window, wishing for grandmother's return. His thoughts are interrupted by a whack to the side of his head. "I am going to enlighten you boy... so pay attention. Have some respect, and close your eyes when I pray. I am a patient man, but do not push your luck. Remember, however long it takes, and mark my words, I will convert you to the Truth. Do not give me reason to use the rod."

Hidden Spirit stares with glowering eyes, and starts to get up, but Preacher Jim knocks him backwards and tells him to stay put. "Let me warn you. I have killed many a heathen in the name of the Lord... on a mission to scourge the earth of your people's wickedness. One night, I heard a voice calling to me. It was God. He was asking me to help you people... you heathens... to help you repent… guide you to the light. I was stunned at first, as my desire to rid the earth of savages was strong. Then, in a blink of an eye, I knew I had another destiny. In that moment of surrender, I no longer wanted to kill the heathens, but, rather, to save as many as possible. That is why I'm here at this school… to convert your souls to Christ. But remember, boy, my arm is the sword of God. I will not hesitate to smite you down."

Hidden Spirit forces himself to remain calm, even stoic — eyes steadfast on the slat at the window.

Softening his tone, Preacher Jim eeks out a smile. "My boy, I tell you that your Great Spirit is none other than the Devil in disguise." He leans in closer to Hidden Spirit. "Don't you know, he's masquerading as the benevolent one, claiming to help you through difficult times? Your Great Spirit is nothing more than an illusion, a pretender."

Hidden Spirit looks at the Preacher and answers with his long, cool stare.

"I don't see anyone in here helping you, other than a bunch of bird feathers." Preacher Jim lets out a loud snort. "Unless they can help you to fly out of here," he says with amusement. "That would be a miracle I'd like to see." He kicks a few feathers, to make his point.

The feathers tremble and fluff their plumage and let off a low hiss, causing Preacher Jim's eyes to widen in surprise.

Hidden Spirit remains silent. Only a twitch in his jaw gives any indication of his mounting anger.

Preacher Jim looks at the feathers warily. "There are demons in this room. I can feel them. Close your eyes, boy, and listen good." He clears his throat. "This is from the Book of Romans. 'If you do wrong, be afraid, for He does not bear the sword in vain — for He is the servant of God, an avenger who carries out the wrath of the wrongdoer…'"

Hidden Spirit can't believe these arrogant white men, spouting their religion. His anger continues to mount as he struggles to free himself of the ropes. Then his gaze catches a movement toward the tiny window where he sees something flicker and waver.

Preacher Jim does not notice.

Hidden Spirit smiles.

A smattering of leaves sweeps into the window, sounding like a chatter of crickets. One by one the leaves flutter gently around the small room in wide circles, swirling, circling above the preacher's head. A small crow with silver wings and searing eyes perched near the ledge, clacking its beak.

Preacher Jim, engrossed in his prayer, talks about his labors and sacrifices. He stops mid-sentence when he hears a squawk — cracks one eye open and looks around the room. Something ruffles his hair. He brushes it away like a bothersome fly, and blinks.

Hidden Spirit keeps his gaze focused on the preacher.

Preacher Jim is annoyed by the sight of a bunch of leaves floating in the air — wondering how they came to be in the room. *Perhaps a storm blew them in.* He looks at the small opening. Then it dawns on him. *It's those blasted crows. They're doing the work of the Devil.* Maybe Opal was right when she told him about those blasted birds following her — attacking her. He had shrugged off her concerns, but now this, this was a whole different story. He could see plain as day they were something evil that he could not abide. Opal blamed it on that heathen boy — said that he had brought the evil with him. *Maybe that boy is nothing more than a curse, a blot upon me,* he muses, *and has been sent to test me.* He fiddles with the scissors in his pocket and draws them out — clicking and clacking the long blades, while pondering what to do. "I'll take away his power, his curse. I will leave him weak, unable to wreak havoc… I'll cut his mangy hair," he proclaims loudly, as he paces back and forth. "I was tricked by him… by his power…

which is surely tainted with evil. I don't need his power. What was I thinking? I have the power of the Lord." Holding the scissors to the sparse light, he says, "I'll teach him a lesson he won't forget!" Grabbing Hidden Spirit's long hair, clacking the scissors furiously... ready to snip, Preacher Jim whirls around as he hears a faint noise. He tilts his head to listen. It was more than a rattling of leaves and squawking of crows this time. It sounded like music — most unusual music. He stands still for a moment, entranced by the sound. *It is utterly decadent,* he thinks... *the Devil's music, no doubt.* Suddenly, his body starts to jerk, back and forth, hips grinding seductively to the sound, feet moving furiously. He is powerless to stop. The sounds seep into his head with the sultry music — his heart pulsing to the fiery sounds and he licks his lips in delight. Then abruptly, the music ends. Preacher Jim steadies himself and wipes his brow in confusion. He can't believe what has just happened, and he feverishly glances around the room listening for the sounds of wickedness. All he can hear is the fluttering of leaves as they circle him and fall to his feet. He opens his mouth to speak, and then promptly shuts it. For once, he's at a loss for words. Then he begins to panic, wondering what has taken hold over him. His gaze falls to Hidden Spirit. The boy is smiling, making fun of him. *How dare he,* he fumes. Preacher Jim envisions thoughts of strangling him. *I'll wipe that smirk off his face. I'll show him what happens when he brings his voodoo... casting a spell over me.* He draws the scissors close to Hidden Spirit's face, and clacks them threateningly, just inches away from the boy's ear. "I have heard rumors and such," he snarls, "about 'the filthy crows... the murder of crows.' How they'd kill a human for pleasure. If I had my gun, I'd blast the whole bunch," he shouts, sputtering in fury. He watches the birds, apprehensively, as the silver winged crow stretches its wings, while others gather... their shiny black plumage glistening in the darkened room.

Overcome with anger, the preacher grabs the boy's hair and yanks hard, ready to clamp down and cut his long flowing locks. But, before he is able, a large crow with huge yellow eyes flies in through the window with a massive beak, zooms over, and snatches the scissors from his hands. The crow sails away, squawking, flying out the small opening, while the crow with the silver wings watches and then whizzes over. The bird's beak is as sharp as a knife and pecks the preacher's head.

Wiping away the blood streaming down his forehead, Preacher Jim curses, hopping around, hollering. "Yee-oow! You nasty, wicked thing. I now have the proof of your malevolence. I will smite you all to smithereens."

Hidden Spirit can't help but laugh at the preacher as he skitters around the room. All the while, the crows are gathering in number. *There must be hundreds of those creatures,* Preacher Jim thinks nervously, as he looks at the birds and backs up against the wall.

The crows squawk and clack their beaks in unison, flapping their wings at the preacher. The noise reaches a fever pitch. "Caw! Caw! Caaaaw… caw… caw!!! Cawcaw… caw!" The sound is grating and unnervingly loud. It reverberates against the walls. The preacher covers his ears and cowers, as beady eyes and long craggy beaks waddle close, snapping their beaks. He shrieks in alarm and holds his chest. He looks at the small window, trying to figure how those birds got inside. *I'm gonna lambast the whole flock when I leave.* He balls his fists in fury, glaring at the boy. "I'm gonna teach you a lesson or two about bringing the Devil's cohorts with you." He whirls around, ready to whack Hidden Spirit, but, to his utter shock and amazement, he can't find him, and cries out, "The heathen is gone!" Stunned, he stands there for a moment, looking around the room. He stomps his feet and hisses in frustration. "That boy has vanished, dear Lord, right before my very eyes. I know the Devil must be near. The crows are his cohorts… demons in disguise." He squints, rubbing his head, and jumps when he hears a garbled whisper echoing throughout the room… and then he freezes.

"Preacher man. Your prayers are going the wrong way. Heading south, if you get my drift. Beware!"

The preacher snaps. He begins to flap his arms, and screech. He feels like he is losing his mind as he flails around the room. He lunges and kicks at the flock of crows. They squawk and flap their wings in agitation. He kicks at the birds again — this time so hard, he spins himself in circles and topples over. Righting himself, he spots the sandwich Opal had made, picks it up, and throws it against the wall, screaming. "You birds and heathens are of the same ilk. A nasty bunch. I know you're in here somewhere, boy," he says, snarling. "When I find you I will cut thy hair and burn it. I will tar and feather you, along with the crows. I'll set an example to the others. As much as I loathe you Indians, I made a promise to do the Lord's bidding. Just remember… the next time I enter these quarters, I'll bring a gun along with the Bible. Maybe that'll convince you to believe in the Almighty…" Fuming, he kicks his foot at the large yellow-eyed crow standing nearby. The crow's beak snaps open and takes hold of the preacher's leg. He clamps his beak hard — drawing blood and ripping the preacher's trousers. "Yeeow-ch," he screams, kicking his feet, trying to rid himself of the crow. He runs as fast as he can out the door, wincing at the stinging gash in his leg. "Trying to save your soul is like trying to convert the Devil!" He hobbles along the path, screeching furiously.

Hidden Spirit smiles as he emerges from the shadows and hears a booming voice. It sounds like Broken Feather, and he calls out. "Grandfather! Is that you?"

"I see you have felt the spirits, Mi-thakoza."

"Yes, Grandfather. It was…"

Broken Feather reaches out and lightly touches Hidden Spirit's face. "Wonderful things happen, when you free yourself of anger… magic happens."

Just then, Hidden Spirit sees an array of shiny black feathers zoom into the room, lifting Hidden Spirit's raven-black hair. The feathers begin to braid his hair into intricate loops, clacking their quills all the while, adorning the plaits with beads and leather, while intertwining the braids into an elaborate style filled with silken feathers. Once finished, they drop to the ground as if on guard, and move against the wall when sounds of footsteps are heard.

Hidden Spirit's eyes shoot to the door as he hears it being unlatched. His grandfather's voice fades away, as he slides once again into darkness, just as three boys enter.

He recognizes the boys from the gravesites — two of which he fought. He watches cautiously as they make their way inside the room and scour the cramped quarters.

The feathers fluff their plumage and stand erect, looking like warriors ready for battle — quills poised.

Zeke walks in first and shakes his head in disgust. "Looks like a flock of birds died in here, with all these disgusting feathers."

The feathers seem to move under his feet as he stomps on them.

Zeke grunts. "I've heard rumors and stuff about crows," he states warily to Abe and Homer. "I heard my mom just the other day telling Mrs. Coons that they were murderers. Been known to kill a man and eat their whole body. Not sure if that's just an old wives' tale or what, but, it made my skin crawl." Then he looks at the narrow opening, and wonders how the crows could have possibly gotten through the small opening. *They're sneaky, for sure. Must have died in here.* Then, almost as an afterthought, he shrugs his shoulders, and laughs. "Who cares about a bunch of stupid crow feathers and made-up stories?!"

Abe takes in the surroundings. He hides his shock at the sight of hundreds of feathers lying on the barren ground. For some odd reason it made his shoulders tense, as he steps further inside, knocks over a bucket of water, and curses as the water spills onto his new boots. Maybe there is something peculiar about the crows, but he won't give in to such ludicrous tales, and walks more carefully now. He is curious enough about the Indian, but he is even more interested in his horse, so he ignores the feathers that seems to hiss as he steps further inside. He wants that animal... bad. He knows that mustangs are resilient, smart, and tough as nails. Most people make fun of them, calling them worthless... good for target practice — but he knows differently. He is completely baffled by how that horse got away, and he is determined to find it... search the area without mentioning it to the boys. *I'm not worried about Homer, but Zeke would want that horse for his own...* his thoughts are interrupted by Zeke's cursing, "Where the Hell are you, Injun? Hiding in a corner?" Angry at no response, he lets off a blast from his gun.

Zeke is still upset about his broken nose, which sits at an odd angle and has swollen to the size of a peach. He's determined to get back at the Indian boy for his broken nose.

Full of bluster, Zeke struts around the room, hollering, "When I find you, I'm going to kick your red ass to kingdom come! Back to where you belong."

Hidden Spirit struggles to remain calm. The urge to kill is overpowering. His eyes burn with fury and, before he can stop himself, the force of anger takes control of his senses. His shadow dissipates and is flung back into the light, and emerges by the window.

Zeke blinks in surprise, and jumps back in shock at Hidden

Spirit's sudden appearance. The sight unnerves him, and his mouth twitches nervously. *Where the Devil did he come from*, he wonders. Still tied up, his surly gaze examines Hidden Spirit's muscular frame. Feeling a little braver now, he shoves his shoulders back, shakes off his surprise and struts forward — hooting next to his face. "Where you've been hiding, redskin? You scared of the dark? Might whip you good this time."

Hidden Spirit seethes and shakes with anger.

"Say, I bet you got yourself a little papoose you're hankering for. Is that why you came here?"

Hidden Spirit struggles to get himself loose, and lunges at the odious boy.

Zeke backs away quickly and sticks his foot out just in time to trip Hidden Spirit, sending him sprawling to the ground, face-first.

"Came to teach you a lesson or two. Need to learn some respect, Injun. Can't believe my Pa is set on saving your worthless ass. If it were me, I'd stuff you full of bullets."

A kick to the stomach makes Zeke smile with satisfaction. He feels a bit vindicated for his bruised and bloodied nose.

The feathers on the floor scuttle a little closer and ruffle their plumage.

"Pa says he gonna save your worthless soul from Hell," Zeke says, mockingly, and he kicks him again — this time harder. A rib snaps.

The quills rise, looking like spiky shards — ready for war. In unison, they fluff their plumage and prance around Hidden Spirit. To an observer they look like a bunch of craggy feathers, weather-beaten, caught in a windstorm. But before Zeke can react, the feathers zoom forth like daggers, piercing his skin.

Homer and Abe look on in disbelief, as Zeke pulls out a long silver feather that pierced his chest.

Zeke yelps and sputters as he plucks another feather out of his tangled hair, and he ducks as another zooms down to peck his nose. It's like being ambushed by dozens of black arrows careening wildly around the room — squawking loudly as they puncture his arms and legs with their sharp quills and draw blood.

Homer and Abe bolt out of the room as fast as they can, leaving the panicked Zeke to fend for himself, as the feathers zip after them. Zeke screams for them to wait as an army of feathers buzz around his head and pin him against the wall.

Then the crows enter, scattering the room, and filling the air with their raucous sounds — squawking noisily as whirling wings and beaks and claws threaten the boy.

Zeke screams, pulling himself away from the birds and quills and goes flying out the door after Homer and Abe as wings and beaks stay inches behind — nudging him along as he frantically swishes his arms in the air.

Homer looks back and grins, and then quickly ducks down as a feather comes dangerously close and grazes the top of his forehead. "I can't believe that this is really happening!" Arching his body, he ducks again, trying to get away from the quills. "Holy cow!" he murmurs. His respect for the boy and the magical powers… is nothing short of remarkable.

SUNDAY DINNER

FRAE BEADLE HAD decided not to go to the baptism on that wild Sunday. He thought Preacher Jim a fool, trying to baptize those Indian kids. Plain ridiculous. He wasn't going to be branded 'an Indian lover.' No sir. He would've drowned the whole lot of them, but kept those comments to himself.

Besides, he has more important things on his mind at the moment. Specifically, Ellie Crumm. Now, *she* is a sight to behold. Her sweet face and tender young bosoms hold him spellbound. He lusts after her… dreams of her nightly, and can barely wait for the day he can possess her. And possess her, he will! He is a man who gets what he wants.

Frae, at thirty-five, has never married. He has held to high standards, and is quite particular. Some say, a little too fussy. He finds fault with most of the ladies who have tried to woo him with their home cooking or some such nonsense. He wants a woman of whom he can be proud. A real looker — someone as fine as his Appaloosa horse—Smokey. Ellie fits the bill precisely.

Being a cunning and strategic man, Frae sets about to make this happen, no matter what it takes, or how much he has to cozy up to the Crumms. He had never been much of a churchgoer, but that has all changed since he laid eyes on Ellie. Now, he's a regular at Sunday service. *Might even be good for business,* he thinks.

Frae puts on a good front and lavishes praise on Preacher Jim for the contributions he has made to their little community. He has even memorized select passages from the Bible and makes sure to discuss them with the preacher. He especially likes the verses regarding women's submission to their husbands. Frae heartily voiced his praise when the preacher denounced the women in church, 'who show signs of independence.'

He thinks Ellie is a temptress, strolling down the road by herself, swinging her hips in a seductive manner. It makes his heart pulse thinking how he would tame the wildness out of her, and how much pleasure he would derive taming her into submission. He is trying to be patient… but, oh sweet Lordy, it takes all his willpower to hold himself in check. Nothing on earth is going to keep him from tasting her sweet, rosy lips. Nothing!

To Frae, Opal is even a bigger fool than the preacher. If he were to tell her a goat meowed… she'd believe it. She is a gullible old busybody, but, for his purpose, it's worth putting up with her. Just the other day, Opal came by the store and about keeled over at the mention of a nice supple rump roast for supper — compliments of Frae, of course. After that, she warmed up to him even more, praising him for everything — from his charming manner to his thriving business. She makes it a point to stop by at least once a week to flatter and gush over him — and praise him for his generosity. "The flavor and tenderness of your meat is like none I've ever tasted. How do you do it?"

A couple roasts and a side of ham is all it takes to win over that fool. Now he can readily switch the subject to Ellie. He asks about the rumors he has heard lately about her and her association with the Indians. "Oh yes, she does like being around them," Opal remarks. Frae is livid at that bit of news.

"I know you and the preacher are doing a great service to convert the heathens… but, what I mean is, to teach the Indians is one thing, but to let Ellie run wild and associate with them is another. I've heard the gossip around town. I find it appalling."

"Oh my, Mr. Beadle. You can't imagine what a trial it is for me to bear." She leans in close and speaks breathlessly. "Between you and me and the Lord, as much as I recognize the good in saving their souls, I strongly disapprove of her consorting with them. I cringe when I see my daughter wanting to make friends with them. She tells me they are just like us, only their skin is a different color. Imagine that… saying they are, 'just like us,'" Opal hisses. She continues to complain about Ellie's independence and the trouble it will cause. "I worry about Ellie, and all the gossip in town, about her favoring the Indians. I surely hope that can be changed," she says, wringing her hands.

You can bet your monkey's uncle it can, he thinks angrily as Opal takes her package and leaves the store with a smile.

Frae is furious with Ellie's friendship with the Indians. *Once I make her mine, she won't be parading her sweet ass around at that redskin school, anymore,* he thinks, with a grimace. *I do like the part in the Bible about women being subservient to their menfolk.* Frae will make that his first rule. Yes, sir. He will set down some guidelines with that girl, right from the start, so there is no misunderstanding. "Thy will be subservient to thy husband, and obey." He will hang that quote on the wall so Ellie won't forget. That's the only quote he has memorized from the Bible, and he hums it to himself. The words roll off his tongue like butter in the sun. As he stands sideways and flexes his muscles, Frae glances at himself in the mirror, admiring his reflection. He grunts in satisfaction at the sight of his bulging shirt. "Well, we'll see how willful she'll be once she's under my roof," he says, hoarsely, taking one more glance at his reflection and wiping away the beads of sweat on his forehead. *Just thinking about Ellie makes me wild. I've got to resist the temptation.* It takes every ounce of willpower to keep his hands off her. Plenty of other women crave his affection, but he can only think of her. And yet, whenever Ellie comes by his store on occasion to pick up a roast for Opal, he finds her to be haughty, even ungrateful, as he hands her the package. Not only does she barely speak to him, she snatches the meat from his hands and practically runs out the door, slamming it in his face before he can engage her in idle conversation. *Her attitude makes my blood boil, and yet…* Another bead of perspiration pops up on his brow as he thinks about her high-and-mighty ways. He arches his jaw in frustration.

Fantasizing about what he would like to do with Ellie, he goes back to work slicing thick hunks of beef, furiously. When Mrs. Coons comes bursting into his shop asking for a nice slice of ham for supper, it startles him out of his thoughts and almost drops his knife.

"Nice to see you, ma'am," he says, forcing a smile as he wipes his brow.

"Sorry to bother you on this fine Sunday, but…"

"No, no. It's no bother at all, Mrs. Coons," Frae says in a reverent tone. "I'm sure the good Lord understands the need to eat. That's why I stay open a few hours after service. Make sure everyone has what they need."

"Quite the Sunday baptism, wouldn't you say?" Mrs. Coons asks, sardonically.

"Yes, I did hear things got a little carried away. What can I get you today, Mrs. Coons?" he asks, while selecting a hefty hunk of ham from the rack.

"That nice ham will be perfect for supper." Mrs. Coons smiles and continues on about the baptism.

"That Miss Snodberry is surely a disgrace to our community…"

Frae has no interest in that homely woman, but Mrs. Coons enjoys the story so… on and on she speaks—first with astonishment and then loathing, while he pretends to listen. She also loves to share the juicy tidbits she hears from the local gossips in the community, and she is not deterred by a listener's indifference. Although Frae is not immune to gossip, today his mind is elsewhere. That is, until Mrs. Coons mentions a snippet about Ellie sitting across the river at the baptism.

At the mention of her name, he can feel the heat rise.

As Mrs. Coons elaborates on the girl, she watches the slice of her ham grow in direct proportion to the length of her story. Beaming, she says, "Of course, Opal is my dear friend... so you can be sure I know exactly what's what in that household."

*

It is five o'clock at the Crumm house. Opal is frantic as she bustles around the kitchen salting the potatoes, stirring the gravy, checking on the roast, and adding the final touches for tonight's dinner.

Turning impatiently to her daughter, she says, "Ellie, I can't believe you're still sweeping the floor, for pity sakes. Hurry up! It's getting late and our guest will be arriving any moment. Run upstairs and change into something decent. And try to act like a lady for once, even if it takes pretending."

Opal jumps at the sound of a knock at the door. "Oh my goodness! He's here!" She quickly runs to the stove where the potato water is boiling over. "This is awful. I positively look a mess. What will he think?" She brushes her fingers through her hair, streaking it with grease, and then wipes her hands on her apron.

"Ezekiel! Answer the door," she says, nearing hysteria. Hearing no reply, she complains. "Where in the dickens is he?" Then she looks at her daughter and, with no other choice, she clenches her jaw. "Ellie! Let Mr. Beadle in, and be polite. Then, for pity's sake, hurry upstairs and change."

Ellie hesitates, letting out a loud breath.

"Shoo," Opal cries, swatting her towel at the hesitant girl. "Get going... *now.*"

Pursing her lips in a grimace, Ellie goes grudgingly to the door, and flings it open.

There stands a surprised Frae Beadle, who nearly drops the bunch of flowers in his fist as he drinks in every inch of her.

He is completely smitten by her youthful beauty and the loose curls cascading along the sides of her face. Even with the smudges of flour coating her flushed cheeks, he wants to take her right there. But, instead, he politely hands her the bouquet of flowers, and says, stiffly, "I picked these daisies just for you. I thought… "

Before he can finish his words, Ellie snatches the flowers out of his hand, turns her back on him, and walks toward the dining room, where she throws them onto the table before heading back to the kitchen. "Our guest, Mr. Beadle, is here," she announces sarcastically.

Opal, in a flurry, welcomes him. "Oh my goodness, Mr. Beadle, I'm so glad you could make it. I know I must look a fright, but I've been running a bit behind. I wanted to make you a supper fit for a king."

Ellie's head snaps toward her mother, not believing her words.

The delighted Opal smiles brightly at her guest. She hurries over to the stove and pulls out a simmering roast, which she places on the counter to cool, all the while gushing over the fine quality of meat. "Just look at those juices bubbling from the center. I swear on all that is holy, that this is one of the finest cuts of beef I have ever beheld."

Frae holds back a snicker. He saunters over and sticks his nose over the roast, and inhales deeply. "Ummmmm. I heartedly agree and it smells like heaven," he says, clutching his chest. "This could give a man a weak heart. I might have to come over for dinner more often." He glances at Ellie, giving her a wink. "The sight of women in the kitchen preparing supper makes my heart race and my stomach rumble. What could be better than that on the Lord's day?"

Ellie chokes back a reply, excuses herself, and races upstairs to her room, fuming. "He's a pig," she moans, flinging her apron onto the floor. "This evening is going to be even worse than I imagined." She mutters angrily as she rummages through a pile of clothes under her bed, and pulls out a shapeless black wool dress.

Staring at it, she holds it up for inspection, and shakes off the dust. "This is perfect!" she says, pulling it over her head, as it immediately falls to the floor in a heap. Ellie does a little spin, smiling at her plan. "This should make Mother's big day just about perfect," she says sardonically, "and… keep Beadle's eyes off me." She hitches up the heavy dress with a dark piece of cloth and ties it around her waist, as it bulges out. The fabric itches like crazy and makes Ellie sweat, but it will be worth all the discomfort to see the looks on their faces.

As Ellie walks downstairs, she hears Frae speaking to her mother. "I can only hope your lovely daughter is as competent as you are in the kitchen and…" He stops mid-sentence as his head swivels over at the sight of Ellie entering the room. He scans her ridiculous outfit, furious at her attire, and bites hard on his lower lip to hold his tongue.

Opal stares in shock at the sight of her daughter who is, *dressed like a street urchin*. She fumes inwardly, as she feels a rush of heat rising up her neck. She opens her mouth to say something, but no words come out. The only sound in the kitchen comes from her spoon, splattering in the gravy.

Opal stiffens her back. *Nothing will ruin this night for me*, she thinks angrily. She has worked long and hard to woo Mr. Beadle's favor for Ellie. But now a slight chill races up her spine, and she frets. *What if he changes his mind about marrying her? There is no one else suitable in this town for her, especially someone as upstanding as Frae.* As a slow burn rages inside her, Opal feels like throttling the girl, but instead she straightens her dress and addresses her as nicely as possible. "Aren't you a little warm in that outfit, dear?" Her eyes shoot daggers at her daughter.

Ellie speaks loftily, ignoring her mother's furious stare, while smoothing her coarse dress. "A hand-me-down from Mrs. Coons. She did say it was a suitable dress for me, didn't she mother?" brushing a speck of dust away as she pulls the plates from the cupboard, and begins to set the table with a big smile.

Just then Preacher Jim enters from the back door, rubbing his hands together, to warm them from the brisk wind. He welcomes Mr. Beadle cordially, and gives him a firm handshake and a slap on the back.

"Glad you could make it for dinner, Mr. Beadle. Opal wanted to make something special for you, and…" He pauses, sniffing at the air, and says, "By the smell of it, I'd say she did just that." Then he slaps Frae on the back one more time.

Ellie notices her father's hands tremble and his eyes twitch ever so slightly.

"You've arrived just in time for supper, dear," Opal says, relieved that her husband has arrived at precisely the right time. She addresses him affectionately. "This has been an exhausting day for you dear, so why don't you and Mr. Beadle gather at the table. Ellie and I will be in shortly with the food."

"That sounds like a mighty fine idea," Preacher Jim says, nodding his head. "Was out in back praying for my flock. Then I prayed most diligently for the children at the school. They'll need all the help I can give them and more." He smiles at their guest and says, "Let's go to the dining room. There you and I can converse before supper," and he guides Frae to the dining room.

As soon as they are both out of earshot, Opal hisses at her daughter. "How dare you wear that… that awful rag? You act like you've had no proper upbringing. I could strangle you. And if you ruin this evening, I will wallop you, but good. Now, you'd better be on your best behavior for Mr. Beadle. I have dinner to finish, and my gravy has lumps." She turns back on Ellie and begins to stir, frantically, slopping the gravy over the sides. "Take the roast and set it next to our guest," she instructs. "He can do the honors of carving the meat, since he so generously provided us with supper. And, hurry back. I don't want everything to get cold."

Ellie rolls her eyes as she carries the heavy platter to the table and then catches Frae's eyes that seem to look right through her dress. His gaze follows her every step. Disgusted, Ellie sets the roast down next to him with a thump, splattering the juice on his lap. *That should fix him*, she thinks, hiding a self-satisfied grin.

Frae bolts from his chair, annoyed, and quickly wipes the steaming juice from his trousers. He feels like slapping the smirk right off Ellie's face, as his mouth quivers with anger. Through pursed lips, he says, "A little careless, wouldn't you say?" He squeezes her arm until red marks appear.

Ellie flinches at his brutality, and yanks her arm away. "It must have slipped, Mr. Beadle," she says curtly, and then hurries back to the kitchen. "I hate and despise him even more than I thought possible," she says under her breath.

Ezekiel comes bursting through the door, giving his mother a hug, and asking hungrily, "What's for dinner, Ma? Smells real good."

"Good gracious, you're late," Opal admonishes, then gives him a warm a smile. "Hurry and wash your hands, and then go sit down. You must be starving. Everything is almost ready!" She turns back to the stove, still trying to get the stubborn lumps out of the gravy.

Zeke goes into the dining room and pulls out a chair next to Frae, which Frae abruptly pulls back. "This seat is for Ellie," he says with a glower, then remembers to smile. "That is, if you don't mind."

"Uh, it's fine." Zeke shrugs, and sits across the table.

Opal pours the gravy into the careen. Pleased with the outcome, she takes off her apron. "Ellie, take these to the table," she says, handing her the biscuits and potatoes. "That should be it. I'll be along shortly. In the meantime, you can entertain Mr. Beadle."

As Ellie enters the dining room, she plops the potatoes and biscuits onto the table, avoiding Frae and his wandering eyes. But before she takes her hand from the bowl, Frae bolts out of his seat and pulls out the chair next to him. "Let me help you get seated," he says. Ellie rolls her eyes in exasperation, realizing she has no other choice. As she sits down, she tries to slide her chair to the furthest end of the table.

But, Frae is quick, and takes hold of her chair and slides it back.

Zeke's eyes widen at Frae's brashness, and grins.

Frae leans in close to Ellie, and remarks so only she can hear. "It's good to finally see you, at home... where proper women, such as yourself, ought to be — instead of gallivanting around the countryside. I've tried to call on you several times, and to my surprise, you were not home. I understand," he says, "that you enjoy the company of Indians. That will not do, Miss Crumm... not in this town."

Ellie starts to slide her chair away again. Her loathing of the man makes her stomach churn.

Not to be deterred, Frae pulls the chair back — so close this time that his hairy arms lean against hers. For good measure he wraps his foot around her chair to lock her and the chair in place.

Ellie wonders how she'll make it through the evening.

Frae leans halfway into her chair, and continues. "You know it's not proper to have the preacher's daughter running around, wild and free... imitating those savages you like so much. People might get the wrong impression of you or... more importantly *me...* wonder why I would consider courting you. After all, I do have my business to think about."

A glint of disgust passes over Ellie's eyes. She imagines heaving his roast —turnips and all — over his fat, hairy face.

Frae contemplates Ellie as he flexes his muscles in annoyance. "I am a man of prominence in the town and..." he stops and exhales his fury. "You realize I have a reputation to uphold in this community..." He stops when Opal waltzes into the room carrying the gravy, and declares with pride, "Dinner is ready at last."

Opal beams at Frae. "We have an honored guest in our house this evening. Mr. Beadle, would you bless us in prayer?"

Frae shuffles a bit uncomfortably at the request, and clears his throat. Then, remembering to bow his head, he blurts out, "Thank you, Lord, for your blessed gifts, and for the honor bestowed upon me of sharing this dinner with such a respectable, family as the Crumms. Thanks, also, for the fine food and the especially the good grade of beef I was able to provide, which I plan to do regularly in the future... Thank you, Lord. Amen! Okay, let's get to it." He picks up his knife and fork, and ties a napkin around his neck.

The room goes still. Opal, for once, is speechless. Zeke holds back a chuckle. Ellie concludes Frae is as stupid as he looks.

Preacher Jim breaks the silence. "That was a, um, quite a prayer, Mr. Beadle."

Opal comes to Frae's defense. "Lovely prayer, Mr. Beadle. Not everyone is as adept at this as my husband." Opal looks at Preacher Jim for affirmation. She clears her throat, clicks her glass, and nods to him.

Preacher Jim pauses, as if recollecting what he's supposed to say, then barks it out. "Oh, yes." He shifts his feet, takes a drink of water, and harrumphs — then he pushes back his chair and stands. "Frae here," he says, nodding his head toward Beadle, "has asked me for Ellie's hand in marriage. I said, 'Praise the Lord. He has answered our prayers.' So, without hesitation, and before Frae was able to change his mind, I gave him my permission to marry my daughter. I know the Lord gives His blessing, as well. It shall indeed be a fine union... so, congratulations! Knowing Ellie as I do, along with my blessings, I also gave Frae my warnings." He gives Frae a wink. "I fear, though, he'll need more of those warnings, and fewer of the blessings, to keep my wayward daughter in line. However, if anyone is up to the task, I'm certain it is Frae Beadle. Should things get out of hand, of course, the mighty hand of God will be at his disposal." Everyone, except Ellie, laughs at his pointed remark. "My wife Opal gives her warmest approval, as well, and I give her my thanks, as she is the one who formed this blessed match. In conclusion, I stress how grateful we are to Mr. Beadle. Congratulations, again, to the two of you."

Frae puffs up his chest looking pleased.

"The wedding will take place on the Sunday after next, following church service," he announces.

Ellie's stomach lurches at the word marriage, and fights to control her emotions. Her mind goes blank... her head starts to spin... she struggles to breathe. The voices sound like an echo around her, reverberating in her brain. When she catches Beadle staring at her, she thinks she might be sick and inhales several deep breaths to calm herself, as something disturbing flares through his eyes.

Frae looks at her with defiance — almost daring her to rebel. Ellie has to fight her desire to get up from the table and flee as fast as she can — before she goes mad from this horrid nightmare. She blinks furiously to hold back the tears... her vision wavers. A knot of fear is wedged in her throat and she digs her fingernails deep into her palms to remain upright.

Silence as thick as mud fills the room as everyone's eyes are on Ellie.

Frae watches intently to gauge what her reaction might be.

Determined that her daughter will not have a say in this matter, Opal purses her lips as she braces for a blow up.

Preacher Jim, oblivious to all, continues. "Following the ceremony, we will hold a small reception at the house. Glad to have a fine Christian man like yourself joining our family. Hear! Hear! A toast to Mr. Beadle and to my daughter, Ellie." Then he adds, "I hope you won't starve," he says good-naturedly. "She might need a few lessons in the cooking area as well as obedience."

Opal stands and says with enthusiasm. "I am very proud to have you as my son-in-law, Mr. Beadle. Welcome to our flock. I knew from the first it was a match made in heaven, and I am so pleased."

Ezekiel sits in amazement, too shocked to respond, and forcing himself not to laugh. He doesn't particularly like Beadle, and has made fun of him with the boys. *He's a braggart... especially about his horse, which he claims is the fastest that ever lived. Whew! Ellie is going to be in trouble with this guy. I almost feel sorry for her.*

The color drains from Ellie's cheeks at the news. She knew they were plotting, but this — this is too much. She clenches her hands together tightly and holds them in her lap to keep them from shaking... determined to stay strong. It takes a moment to regain her composure, and then she says, her voice light and sweet, "The meal looks delicious, mother," forcing a big smile. "I'm starving."

Everyone is stunned as a hush falls over the room, and they glance at one another in surprise. Then suddenly everyone begins talking at the same time, while passing the food around the table.

Seemingly unfazed on the surface, Ellie slides her shoulders back, ignoring her fears, and forces herself to act calm. She eats numbly, as though this is just another Sunday dinner.

Opal exhales a sigh of relief, even if a bit taken aback by Ellie's agreeable response. *Could it be that she cares for Mr. Beadle? Well, whatever her feelings, it's too late for any objections.*

After what seems like an eternity to Ellie, supper finally ends. Preacher Jim is regaling Frae with stories of his days in the Civil War and the two men chuckle, like old buddies. Ellie's nerves are ready to snap... she can't sit there another moment, and jumps up from her seat. She says as politely as she can muster, "I will take the plates to the kitchen for you, Mother so you can relax."

Opal is stunned by Ellie's attitude. "Why, I do believe she'll make a fine wife for you after all, Mr. Beadle." They both smile a secret smile.

Beadle's eyes light up as he watches Ellie clear the dishes. *Well, if that's all it took to turn her around, I should have asked for her hand in marriage, long ago,* he thinks. Whatever was the matter with her earlier seems to be gone, he surmises, feeling assured of the wedding. He leans back in his chair as she clears his plate. "Just what I like to see," he adds appreciatively, "a submissive woman at work in the kitchen," and rubs her arm possessively. Ellie flinches at his touch. Her thoughts alternate between panic and despair, or smacking him with his plate. She wavers, as she clings tightly to the dishes to stop herself from carrying out her thoughts, and thinks she had better hurry to the kitchen before she explodes.

Opal comes directly behind into the kitchen, beaming with joy. "I'm so pleased with your acceptance of Mr. Beadle, my dear. He will make you a fine husband. Why don't you take the evening off, and spend some time outside... alone, with your betrothed? I'm quite sure the Lord will understand... this once." She gives Ellie a pleasing look.

Ellie, unable to reply, runs outside, and breathes in the brisk autumn air. She tries to steady her nerves, but she is so rattled she can hardly think. Her hands are still shaking as she bemoans her state. *What am I going to do? Mother is so determined that I marry that lout, she will stop at nothing… even if it means locking me in my room if I refuse. I must be careful, and not raise any suspicions.* Her head starts to spin tormented by the news.

Frae comes outside a few moments later and stares at Ellie standing against the rail. She ignores him. Her aloofness makes him want her even more. *She is going to be a wildcat,* he thinks, as adrenaline surges through his veins.

As Frae approaches, Ellie cringes inwardly. He had been longing to kiss her from the first moment he laid eyes on her. Now that they are officially betrothed, he can barely control himself. He walks up behind her, puts his arms around her waist, and nuzzles her neck. Ellie shoves him away. Not to be deterred, Frae grabs her roughly and kisses her on the lips.

Ellie is so worked up that, without thinking, she slaps him soundly across his face. "How dare you? Until after the wedding, you will keep your hands off me!" She explodes, her face burning with anger.

A mask of rage shrouds Frae's face. Before Ellie can move, he lunges at her, swings her around, and kisses her so hard, she almost suffocates from lack of air. Breathing heavily, Frae pulls himself away. "Just giving you a little sample of what's to come," he growls. "Once we're married, I will have you whenever and wherever I want. If you ever strike me again, I will take your father's advice, and use the hand of God. You will remember… being subservient is the first rule of my wife!" Then he stalks off in the direction of home.

Ellie falls against the railing, thinking she might collapse, and clings in desperation. Her mind is in turmoil as she fights to hold back the tears and regain control. *I have to get out of here or I will die a miserable death,* she thinks. She flies in the door, and runs up the stairs.

Opal catches sight of her, and calls out. "Not having a lover's quarrel so soon, are we? Mark my words, with a sturdy man like that, I foresee many children in your future. I am truly blessed to have that man join our family."

SWEET FREEDOM

ELLIE IS UP early the next morning, thoughts racing through her mind. *How will I get through this week? I must put on a good front, and be as agreeable as possible... even let Mother think I would actually marry that pig.* Her stomach lurches at the thought, and she quickly puts it out of her mind. She flies out of bed, throws on a dress, and hurries down the stairs. She finds her mother in the kitchen. "Good morning, Mother," Ellie says sweetly, flashing a smile.

Opal is completely taken aback by Ellie's agreeable mood and looks skeptically at her daughter. "Well, you seem chipper this morning. Must be it's the thought of your wedding day giving you all that excitement. And with a very fine man, I might add."

Ellie grimaces at that thought and keeps her voice calm. "I couldn't sleep, so I thought I might as well get up and keep busy. I was thinking this morning that we should give some of our apples to the teachers at the school. The limbs are practically drooping to the ground. I could take a basketful to Mrs. Barlapp on this fine day." Ellie watches for her mother's reaction. "Maybe she would make a few pies for the teachers, and some apple butter, too."

Opal's mouth drops wide open. "Well, praise the Lord for such a wonderful thought. I wasn't sure you were capable of..."

She stops herself. "What I mean is, this seems unlike you... that's all."

"I must have come to my senses, to marry that evil..." Ellie replies, with a venomous edge, then catches herself. "I mean to say... marry that ev... vangelical man is a blessing." Before Opal can reply, Ellie quickly adds, "I see Homer is already out back raking the leaves. Have him pick some apples for you, and ask him to fill a bushel for me. I'll be making pies for next Sunday's supper. Can you believe it? There's only one week left before you wed. I'll be on pins and needles trying to get everything in order for your blissful day."

"Yes, of course, Mother." Ellie replies, gritting her teeth, trying to keep the sarcasm out of her voice. "I can hardly wait."

Opal is still perplexed at Ellie's sudden change of heart. She is convinced it's her prayers that made all the difference. *Well, the good Lord certainly works in mysterious ways,* Opal thinks, *and, this is indeed a mystery.*

"Well, to be honest, my dear, I thought you'd put up a fuss about marrying Mr. Beadle. I know the wedding is a bit sudden... but it's all for the best. This union certainly makes up for all the trouble you've caused me. Now that it's all settled, I'll be able to hold my head high, once again, in town. I'll be particularly thrilled to see the surprised looks from everyone now that my daughter is betrothed to the most eligible bachelor for miles around. I've heard tongues wagging about it already. Most folks thought you were a foolish girl, with a wild streak. Very unflattering gossip for a preacher's daughter." She bustles about the kitchen, like a rooster ready to pounce on a chicken.

Ellie glares at her mother. She can't help herself.

Opal catches the look. "Now, no need to get into a dither," she admonishes. "It's what proper women do. Marry and have offspring. Can you imagine what a thrill it will be to have little ones running around? Maybe even several? I so often tell you, but you don't listen… prayers are a powerful path to God's ear. Remember that."

Ellie furiously scrubs the sink as thoughts of strangling her mother looms in her mind. Her skin crawls at the thought of having that man's offspring.

Still amazed at her daughter's turnaround, Opal says, "You may go and deliver apples to the school, after you wash the dishes and tidy the kitchen. This will soon be your position you know… as a wife. So do a proper job and make your husband proud. And your mother, as well."

Ellie wants to blurt out, "You disgust me as much as Beadle," but she bites her tongue and starts sweeping the floor, to vent her anger, sending dust and debris high in the air.

"Good heavens to mercy," Opal says, waving away the dust, coughing. "You're making a mess. There is dirt on my counters and in my dough. You must learn how to navigate in the kitchen. This is part of your wifely duties. Your husband will surely disapprove of your slovenly work."

Ellie feels the fury rise up inside and feels a small vein throb in her temple. She wants to throw the broom down and run out the door and never come back. She shoves her anger back down and smiles sweetly at her mother, not able to reply.

Opal wonders why Ellie couldn't have been this agreeable before. *Well, maybe that's what she needed all along… a fine young man to wed her. She'll need to learn obedience, though. Frae will be just perfect.* "Now, I'll be back within the hour, so finish your chores before you go to the school and stay away from those heathens. I have to run into town now. Goodbye, dear." She walks out the door, a smile covering her face.

Ellie continues to scrub furiously, until her fingers are red… incredulous that this is really happening. Once she finishes her work, she throws the bucket in the corner and hurries out the door.

Homer has raked up a huge pile of leaves, and is piling more on top as he turns around and sees Ellie coming his way. His rake clatters to the ground as he stares... cheeks burning the color of the mottled apples that are hanging from the tree. His blush deepens even more as he opens his mouth to speak. "H-h-hello, Ellie," he says awkwardly, smiling shyly.

Ellie waves casually as she walks up to him. "Hi, Homer. Could you pick a basketful of apples for me? I'm in a bit of a hurry. And when you're finished with that, Mother wants a bushel full, as well." She looks toward her father's shed. "You can put Mother's by the front door."

Homer shuffles his feet nervously, trying not to stutter. "I... uh, I... uh... anything y-you want... uh, I'd b-be glad to..."

Ellie turns her back on Homer, and walks away.

Homer stumbles backwards as he watches Ellie walk off, and lands in a pile of leaves. He pounds the ground in frustration. He hates that he always makes a fool of himself whenever Ellie is near. Pulling himself up, grateful that she is gone, he kicks the leaves in frustration before taking the basket, scrambling up the side of the craggy old tree, and plucks the ripe apples.

Ellie hurries over to the shed, hoping to get inside while her mother is gone. No luck. When she hears her father talking, she peeks through the window. No one is with him. Ellie stands for a moment, and listens with great curiosity.

"Heathens are the cause of my angst, dear Lord. I do my best, and all I get is weird goings-on... like that heathen who came to haunt me during my Sunday service. I didn't kill her," he cries out. "She did it to herself... I just tried to stop her from leaving." Preacher Jim strides across the room. "And, I think that Indian boy to whom I have given my heart and my time... practices witchcraft with the Devil."

Ellie can't believe it as her father falls to his knees and begs,

"Please forgive me. I am doing my best around here." Abruptly, he stands, and shouts. "I gave the boy my dire warnings of Hell... what would happen if he refuses to *BELIEVE*! Does that kid listen? No! Maybe it's time for more drastic measures. I have been too soft on him... coddled him. I will take my gun with me the next time I see him. Maybe that will spark some fear in him, make him repent." Preacher Jim paces back and forth, in the musty old shed. "And dear Lord... that heathen who died in my office, why did she come back? Why did this happen? Why, oh, Lord? Why?"

Ellie watches as her father holds the Bible close to his chest. He has been acting strange of late, and now she knows why... he's even worse than before. She must free Hidden Spirit, and soon, for his safety as well as hers. She scurries back to the tree where Homer has the basket waiting. He shyly asks if she needs any more.

Ellie shakes her head, takes the basket, and, as an afterthought, calls out, "Thanks, Homer." Then she turns and starts walking down the road.

Homer gets up his courage and runs over to Ellie, breathless. "M-may I walk with you a ways?" Before she can answer, he shyly takes the heavy basket from Ellie.

"No, Homer. It's not necessary," and she starts to pull the basket back. "I'm in a hurry." She sees the dejected look on Homer's face, and she isn't certain she can trust him. But the basket is heavy, and she relents. "Well, just a ways, now. I have things to do, and I really don't feel like company."

Homer doesn't care. Being near her even for a moment is heaven to him. He wills himself not to look like a fool, and holds the basket tightly. Sneaking a look at her, he sees that she seems preoccupied. He tries to ask her a couple of questions, but she just stares ahead as if she doesn't hear him. Homer cannot believe the gossip circulating around town. He has to find out if it is really true. *Is Ellie going to marry Frae Beadle?* He hopes not. He doesn't like the guy. His parents had a run-in with Beadle at their newspaper office in town. Beadle asked them for free advertising in exchange for a leg of lamb, and his parents consented to a month's worth of advertising on the second page. But that wasn't good enough for Frae, and he became more demanding. He wanted a whole section dedicated to his butcher shop. Seeing how unreasonable he was, Homer's parents decided to end their agreement. Frae was so furious he threatened to tell his customers not to buy their newspaper... claiming their news was fake, made up by some Indian-loving, slave-freeing members of the community. Frae was still making a fuss when he was escorted out of their office.

Knowing the kind of guy he is, Homer can't believe Ellie would actually marry him, but he has to find out for himself. Finally, he gets up the courage and simply blurts it out. "Are you really going to marry Beadle?"

Ellie's soft features turn to stone, and her face freezes. She whirls around and confronts Homer. "Where did you hear such news, and what business is it..." Ellie doesn't bother to finish her sentence. She snatches the basket from Homer, furious, dropping a few apples on the way as she cuts through a wooded patch, and runs toward the school.

I'm a fool. Homer chastises himself, wringing his hands. *I'm just a great big stupid fool.*

Ellie is shaking. Just the mention of Frae and the rumors swirling about, sends her blood boiling. She tries to control her emotions. She has to. Too much is at stake. Plus she has to help Hidden Spirit. She had heard her father telling her mother that he was locked up on the boy's side of the yard... once used to house prisoners. The building is set near the edge of the grounds. Luckily it is surrounded by a bunch of low-lying bushes and thick shrubs. As she nears the oddly shaped structure, she hides behind a towering oak tree and stays put, as she looks around the grounds and listens. With no one about, she cautiously makes her way to the back of the building, stands on tiptoes and peeks inside the small opening into the darkness. Softly, she calls out, "Hidden Spirit… it's me, Ellie … the one you saw the other day." She waits for a long moment before hearing him answer.

"Why have you come?"

Relieved to hear his voice, she says, "I want to help you… get you out of there." Then she tosses a small knife through the window. "I wasn't sure what to do, so I thought this might help. I could come back later tonight and unbolt the door… that is, if you would like my help."

A little more friendly now, Hidden Spirit says, "Yes. I would… thank you. Tell Morning Star what has happened and not to worry. I will wait for the girls by the stream tonight when the moon rises."

"Will you take me with you?" Ellie asks, crossing her fingers. "I beg you. I will do everything you ask and will do my best to bring a horse."

After what seems like an eternity, he answers. "It will be very dangerous… but… yes."

Ellie almost collapses in relief. Her mind has been in utter turmoil since he has been locked up and she jumps for joy. "I'll be sure to tell Morning Star the news," she bubbles. "I'll do it right away, and thank you a thousand times over. I owe you my life…" Then she stops. Her words fade to a whisper, "If anything happens, I will…" A strange and unexpected sensation hits her in the stomach with a huge jolt. The brief feeling of euphoria has vanished, and she murmurs, "If I can't make it… go without me." She doesn't understand why a sudden cloud of doom overtakes her. Her freedom is so close, but she can't shake this uneasy feeling. Just then, Ellie hears voices, and jerks her head toward the school, and says, "I'd better leave. I hear someone coming. Goodbye, Hidden Spirit. I'll be back."

Ellie races away from the building just as Mr. Darrell is coming around the corner, instructing the boys on gardening. "These weeds are thick and overgrown. Start cutting them down. Bears or some other wild beasts could be lurking in there."

She wishes she could help the boys escape, as well. Maybe once she's far away from here, she could tell someone about this place. How unfair and cruel it is for the children. Looking back over her shoulder, she sees the coast is clear and takes off in a run. As she winds her way through the wooded area, she feels guilty for her excitement, considering the pain that surrounds this place.

Just then, fear grips her stomach, and she swallows hard. *It might not be so easy sneaking Frae's horse out of the barn,* she thinks. *If he catches me, I'm not sure what he would do to me.* She groans, knowing that once she gets to Frae's place, she'll have to pretend, put on a front, like she has never done before. *I'll have to apologize for my behavior last night... maybe I'll even have to kiss him. What a nauseating thought!* "Just keep my mind on leaving," she reprimands herself, not wanting to lose her courage.

Nearing the school, she sees Mrs. Trimble standing outside talking with Mrs. Burns. They look at Ellie with suspicion, as she walks up to them. Mrs. Trimble is wondering what she is up to, and purses her lips. "I hear congratulations are in order. Well, I must admit I am surprised... but really quite pleased for Preacher Jim and Opal. They must be so relieved that you found a betrothed..." and coughs out, "relieved that someone would have you. Mr. Beadle is a fine man, and a devout Christian. So I say, well done I'm still a bit flabbergasted at the news, though. It was quite sudden."

Ellie's face burns at the mention of Beadle. She forces a pleasant smile, while desperately wanting to hurl some of the apples at both women... and knock them in the head. Instead, she gives the ladies a courteous bow, and says, "I'm surprised myself."

"How on earth did you manage to snag that fine man, young lady?" Mrs. Trimble says with an edge to her voice.

Ellie's face burns at the woman's remarks. "I convinced him I was an angel... one of the Lord's divine harlots," she smiles. "Then, to make sure I snagged him," she adds, wickedly, "I gave him a peek at my legs... all the way to my knees, and that was all it took." Ellie watches in amusement as the women gasp at her vulgar remark.

Mrs. Trimble's eyes bulge, shooting her daggers. "You are shameful, simply shameful."

Ellie says, "I know. Mother has told me so often that she's even convinced *me* how shameful I am." Delighting in her mischief, she holds up her basket, and smiles broadly at the shocked women.

"I simply can't believe her nerve," Mrs. Trimble huffs in indignation.

"The reason I came here... Mother asked me to bring these apples over for Mrs. Barlapp..." She picks a rotten apple out of the batch, and throws it on the ground. "She thought she might make a pie for your dinner. She tells me that you ladies work so hard, you need something to ease your burden, and give you joy."

"Opal is most generous and thoughtful," Mrs. Trimble says warily, still miffed at the brazenness of the girl. "You could learn a lesson or two from her," she admonishes. "I will relieve you of the basket," she says, holding her hands out. "Thank your mother for her kind thoughts."

Ellie holds firm to the basket. "I'll take them to Mrs. Barlapp for you. The basket is heavy, and, I'm supposed to get the recipe for her flaky piecrust. Mother's falls apart every time... and it's so dry and tasteless. She wants things to be perfect for Sunday... for my wedding. You'll be there, I'm sure... I hope," she says with a sarcastic tinge. "It's really too bad Miss Snodberry won't be coming."

Mrs. Trimble bristles at those words, and hesitates. She wishes she could prevent Ellie from going to the kitchen, but what is she to do? She would like to wallop her, but good, but it's not her place to do so. Besides, Opal did send her over with a wonderful gift. She pauses. "Well, I suppose that would be fine. Yes… go ahead. But don't stay too long, and do not interfere with the girls and their chores. They have much to do." She gives Ellie a withering smile, and continues. "I know how you like to mingle with them. The whole town knows."

Ellie flinches at the remark. She would like to tell Mrs. Trimble to go to hell, but, instead, she thanks her and saunters inside the building. She shivers as she walks in inside, the building, *where dingy walls and gloom await.* Ellie can feel the sadness in the walls, and she rubs her arms to ward off the chill. She could have sworn she saw dark shadows hover overhead, so she hurries down the hallway and into the kitchen, to get away from the icky feeling. She stops abruptly at the doorway, where she sees Morning Star being lectured to by Mrs. Barlapp. *How lovely she is, and poised even while dressed in misshapen clothes,* Ellie thinks.

"How many times do I have to tell you not to take half the potato when you peel it," Mrs. Barlapp barks, holding the potato inches from her face. "Watch how I'm doing it. Now, you scrape the knife lightly over the peel and use your finger to hold it in place. You don't dig into it, mind you, and take the potato with it. Considering how long you've been here, you should be much better by now. And, who knows? You might someday apply for a position as a servant, or, God forbid, a cook… then, what? I'd be the one blamed for your slovenly work." She slaps the potato onto the table, but stops when she sees Ellie. Barely able to control her temper, she says to her, "We're busy here at the moment... what is it?"

Morning Star glances at Ellie. Her face lights up perceptibly as she watches the girl enter the kitchen with the basket of apples.

Ellie purposely ignores Mrs. Barlapp's sour mood, and politely hands her the basket, and smiles with a confidence she doesn't feel.

"Mother asked me to bring these over for you. She thought, if you have time, you might want to treat the teachers to one of your delicious apple pies for dinner."

Suddenly, Mrs. Barlapp's mood lifts. "Opal is a fine woman, very fine. I'm sure the teachers will be delighted... and it will be no trouble..."

Ellie interrupts, trying to keep the edge out of her voice. "It would be a nice treat for the girls, as well."

Mrs. Barlapp's demeanor shifts abruptly, and she frowns at her suggestion. "The girls get plenty to eat around here, so don't worry about that. You can be on your way now... and thank your mother for me."

Ellie stands her ground and refrains from sticking out her tongue at the woman. Instead, she says politely, "Yes, I will tell her." Looking around the kitchen, she puts forward a suggestion. "I could teach Morning Star how to peel properly. Mother showed me ages ago how to remove just the skin and leave the apple intact. She said if I ever want to be a good wife, I must learn my way around the kitchen, reminding me that cooking is the way to a man's heart."

Mrs. Barlapp's eyes widen at the girl and her suggestion, and she pauses briefly, wondering what in the world has come over her. *Maybe it's because she's betrothed now, and needs to keep her man around home. About time, is all I can say! She's a handful. But you never know when a snake might change its stripes.*

"Well," she says hesitantly, "I suppose it could do this one some good to learn how to tend to meals and such." She thumbs her finger at Morning Star. "So get on with it. I'll be back to inspect your work shortly. Just make sure you don't cut all the apple away with the peel."

As soon as Mrs. Barlapp is out of earshot, Ellie whispers excitedly to Morning Star. "I saw Hidden Spirit... just before I came here." She squeezes her arm in excitement. "Do you know where that big oak tree is by the fork in the road?"

"Yes," Morning Star says softly, and takes in a deep breath — filled with nervous anticipation. "I see it on the way to church."

"You and Little Moon are to meet him about a mile south of there, down by the river. Tonight, Morning Star... you will be free! Go after everyone is in bed and follow the willows to the river." She quickly draws a map in the flour showing her the location. "He'll be waiting for you."

"Is it really true?" Morning Star says in disbelief, hands trembling.

"It is really true," Ellie reassures the girl. "I'm going to help get him out tonight. I hope you don't mind, but I'll be coming with you."

"I would love it," Morning Star says with pleasure.

"We'd better get to work on these apples, before the old bag comes in here and catches us talking."

Ellie is so jittery that she peels away half the apple from the skin. "I'm terrible at this, Morning Star, but who cares."

"I can't believe this is really happening. I prayed to the Great Spirit every night, and now..." Morning Star looks at Ellie, and then bursts into tears.

Ellie hugs Morning Star, and tries to console her. "I know it's been terrible for all of you. I feel ashamed of what my father has done, saying he's doing God's work. There is no changing his mind. I'm grateful to be leaving with you. Only a little longer now, and we will both be free. You must hold on and tell Little Moon the news."

Morning Star wipes her eyes with her apron, sniffling, unable to control her tears. Mrs. Burns enters the kitchen with Mrs. Barlapp, and they catch the girl crying. "What on earth is the matter with you?" Mrs. Barlapp demands, smacking Morning Star with her towel. "Carrying on, blubbering like this? You're just peeling apples, for pity's sake. I don't have the time for this kind of nonsense… boo-hooing and such." Mrs. Barlapp inspects Ellie's work, eyeing the apples, and then shakes her head in dismay. She looks at Mrs. Burns, in exasperation, and then scowls at Ellie. "Why, you aren't much better than this one," she grumbles, and shoves Ellie out of the way.

"Let me show you how it's done," Mrs. Barlapp announces with authority, as she whips out a knife and starts paring. "You will have to do better than this, if you want to succeed as a wife." In less than two minutes, she peels the apple to perfection, skin intact, and holds the perfectly pared apple up for inspection. "This is how it's done. You leave the apple, and you take the skin. Gotta lot to learn there, young miss, so you best start practicing. And you best be a fast learner if you want to keep that man of yours coming home in a timely manner." She continues to peel the apples with ease and tosses them into a bowl. "I'm not meaning to be nosey, but, I heard rumors in town that Mrs. Coon's daughter, Beatrix, was going to be Mr. Beadle's intended. Can't see for the life of me why he changed his mind," she intimates to Mrs. Burns, lowering her voice. "Now that girl can cook, and, she's very polite. Every time I see her in town, she always asks about the school and how I'm faring among the savages…" Catching herself, she says, "I mean, the heathens."

Ignoring Ellie's glare, she continues on. "That Beatrix has a little meat on her bones, too." Looking at Ellie's thin frame, she pats her belly. "Might need to put on a little flesh there, dear. You're skinnier than a rail. A man likes something to hold onto… not just a sack of bones."

Mrs. Burns nods her head at the woman's comments, and heartily agrees.

"Thank you for the advice," Ellie says coldly. "How did you know my dream in life was to find a man like Beadle, so I could peel apples, cook and clean, and then have a passel of homely kids to look after?" Turning to leave, Ellie adds cynically, "Guess my dream just came true. Just a lucky girl, I suppose!"

The two women are so stunned by Ellie's comments their jaws drop in shock. When Mrs. Barlapp is finally able to speak, she expresses her outrage. "That girl is despicable. I feel for poor Mr. Beadle, marrying that one. He'll be sorry he didn't pick that nice Beatrix… you mark my words."

"Acts like Jezebel's twin… that's certain," says Mrs. Burns.

Ellie grins at the thought of her naughty comments as she races out the door. I'll be out of here soon, she thinks happily. A thrill of excitement rushes through her body. She can't wait. But the excitement diminishes quickly when she remembers her next stop. She grits her teeth and braces herself for the encounter. *This will be awful, but, whatever it takes to get out of here, I'll do.* Summoning up the courage, she continues on down the road, repeating over and over to herself, "Whatever it takes, I can do it."

Ellie knows she is embarking on a dangerous mission. Maybe she was too quick to offer her help in getting a horse. She doesn't know a bit from a halter, let alone how to saddle a horse, or ride one. As nervous as she is around horses, she reminds herself that all she has to do is lead the animal out of the barn, and walk it down the road. She really hopes Morning Star can ride, and she chides herself. "You must do this, if you want to leave."

Then the ominous thought comes storming back, and she gets

the chills. She tries to shake her fears. *What if Frae suspects something? I hate him. It will be hard to pretend that I like him. He'll see it in my face that I'm pretending.* The closer she gets, the more anxious she becomes. Frightful thoughts swirl around in her mind and she almost turns back. She keeps her thoughts focused on her dreams of living in New York. *If I don't do this I will be forced to marry that pig.* She thrusts her shoulders back, and, with a big breath, she thinks, *I can do this. I'll soon be on my way. Stay strong.*

Ellie's knees start to wobble as she nears his house. She forces herself not to run away as she sees Frae standing near the barn, mending a barbed wire fence. It is as if he can sense Ellie standing there as he suddenly turns around and looks at her. A brief look of surprise crosses his face. He wipes his brow, which turns into a deep furrow, then frowns. *He doesn't look too happy to see me,* she muses, watching his jaw clench.

She breathes out nervously as she nears him. "I... uh... wanted to come over and apologize for my behavior yesterday, Mr. Beadle... I mean... Frae. I was very rude."

Beadle's piercing eyes widen in surprise. Then his gaze travels over her entire body, and he licks his lips.

Ellie suppresses a shudder.

"I thought you might be unwilling to marry me. Wouldn't even give me a little kiss," he says with annoyance, as he saunters near, touching her arm. "But I got a good enough taste to wet my appetite. I'm a forgiving man."

Ellie winces at his closeness and involuntarily backs up.

"Must say," he remarks with a trace of annoyance, "I'm mighty glad you came to your senses. Couldn't believe you'd refuse my proposal," and caresses her arm. "Most women, from at least twenty miles around, would jump at the chance to have me. I even attracted the pious Beatrix Coons. I swear she was pining after me."

Frae was so close now she could feel his breath on her neck. "Been holding out for you, though, Ellie. There's no one like you."

Ellie flinches. She feels her skin crawl, but she forces herself to stay put. "I wanted to apologize," is all she can manage to say as she turns her head, stiffens her back, and looks directly at him. "I was taken aback by the announcement, that's all." Scarlet stains rise on her cheeks, "but-I..." she falters. "It... it was so sudden, and I... I wasn't prepared for such... an announcement, and... well... it took me by surprise." Her voice betrays her... she's close to hysteria, and fights her desire to run.

Beadle's eyes smolder. He grins at the sight of Ellie's flushed cheeks.

Ellie tries not to grimace as Frae flexes his bulging muscles and says, "I knew you would come around." Beadle's clothes always seem a size too small, as his shirt stretches across his barrel chest, revealing a thick curly tuft of brown hair.

Ellie imagines a rat hiding among the bristles of hair. She covers her mouth, and tries not to laugh at the thought as she keeps her eyes focused on the barn.

Frae snatches her hand, wrapping it tightly in his, and kisses her palm. She feels the tip of his tongue dart across her fingers. The feel of his flesh is unbearable. It takes a force beyond words to refrain from pulling away and scratching his eyeballs out. So she pastes a smile on her face, and then jerks her hands away, in defiance.

"Well," he says, in disapproval, "my feisty temptress is trying to be coy with me." He mouth flattens into a scowl. "I will allow that for now, but don't make it a habit. Remember what the Good Book says about obeying your husband... and submit to him whenever he wants. Pretty good advice from the Good Book, I'd say." Frae thrusts his face close to Ellie's, and says with a ruthless

smile. "Just remember that, and you'll have a real happy home."
A warning squeeze follows.

Ellie predicts a bruise to emerge shortly.

Then, he puts his lips right next to her ears and adds, "I don't
want you hanging around those heathens anymore, either. I'm a
tolerant man, so take this as fair warning."

Ellie thinks her legs might give out, so she takes hold of the
fence — hands trembling. She wants to run, but she is so frightened that she can only stand there.

Beadle is quick to notice the fear in her eyes and it makes his
heart beat a little faster. His lips curve into a half-smile. "I think
you and I will get along real fine." *Gonna have no trouble control-
ling this one*, he thinks, relaxing his jaw.

Desperate to remember why she came... trying to squelch
her fear, Ellie forces out, "I-I was wondering... Frae, if I could
see your horse. I've heard people talk about him. They say he's a
beauty. Fastest horse around."

Frae's eyebrows shot up at the news. "I believe some people are
envious," Beadle says, throwing Ellie a wink. "Since you're going
to be my wife soon, I might as well show you around the barn."

She wants to tell him he is repugnant, but she smiles dimly,
instead, and watches him throw his shoulders back. His barrel
chest expands to the point where she expects his shirt to split
down the front. She stifles a laugh as he struts toward the barn
and says, "Now don't be gettin' any silly notions about Smokey.
He's my horse and he's off limits. He's my pride and joy," and
cocks his brow. "As for the barn, it's man's business. Better keep
your thoughts on women's work... which belongs in the kitchen
and... elsewhere." His pale eyes narrow, assessing Ellie. "That'll
be your special place," he grins. "The 'elsewhere'."

Ellie chokes back a retort, and feels her cheeks burn but manages to speak calmly. "It's very nice of you, Mr. Beadle... I mean, Frae... to show me around."

The barn is cool inside and she doesn't mind the smell of hay that fills her nostrils. Carefully scanning the area, she pays attention to the location of the hooks, racks, saddles, blankets, and halters. She makes a mental note as they walk to Smokey's stall.

Forgetting about Frae, Ellie can't help herself as she runs up to Smokey. "Oh, he's so beautiful," she says, admiring the sturdy gray and black appaloosa. She timidly reaches up to pet him. Smokey bends his head, and gives her a sniff. She smiles and rubs his silky nose, which quivers to her touch. Ellie had no idea how soft it would feel, and as she puts her nose close to his, her fear vanishes. "You are indeed a beauty," she says in a murmur while looking into those huge round eyes. "I think we'll be good friends."

Frae frowns his displeasure at Ellie. *She gives that horse more attention than she does me.*

Ellie senses Frae's irritation but still gets up her nerve to ask, "How on earth do you use a bridle?"

Frae looks at her, dubious, wondering what she is up to, but he grudgingly obliges and shows her how it's done. His thoughts remain steadfast on their wedding night.

Ellie looks out the barn door, and is relieved to see the house is quite a distance away. She quickly calculates in her mind how long it would take to get Smokey out the barn and down the road.

Now that Smokey is wearing his bridle, Ellie asks, "I bet he's a hard one to handle." She knows that Frae likes to boast and he takes tremendous pride in his horse. He answers skeptically. "Smokey needs a firm hand, but he's intelligent. Smarter than a lot of people."

Ellie asks a few more questions, and when she hears all she needs, she looks around, memorizing the layout of the barn. Feigning politeness, she says, "Oh, my goodness, Mr. Beadle, I've lost track of time. I'm going to be late. Mother wanted me home ages ago."

Before Frae can snatch her up for a goodbye kiss Ellie whirls around, and runs out of the barn.

He hollers after her, knocking the halter out of his way, "You could've been a little sweeter... maybe a little peck on my cheek for my trouble." Hearing no reply, he kicks the stool in the barn, and then heads back out to the fence. *I'm sick and tired of her haughty ways,* he fumes inwardly. *We'll see all that change soon enough.*

Out of his reach and safely at the gate, Ellie turns and waves, almost giddy. "You'll get your thanks later, Mr. Beadle." She races down the road — grateful to be away from his lecherous eyes and groping hands.

Now I need to get into the shed, she ponders. *I should have taken more coins the last time I was there... but I would have gotten caught.* She is so excited about leaving tonight she wants to sing, but refrains. *Singing is always forbidden in my house, unless it's Bible verses,* she thinks grimly.

Yesterday, Opal walked into the kitchen and caught her twirling in circles, lifting her dress, and singing while she worked: "Camp-town ladies sing this song, doo-dah doo-dah..." But she was abruptly stopped by a resounding slap from her furious mother. "That song is utterly sinful. Camp-town ladies are nothing more than whores. You should know better. I have told you that, singing is for praising the Lord, not for doo- dah-ing nonsense. If you weren't getting married, I'd have your father wash your mouth out with soap!"

Ellie grimaces. *Hard to keep track of what's a sin around here,* she thinks incredulously as she hums "doo-dah" under her breath, sweeping the floor. *Soon enough, I'll sing whatever I choose.*

"Never are you to utter those vile words in this house, again. Your father would faint."

Ellie thought when she is gone from this place it will be one of the happiest days of her life. But, for now, she will control her temper and try to act normally — whatever normal is in this house. Mother can spot suspicious behavior a mile away, so she has to be careful and remain on guard.

*

Ellie arrives back home and eases her way around the back of the house, about to scurry to the shed, but she hears Opal screech and sees her poke her head out the door.

"Where on earth are you going? It's well past two o'clock and I need some help. Get in here now."

"Darn," she mutters and walks back to the house, frustrated.

Opal frets, leading Ellie to the study. "I was trying to surprise you with a wedding blanket, but I won't have it done on time, and I'm about at my wit's end."

Ellie replies casually. "I have a blanket, Mother. I don't need a new one."

"Fimble-famble. You don't have one like this. Look at the pattern. It's designed to encourage fertility."

Ellie almost falls over at those words.

On the floor, lies the large quilt strewn out. Its edges are trimmed with yellow lace and pink gingham squares with a hand-stitched cross in the center made of burlap sacks and what looks like some tattered curtains from her old room in Kentucky. Ellie can hardly keep a straight face as she looks at the ridiculous thing. It takes all her will power to keep from yanking the blanket from her mother and throwing it out the door in a trash heap, where it belongs.

"You must be fruitful and multiply, young lady. I'm praying for a grandson… big and strong, just like his father."

Ellie wants to gag and thinks, *one horrid beast is more than enough in my life.*

"Make us proud..." Opal says, chortling with excitement. "I'm certain Frae will be anxious to have many sons."

All of a sudden, Ellie starts to giggle from a combination of pent-up emotions — relief and fury. It feels like being scared and excited all at once — sitting on pins and needles, waiting to leave — and pondering the consequences, should she get caught. That thought gives a jolt to her stomach as she sits down on the floor, in a plop, resigned to help. She threads the needle, barely noticing a prick on her finger, as she starts the tedious task of sewing the ugly blanket. She pays no mind to the blood staining the quilt as she works. Gathering the edges together she stitches large loops, but the thread gets tangled and the edges bunch in the middle. Frustrated, she yanks the thread out, unable to concentrate on this miserable job.

Opal about jumps off her chair when she spies blood on the blanket and moans, "Good gracious!" She snatches it from Ellie's hand. "You have created a mess," she says, with annoyance. "What is *wrong* with you? I know you have a lot on your mind, but look at what you've done. Now I have to redo all your work. Why don't you go scrub the floors or do something useful that you can't ruin. It's like Lucifer has reared his ugly head... making you act this way."

"*Whoo*-hoo," calls a voice from the door. "Anyone home? It's me, Ethel."

Opal is thrilled to see her friend, Mrs. Coons, and she jumps out of her chair to open the door and welcome her. "Thank goodness you came over. You couldn't have arrived at a better time. Ellie is having a case of the nerves, and it's driving me batty. She splattered blood on the quilt, making more work than I had before. Honestly... I'm at my wit's end with her."

Mrs. Coons looks at Ellie in dismay, then back at Opal. "Thought I'd come by and see if you need any help... and by the looks of it, I see you need plenty." She casts her critical eye on Ellie's sewing, and shakes her head. "For pity's sake, girl... you'll need to stay home a lot more if you want to learn how to run a household. And, most important, learn how to be a lady and keep your nose in the home... like my daughter, Beatrix."

Opal nods her head in agreement and says, "That would take a miracle. She's practically wild. That soon will change though."

"I'd say Frae is the miracle. Now, let me look at this mess. I'll tell you what, my dear friend... I will take this home and have Beatrix help me with it. We'll have the blanket whipped up in no time. No need to thank me, Opal. Just doing what the good Lord would expect of me."

Mrs. Coons puffs up her chest like a peacock, and then turns to Ellie. "Are you any good in the kitchen?"

"Land's sake, no." Opal says. "I tried to teach that girl how to bake bread, but it turned out as chewy as a leather strap. As for her rump roast... burned to a crisp on the outside, raw in the middle," Opal is exasperated. "I don't know what else to do. I'm ready to give up. Mr. Beadle is welcome to come over for supper if he gets hungry... which I suspect he will."

"Well, in that case, there might be some trouble... " Mrs. Coons adds, looking off momentarily, thinking, *there might be more trouble brewing elsewhere, besides the kitchen.* In a whisper, she says, "Have you ever thought the girl might be a bit daft?" She touches her head, to clarify her point. "Well, whatever the problem, it's got to be a relief getting her out of your hair."

While Ellie suffers the remainder of the day in the company of these two women, she keeps her mind on leaving. Looking over at Mrs. Coons, she thinks, *it can't be soon enough.*

Fortunately for Ellie, Mrs. Coons declines Opal's invitation for dinner. Ellie's nerves have been on the verge of splintering, and she is relieved to see the woman go.

*

Ezekiel didn't come home for supper, so Opal saves him a plate for later. "You know how boys are, dear… full of adventure. Your father is still in his private room outside… praying for the lost souls, I'm sure. I do hope he comes in soon."

Ellie ignores her mother for the remainder of supper. She barely takes two bites from the ham, and pushes the rest of the food around on her plate. Opal frowns at Ellie, but holds her tongue. Briefly, she considers confiding in her daughter the perils of the wedding night… but then thinks better of it. *Best she finds out on her own, like I did.*

Ellie asks, "May I be excused from the table, Mother?"

Opal nods her head as Ellie takes her plate to the kitchen, and tidies up. When she finishes, she tells Opal, "I need to take a walk, Mother. To calm my nerves."

Reluctantly, Opal agrees. "Yes, yes, go ahead. Don't want a skittish bride… but don't be late."

Ellie needs a coat, so she runs upstairs. Her knees are shaking as she enters her room and looks around. This will be her last night here. After she frees Hidden Spirit, she will come back and wait for everyone to fall asleep. Then, she will be gone — forever. From under the bed, she pulls a bag containing her few belongings, and tosses it out the window, where it lands in the bushes below. Then she runs down the stairs, says goodbye to her mother, and hurries out the door. Grateful to be outside, she sucks in the night's air, loving the freshness and lets loose a long exhale. *This is it*, she thinks, nervously. She can see a dim light burning in the shed, and she knows there is no chance of getting inside. "I'll make do with what I have," she tells herself, then takes off in a run to free Hidden Spirit.

A full moon illuminates the path as she runs as fast as she

can. Nearing the building, she stops by the towering oak tree, to catch her breath and to look around and make sure no one is about. When she hears voices, she slides further behind the tree and wonders, *who is it?* A lump clogs her throat as she peers slowly around the side of the tree and catches sight of her brother, Zeke, with Abe and Homer.

Zeke is saying, "I'm gonna shoot me some crows… for stew. Teach those nasty birds to stay away. If that lousy Indian gives me any trouble, I'll blast him, too. Let's see if any crows or feathers try and stab me this time. Come on, boys." Heading toward the door, Zeke hears hoof beats coming fast. He turns and sees a horse charging at him, seemingly out of nowhere. He barely manages to get out of the way as he scrambles behind a large maple tree.

Abe looks on in amazement. "It's that Mustang. What's he doing?"

The boys look on, stunned. They see the horse, battering its hooves against the door. Before they can react, splinters of wood go flying into the air, knocking the hinges off their sockets. A moment later, the door goes crashing to the floor with a thud.

Zeke cocks his gun.

Ellie hears the commotion, puts her hand over her mouth to stifle a scream, wondering what is going on. She lowers to the ground and peers around the tree. The glow of the moonlight is bright, and she sees the faint outline of a horse at the door. It must be Hidden Spirit's horse, she thinks in relief and smiles — watching incredulously as the animal prances inside the room.

"Ghost Dancer!" Hidden Spirit says in delight as he sees the horse's long neck arch around the doorway, then trots into the room and lets off a shrill whinny, as if to say, "I found you." Hidden Spirit runs up to the horse and says, "I was expecting someone else—someone with hair the color of sunshine, but I am glad you found me. I see you hid well from the white eyes," he says warmly. "I fear some might want to keep you for their own, while others want to harm you." He pats the horse, admiringly. "I am grateful you came," he says, kissing the horse's nose. "Did Grandmother send you?" Ghost Dancer nuzzles the boy, bobbing his head as if saying, yes. "We'd better get out of here, before more trouble follows. Time to go, fella."

The horse snorts as Hidden Spirit hops atop his powerful back and leaps out the door, in one long graceful movement.

Ellie cannot believe her eyes, as she watches this incredible scene. Hidden Spirit, flying out the door atop his horse… hair and feathers billowing in the wind. It's a sight she will never forget. *Thank goodness, he's free.* Then she hears a chilling cry. "Hey-hey-hoka-hey." It sends shivers down her spine. She moves away from her hiding place and feels her breath quicken in her chest as she watches Hidden Spirit whirl his horse around, and come to a stop near the boys.

Zeke shouts a threat to Hidden Spirit. "You're not going to run away again, Injun. I'll shoot you first, then I'll drag your ass into town. Show my Pa what you're made of… a coward and thief. He furiously shoves the barrel of his gun at the horse's head. "Make a move and I'll shoot. First your horse, then you!" Ghost Dancer squeals and tosses his head. He butts up against the boy with his hindquarters… then with one swift and powerful motion, he knocks Zeke and his rifle backwards into the dirt. A stunned Zeke quickly pulls himself off the ground and backs up in fright, not wanting to get trampled by the wild horse.

Ghost Dancer clacks his teeth ominously, at the boy who is shaking in fright. Zeke slithers away as fast as he can, not wanting to get kicked, by the wild horse. Ghost Dancer rears up, and whinnies as the boy and horse take off in a gallop.

Ellie giggles, as she hears Zeke cuss. "A lot of help you guys were," he shouts angrily. "I told you we should've shot that lousy horse when I first saw him. But no one would listen."

Abe grins broadly. "I guess the horse is smarter than we are Zeke. No need to be sore. I told you Mustang's are smart as a whip and cagey. That Indian kid deserves him. He didn't do anything wrong, but come here looking for his family. Your dad has no reason to keep him locked up.

Zeke grabs his arm, irate. "I can't believe you'd take the side of the Indian over me! When did you become such an Indian lover?" Zeke is out of control with anger and throws a wild punch with his ham-sized fist at Abe, and misses by a long shot. Zeke pants heavily as the two friends stand face to face.

"Look Zeke. I'm not an Indian lover. I just don't care about them, one way or the other. No need to be sore. I told you that Mustangs are smart as a whip and cagey. You need to settle down. Let's go tell your pa that he escaped. I don't know why he keeps him locked up anyways." The boys' turn to leave, while Zeke, still miffed, stalks off ahead of Abe, heading toward home.

Abe changes his mind about wanting the impressive horse. *That Indian kid deserves him,* he thinks, hiding a smile.

Homer stands silent surprised by everything tonight… Abe's comments about the Indian… the fight between the two boys. He wonders why he hangs out with them. *Zeke is becoming too much like his dad.* But on the other-hand watching this incredible sight of the horse fighting to get the Indian boy out leaves him awestruck. He swears he saw Hidden Spirit by the edge of the trees riding off in the dusky light. "Please be careful," he whispers. Then he hears, Zeke calls out, "Where the hell are you Homer? Time to go."

Ellie falls against the tree, trying to take in what just happened. She sinks to the ground, in wonder. For some odd reason, that similar feeling comes back—that Hidden Spirit should leave without her. She feels her muscles tense. Morning Star and Little Moon were his reasons for coming. She had no right to ask for help that could get him into really big trouble. As hard as she tries... the troubling image doesn't go away.

She stands slowly, ready to leave, but just as she does, she sees Hidden Spirit... standing right beside her. She didn't even hear him come. It's as if he appeared out of the blue. Ellie almost faints at the sight of him—the smell of his musty fragrance is intoxicating, as she feels his long braid brush against her cheek. His closeness is like an aphrodisiac and she wishes she could stay with him as her eyes drink in his well-defined profile. For a fleeting second, she feels jealous of Morning Star, but chastises herself at the thought. She feels a burning sensation where his hand touches her arm. Unable to move, she is completely at a loss for words.

He holds his hand up to keep her from making a sound. "Have you told the girls where to meet?"

Ellie can only nod her head.

"Thank you for coming to help. Ghost Dancer found me and decided to get me out. I have something to do first then I will meet the girls by the stream. I must go now. Do not worry if I'm late." Hidden Spirit briefly touches Ellie's arm, then just as silently as he appeared, he fades into the shadows. Startled by his appearance she is overcome with... well, she's not sure she can put into words. She can still feel the intensity of his touch, as waves of heat ripple throughout her body. She can barely breathe, and holds onto the tree for strength — fearful her knees might give way. Ellie stands for a moment to regain her senses. *The thrill of seeing him... wild and fearless will be forever imprinted in my mind.* "Be safe," Ellie calls out after him in the darkness.

She waits a few more minutes before leaving and thinks, *I need to focus on what's ahead. I can't be careless now,* she chides herself, as she walks back home, concentrating. She hopes to find that her father has retired for the evening, so she can get into the shed. But, to her frustration, a dim light still burns inside.

Ellie is so wound up, she can't think, as blood courses through her brain. *I really need the money!* She stomps her foot in frustration, then walks inside the house, where she finds her mother still stitching and sewing. She wonders what awful thing she is making now.

Opal's bleary eyes regard her with impatience. "Wedding's less than a week away and I could use some help pulling it all together. I certainly hope you get over this nonsense soon."

"I'm sure it will pass," Ellie says, crisply. "Maybe you should go to bed, Mother. Tomorrow's another day, like you always say."

"Yes, yes... soon as I finish this row."

In her room, Ellie pulls out a feed sack that she had kept hidden for this day, and stuffs a few clothes inside — glad to leave her unflattering dresses behind. She quickly changes into a pair of pantaloons, which she had sewn ages ago. *Now it's perfect for my first adventure,* she thinks, admiring her handiwork with a gleeful smile. *Imagine if Mother saw this. She would call me some awful name, and then lecture me on my brazen behavior.* Sitting on her bed, she waits for all to be quiet. After an hour or so, she sneaks down the stairs, and eases open the back door to step into the brisk, star-filled night. She fills her lungs to the brim, trying to control her jitters. Then she walks quickly to the shed, hoping to find it unlocked. The door handle doesn't budge — and she would need a sledgehammer to open it. Disappointment fills her as she pauses for a moment, wondering if she should dare smash the window, but decides against it. Instead, she turns and hurries down the road. *Leaving home is more important than taking Father's hidden treasure,* she thinks, continuing down the trail to Beadle's house.

Nearing the back porch, she pauses, and then groans in frustration, as she sees a light still burning in the window. She eases closer to the window and sees Frae, sitting in a wingback chair with a book in his lap, reading. His head bobs. He seems to be drifting off to sleep. She waits as anxiety starts to creep in, and she jumps at every little sound. She hopes it won't be much longer — her nerves are about to snap. Finally she sees his head hit his chest and remain there, unmoving. Seconds later, a loud snore breaks through the silence. *I think it's safe to go and get Smokey now.* She crosses her fingers, praying he stays fast asleep.

Approaching the barn she hears the low bellow of a cow, and she deposits her bags beside the post. Inside the gate, she steps carefully around the steaming piles of manure.

Upon entering the barn, Ellie panics. "It's so dark in here, how am I ever going to find the halter?" she sobs. "I wish I'd thought of that earlier." She shoves the door open as far as she can, allowing the moon to shine in. Eyes adjusting to the darkness, she spies the halter on a peg next to the door. Wielding a carrot, she approaches Smokey. She lets him take a nibble, just as she saw Beadle do — all the while rubbing his smooth, sleek neck, and talking quietly. She loves the silky feel of his coat and his smooth nostrils that blow warm air on her cheeks. As Smokey crunches his carrot, she smiles at him, admiringly. "You are magnificent, but your master is awful. I hate him." He nickers, nudging her hand — wanting another carrot. When she sees he is content, she places the halter over his head — but he snorts and backs away. Ellie tries once again with the halter, handing Smokey another carrot, hoping that will work, but the horse whinnies, and shakes his head. Ellie decides to give up on the halter. Maybe a rope around his neck would be easier. She flounders in the dark, trying to find her way to the wall, where she manages to get the rope and then make her way back to the horse. "It's okay, Smokey. We're going for a walk," she says, nervously, "so please be good." Standing on her tiptoes Ellie throws the rope around his neck. "Whew," she says with relief. She had no idea horses could be so difficult. "Come on, boy," she says, clicking her tongue as she opens his stall. But Smokey refuses to budge and Ellie is getting frustrated. "Please, boy, come with me… please," she says in desperation, yanking on the rope. "I'll give you another carrot." As much as she tries to cajole the stubborn animal, Smokey won't cooperate. He snorts loudly, and tosses his head, trying to free himself of the rope. Ellie starts to panic. "You must come with me," she says urgently, as she looks for another carrot.

A chilling voice rumbles in the darkness. Ellie stops mid-stride, and freezes. "Thought you fooled me earlier. Pretending to be all sweet-like, coming over to apologize. I knew something was fishy right off, when you pranced up to me, parading your sweet ass around my barn, thinking I was stupid… pretending interest in my horse. But I got onto you and your whopping lies. Well, Miss High and Mighty… here's what I'm going to do. I don't want to disappoint your good mother… so the wedding's still on. And when that happens, you'll be my property to do with as I wish. I could even charge you with horse theft, if I wanted, but I wouldn't do that to my darling Ellie. Of course, you know stealing's a hanging offense, and I have good reason to turn you in. I don't have to tell you, most folks think you're a mite more trouble than you're worth. But, when I'm finished with you, you're gonna be sweet as apple pie. Anyhow, I'm gonna have a real good time taming you… my wild little filly." Beadle yanks a handful of Ellie's hair and twists it until she is ready to keel over in pain. "Trust me. All I need is about a month, and you'll be singing a different tune."

His words hold a dark, forbidding warning that sends Ellie's heart thumping. She holds her chest to calm the frenetic beat while looking at Frae, begging him with her eyes. A fierce blow lands solidly across her face, then another punches her in the stomach. She lurches sideways, falling to the ground. Her ears start to ring. Frae yanks her up by her wrist, and drags her down the road. Ellie is helpless to free herself of his powerful grasp. She feels like she is living a nightmare, from which there is no escape. Her mind numb, she loses track of time and how long it takes to get to her house. When she hears Frae pounding on the door, she comes out of her pain-filled stupor.

The door swings open. At first, Opal looks at Frae in surprise, and then over to Ellie. She gasps at the sight of her daughter's black eye, bloodied lip, and ripped clothing. Swinging the door open even wider, she motions for him to come in — afraid to ask what has happened.

Frae blurts out angrily, "Your daughter is a horse thief. She came skulking around my house in the night. Luckily, I woke up in time before she rode off with Smokey. I won't be made a fool by her again. She'll pay the consequences soon enough. She's lucky I don't call for a hanging, but," he snarls, "it's getting late. I'm not even sure I want her anymore, but, if I do, I'll teach her a lesson she won't forget." He stomps out the door.

Opal looks at Ellie, dumbfounded by her daughter's behavior. She knows she is headstrong and defiant, but this is outrageous. She glowers at Ellie, then shoves her into her room, and slams the door behind her. "You will stay here until your wedding day. Any more shenanigans like that and I'll have your father whip the evil out of you. The only reason I don't do it now is I want you presentable for your marriage vows. I'll make a salt pouch for your eye to take away the bruise. In the meantime, you have five days to pray to the Lord for His mercy on your soul, and, your ill-begotten ways. I'm surprised Mr. Beadle would still consider you after this, but he is a fine Christian man."

Ellie sits silently — too distraught to say a word as her mother continues to berate her.

"Tongues will be wagging about your outrageous behavior. And just when I thought I could hold up my head in town, and be proud of my daughter… for once, mind you. Now, look what's happened. And I'll be the one blamed for your wicked ways." Opal's normally colorless face burns brightly as she raises her hand to strike Ellie, resists, and storms out the door and locks it. "Satan's spawn… certainly not mine."

DANCING ON THE GRAVE

THE BOYS HAVE left and Zeke has gone to bed. Preacher Jim stays up rehashing what they had said about Hidden Spirit, who escaped earlier. Their words are all jumbled up, each one telling a different story. Preacher Jim can barely make sense of what they are saying — something about a horse knocking down the door. "How could that be?" he grumbles. "They must have been seeing things. That door was locked up tighter than a drum." Preacher Jim is furious and thinks he had better take a look around, see what's going on. "I might just find the Indian boy where that sissy kid, Homer, said he might be. He mentioned something about the burial grounds. What would he know about the dead? That kid hardly ever attends service, and his family's plenty odd."

Preacher Jim grabs his rifle and extra shells from the gun rack, and slams the door behind him. Hurrying along, he shivers, lamenting the fact he has forgotten his coat. *Well, it's only a couple of miles,* he thinks, and the time will give him an opportunity to sort things out. He's a little rusty with his gun, but he used to be a crack shot in the army. *Just like riding a horse,* he thinks. *You never really forget how.*

He can't have the parishioners thinking he couldn't control the heathens — especially now that a runaway is lurking somewhere in the area. They'd be nervous. Might blame him. If he gets his hands on that Indian kid, he just might shoot him. "The hell with trying to help him," he mutters. "I just wanted him to see the light. Ha," he says with a snort. "He'll see the light at the end of my barrel. That's what he'll see."

Engrossed in his thoughts as he walks along, a large horned owl swoops down with its enormous wingspan, brushing the top of his head and knocking his hat to the ground. It startles the preacher, causing him to trip over his feet and stumble over a rock. He clutches his gun closer to his side. Looking around nervously he realizes he'd better pay attention to where he's going.

Maybe the task of trying to save the kid was too much...not worth the effort...he fights me every step of the way... making me think I'm seeing things. I've got to be on guard, at all times. Well, he's not going to ruin the fruits of my labor. Maybe I ought to pray mightily, right here and now. The Lord will guide me.

Preacher Jim kneels down on the side of the road. Hands clasping his gun, he begins to pray. "Dear Lord. These Indians are driving me to distraction. Help me find the heathen that escaped... I'll not be fooled by him the next time." He stands, bowing his head, saying a brisk, "Amen."

After shaking the dirt from his pants, the preacher takes off in a sprint, his long legs taking great strides. Before he knows it he is at the top of the hill, and stops to catch his breath. He carefully surveys the area, grateful for a bright moon and a clear night. At first, nothing unusual catches his eye. He walks silently out from the cover of the trees and stops dead in his tracks, quickly step-ping back behind the towering oak. Peering around the tree, he can't believe his luck. There he is — the same Indian! He would recognize that buckskin get-up and long hair anywhere. He is so excited, he doesn't know what to do first... jump with glee, shoot him, or wait a minute and see what he's up to. His curiosity gets the better of him, so he chooses to wait. Inching his way forward and standing in the shadows of the trees, he quickly slides back, feeling a tingling sensation in his foot, and gives it a shake. *It's like that Indian kid knows I'm here.* Slowly, he eases back around the tree, and watches as Hidden Spirit walks around the grave. He squints to get a better look and sees the kid throw something inside one of the graves. Sticking his head out a little further, he curses. "By God that Indian kid must be stealing the dead heathens." He almost laughs out loud. "Well, let him have the rotten corpses. Where they end up is no longer my concern. "

Engrossed with watching the boy, he jumps about a foot into the air as something or someone floats past his face — looking like a bunch of skeletons. Then he feels a cool blast of air waft over him. His knees buckle. Eyes glued to the images floating past and over to the grave, he quivers with fright, and ducks back into the shadow of the trees and grabs his gun.

The preacher feels his face start to burn as he shakes his head in dismay. "Well, this is going to be your last prayer, buddy boy, so you might as well make it a good one. Maybe you can have a nice little gathering with your dead friends… down in the cold grave. Be sure to give them my regards." He raises his gun, carefully taking aim, and pulls back on the trigger. But, it is stuck. "Blast it," he mutters, jerking the hammer back and forth, frustrated. When it finally releases, he cocks the gun and once again takes aim at the boy. "Okay… say 'bye-bye,'" and he squeezes the trigger once more, ready for a loud bang. Instead, he hears a click-click. Oddly, his gun won't fire. He curses his luck. Hoping to dislodge the bullets he angrily whacks the gun against the tree, when suddenly it triggers a deafening boom, shaking the ground beneath him. The preacher covers his ears from the noise. He doesn't know if it was his gun or the thunder that caused such an explosion. He looks at the ravaged gun — now bent and smoldering. He isn't feeling nearly so brave in the wake of the commotion.

Suddenly a high-pitched wailing catches his attention. Clinging to the tree, Preacher Jim peers around to see what in the world is going on. Sure enough, it's that same Indian boy who is singing and dancing wildly around the grave.

The wind starts to rise, slightly at first, then it turns into a high-pitched gale as the branches from the trees rustle and sway to the boy's mournful song. The leaves on the ground gather momentum and swirl about, eerily encircling the grave. Jagged streaks of lightning flash through the sky, threatening to strike anything in its path. Unable to look away, the preacher watches this bizarre scene in dismay, as the leaves seem to follow the boy's every move. Without warning a dazzling bolt of lightning shoots from the sky and sizzles, striking the tree under which he has been standing. The electric bolt causes his body to contort in pain as he lets out a howl — causing his hair to stand on end. A large branch above him groans and he looks up just in time to see it crash over him, knocking him to the ground, out cold. When he comes to, the neon moon is shining brightly again. The night is quiet. Chest heaving, he slowly moves his arms and legs. Since nothing seems to be broken, he hauls himself to his feet. He looks around trying to figure out where he is and what the devil he is doing out here, anyway. He starts to walk, to clear out his head, shaken and bruised by some strange phenomenon. His thoughts return to the Indian boy... he wants to get out of this place as quickly as possible. He walks unsteadily at first, then he gets his bearings, and scurries off into the darkness. In his haste he trips and falls headlong into a grave. "Oh blast it!" he mutters and cringes as he lies inside the damp hole. Preacher Jim starts to climb out of the eerie grave, when he feels something or someone holding him down. Eyes swiveling back and forth, he doesn't see a soul, so he starts to panic. He tries once again to get up, and is unable. It's as if his limbs are frozen stiff. He feels something cool and slippery move across his body. Horrified, he screams shrilly. "Oh, dear God, please help me!" He cries out, as he struggles to move his long frame. A strange, unnatural sounding voice whispers in the darkness, "You called?" The preacher looks frantically around the grave, and pleads. "Please, whoever you are, I need help." A hissing sound follows as he spies three black ghouls float into the grave — the moonlight outlining their forms. A raspy voice says, "Good evening, Preacher Jim. We saw you take a little fall, and then we heard your call. So, we came forthwith. Your fiery friend sends his regards," the raspy voice mocks.

Quivering with fright, Preacher Jim pleads. "I'm glad you came, whoever you are. I need help."

The raspy voice hovers over the preacher. "Looking for the Lord, I hear…?"

"Y-yes," he says as he looks in alarm at the wavering shapes pointing their sharp long talons close to his eyes.

"B-but… I didn't call for you." Preacher Jim starts to sweat. "I was calling for the Lord. You must have misunderstood."

Wails of laughter erupt. "Ooooopsies… The Lord, you say? Well… we're headed in the other direction."

Preacher Jim winces. "Wh-wh-who are you?"

"Oooooohhh," says the ghoul with a ghastly grin. "Always on the lookout for pious preachers, skulking around in the night. Say… you out looking for some action? I know a real hot place that'll serve up anything… quick and slick, and slimy as you like."

Increasingly frustrated, Preacher Jim responds. "I'm not looking for action, you nitwits. I'm calling for the Lord."

A low guttural sound emanates from its mouth. "Most ungrateful," the ghoul says, as his bony finger with inch-long nails slides out and scratches him across his face.

"Ou-ou-ou-ch… that hurts."

"Need to be a little more grateful," the ghoul snickers, putting his face next to the preacher's. "Pain makes me feel alive! Here, scratch me… I love it!"

"No-o-o-o. I don't want to scratch you—I just want out of here. Dear God in heaven… please… help me."

"What is it with all you holy-rollers begging for help? 'O-o-o-oh, Lord… I have sinned.' What a load of malarkey. Where we're going… We LOVE sinners! Love 'em to death. Good times are gonna roll."

"I wasn't begging," Preacher Jim says irritably, "or whining. I was praying to our Lord in Heaven!"

"Heaven?" The ghoul contorts with laughter, "That's not where *you're* going, preacher man. And speaking of going… "

A slippery hand reaches out and grabs Preacher Jim by the throat. He struggles fiercely to free himself, but the ghouls merely laugh at his awkward gestures. "Come! Let's take a glimpse of what'll be awaiting you," a ghoul says wickedly. "You might call it a little sneak preview. It's our pleasure to escort you, Mr. Preacher." They grab Preacher Jim by the scruff of his neck and off they go, flying into the night sky.

The preacher looks at the ground beneath him as he flies through the air — and abruptly faints. A moment later he awakens to a burning slap in the face.

A sinister voice booms out. "Welcome, to Hell, Preacher. I have heard your sermons and thought you might like to join us for a little fun… be with a *real* man! Live on the wild side. Know what I mean?"

Preacher Jim stares into a cadaverous face with orange hair and burning eyes — its sockets filled with red-hot embers. "You can call me Mr. D.… I only let my special friends call me that… I am pleased that you speak of me so often to your followers. I especially love it when you tell them where they'll go if they don't follow your words, but you forget about yourself, Preacher Man. Take a look around, my friend. I thought you might be curious about your roasting… oopsies… I meant to say *resting*… place." All the ghouls slink toward the preacher, grinning with malice. "I think you'll find this place to your liking… your description is sooooo accurate. Like you say, 'IT'S SMOKIN'!" The Devil causes a searing flame to crackle and shoot upward, burning the Preacher's foot, causing him to scream out in pain. The empty voices laugh ominously. "Come!" the Devil whispers, hoarsely. "I want you to take a closer look." As he opens his mouth, bright orange flames shoot out, outlining his jagged fangs. "Sooooo. What do you think, Preacher?" His mouth opens wider, revealing lurid pictures of people wailing and screaming out. "Please help us. Don't leave us here!" A guy with a pitchfork jabs them in the backside, as more screams and laughter echoes in the darkness. The heat grows intolerable. Preacher Jim watches in horror as the ghouls encircle his head and dark figures swoop in and out of the fire, laughing raucously and mimicking him mercilessly. "Ooooooohhhhh, I'm so sc-sc-sc-aaaaaared," they shiver, as flames leap up, singeing the preacher's brows.

"I've heard your sermons so often… I thought it was time we meet. You speak of me—so-o-o-o-o often," he says, puffing on his big fine Cuban cigar. "They actually believe that crap, Preacher Man? Amazing!" He burst out laughing again.

"You and I are two peas in a pod—we could piss snake oil and sell it for a cure. My tongue drools at the thought of all your parishioners calling themselves 'believers.' What a racket! Send me your money! You'll be saved. Half of them will be visiting me down here one day… but don't forget, my lying preacher… you and me. We're just the same, with a different name."

Preacher Jim shudders, and his eyes rim with fear. "That's not true. I am not like you."

"Oh, my wicked one, but you are. You try so hard to be righteous, and yet it eludes you. Don't you tell your flock to give until it hurts? Well I'm going to give you something that hurts." He jabs him in the backside with his pitchfork. Then, he jabs him again, this time even harder.

"Ooooooww-weeee stop. Please!" Preacher Jim implores.

"When I heard your call, it was like music to my ears. Now it's collection time, my friend."

"I-I-I need the money… I'm going to build a great big church that will reach to the sky and save souls. Listen… Take all the money. Just let me go."

"Don't you know this is where you belong, preacher man… down her with me?" He crooks his bony index finger, and twirls it. With some delight, he summons a song.

"In Hell with me, you'll always be.

The depths of despair, but you won't care.

You'll be surrounded by sinners, who used to be winners.

Impressive, no doubt, for a lowly beginner.

So, go and save them with your pious prayer.

But look out behind you. They're everywhere!"

The Devil, wheezes, and laughs so hard he turns into an orange, fiery ball. "Here you can preach to your heart's content. But you know WHO I really want to meet, is your wife, Opal," he says hoarsely. "Love those pious bitches. You can keep that tub-of-lard, Mrs. Burns and that scrawny Snodberry. I see she left your school for someone like her. Smart woman. I'd bet you'd say, that's a real big sin. Who the Hell cares? Wouldn't mind that cook though… could use some imagination on my menu. I like my meat raw and a tad singed… so when I take a bite its still got some wiggle in it. Maybe even cry out. Imagine the good times we'll have. None of that stuffy nonsense, you preach about… we'll drink and dance and shake our pants." He starts to gyrate, thrusting his hips in a seductive, vulgar motion. Then slithers between the preacher's legs, snapping his boney fingers.

"God help me," Preacher Jim says, stumbling backwards.

"Little late for that, wouldn't you say, Preacher? Hey, take a little look around the place. Pretty impressive, isn't it?"

"Well," said Preacher Jim, nervously, starting to sweat. "Not really..." His lips are so parched and dry, he can barely speak. With a hoarse voice, he asks, "C-could I have a drink?"

"Got some nice Black Daniels for you." He sniggers, jowls flapping. "Unless you prefer Tanqueray Sin."

"I don't partake... I don't drink alcohol." He tries to moisten his cracked lips. "I'm a Christian."

"Ha! What a load of crap that is. Might loosen you up a bit. You could use a little unraveling." The Devil laughs as sparks shoot out of his mouth, singeing the preacher's pants. "Having a Hell of a time."

"Damn it," Preacher Jim says, jumping back. "I'll take that drink." A tinge of exasperation fills his voice.

"I love it when you curse," says the grinning Devil, pouring a large glass of whiskey. "Makes my heartless body writhe in delight."

The other ghouls slink over, grinding their blackened teeth.

Preacher Jim's hands shake as he takes the glass of whiskey, spluttering as he swallows the strong elixir. He hears gales of laughter roll down the darkened hall.

One of the ghouls hisses at him, waving him over to join the others in a cauldron of boiling water... splashing steaming droplets in his direction. "Hey, come on in," they shout. "The water's fine... if you don't mind a little scalding. Hee-hee-hee!"

"Come!" The Devil materializes next to the preacher and whispers, his voice shallow. "I want you to take a closer look. This place awaits the really big sinners. The kind that will pray now and pay later."

Bright reddish flames shoot out of his mouth as he opens wide, and hacks. "Gotta cut down on cigars. Those things'll kill ya. Then, where will I end up?" He howls with laughter, and opens his mouth even wider, this time revealing even more lurid pictures of people wailing and screaming. "Please help. Don't leave us here!" A short man with searing eyes, a short bulbous tail, and a burning pitchfork jabs the man in the backside and tells him to, "move it, pansy." Then more screams and shrieks are followed by waves of laughter, as a scalding mist soaks the masses.

"You can save these wretched souls, my man. Your sermons could make them remorseful. Like me! Can't you see, I'm drowning in a pool of remorse? 'Oooh... save me, save me,'" he says derisively.

The heat is intolerable. Preacher Jim watches in disbelief as the ghouls circle his head and dark figures swoop in and out of the fire, laughing raucously, mimicking him, "Oooooohhhhh, I'm sooooooo s-s-scared." He shivers as flames leap up, singeing his hair and eyebrows, and the ghouls start singing a macabre song.

"Preacher Jim, you have sinned,
The gates of Hell will let you in.
You'll cook and fry, but never die:
You know you've lived a lie.
You'll bask and bake in this hellish place...
And live with ghouls who loooove this place.
Then off you go with a searing glow,
Alas-ss-ss... we have your soul."

The ghouls click their skeletal fingers in sync with the sinister tune.

"A song just for you, Preacher Man."

Preacher Jim screams out in fear.

Everyone howls maliciously.

Suddenly the preacher is yanked back into darkness. He whirls through the air and lands with a thump in the empty grave. He awakens with a moan, looks around cautiously, and pants with fear. He sits up and feels sweat pouring down his back. He manages to stagger out of the grave, quaking. *What in the Hell just happened?* he wonders in alarm, blinking his eyes. Preacher Jim reaches out and feels familiar blankets beneath him. Shaking uncontrollably, he finds himself on top of his bed. He smells smoke… maybe a trace of sulfur? He touches his eyebrows, and passes out.

DAYS OF DESPERATION

IN HER ROOM, Ellie paces back and forth, nervously. After staying up most of the night, she has a splitting headache. Panic seeps through every pore of her body. Her mind is filled with troubling images of all the brutal things Frae has threatened to do to her, after the wedding. Her heart is pounding so hard she has to hold her chest to calm the beating, so it wouldn't explode.

She slumps to the floor, in a despondent state, and stares blankly at the wall. *It's all my fault,* she thinks miserably. *I forgot about how cunning he can be. I'm so stupid.* Ellie is angry at herself for foolishly thinking she could get away with stealing Frae's horse. As her thoughts become even more troubled, she imagines Frae might kill her and get away with murder. She is so frantic by now, she doesn't hear the key turn in the door, and she looks up in surprise as Opal comes bursting into the room with a tray of food, scowling at her.

"You might as well eat, as you will not be leaving this room… under any circumstances," She sets the tray on the bed, and continues. "You will stay in here until your wedding day. I don't care if the house is on fire. News has already spread about your escapade last night. I don't know how I will survive the gossip." Opal's mouth flattens into a hard line as she glares at Ellie. "I could wring your neck. I'm certain Frae wouldn't object, but then I would be depriving him the opportunity to do it himself." Seething with anger, she shoves a plate of food at her daughter. "You'd better eat to get your strength up. I have a feeling you will need it."

Ellie looks at the food, and at her mother, then picks up the sandwich and throws it out the window. "Let the squirrels eat it."

Opal throws her hands up in the air. "You will get what you deserve, young lady," and huffs out the door, with a bang.

Ellie hears the key turn in the lock, and then a click. She continues to pace — worried about Morning Star and Little Moon, and wondering if they made it out safely. "I have to get away from this place. I just have to." She knows it is more imperative than ever. "I'm sad I couldn't leave with Hidden Spirit and the girls," she whispers to herself. Then, it dawns on her. If she had gone with them, they would be in greater jeopardy.

Her mind races with uncertainty. *If they force me to marry Beadle, I'll do something extreme.* She entertains the idea of finding the most lethal, poisonous mushrooms in the area and feeding them to Beadle. She smiles at her image of him in the aftermath — squirming on the floor in torment. *My magical mushroom dish… that should do it,* she thinks with some satisfaction. She holds her head. *I need to stop these crazy thoughts.*

Seated by the window she looks out at the bleak, overcast sky. The dark clouds loom near. It looks like rain. She is trapped. Feeling defeated and sorry for herself, she rubs her fingers on the foggy window and stares blankly outside. Her swollen eye still aches from Beadle's punch. *I must never give up my resolve to leave. I can't let them do that to me.*

Suddenly a flash of red crosses the yard. She sits up and takes notice. "It's Homer."

She bounced up, ready to open the window and call out to him, but stops just in time — at the sound of her mother's voice below.

"Homer, I need more wood chopped before you leave. Then get the leaves raked. They blew all over the place last night. Put them in a pile by the shed, and burn them before they scatter all over again."

"Yes, ma'am."

Ellie brightens. She had never given Homer much thought before, always thinking of him as her brother's friend, a nuisance. But now her mood elevates. Homer seems nice enough, after all, and she knows he likes her. Well, now... ideas are swimming around in her head. She cracks open the window and peers below, looking for her mother. She thinks the coast is clear, so she bends her body out a little further until she feels dizzy, then quickly pulls herself back inside. Heights frighten her. "It's a long way to the bottom," she frets. Her thoughts come flooding back from a time when she was eight years old, fell from an apple tree, and broke an arm. "If I tried to jump from here, I'd probably break a leg," she says, shakily. "If I want to leave, I must be brave." She takes a deep breath, and cautiously leans a little further out the window to make certain her mother is gone. "Good," she says, and then calls softly out to Homer, who is on his hands and knees, busily collecting scattered walnuts from beneath the large tree. He doesn't hear, but she watches intently, waiting for him to look up. She feels a faint rush of hope radiate inside of her as a plan comes alive in her mind.

*

Darkness settles in now as lights are turned out and everyone drifts off to sleep. Everyone but Morning Star, who sneaked into bed earlier with her clothes on, and waited patiently for this moment. "It's time," she breathes out. With trembling hands, she tosses her covers aside, and climbs out of bed. She pinches herself telling herself, "this isn't a dream," as she tiptoes into the darkened hallway where Little Moon is waiting, anxiously. As soon as Little Moon sees her, she runs up and hugs her. Both shake with a mixture of fear and excitement. They clasp each other's hand tightly for comfort, as they walk down the darkened hallway. '*To the door that will take them to their freedom.*' Little Moon is so happy she starts to skip. Morning Star smiles at her sister, warmly. *Let her skip.*

The door is huge, old, and sturdy. Morning Star turns the handle and, to her surprise, the door is bolted securely.

Little Moon looks at Morning Star in alarm, and whispers, "what's wrong?"

Morning Star can't believe it. How did she not know they bolted the door at night? She starts to panic. "I... they... it's locked, Little Moon. I'm not sure how to get it open." Morning Star looks for another way out, and the only possibility she sees is a small window at the top of the wall. The girls heave and tug as hard as they possibly can on the solid door. Desperate now, Morning Star lunges while Little Moon shoves and pushes so hard, she hurt her shoulder from the force. But still, the stout boards don't budge.

"Oh, no," Morning Star says, frantically. "We're trapped in here." Wringing her hands in frustration, she looks at the door and shakes the handle — then she bangs her fists against the wooden structure, and finally kicks it. "There has to be another way out of here," she says, panting.

Before the girls can figure another way out, they see Mrs. Trimble stumble out of her room and hear her shout. "Get away from there!" Her voice cuts through the night like a razor. Shoes clacking and eyes agog, she goes flying down the hallway, her voluminous gown flapping furiously behind her. "What are you doing out of bed this time of night? Why are you girls at the door... trying to run away, are you? This is an outrage, you ungrateful..." Unable to finish the sentence, she splutters, "savages."

Morning Star and Little Moon stand, rooted to the spot. Drenched in fear, Little Moon shakes uncontrollably. Morning Star feels like a cornered animal and tries to run, but with nowhere to go she whirls around in circles, and freezes.

Mrs. Burns, for all her bulk, flies out of her room, and hustles down the hall toward Mrs. Trimble, frightened and still half-asleep. "Is someone trying to break in?"

"No, you ninny, someone's trying to escape."

"Escape? Why in the world would they…?"

"Oh be quiet, Mrs. Burns. For the life of me, I don't know." She glares at Morning Star and Little Moon.

"We have devoted ourselves to helping you girls… help you to have a better… Oh, why bother," she says, fuming. Staring hard into Morning Star's face, she clutches her chin, forcing the girl to look at her. "Preacher Jim informed me, and rightly so, that the boy who came here would be trouble, and, most likely, he came to get you. How could you associate with a savage like that, who breaks our laws? He'll ruin your life. And if they catch him, they'll hang him."

Morning Star stares in silence at the woman, as a bitter taste rises in her throat.

"I am disappointed in you. I thought you liked it here. I prayed that you would amount to something."

Morning Star finally finds her voice, and speaks calmly and clearly. "Did you think we wanted to come? Did you ever ask how we felt about leaving our families or how we feel about living in this place? I'll tell you how I feel. I HATE IT HERE!"

Mrs. Trimble is so appalled at the girl's remarks, she practically trips over her feet as she whips around to face the girl and slap her soundly across her cheek. She struggles to maintain control of her fury. "Oh, I could wring your neck," she says angrily, and motions for Mrs. Burns to come over. "Take this girl to your room, and bar the door. There will be no more of this nonsense tonight or there'll be 'H' to pay. I'll take the other one."

Following her order, Mrs. Burns ushers the girl into her room, and throws a couple blankets on the floor. Stifling a yawn, she says, "This is where you will sleep."

Morning Star stays awake all night, tossing and turning — her body aching from the cold floor. She is too despondent to sleep, but, before she knows it, morning is here. She hears a creaking sound as Mrs. Burns gets out of bed and comes over and shakes her roughly. "Time to get up, missy. And no more of your she-nanigans like last night… you hear?"

Morning Star doesn't respond as she pulls herself up out of bed. Numbness fills every square inch of her body as she goes to her room and puts on a worn-looking dress, thinking, *I feel just like this dress… ugly and tired.* She trudges down the hallway and walks into the kitchen where a dour Mrs. Barlapp is stirring up batter.

Seeing Morning Star, she raises her eyebrows and frowns. "I will be fixing pancakes and ham for the teachers this morning. But you are no longer allowed to collect eggs from the chicken coop… not until that runaway has been caught. Just giving me more work to do…." She grumbles, as she beats the batter into a frenzy. "You, with your shameful actions, have made a lot of extra work for me now. You think I enjoy working my tail off while you… ?" Her rant drones on.

As if in a daze, Morning Star walks past the woman, ignoring her remarks. She gathers ingredients for the girls' breakfast, and starts to prepare the oatmeal. This gloomy feeling pervades her senses and reminds her of the time she and the others were forced to leave their homes. She feels her stomach knot. Lost in misery, she frets about Hidden Spirit, wondering where he is. As tears begin to drip, she prays they won't find him. A dark cloud seems to have permeated this place, extinguishing the spark she felt earlier. Mrs. Barlapp whacks her with a towel, and she jumps. "What's the matter with you?" she demands, as the oatmeal starts to boil over the pot. The frothy mess bubbles up, then dribbles down the sides, onto the stove.

Morning Star quickly pulls the pot off the stove, almost dropping it, and scalding her hands.

"Are you daft?" Mrs. Barlapp screeches, seething with indignation. "You have been at this long enough to do a better job." Pursing her lips tightly, she says, "Well, the children will have less to eat today because of you."

Holding back her tears, Morning Star starts to apologize, then stops. *There's no use trying to apologize to these people. They will never understand us, or why we don't want to be here.*

"I heard about your escapade last night young lady. You should be ashamed. I feel truly sorry for Mrs. Trimble having to put up with all you… you heathens. Waste of time, I'd say. I would tell her my opinion, but I don't want to upset her even more."

Morning Star bites her tongue and chooses not to respond — preferring, instead, to ignore the woman.

"If it were me running things around here, I'd tan both your backsides, but good. Now get back to work," and smacks her with the towel again.

Morning Star endures the glares and nasty looks from the teachers as she sets the food on the table, trying her best not to drop or spill anything. The morning seems endless. Just like every other miserable day in this place, only worse.

After lunch, Mrs. Trimble marches Morning Star and Little Moon by the napes of their necks down the hallway, out the door, and directly to Preacher Jim's office. She knocks loudly and waits for the preacher to answer. The door swings open abruptly to a frazzled-looking preacher standing in rumpled clothing — looking as though he hasn't slept in a week.

At a momentary loss for words, Mrs. Trimble chews on her lips, and then speaks hesitantly. "I must report an incident that happened last night. It's a bit unsettling I have to say. I don't know what's come over these girls of late... and I hate to add more burden to your load... but these two..." She pushes the girls forward. "They tried to run away last night."

Preacher Jim's brows arch in annoyance. He strokes his eyebrows nervously, and paces back and forth. Whisking his Bible off the table, he raises it high in the air, as if ready to deliver a high-minded speech to his parishioners.

"I'll tell you what's happening," he bellows, while brushing a strand of hair from his face. Unaware of his fidgeting, he paces across the room. "It's the Devil, that's the problem." He looks accusingly at the girls, wagging his pointy finger in their face. "You have brought the wrath of the Devil upon me." His large yellow teeth seem to flicker in the scant light. "I have seen the burning pits of Hell, and it's not a pretty sight." He yanks at his eyebrow hairs so hard that a couple of them break loose.

Mrs. Trimble is momentarily stunned by the sight of the frazzled, peculiar-looking man, and steps back. She could swear his eyebrows seem somehow different, even odd-looking. And, no wonder — they are sticking straight out, like porcupine quills.

The preacher paces back and forth, escalating his tirade. "It's the fault of that runaway," he roars, holding the Bible in the air. "The one who showed up here looking like the Red Devil himself, trying his best to bait me... trick me... send the demons after me. I should have killed him on the spot, but, no! I wanted to save his Godless soul, show him the true face of our Lord... and this is my reward... more deceit." Crossing the room in long strides, he laments. "That boy has ruined my life."

Startled by his venomous outburst, Mrs. Trimble backs away. "Well, thank you for your time, Preacher Jim. Sorry to bother you. Please forgive my intrusion." She motions to the girls to leave, and they hurry out the door. His thundering voice follows them down the path as they head back to the school. Mrs. Trimble wonders what on earth has happened to the man. Aware of the toll this place has taken on all of them, she must be understanding and tolerant of his erratic behavior.

*

Ellie raps lightly on her window, praying Homer will hear her. She watches as he busily gathers baskets full of walnuts that blanket the ground. Homer picks up the damp leaves and puts them in a large pile as he shakes out the walnuts. "Please, please, look up," Ellie whispers, and she raps on the window again, a little harder, pleading with her eyes. Her breath catches as she hears footsteps coming down the hallway and a key rattling in the door. She flies to her bed and pulls up the covers just as the door opens.

Opal scowls as she looks around the room, and eyes Ellie with a mixture of contempt and suspicion. The girl stares at the floor, her face flushed, as she tries to hide her look of guilt. "This is a note from Mr. Beadle, your betrothed," she says in a huff, and drops the envelope onto the bed. "I will bring up a pack for your eye and lip. Make you as presentable as possible, for your wedding on Sunday. I must say that I can't wait for that day to come. Then you'll be out of my hair, for good." Opal sniffs and moves over to the window, where she sees Homer, then turns to Ellie. "I do not want you talking to that boy or disturbing his work. Talk to the Lord, if you get lonely." She carefully scans the room one last time before leaving.

After her mother has left, Ellie looks at the crumpled envelope. She can tell Opal has read the letter, but she couldn't care less as she glances at the scribbled words.

Ellie, after your outrageous behavior ... making a mockery of me ... you're lucky I still want you. You have put me in an awkward situation. I have a business to run and a reputation to uphold in the community. People are gossiping, saying you tried to steal my horse. They wonder how I will handle such a reckless girl with heathen associations. I will not be made a laughing-stock in town. After we wed, this will be your only warning. Take my words as law. Yours, Frae.

Ellie furiously rips the note into shreds, and then hurls the tiny pieces out the window, sending them scattering in the wind and landing near Homer and his basket full of walnuts.

Homer pulls at a scrap of paper that sticks to his hair and glances around curiously and sees fragments of paper still fluttering in the air. He looks up and catches Ellie staring out her window waving and motioning to him.

Is she calling me over? Homer wonders as his heart starts to pound. He hurls himself to his feet, and, in his haste, stumbles over the basket full of walnuts. Frantically trying to right himself, his arms look like a wobbly windmill blowing unsteadily in the air. His face burns with embarrassment, he knows he looks like a fool as he hurries over to the window. "D-did y-y-you want something, E-Ellie?"

Honey blond hair cascades alongside her lovely face, as she leans further out the window. Homer thinks he might faint from excitement as he stares up at her beauty.

"Homer," she whispers, "my parents have locked me in my room. Could you help me get out of here?"

Homer's entire body is quaking as he strains to hear her words, hoping the pounding in his ears subsides. All he can do is nod his head.

Ellie is not sure he understands, and decides to write a note.

She scribbles as quickly as possible and then tosses it down to Homer. As the wind picks up, he chases after it as though it was a valuable treasure — and plucks it in mid-air. He gasps as he reads Ellie's words:

Please help. I need to escape from here. My parents have locked me in my room. Can you find out if there's a train close by? P.S. I need you to get inside the shed. There is money hidden in there. I hope I'm not asking too much. Thank you. Thank you. Ellie.

A door slams. Homer jumps as Opal comes outside to dispose of the potato peels.

He quickly shoves the note into his pocket, picks up the rake, and starts raking — acting as if he is absorbed in his work.

"Aren't you finished with those leaves yet, Homer? And what about those walnuts?"

Homer clutches the rake and forces himself to answer in a calm voice. "Y-yes, ma'am... I'm almost finished. The tree is so full of nuts... um... it'll take some time before I can get to them all. Then, they need to dry before I can shuck them."

Opal glances up at Ellie's window, then back to Homer. "You are to have no communication with my daughter," she says, eyeing Homer suspiciously. "Come inside when you're finished, and take the ashes out of the stove. Then you can bury these peels before they attract the rats." Once again, she looks up at Ellie's window, and then goes inside to the kitchen.

When Ellie hears her mother leave, she pokes her head out again, cautiously.

Homer continues to rake — just in case Opal returns.

Ellie speaks softly. "Homer, I have to get out of here. Would you help me?"

Homer shakes from head to toe, eyes agape as he stares at the beautiful sight that fills his dreams each night — her soft golden curls fluttering around her face. He sighs at the vision, not believing she is really talking to him, or that she is asking for his help.

"Y-yes, I-I will," he says, as a lump forms in his throat. He swallows hard.

"I only have a few days, five to be exact, before they marry me off. Is tomorrow night too soon? I have to leave, as soon as possible," Ellie frets, near tears, "or else I will go mad."

Homer's head bobs up and down, too afraid to speak… afraid he'll sound stupid.

Looking at the steep drop, she says. "I'm not sure how I'll get down from here. Maybe you could get a rope. That's the only way for me to get down."

"I-I'll a-ask my dad for his h-help," Homer says apprehensively. "He's pretty handy. I-I'm sorry they did this to y-you."

"I am, too," Ellie says urgently. "Don't forget the money in the shed. It's kept locked, so you'll have to break in. There's lots of it in there so bring a bag." Ellie then describes where the money is hidden as Homer's eyes pop in amazement.

*

Morning Star sleeps fitfully, tossing and turning. Each time her eyes close they suddenly jerk back open and she continues tossing and turning. Her mind is full of troubling thoughts while she lies awake wondering what will happen now that she and Little Moon are unable to escape.

Mrs. Burns has instructions to: "Keep a sharp eye out, day and night. She might try to run away again. So, sleep with one eye open, if need be."

Morning Star shifts uncomfortably, her bones aching from the damp, hard floor. She lies on her back, hands under her head, and sighs. She feels something caress her face, ever so lightly, drifting lazily, circling her brow. Her eyes fly open, at first in alarm.

Then, as she feels the soft caress again, she smiles and sits up in wonder. "It's him!" she whispers. "Hidden Spirit is here! He has to be." She feels almost giddy. A sense of elation fills her and she squeezes herself to stop trembling. She slips from under the covers and tiptoes past Mrs. Burn's large frame, gusting with loud snores, as her mouth ripples with her exhale. Morning Star follows the feathers, as they glide silently. *It's like they're dancing in air.* She feels as if she is floating along with the feathers, as a downy tuft swirls around her body, guiding her to the door. Great plumes of quills twist and turn in the tiny opening of the lock, before finally unlatching. The hinge lets out a low squeak as Morning Star slowly pushes the door open, then waits, holding her breath. Mrs. Burns lets off a snort and the sound of breathing stills. Then, after what seems like an eternity, a loud snuffle erupts. To Morning Star's relief, she slips outside the room and slumps against the wall — shaking and unsure what to do next.

Morning Star blinks a couple times before her eyes begin to focus in the dim light. She sees the faint outline of feathers and excitedly follows the sight down the hallway. Along the way, muscular arms come from out of nowhere and surround her thin frame — bones protruding where flesh ought to be.

Ready to burst into tears, Hidden Spirit whispers, "Shhhh." She flings her arms around Hidden Spirit's neck and holds tight, overcome with relief at his touch, and his nearness. Her delight is almost unbearable as she traces his outline with her hand. Making sure this is not a dream, that it's really him. She covers his face with kisses. "Oh, Hidden Spirit. I was sick with worry when they captured you," she says, and bursts into tears.

Hidden Spirit gently shakes her and whispers, "Morning Star, we must be calm. We have to free Little Moon. Do you know where she is?"

"Yes," Morning Star sniffs. "Down there," pointing to Mrs. Trimble's room. "She has her locked in her room."

Hidden Spirit's brow creases into a frown, as he ponders how to get her out. A tiny spark whispers in his brain. He closes his eyes to contemplate and before he knows it, feathers are flying wildly around the hallway. They seem to come alive as they whizz down the hallway, zooming in front of him — like geese in formation. Then they form into a thin straight line, like an arrow — sharp and precise. The feathers hurl into the lock, burrowing furiously. A clunking sound follows… the door opens.

Mrs. Trimble hears the racket, and bolts up in alarm, quickly lighting a lantern. Holding it high in the air, she blinks furiously at a swarm of feathers near the door — looking like an angry hive of bees. Then she clutches her chest as she sees an Indian boy race into the room, appearing wild and ferocious. *It must be that brazen one Preacher Jim was talking about,* she thinks, as her head reels in shock. Before she can scream or think what to do, the Indian scoops up Little Moon from her bed, and is gone before she can manage to get a word out, or even to yell for help. Gathering her wits about her, Mrs. Trimble flies out of bed, screeching. "You get back here, you wicked…" Her words freeze in her throat as she watches the swarm of feathers whirl around mid-air and head directly toward her face. The mass of feathers hovers inches away from her eyes and her head, and she quickly falls back — shock rumbling through her body. One of the black feathers flutters near the tip of her nose and she swats it away, wishing she had her scissors in hand. She'd snip the whole bunch of them, she thinks, beginning to wonder about her sanity. *All sorts of witchcraft and evil goings-on here,* she thinks furiously.

*

It's nearing ten o'clock, Tuesday night. Homer is a bit giddy as he gathers a coil of rope, a satchel full of food his mother made, and a hefty burlap bag. Luckily his parents are sympathetic to Ellie's plight and give their blessings. His father even shows him how to break the lock. He also gives him a pair of pliers, just in case.

Homer set out on this brisk autumn night, perspiring. The closer he gets to Ellie's house the more nervous he becomes. He even wonders if he can really do this. He has thought about this moment non-stop since she asked him for help, hoping she would be impressed with his willingness to help rescue her. Who knows? He might even get a kiss for his troubles. Wow! That thought makes his face blister with heat. But, then doubt starts filtering in, buzzing around his head. *What if I can't get Ellie out? What if I get caught? She'd have to marry that oaf, Beadle, and it would be my fault — and then she would hate me. Oohhh, I'd better stop thinking before I lose my nerve.*

By the time he reaches Ellie's house, Homer is shaking. He waits by the foliage to calm down and listens for any sounds of Preacher Jim or Opal. Walking closer, he bends down low, and peers inside the window, where he sees a dim light burning in the study. *No one's there!* He hesitates for a moment, wondering where they might be and hoping they are getting ready for bed. So he eases his way to the fence, and scuttles down the yard.

As Homer nears the dilapidated building, apprehension sets in. *It looks haunted.* Hackles rise on the back of his neck as he takes the pliers from his pocket, and steadies his hands, which begin to shake. With much concentration he jimmies the lock, like his father instructed, and to his amazement, it unlocks. Homer's heart thuds as he pushes the door open. It lets off a woeful groan. A feeling of dread rises as a blast of musty air floats out and assails his nostrils. He knows the shed must be crawling with spiders — large ones. Feeling woozy, he almost turns back. His nerves are ready to snap. Ellie never paid him any attention until now, and the thought of her sets his mind reeling. Maybe things could be different now. He imagines himself like the Indian boy —tomahawk in hand, ready to save the damsel in distress. *Well, that's not likely to happen. Must have read too many books,* he thinks, miserably, and hesitates at the door before forcing his feet to move inside the musty shed. All the while, he is keeping his thoughts focused on Ellie's lovely face. He bends down and starts to crawl on his hands and knees into the foreboding room. It is so dark, he can't see his foot in front of his face and has to feel his way around, hands skimming the floor. As he inches his way forward, looking for the loose board, he is desperately trying to remember Ellie's description. Jars rattle and shake as he bumps his head hard into a cabinet and chokes back a yelp. Sitting back and seeing stars for a moment, he rubs his head, which is sore and already forming a lump. "I must be stupid to do this. I know she doesn't really even like me. She just needs me. I must keep my promise," he moans. Homer continues to inch his way forward, fumbling, hoping soon, he will find the chest full of coins. *The place smells like something must have died in here long ago. Whatever it is, I hope I don't bump into it.* He holds his breath, making his way across the floor. For just a brief moment a half-moon slips through the clouds outside the window, and a glint of light filters in. His eyes are starting to get used to the murky darkness and he is grateful for the bit of light. Making his way further into the shed he hears a board creek, then a groan. *This must be it,* he thinks excitedly as he feels around for the loose board. Exhaling deeply, a wave of excitement trickles through his veins as he slowly lifts the board. His hands slide inside the hole, and he finds the dusty chest. *This weighs a ton,* he thinks, as he struggles to pull the chest out. He finds the clasp, and quickly pries open the lid. The moonlight bounces off a pile of silvery coins. He runs his hands through them. They feel cold and hard against his sweaty palms. As he runs his hands deeper inside the box, he is shocked at the amount of money inside. "There must be hundreds of coins in here. Where did the preacher get it all?" Anxious to leave this murky room, he gives it no more thought, and simply stuffs his bag full. He feels like the bank robber, Billy the Kid, and grins as he drags the bag out the door. Homer gulps in the chilly night air, glad to be out of that place that sent goose bumps rising up his spine. He wraps some twine around the heavy sack to secure it, and then heaves it over his shoulders... he instantly topples backwards, and lies sprawling on the ground—coins spilling out in every direction.

"Dog-gone-it," Homer grunts, pulling himself up. Not feeling quite so proud now, he scurries to locate the coins fallen into the dirt. He decides it's best to drag the heavy bag behind him, and rushes as fast as he can to Ellie's house.

Out of breath, Homer drops the bag under the tree and uncoils the rope, looking up at the window. He doesn't remember it being that high, and to climb up it appears, well, harder than he had thought earlier. He wishes his father had taught him how to throw a rope, as well, but — too late for that now. His stomach muscles bunch into a knot, as he tries to whistle, but his throat is so dry he can barely get out a squeak.

Homer is inept at hunting and at pretty much anything to do with the outdoors. He is a painter, however, and can draw remarkable images. But this... this is beyond his capabilities. *How am I supposed to get the rope to her?* His pulse does a quick thump as she peers out the window and waves to him.

Homer waves back and takes the rope. He twirls it above his head like he has seen Abe do, trying to look impressive. But his palms start to sweat, and his hands jerk oddly, and when he finally throws the rope, it does a lopsided twirl, and then falls on top of him. Homer's face darkens with embarrassment — he is fully aware he looks like a fool… again. He hears Ellie whisper, "Homer, look where you're throwing."

He wishes he had something clever to say, so he wouldn't seem like such an idiot, but the only thing that comes out, is a timid, "okay."

Homer tries again, but the next throw isn't much better. He could kick himself. This time, he gives it a mighty twirl, but the rope simply wobbles a few feet in the air, and then lands in the brush. He can't think what to do next. *Maybe I should climb the tree and hand it to her.* Since he is afraid of heights he quickly dismisses that idea. How will he ever get the rope to her? Ellie is getting increasingly annoyed. She says, "Concentrate, Homer."

Homer starts to panic. He looks up at the flustered girl, and is now completely humiliated. He whispers to himself, "Don't worry, I'll get it to you, Ellie. I was just practicing." But clever is not how he feels. His stomach does a couple flips as he picks up the rope. Determined to get it right this time, he is jarred by the sudden sound of a door slamming open, and he falls against the wall, and lands into the bushes. He sees a flickering light weave around the steps like a firefly.

"Anyone out here?" Preacher Jim calls out, nervously, toting his gun in one hand and a lantern in the other. He sets the light down on the porch and walks down the steps. Cocking his head toward Ellie's window, he hears a rustling in the bushes and, without hesitating he let off a loud blast. *Not taking any chances this time. After all, one never knows who or what might be prowling about. Maybe they're looking for me.* He clutches his gun closer.

Homer feels faint with fear, his heart hammering uncontrollably, as the bullet whizzes past, just a few feet from his head. He struggles to move from the bushes, but is caught in the shrub.

Opal comes flying out the door, dismayed. "Did you see someone?" She frets, standing behind the preacher, breathing heavily. "Scared the daylights out of me."

"Wasn't sure. Thought I heard someone lurking in the back. Wasn't taking any chances. Wanted to scare them off." He whirls his gun to the left then to the right, eyes swiveling.

"Just coons, dear," Opal says, placating the preacher. "Come inside. It's getting late. We'll get that boy, Homer, to set some traps."

"Make a good meal for the heathens," Preacher Jim comments idly, more to himself — not really believing it was coons. Trying to decide what to do, he steps down once again from the porch, and looks into the yard, and hollers. "I'm still a pretty good shot, you know." Whirling his gun back and forth, he scrunches his eyes, peering into the darkness, hoping it wasn't the demons, and let off a shudder—his head moistening with sweat.

Finally, after Opal's insistence for him to come inside, he turns abruptly and walks into the house, banging the door behind.

Homer untangles himself from the prickly bush and stumbles free, ripping his pants in the process. At this point he doesn't care what he looks like. He's just glad he didn't get shot.

Homer sees Ellie looking down. She hisses. "What are you doing? We'll get caught if you don't hurry, and my father will shoot you. He's acting peculiar of late."

Homer had always wanted to do something that would draw Ellie's attention … maybe even admiration, but instead, he feels humiliated.

He picks up the rope, and shakes it off. "This is my last chance," he breathes out, smacking it against his leg. Suddenly, in the distance, he sees movement. An outline of feathers and hair appears in the moonlight, looking something like a crimson mist, floating in the air. A mysterious figure appears. Homer sucks in his breath at the sight of the Indian boy racing toward him in the moonlight. He isn't sure what to do. He wants to warn Ellie, so he jumps up and down, waving the rope. "L-L-Look!" That's the only word he can manage as his throat constricts. He doesn't know if he should run or confront the boy. So he stands in the open, fists raised, and, before he can react, Hidden Spirit races past and knocks him into the shrubs, once again. Homer falls hard. He feels the rope being snatched from his hands. He curses his luck as he looks up at the moon peering out from behind the clouds. It seems to taunt him with a smile.

Hearing Ellie gasp, he looks up at the window and quickly scrambles to his feet to see the agile young Indian in motion. In one graceful twirl, the rope flies into the air and lands inside Ellie's window. Homer feels a mixture of jealousy and admiration for the boy. He lets loose a sigh, and sinks to his knees, wishing that it were him rescuing Ellie. Once again, all he had managed to do was look foolish. He realizes his dreams of impressing Ellie are now, officially, over. *It was a nice dream while it lasted.*

Watching the scene below her unfold, Ellie can hardly believe her eyes... shocked at the sudden appearance of Hidden Spirit, looking wild and handsome as ever. He swiftly climbs the rope and slides into her room. She is at a loss of words. *How did he know,* she wonders.

Hidden Spirit motions for her to hurry. Gathering her wits about her, intent on not wasting another moment, she grabs her satchel and tosses it out the window. In the next moment she feels muscular arms surround her, swoop her up in one swift motion and lift her out the window. Forgetting her fear of heights she grabs hold of the rope and sails down, pantaloons billowing out. She doesn't care how she looks as she tumbles to the ground, landing with a whoosh. She is so grateful to be out of her house, she twirls in circles. "This is a miracle! I made it!" she whispers, and kisses the ground. Looking at Hidden Spirit, tears of happiness fill her eyes. Before she can stop herself, she runs over and gives him a hug. The feel of his muscular body was a masterpiece, savoring the moment. "Thank you. I know it would be dangerous to take me... so I will leave with Homer."

Hidden Spirit nods his head. With a faint smile, he says, "The girl with the sunshine hair. Travel safe."

Before Ellie can tell him, 'I have never met anyone like you before. I would have done anything for you,' he suddenly disappears as silently as he had appeared — into thin air. She blows a kiss to the vanishing Indian boy who just saved her life. *He is my hero*. She thinks with a shiver. Her mind is still reeling from his actions and his touch.

Ellie looks irritably at Homer, who is shuffling his feet. She can't contain her growing annoyance at him any longer as doubts begin to surface. "Let's hurry, before you trip on your rope... or your feet."

REUNITED

IDDEN SPIRIT AND the exhausted girls arrive in the hills a few weeks later... in the quiet of night. As they ride up, Plenty Feathers is sitting by a small campfire, smoking his pipe.

He didn't seem surprised to see them... it was as if he had been expecting them, and he cries out in joy. "I see the Great Spirit has answered my prayers, and blessed me generously with your return." He hurries over to Hidden Spirit, and gives him a warm hug. Then he helps Morning Star and Little Moon off the horse, and holds them close. "My children, it is good to see you. My heart sings with happiness to have you back among our people." He studies each girl closely. "I can feel your bones, where flesh should be. Come inside, I have a stew simmering."

The exhausted girls follow Grandfather as he opens the flap to the tepee, motioning them inside. "I see your journey at the white man's school has been filled with many difficulties. My heart grieves remembering our Chasing Rabbit. I pray every day to keep the anger from my heart — what the white eyes took from us." His voice cracks with emotion. "Come and sit, my children."

Morning Star and Little Moon can barely believe they are home as they sit down on the soft buffalo skins, soaking in the warm and beautiful surroundings. A soft light flickers from the fire, and the smell of elk stew simmering sends their bellies rumbling. Not a detail escapes the girls' senses. After enduring such a stark and unpleasant environment, this familiar setting seems almost unreal — like a dream.

Grandfather walks toward the fire and stirs the stew, adding a few sprinkles of herbs to the pot.

Little Moon whispers to Morning Star, "I hope this isn't a dream and that tomorrow morning I find myself back at the school."

"I think this is real, Little Moon. We're home," Morning Star assures her sister. Then the girls fall into silent contemplation, deep in their own thoughts. Grandfather watches the girls with hooded eyes, and smiles as he hands each of them a steaming bowl of the stew.

"Thank you, Grandfather," they say in unison, grateful for his thoughtfulness.

The aroma wafts through the air, as each girl inhales the savory food for a moment as they silently say a prayer. Little Moon can hardly wait, and she breathes in deeply before taking her first bite. "This is delicious," she says, smacking her lips between mouthfuls, blissfully happy.

Grandfather looks pleased at her enthusiasm. "It will warm your thin bones from the cold night, my child."

Morning Star looks at Grandfather's thin but muscular frame, noticing he has aged well since she last saw him. Then the smell of food calls to her and she eats slowly, savoring each bite — feeling at peace, at last.

Having tended to Ghost Dancer, bedding him down for the night, Hidden Spirit comes inside. Tonight, there are no shadows crossing his heart. He is grateful the girls are back among their people, and in his company. His heart tugs at the sight of Morning Star, but he pulls his eyes away, carefully looking around the tepee. He walks over and hugs his grandfather tightly as he looks at the medicine bundle hanging near the wall. "I notice you have some new additions. They look powerful. It's good to be back with you, Grandfather. I am grateful you fared well while I was gone."

Lighting his pipe, Plenty Feathers waits until it is fully lit before speaking. "I had a visitor not long ago. The man came looking for you, but he didn't stay long. Seemed to be in a hurry to leave," Grandfather says, with a mischievous smile. "He looked frightened... like he had seen... a 'niya'."

Hidden Spirit looks admiringly at Plenty Feathers, and laughs. "I see you have been up to some of your old tricks." They talk for a while about his time in the hills. Then, after the girls finish eating, Plenty Feathers takes note of the girls' exhaustion. With Little Moon's eyes drifting shut, he hurries over to take their bowls.

The furs spread across the floor look inviting to the weary young travelers, who can barely hold their heads up or keep their eyes open. With thoughts of sleep, Little Moon crawls inside the luxurious furs and is slumbering the second she lies down.

"We can talk more in the morning. I want to hear about all that happened while you were away," Grandfather says quietly. He motions for Morning Star to get to sleep.

Gratefully, Morning Star crawls between the soft pelts and nods off a moment later, followed by Hidden Spirit. Grandfather stays awake, contemplating what will happen now that his grandson is back.

Hidden Spirit awakens at first light, and slides from between the buffalo skins, looking at the faces of the sleeping girls. In the pre-dawn darkness, a rosy pink glow eases its way up — awakening the east. A morning star is etched brilliantly above in the sky, as the boy steps quietly outside into the crisp morning air. He is greeted by his Grandfather who is tending to the fire and smoking his pipe. "Grandson, I hope you slept well."

"Yes, very well. It's good to be back, Grandfather," Hidden Spirit says, sitting down next to Plenty Feathers, who hands him a cup of coffee. "It has been a long journey and now I have things I must attend to in town. I wish I could stay with you and the girls a while longer, but I cannot. Please watch over them. I'll be back as soon as I can."

Grandfather nods as he pours Hidden Spirit more coffee, and talks quietly. "I know, Grandfather, things are not good on the reservation and I worry for our people. I must find a way to bring all the children back home. It is not good at that white man's school. But, first, I have other matters to take care of."

Plenty Feathers studies Hidden Spirit, his hooded eyes fill with concern, "Be careful of those palefaces, Grandson. The one I ran into up here was bad."

Looks like Grandfather handled that one well, Hidden Spirit thinks in admiration. He has an inkling who Grandfather was talking about. And he's right about him being bad, but he would talk with him about that at another time. Right now, he has other pressing matters on his mind. Once Hidden Spirit finishes his coffee, he says, "Goodbye, my Grandfather. Be safe up here with the girls." Then he and Ghost Dancer set off down the hill in the early morning hours. A short time later, he nears town, and leaves his horse near the edge, nestled in some trees. "Stay here, boy," he whispers to Ghost Dancer. "Keep your ears alert." He rubs his neck and walks carefully to his parents' house.

As he enters through the back entrance, he waits for a moment, watching his mother, noticing her shoulders are slumped. He can feel her immense sadness as she stands at the stove, stirring the pot. White Tail senses someone is there, and, when she turns around, she screams at the sight of her son, drops the pan she was holding, and beams with joy. She suddenly looks years younger. Hidden Spirit races over and scoops her off her feet, hugging her tightly.

"Oh, my son. I was so worried about you. The Great Spirit blesses us with your safe return. You cannot know my relief. I am so happy you are back." She burst into tears, overwhelmed by his return, and then blots her tear-filled eyes. "Seeing you lightens my heart, and gives me hope."

White Cloud emerges from the back room, and his throat constricts at the sight of Hidden Spirit. Emotions flow deeply through his bones. He stands for a moment to quiet his pounding heart and, in silence, observes his son. *Hidden Spirit is different, somehow. The journey has changed him. He has grown full of wisdom. He is now the man he was destined to be.* But still — White Cloud is worried for his headstrong son. He notices a line that has deepened around his mouth — and yet his demeanor has softened. *This combination will make him a formidable force to be reckoned with. The people on the reservation need someone like him*, he thinks proudly.

White Cloud walks up to his son, and hugs him tightly. "Come, tell us of your journey." He pulls out another chair so they all might sit at the small wooden table. A vase filled with lemon verbena sits in the center, reminding Hidden Spirit of his beloved sister, Chasing Rabbit. He traces the outer edges of the silky flower and puts the fragrant blossom to his nose, inhaling the lovely scent.

"How are things at that white man's school, my son?" White Cloud asks, solemnly, even though he already seems to know the answer. "Most importantly, how are all the other children? I have prayed to the Great Spirit for their well-being."

Hidden Spirit pauses before answering — his stoical face fills with pain. "There is sadness and death at that place. They are intent on taking our culture away from our children and filling their minds with white ideas. I was captured while I was there, and the preacher lectured me from his Bible, telling me I worship the Devil. He tried to convert me. I think it was the other way around. The white man speaks with two tongues. They say their religion is kind and caring, but their actions say otherwise. The children seem confused and afraid… afraid to believe in the white man's religion… afraid they will be punished if they believe in our Great Spirit. Little Moon was very brave at that place, but I'm not sure how much more she could take." His voice lowers. "Morning Star is so thin, I hardly recognized her. They cut her hair… they cut *all* the girls' hair… and dress them in the white way."

White Tail brings fried bread, dried jerky, and bitter coffee to the table. She listens closely to Hidden Spirit — and her eyes fill with tears at the memory of her daughter. Finally, she manages to clear her throat, and speak. "Everyone walks around this place with long faces. With our children gone, hope for our future, I fear, is fading."

Everyone is silent for a while, sipping coffee — lost in their own thoughts and contemplating White Tail's words.

Then, Hidden Spirit turns to his father and tells him about his journey to the school, and how, "Wigley came upon me while I was tending to Ghost Dancer's leg, and almost killed me. It was my carelessness that caused it. He dragged me at the back of his horse until I was unconscious. I was in the throes of death and walked between the two worlds. I saw our ancestors there. Crazy Horse sat with me for I-don't-know-how-long, not saying anything. He just looked at me. I could feel his eyes burrow into my heart. And then, I saw Broken Feather. He spoke to me of my choice… to stay in the world of the living or go to the hereafter. I chose to come back and walk in the world of the living. My time is not finished here."

White Cloud grasps his son tightly. "Oh, my son, I am grateful Broken Feather came to you. I will thank him in my prayers. And now," he smiles, "you say the girls are back… a blessing from our Great Spirit."

"They are staying with Plenty Feathers in the hills. I have things to take care of here, in town, with Peale, and I don't want them to get caught. They will be safe there. I must prove to Peale that Wigley is stealing our supplies, and worse. I must convince him that Wigley is no good."

White Cloud worries that it might not happen. "Peale won't lift a finger to help us. I went to see Wigley a while ago, on our supply day. There was no food. I questioned him why we have nothing, and I came away with a black eye. He told me not to come back until he says so. Then he shoved me away from the door. He told me to go beg elsewhere, if we're hungry. I'm pretty sure there was food inside. Our people are starving, my son, and Peale does nothing. It will be hard to convince him about Wigley."

Hidden Spirit feels his insides burn. White Cloud notices his son's eyes darken, and he worries. "Father, I must go to town and find out what is happening to our supplies. I have never trusted Wigley from the first time I saw him, and now he thinks I'm dead. So…"

"It will be dangerous for you, my son. Wigley is a man with no conscious. You have already seen that." White Cloud looks at his son's eyes and sees his determination. A flicker of pride fills him, and he says, "Be careful."

Hidden Spirit assures them he will. He stays with them the rest of the day, and then, when the sun sinks low, he says, "it is time to go now." He hugs his parents' goodbye, and walks silently into town. With dusk fast approaching, Hidden Spirit blends into the night shadows.

A half-moon lights the way on this calm and serene evening, with crickets and katydids filling the night air with their song. Hidden Spirit walks unnoticed into town, and crept around the red brick building where Wigley resides. He stops and listens as he approaches the storage room. All is quiet. He pries the shutter open and deftly climbs into the small window. As he steps inside, his eyes bulge at the sight before him. He can't believe the amount of food he sees — bags of flour, sugar, and wheat piled high to the ceiling along with beans, coffee, tins of sardines, and numerous barrels of other goods. He picks up a few cans, wondering, "What is Wigley up to?" There is enough food stored here to feed his people for a very long time. Filled with disgust, Hidden Spirit tries his best to keep his anger under control as he deftly climbs out through the window.

Rage fills him as he walks. *My people are starving, and Wigley is stealing our food.* Once again he slides into the shadows, determined more than ever to find out what is going on. With as much control as he can muster, Hidden Spirit walks around town searching for Wigley.

It didn't take long to find him. Up ahead he sees Jeb, hooting and crowing about some big plans. He follows close behind, listening. "Wait till Peale finds me gone... an the supplies. He'll be madder than a hen in heat, thinkin' I was so upstandin'. He'll have sniption fit fer certain." Wigley and his friend, saunter down the street, laughing.

Hidden Spirit flings his hands in the air.

Wigley thinks he sees something, and falls silent, his mouth hangs open. It's a bunch of feathers floating in the air, zipping along like a predator on a hunt. Not a hint of breeze is blowing. His skin prickles — a peculiar kind of feeling. He looks carefully into the darkness, his eyes scrunch sharply. "It can't be," he whispers, and sucks in his breath. He looks closer... but the outline is hazy, and he sees the shadow move... like it's coming right at him. Wigley jumps back, holding his chest.

"You see anything?" Jeb asks, craning his neck.

"I-it-was nothin'," Will says. "Musta been my 'magination. Thought I saw a ghost... with a bunch o' feathers or somethin'."

He feels the hairs rise at the back of his neck and mutters. "I swear it was that Injun... the one I killed a while back..."

"Say, it's black as the ace of spades out there. I can't see a damn thing. Ya must be seein' stuff, partner. I told ya... this place is spooky as hell, but ya didn't believe me. Those Injuns got some potent shit up their sleeves... I seen it too!"

"Guess I got the willies, is all." Suddenly Will's hat lifts slightly and wobbles on top of his head. Then it blows clean off, landing on the ground. His eyes swerve nervously around toward Jeb. He hollers, "Let's get going. When we finish our business here, I ain't ever comin' back to this place ... no matter what." Retrieving his hat, Will joins Jeb, who is already hustling down the road. "I need me a bottle of whiskey."

"That makes two, partner."

Out of breath, Will quickly unlocks the door, and scoots inside, where he grabs a bottle of booze. "My nerves are rattlin' like a great big caboose," he says, taking a huge gulp, as it trickles down his chin and onto his shirt. Not caring, he wipes his face with the back of his hand. "There, that oughtta help."

"Hand it over partner," Jeb says irritably. "You ain't the only one in need."

"Let's sit down and go over what we gotta do. We got some serious plannin' to ponder," Will says thirstily, and grabs for another bottle. "Elmer's gonna be waiting for us. It's a four-hour ride, an we can't be late.

Hidden Spirit hides by the door, listening to the details with clenched fists.

"Just a few more days, Jeb, and we're outta here. We gotta get up with the roosters tomorrow, so you'd better take it easy on this bottle... ain't getting any more neither." And he bangs the bottle down on the table.

*

It's nearing 7:00 a.m., and Will is getting real anxious about leaving. They have to meet Elmer at the crossroads, near Wallis at noon, and he can't seem to wake Jeb for nothing. He's snoring so loud, it sounds like someone's sawing a stack of logs. Will's eyes are a bit hazy, as well, after drinking all that hooch with Jeb last night. "That Jeb's a serious drinker," he grumbles. "Had ta hide my whiskey or else he'd drunk it all up." He kicks the side of the bed. "Blast him, anyways. I don't know what's worse — his drinking or his snoring." Will looks sideways at his passed-out friend. "I'd like to plug his snout, that's for dang sure." He paces the room, rubbing his head. "I've gotta get him up, somehow… we're gonna be late." Will spots a bucket sitting in the corner, half-full of water — thinking that ought to do the trick. He hollers one more time. "Jeb, you best wake up, or I'm gonna douse ya, but good. Hope this is just water," he grins, holding the bucket. "Looks a might yellow if'n ya ask me."

Jeb grunts, rolls over, and let off a big snore.

Will shrugs his shoulders, and then heaves the yellow water onto Jeb, bucket and all. He watches as Jeb roars in disbelief and falls off the bed, tangled in the blankets, shouting, "What the hell's going on?" He wipes his eyes, and sees Will snickering. "What's the matter with ya, anyways?" Jeb sputters, wiping his eyes. "Throwing water on me like that… ya made my ticker thud real hard."

"I had to wake ya somehows… so put a whistle in yer giddy-up an get dressed. We gotta get a move on. Elmer's a fussy old codger and won't wait for nothing or nobody. Got somethin' strong a-brewing on the stove, an' it ain't liquor… so grab a cup while I get the horses." Before Jeb can finish saying, "What's the hurry? My head's buzzin'," Will zips out the door, and bangs it shut.

Jeb forgets the coffee and staggers out the door scratching his head, looking blurry-eyed and ruffled. Will brings his horse around, and Jeb hops atop his mount, reeling in the saddle. He smacks Jeb's horse and they take off in a flurry of dust with Jeb hollering, "Whoooaaa there, Nelly, not so darn fast," while he clings to the saddle horn as they go galloping out of town. "I told ya not ta drink so doggone much last night!" Will yells. "You'd better hang on good and tight, and stay in your saddle, 'cause we got a four-hour ride ahead of us."

Finally making it to their destination at the crossroads ahead of schedule and with the sun blaring down, Jeb hops off his horse, and wipes his brow. "I'm hotter than a stick on fire. How 'bout we take a snooze over there under that big ole tree, before Elmer gets here? I'm plumb wore out," he says, rubbing his backside.

"Sounds like a mighty fine idea, partner," Will says, heading to the shade.

"Man, that was one long, miserable ride," Jeb groans, stretching his right leg, trying to get his britches unstuck. "I think my pants are fried to my butt." He gives a tug to loosen them and takes off his hat to fan himself. His head hurts like a hammer had a whack at it, and he hopes he'll feel better by the time Elmer Fink arrives. He isn't keen on that old corker, but he is too tired to care. He yawns widely, and soon falls asleep.

An hour or so later a wagon rumbles like thunder down the road. A trail of dust is blowing a mile thick as the driver cracks the whip, looking like a wild man possessed. "Gee-haw!" he yells.

Will hops up, staring at the sight — hollering and jumping around like a rats in his pants. "Wake up, Jeb. Pronto."

Jeb is still groggy. He rubs his eyes, tries to focus, and is having a hard time getting up. Will smacks him to his senses. "Hurry up, partner."

"Just give me a dang minute," Jeb says, as he grabs his canteen and quickly douses himself with the water, letting the cool liquid clear his head. "Ooooh… that oughtta do the trick," he groans.

Will is elated and waves his hat, shouting, "take a look at this glorious sight!" He runs lickety-split down the road to greet Elmer.

Elmer is a mean-looking, grizzled old man of about sixty, but looks closer to eighty. His dirty white beard and long stringy hair billows out behind like a tired rag. He looks as though it has been a year or better since any part of him has seen a trace of soap or water. He has long since lost most of his teeth, except for a shiny one on top and a couple of ragged ones on the bottom — stained with tobacco juice.

Will doesn't think Elmer has changed much from the last time he saw him. Except maybe his beard has gotten longer and dirtier, and his hair a might thinner. His one gold tooth in front glints in the sunlight as he says. "Howdy, Will. Been awhile. Glad to see you made it on time."

"Yessirree, I weren't gonna be late for my booty," Will says with a cockeyed grin.

"How's those Injuns on the res treating you these days?"

Will's grin broadens. "I gotta say… treating me real nice-like."

Elmer scratches his beard. "I'd say you did pretty well for yourself on that dirt patch in South Dakota, huh?" He gives Will a wink, and grins. "Say, get friendly with any them squaws?"

Will's face reddens, thinking of the one that got away. He is still fuming over that redskin bitch. Too bad he didn't finish what he started with her. He looks over at Elmer, who is staring a hole right through him. *Better forget her*, he thinks, then slaps his britches, and forces out a grin. "Squaws ain't much to my liking." Before Elmer can ask any more questions, Will scoots over to the wagon, and sees the canvas piled high.

"You're gonna make a tidy profit," Elmer says, in admiration, looking at the bulging wagon. "Gotta load of hootch that'll keep you and the men happy for a spell. Got yer liquid gold tucked away nice and neat. I'd say ya hit the mother lode."

"Poor old Injuns," Will smirks, looking pleased at the amount of whiskey in the wagon. "They're gonna be a sorry bunch when they try to get their handouts."

"What ya planning on doing with all your loot?" Elmer asks.

"Gonna be headin' down to Texarkana, near the border, and set me up a fancy whorehouse. I'll keep a nice pile of hooch for the saloon, an sell the rest to the boys down in Henderson. They're always a thirsty bunch. Plus… I gotta big load of goods I been stashin' away in my warehouse. Puttin' the Injuns on smaller rations, ya might say. Didn't want 'em getting fat an' lazy sittin' around beggin' for food an gettin' used to the good life." He lets off a snort at his cleverness.

Elmer walks around the wagon and lifts the canvas, pulling out a bottle of whiskey. He holds it to the light and takes a drink. "I had to give it a tester, to make sure the goods weren't sour." He smacks his lips in satisfaction. "Real good tasting, too." He looks over at Jeb, glares, and spits out his tobacco juice. The juice lands near his boots, causing Jeb to jump. The old man grins, revealing his bright red gums.

Elmer isn't keen on the boy, and wonders why Will has him for a partner. *That kid is a spineless ninny, and stupid as hell.*

Elmer lowers his voice. "Say Will, whatcha doing with that fella over there? He's got shit fer brains an' drinks like a fish. He's gonna guzzle away all your profits, if you ain't careful. I saw 'ole Jeb at the bar in Henderson and he was a'crowing how he's gonna be your partner. I about fell off my perch when I heard the news."

Will twiddles his thumb and says. "Jeb's quick as a whip with a gun an' he can shoot real good, hit a tin can a mile away. I'm the brains, an' Jeb's the gunslinger. So I figure, he's good for sumpthin'. Ain't all bad."

Elmer notices Jeb walking to the wagon, eyeing the content under the canvas. Just as he lifts it up, Elmer spits. This time his tobacco juice lands directly on Jeb's boot. The old man sidles up to Jeb, and gives him a glare with his beady eyes. "What are ya standing 'round the wagon for? Waiting to snatch a bottle a whiskey when we ain't looking?"

Jeb glares right back at the grizzled old man, and fingers his pistol. "I ain't snatchin' nothin'," he growls menacingly, thinking, *if that old coot spits on my boots again, I'll lamblast him, but good.* Puffing up his chest, he hollers. "Ain't no reason to accuse me, neither… an' you should mind yer own beeswax, or else I'll land a bullet…"

Will quickly intervenes, and steps between the two before a fight breaks out. Elmer is a tough old codger, and mean as a rattler, so Will says, "Whoa there, fellas. No need to get your britches in an uproar. Why don't ya boys shake hands and forget 'bout all this? Here ya go, Elmer." Will pulls a leather pouch from his pocket, and hands it to Elmer, shaking the bag. "That should cover your expenses."

Elmer feels the heavy pouch. "This'll come in handy for my triple dilly poker game tonight with the boys back in Tucker."

Jeb wonders what the old coot means by a triple dilly poker game, and scratches his chin while glaring at the grizzled old man out of the corner of his eye.

Elmer goes on talking to Will. "I'm gonna splurge on this fine gal, Dolly Doolittle. I been hankering for a taste of her for quite a spell — chomping at the bit to get my hands wrapped around her, good and tight."

Will grins. "Sounds like a good time, Elmer. Give Dolly a squeeze for me, too." Standing between Jeb and Elmer, the old man glares at Jeb one last time before untying his horse. "Say, Will, on your way outta town, why don't you stop by and we'll have a snort or two to your new beginnings. Too bad you're heading to that dusty place in Texas. Almost got myself shot down there a while back in Waco, playing cards. Those guys don't mess around. Well, good doing business with ya. Just watch out for that partner of yours," Elmer says, as he tips his hat to Will. "He'll drink ya dry."

With surprising agility, the old man climbs atop his horse like a spring chicken, gives Jeb the finger, and rides off down the road, trailing a cloud of dust.

Jeb returns the same gesture. "Hope ya don't lose another tooth. Ole Dolly might not like yer yacking with yer gums." He looks at Will. "I can't stand that ole coot. He's nastier than a hornet's nest and about as ugly, too. An' what's he talkin' 'bout... a triple dilly poker game?"

"How the blazes would I know, and I ain't gonna worry about that, 'cause we gotta get down to some serious business."

After the dust settles, Jeb wipes the dirt from his face, then hops into the wagon, eyeing the whiskey, and pulls out a bottle to sample for himself. Will hollers over. "Take it slow on the drink, Jeb, our work here ain't done yet, and I don't want ya guzzling all our profits before they make it to Henderson. Skeeter McFee'll be waiting at the fort with a bunch of thirsty soldiers, and we got a long drive ahead of us. I don't want you drunk while yer driving the wagon. We stand to make a big profit this time!" Will shoves the canvas back further as he goes through the goods, and whistles. "It looks as if they sent extra rations, too — for the poor 'ole Indians. Boo-hoo." He laughs, looking at the overflowing bags of food. "Musta complained they didn't have enough to eat, so the government kindly sent more. That was real nice of them. Helps us out e-mmensely. I gotta be sure an thank the Injuns. I shoulda had 'em get on their bony knees, and beg for their rations... tell 'em to eat dirt if they is hungry," he says with a sardonic grin.

"Let 'em shoot a coon or possum. The good rev pays no attention to their complaints. He tells them to see me… thinks I'm a real trustworthy man, bein' ex-military, and all."

Licking his lips, Will calculates all the money he'll make this time, along with the tidy bundle he already stashed. "A good haul this time. Can't wait to get outta that hellhole." And he kicks up his heels in a jig. "Now, Jeb, I want you ta count the cases of whiskey and see how many we got. And remember, we're sellin' a bottle for two bucks apiece. So get ta countin', slick. I'm gonna take a drizzle."

"Ya mean a piss? Can't you just say you gotta take a piss? Drizzle sounds like it's gonna rain."

"Well, never you mind what I gotta do. Big words keeps me sharp. Just get started countin' now." Will walks off as Jeb scratches his head, looking bewildered. "That's a whole lotta addin', partner."

Will sneaks behind a tree to see how Jeb is doing, and waits.

Jeb is busy rummaging through the wagon to see how many cases of whiskey they have, trying to figure how much money they'll make if they sell each bottle for two dollars. "Now let's see what we've got here…" He starts counting, using his fingers. *Will says there's twelve bottles in a case. So, I figure I've got just enough fingers to cover it. I'm glad my counting is getting better. I gotta be sure Will doesn't cheat me.* "Now, let's see here. One, two, three, four, five, seven, eight, nine, a dozen…" Jeb scratches his head trying to figure out why his fingers doesn't match the bottles in the case, and he tries again. No luck. "Well, ta hell with this," he grumbles, and yanks out a bottle. He doesn't see Will, so he uncaps it, tilts his head back, and takes a real big swig. "Woo-wee! Gonna need it for all the work I gotta do."

"I knew it," Will fumes, while hiding in the bushes watching Jeb. "He's gonna drink me dry."

"Hope it clears my clacker," Jeb says, starting to count once again. "Now lemme see what we got here." He holds up his fingers.

"Okey-doke. I got me ten fingers, that's easy 'nough." He resumes his counting, getting frustrated.

Will holds back a snigger, as Jeb looks confused. "Now wait a minute, here. I must o' messed up, I gotta couple extra bottles."

"Man, this is like takin' candy from a young 'un," Will grins. "What he don't know ain't gonna hurt him. 'Sides, I done most of the work."

Jeb takes another drink, and moans. "That dang Will… makin' me do all the figurin'. I bet he's tryin' to cheat me outta my share, an my noggin's gettin' fuzzy."

Jeb about jumps a foot in the air, when he sees Will emerging from the bushes, and walking up to him.

"Lookee here, Jeb. You need ta take it easy on the whiskey, an' keep yer mitts outta the hooch."

"I thought ya had ta take a piss," Jeb hollers. "Why don't ya leave me to my business and you tend ta yer own."

"Was just checkin' to see if you needed any help with yer countin'. See yer doin' real good." He sets off, chuckling. Will squeezes himself. "Oooh… I gotta go real bad," he grunts, and hurries off into the woods. He makes his way to a nice thicket of underbrush, and begins to yank his britches down when, suddenly, he feels a ruffle in the breeze, and his skin begins to prickle. He looks around to see if Jeb is spying on him, and he hollers, "Is that you, Jeb? Whattaya doin', followin' me?" Will quickly pulls up his pants and looks carefully through the bushes, but no one is there. He decides he'd better look elsewhere, and continues walking. Up ahead he thinks he sees some feathers… floating in the air and rubs his eye, thinking. *Damn things looks like they're flying.* Astonished by the sight, he stands real quiet, looking and listening. He doesn't see a thing, or hear a sound. A bead of sweat pops from his brow. "It musta been an a'lusion… or… probably Jeb, tryin' to be funny," he whispers. Made him a bit skittish, though.

A few moments later, Will is starting to relax. He finds another spot, ready to get back into the "going" business, when he sees those feathers again. This time, it's a great big flock of them, quills pointed directly at him. He screams in fright, and falls backwards into the sticker bush with his britches halfway down. "Yee-owww-eee!" He cries out, all entangled. As he tries to get to his feet, an arrow comes whizzing right out of nowhere, and sails straight through his hat — pinning it to the tree. Not knowing what to expect next, Will panics. "I best get on outta here." He pulls up his pants. "I gotta find Jeb and tell him to get his gun ready and shoot the sons-o-bitches hiding in those feathers."

Will's feet are flying down the road, quick as a racehorse, when out of nowhere a rope glides around his neck and yanks him off his feet — before slithering backwards. Will screams for Jeb. For a second, a face flickers in the center, and then, in a poof, it's gone. "Musta been a ghost or somethin' worse," he moans. Will blinks his eyes real hard as a bright row of feathers dances toward him, looking like the Devil as they circle him, tips clacking. Will's thinking he's about to get scalped, and lets out a yelp. Then he sees a wizened old face appear in the center of the feathers, still floating, until it's a few inches from his nose. *Maybe Jeb was telling the truth about those Indians in the hills, after all,* he thinks, *with their wicked power.* Just then, a hand reaches out and grabs Will by the throat. Will crumples to his knees, and blacks out.

Jeb's getting tired of all the counting so he scrunches down beside the wagon to steal a drink, hoping Will won't see him. "Darn, my pipes are bone dry, and I can barely swallow." The coast is clear, so he tilts his head back and takes a nice long drink of the tantalizing brew. "Whooo-weeee… that's more like it! That should clear the dust from my swallower." Jeb smacks his lips, wondering what Will is up to. It dawns on him that his partner hasn't said anything for a while, or yelled at him for taking a drink. So he shouts, "Hey, Will, where ya at? Are ya still takin' a leak, or doin' the big one?" He slaps his knee, laughing at his comment, and looks around for Will. He almost jumps out of his britches and his laughter freezes when he sees a young Indian staring right at him. *Has a glint of anger in his eyes, and looks wild.* Caught off guard, Jeb isn't sure what to do, so he starts for his nose, then changes his mind. "Hey, Injun, are ya' thirsty?" As Jeb offers him the whiskey, the bottle is knocked out of his hand.

"Hey," Jeb whines, "you coulda' just said no. Wasn't necessary to break my jug o' feel-good and…"

Jeb stops when he sees a stick twirling in the air, hovering inches away from his head. He flinches. "Will! Get over here. I could use some help." He doesn't hear any response, and the Indian boy's piercing gaze makes him jumpy and he looks around uneasily. His voice cracks when he notices an old Indian hiding in the bushes, and quickly opens another bottle of whiskey, chugs another shot before taking a closer look… to his dismay, he finds the Indian gone. *I must o' been seein' things,* he thinks. *What else could it be?*

Nervously, Jeb looks at the young Indian and says, "Hey, whattaya doin' out here, anyways? Ain't Injuns s'posed to be on the reservation?" He asks anxiously, while dancing from one foot to the other, unsure of what to do next. "You might git in real big trouble if'n ya get caught out here. Might get yerself thrown into the ole clinker."

The boy stares back with unflinching eyes.

Jeb's eyes swerve to the side as he looks again in disbelief. Behind the kid is that old Indian, this time dressed in war regalia, carrying a tomahawk, sitting atop a white buffalo. "What the heck is this? Maybe I'd better lay off the whiskey for a while." His hands are shaking too much to get hold of his gun. He thinks that Indian on the buffalo has a real strange look in his eyes, like maybe this one is half-crazed or something. Now he sees that old Indian holding Will's gun… the kid has a stick. He tries to look away, but his eyes seem to be locked on the frightful image of the Indian wearing a load of feathers around his head. He feels an odd prickling sensation on his scalp, which continues down his arms… and, before he knows what happened, a sharp jolt knocks him off his feet and lands him hard on his backside. Not trusting himself to speak, he starts to pull himself up when he feels a wet trickle run down his pants. Thoroughly spooked and feeling foolish, he thinks miserably, *these Indians practice some real powerful magic. This is the second time I've been knocked over by an Injun and hit in the head… scared the living daylights outta me.* Frightened to think about what might happen next, he hollers out. "Will, I need some help here!" Looking around nervously, he kicks the dirt. "Where the devil are ya, anyways? Hidin' in the bushes, you chicken shit? C'mon, there were a slew of Indians out here ready to scalp me. One of 'em just about blew my britches off!"

Jeb's skin prickles as he hears a rustling in the bushes. He grabs the side of the wagon to steady himself, as he now sees the big white buffalo standing in the brush, snorting. Its massive head lowered, sporting two deadly horns, ready to charge at the quaking Jeb. The last thing Jeb remembers is monstrous eyes glowering, thundering toward him as he grabs his chest and slithers down the side of the wagon, where he passes out from fright.

The next thing Jeb sees is Will, standing over him as he lies sprawled out on the ground. Will is hollering for him to get up and gives him a good smack to roust him. "What the devil happened here, and where the blazes is the wagon? I 'bout got strangled by a vicious bugger back in those bushes, wearing a bunch of feathers. I was yellin' like hell for help. Figured you musta been drunk."

Jeb rubs his head and staggers to his feet, wondering what's going on. As his eyes clear, thoughts come leaping back. "Look,

Will, we best hightail it outta here. Might be more Injuns comin' ta kill us this time."

Jeb wobbles as Will catches him and helps him to his horse, hoisting him onto the saddle. Smacking the horse, Jeb grabs the reins and takes off in a flurry of dust. Will follows right behind as they gallop away at breakneck speed. Jeb hangs onto the saddle horn, babbling on about an old Indian and a white buffalo.

THE VISIT

OTIS PEALE IS sitting at the table waiting for his supper, exasperated by Mrs. Stover's insolent behavior of late. *I should give her a good talking to. Remind her who is boss in this house,* he thinks, starting to fume as he checks the clock for the third time. "Forty-five minutes late. I should take it out of her pay for insolent behavior."

Stomach rumbling, he finally sees Mrs. Stover marching into the room like nothing is amiss. Peale gives her a withering glare, and involuntarily, his nose sniffs the air as she sets down a large platter filled with a mouthwatering roast and all the trimmings. His attention is now focused on the food, and, with fork and knife in hand, he slices off a large hunk of pork, and adds it to his plate — along with potatoes, rutabaga, and greens. He is so anxious to start eating he almost forgets to say his nightly prayer. So he quickly adds, "Thank you for this food. Amen." And quickly begins digging into the roast with relish, almost forgiving Mrs. Stover for her tardiness. *The food is simply delicious tonight. Maybe she has seen the error of her ways,* he thinks. While savoring his meal, a loud knock rattles the door and, suddenly jarred out of his reverie, he drops his fork. "Damndest time for someone to come calling," he groans. *It better not be that darned Mrs. Comford,* he thinks with alarm. She has been driving him batty with all her pestering about church and such. He wasn't liking the way she's been looking at him of late either. *He'd had enough of her for one day.* He picks up his fork and hollers for Mrs. Stover. "See who's at the door, and tell whoever it is, I'm eating my supper."

No response.

What is it with help these days? Maybe I'll just fire her for disobeying my orders. "Damnedest time," he grumbles as he sets down his fork and grudgingly gets up and walks to the door. As he swings it open, he almost falls over in surprise. There stands an Indian boy about eighteen years old with a stained deerskin shirt and hair and feathers blowing around his face — wild-looking as all Hell. Peale gives him the once-over and glares at him, steely-eyed. *Should've brought my gun,* he thinks, as the boy inches his way closer to him. Recovering from his surprise, Peale struts forward and barks, furious at being disturbed at suppertime. "What the devil are you doing at my house? Can't you Indians read? The sign plainly says: 'NO INDIANS ALLOWED', and that means you!"

The boy starts to speak, but Peale quickly interrupts, pointing back to the sign and wagging his finger. "'FOR ANY REASON', it says. Now go away. My supper is getting ruined and I don't want to be disturbed any longer." He starts to slam the door shut, but Hidden Spirit is quick and shoves Peale aside, and enters the house.

Gasping at the boys' insolence, Peale's face turns a deep scarlet. "What are you doing, bursting into my house? I could shoot you for trespassing!" He hustles inside after the boy, panting. "What the devil are you doing?" and pokes him in the chest. "I ought to have you arrested for disturbing me. If you have any complaints, go tell Mr. Wigley."

With glowering eyes, Hidden Spirit dares Peale to touch him again. The man falters and backs up a couple steps.

"I need to talk about Wigley, Mr. Peale."

Over his shoulder, Peale hollers frantically to Mrs. Stover. "We've got a wild Indian in here. Run and get help. Hurry!"

Mrs. Stover runs out of the kitchen and peeks around the corner to see what all the fuss is about. Her jaw about drops and so did the towel she was holding. She is startled by the presence of the dashing young Indian boy, with his intense demeanor and his fearlessness. As she looks a little closer she thinks, *this young Indian is certainly brave to come in here like this. Plus, he is so very handsome.* She strains her neck even further around the corner, and smiles, hoping he gives Peale a piece of his mind. *Just what he deserves!*

Mrs. Stover has always hated the fact that Peale sent the Indian children away without a second thought, or care — not to mention the grief it brought to the families. *It was despicable, what he did,* she fumes, inwardly. After the children left the reservation, she began to notice how subdued the parents had become — their smiles diminished and their expressions sad. Plu*s, they always look hungry.* She doesn't trust that Wigley one lick, either, and wonders why Peale ever hired that awful man. He speaks so belligerently to the Indians, and trots around the reservation like he is someone to be feared. It's clear he doesn't like them. *And those missionaries are not much better,* she thinks angrily. She could wring their necks, calling the Indian people devil-worshipers and such — declaring their religion barbaric nonsense and un-Christian like. Mrs. Stover fought hard to resist the temptation to box those ladies right in the ears for saying such things.

Furthermore, she hates that Mrs. Comford and Mrs. Green come every Sunday for supper. Mrs. Comford is a fussy old bat, always complaining that the soup is cold or the chicken is still pink in the middle or the pork chops are tough as a board. She told Mrs. Stover on one occasion. "You should come to my modest dwelling one evening. I will not only teach you how to cook, but

I'll acquaint you with some verses from the Bible as well. Might do you some good," Mrs. Comford preened.

Mrs. Stover had been close to losing her temper with that fussy bat, but when she overheard the woman's remarks to Mr. Peale, she nearly came unglued.

"That cook of yours is a non-believer, dear Mr. Peale. I don't know why you have her working for you, you poor man. I know you need someone to look after your needs and run your house, but, really, she can't cook a decent meal, and, she has a nasty temper, besides."

Mrs. Stover couldn't believe what she was hearing. And, what was worse, Peale didn't even defend her. He should have told that woman to mind her own business. Instead he smiles at Mrs. Comford as she prattles on. "I'm a noble and enterprising woman, Mr. Peale, sent here by God to teach the lesser ones." That was too much for Mrs. Stover, so a few weeks ago, while she was serving supper, she spilled a ladle full of gravy on Mrs. Comford's Sunday dress. Peale, outraged, knocked his chair over as he jumped out of his seat, demanding an apology be made to the furious woman. Hiding her smirk, Mrs. Stover says, "I'm sorry for my clumsiness. Forgive me," and then hurried to the kitchen.

So, now, Mrs. Stover decides to ignore Peale. *Let him squirm a bit. Do him some good,* she thinks, wickedly.

Hidden Spirit strides further into the study. Mrs. Stover can hear the anger rising in his voice. "Like I told you, Mr. Peale, we have no food and our people are hungry. The hardship is..."

"I have my own pile of troubles around here," Peale shouts, almost apoplectic. "And on top of that the missionaries are fit to be tied with you people. Now that's a real hardship! So, leave!"

Otis fumes at the intruder, as he flails around the room. *I know this one is trouble.* But Hidden Spirit will not be deterred. "You will listen to what I have to say," he threatens, standing nose-to-nose with Peale. "Wigley is stealing our supplies. I caught him and his friend. Our people go hungry while…"

"Hungry?" Peale balks. "You people get plenty to eat. I see loads of food in the storage house. We'll get this straightened out tomorrow with Wigley, so, go."

"Our supplies are being traded for whiskey and…"

Otis is in no mood to listen. "I don't want to hear any more of your stories tonight… or ever!" Pointing to the door, he raises his voice. "Now, leave my house… at once."

Hidden Spirit refuses to budge.

Peale begins walking stridently, back and forth, trying to figure out what to do. *That boy gives me an unsettling feeling*, he muses, looking at him sideways. *He shows no fear… seems arrogant. Maybe he'll listen when I show him my gun.* He moves for his pistol inside the desk drawer. But when he pulls it out, he feels a fist barreling into his stomach and bends over howling in pain. Hidden Spirit pushes him backwards, and he falls into a chair with a resounding thud.

Peale's eyes grow large with fright and he starts to sputter indignantly, but Hidden Spirit motions him to be quiet. "You will listen to what I have to say."

Mrs. Stover gasps at the boy's boldness and, piqued by her curiosity, peers further around the corner. Smiling. *It's about time.*

Hidden Spirit's eyes spark dangerously. "Wigley is stealing our food." Peale opens his mouth to respond, but the boy shoots him a menacing glance. "I caught Wigley with some guy at the crossroads near Wallis… four hours south of here. They had a wagon full of whiskey and supplies. Whenever my people go to Wigley for their rations, he tells them to come back another time. It's been going on for months and the people have no food. You must do something."

Peale interrupts, agitated. "Look, we're doing all we can to help you people. Now, I don't want to hear any more about your hardships, real or otherwise. Wigley is a good man, and a hard worker. You think my life is easy living here? I came to this miserable place out of duty to my country. Now, I insist you leave my house at once… before I… " A loud knock at the door vaults Otis from his chair. He barrels to the door and swings it open. Relief crosses his face at the sight of Will Wigley, accompanied by Jeb. "Get in here," he says, waving them inside. "I'm glad Mrs. Stover found you… and in the nick of time. I've got an emergency going on here. Some wild Indian's parading around my house, threatening me. He refuses to leave."

Wigley stomps into the room and almost falls over at the sight of the Indian kid. He came here with a good story to tell Peale, but now his head whirls at the sight of the Indian glaring at him with murder in his eyes. His stomach muscles knot up, and he gulps in a breath of air. He's trying to think, but his words wouldn't come. "Uh…uh…" His legs begin to buckle, and he grabs ahold of the table to steady himself.

Jeb looks at his partner, perplexed by his behavior. "What's the matter with you, anyhows? That Otis is lookin' at you like yer daft."

Maybe that was the sons-a-bitch hiding in them feathers, he thinks, as his head spins again. "I… uh…I… that kid's s'posed to be dead," he says in a hiss. "Killed him myself a while ago."

"Well, looks to me like you didn't do so good. He's standing right here."

"I know it was him back there by the wagon, trying some funny stuff…"

"Seems like he's itchin' for a fight, too," says Jeb, eyeing the boy. "Lay low, Will. I'll finish the job on him."

The exasperated Otis can no longer control his frustration, and he cries, "What the dickens is wrong with you, Will? I've got a wild Indian in here threatening me, and you look like you're ready to faint."

Will struggles to say something, but he gasps in terror, recalling those fearful images the boy brings back to mind. "This here Injun is dangerous... he's a killer."

"I know, for Pete's sake. That's why I sent for... well, never mind. Just get him out of my house."

Jeb, feeling a bit braver, hollers out. "Stick 'em up, ya yeller belly!" He reaches for his gun, and then, just as quickly, slides it back into his holster. He winces when he sees a couple of feathers sail through the air and then stop — just inches above his head. It makes Jeb skittish. Suddenly he feels his arm being jerked. His eyes lock with the Indian boy, who breaks into a grin.

Peale looks strangely at Jeb and wonders if he is a bit off in the head — like he's seen a phantom. Well, he doesn't care about crazy, if that nitwit can help get him out of this predicament — strange or not. Then he turns his attention to Will. "This Indian kid says you and your friend are stealing their supplies. He claims he saw you and some other fellow at the..."

"Now, just hold on there a doggone minute," says Will, finding his voice and getting his nerve back. "This here Injun apprehends me an' Jeb as we're pickin' up the supplies, and he comes along and steals the whole darn wagon load. We're lucky ta be alive. I think he's sellin' the goods for whiskey, and ya know how wild those Injuns get when they've had a taste of the stuff."

"Oh, my goodness," says Peale, all a-twitter, pacing the room.

"We rode at breakneck speed to get here an' tell ya what happened... an' now, lo an' behold, the crook is right in front of us. Best be careful of this one, Mr. Peale, he's wicked and he does some kinda funny tricks with feathers and such. Evil ones, fer sure!" He looks warily at Hidden Spirit and wonders if any more of those feathers are hiding somewhere. Then he howls. "Maybe he's planning on scalping ya for sending those brats off to school. We seen a whole passel of redskins tryin' to follow us, but... being clever... we lost 'em!"

Otis jumps up, and scurries for his gun. "Tie him up," he shouts, as pandemonium breaks out. Will's and Jeb's feet go flying across the room, knocking Hidden Spirit to the ground. Fists start to fly every-which-way, smashing and pounding furiously, as Hidden Spirit seizes Will's hair and yanks hard. Otis jumps into the middle of the fracas, trying to break it up, and gets whacked on the head. Then Hidden Spirit kicks Jeb squarely in the ribs... a crunch follows and doubles him over. Full of fury, he grabs Wigley around the neck and squeezes with tremendous force. Will gasps out a faint, "Help."

Jeb holds onto his ribs, trying to catch his breath, unable to help Will.

Otis fires a warning shot. "Put your hands up in the air or I'll land a shot right through you."

Hidden Spirit reluctantly lets go of Will, and stands calm as a warm summer day. But his ominous expression hints otherwise.

Will is holding his throat, gasping for air, as Jeb helps him to his feet.

"Okay, everyone, simmer down," Peale says, his hands shaking. He looks angrily at Hidden Spirit, wiping the blood off his forehead, and then turns to Wigley. "I thought you said you could handle these wild Indians. Doesn't look like it to me!"

"He's a cagey one!" Will coughs, holding his throat. "And strange as all get out..." A shiver of fright engulfs him, and he pauses, recalling the earlier events.

"Yeah, his nuts must be big as..." Jeb glowers, holding his ribs, but quickly backs off as he sees Hidden Spirit's body tighten, ready to pounce, eyes flashing dangerously.

With a trace of hysteria, Will says, "I think there's gonna be some kinda revolt with the Injuns, Mr. Peale… if we ain't careful."

Otis squeals in alarm. "For Pete's sake! Why are you standing here babbling on like two nincompoops? Take him away, and lock him up. We'll see about a hanging later." He grabs his firearm, brandishing it about. Will and Jeb duck, afraid the gun might go off again.

Will is liking the turn of events, and speaks with a bit more bluster. "He probably was gonna murder you and the missus, or scalp us in our beds as we sleep."

Otis grabs his heart at the news and hurries to a closet, and finds some rope — which he throws to Will. "Tie him up and lock him in the cellar beneath the storage building. Just get him out of here!" He mumbles, still shaking. "I don't know if I'll be able to finish my supper after this. Dreadful to think what might have happened."

Will grins wickedly, happy to oblige. He ties Hidden Spirit's wrists tightly behind him while Jeb wraps the rope from his neck to his feet.

Otis ushers them to the door, and yanks it open. "Goodnight, boys. If you have any trouble with that one, knock him on the head or something."

Will grins. He can't wait to teach the kid a lesson or two.

GHOSTLY FIGURES

RELIEVED THAT ORDEAL is over, Otis sits down at the table and picks up his fork. Hands trembling slightly, he is dismayed by the events that have just taken place. "That was a dangerous-looking Indian," he mumbles to himself, as he cuts into the cold roast. "And in my own house. I could have been scalped to death... maybe even worse." He shoves a forkful of meat into his mouth, and chews furiously. Now, another knock is heard at the door... Peale almost chokes on his food. His eyes swivel nervously at the sound, and he reaches for his gun. "They try anything this time, and I'll blast them right back out the door." He cocks his ear, listening. There is nothing. He breathes a sigh of relief, and wipes his forehead. His nerves are on edge, and he wants no more interruptions this evening. Whoever it is, they can come back tomorrow — as long as it isn't another Indian. Then he hears another knock, a little softer this time. Peale clutches his gun, and shouts irritably. "Mrs. Stover! Get the door, and be quick about it. Tell whoever it is to go away, I'm eating my supper."

Mrs. Stover huffs to the door, towel in hand.

"It better be no more Indians, either. Had enough of them," he grumbles, to himself... knocking over a bowl of green beans in his fury, and simply brushes the spilt food onto the floor. *Mrs. Stover can deal with the mess later. She's almost as annoying as those Indians.*

Mrs. Stover opens the front door, looks around, and sees no one. *It was probably that old goat's imagination,* she thinks, and slams the door shut.

Otis calls out. "Who was it, Mrs. Stover?"

"Most likely the wind, Mr. Peale. No one was there."

"Bolt the door shut. I want no more interruptions tonight."

Mrs. Stover slams the door shut, checks that it's secure, and huffs back to the kitchen.

Otis stops chewing for a moment, and listens closely. He would swear someone is rapping at the window. He runs over, and peers out... his eyes bulge in shock. *Something is moving in the bushes next to the fence. It looks darn near like a white buffalo. No. It can't be. My eyes must be playing tricks on me, that's all.* Nerves in a dither, he sits back down at the table, eyeing his supper. It isn't quite as appealing anymore, but still — it's a shame to let it go to waste. He slices a nice-size piece of roast onto his fork and adds some rutabaga, ready to take a bite when his fork clatters to the floor. Otis looks up in alarm.

There stands an Indian, all decked out in some kind of war regalia with bird feathers covering his head cascading all the way to the floor, and wearing some sort of rawhide shirt with a life-like image of a white buffalo embroidered on front. *I swear to God that thing just snorted,* he thinks. Grabbing his gun, he squeals in fright. "What the blazes do you want?"

The Indian merely smiles. "Didn't mean to startle you," he says in a silky voice, "or ruin your supper."

Dumbfounded, Otis stares in silence, his mind whirling. *How the blazes did that old Indian get in here? Mrs. Stover must have left the door open. Careless woman. Well, I've had enough of these Indians for one night. No... a lifetime.* He stares at the unusual-looking Indian and wonders if there are any more like him lurking about his house. Just thinking about it makes his heart race faster.

Clearing his throat with a "harumph," he pushes his chair away from the table, and shrieks out. "What are you doing in my house? Get away from here, or I'll shoot you for trespassing."

Otis is so flustered he thinks a vein might pop, so he hustles to his desk and pours a shot of whiskey, which he downs in one gulp. *Just the remedy for my nerves tonight!* He quickly pours another, feeling a soothing warmth spread throughout his body. It takes a couple minutes before he can gather his wits about him and regain his composure. "How the devil did you get in here? What do you heathens want from me, anyhow? This is the second time tonight that one of you has come barging in with wild accusations, blaming me for your troubles and…" Before he can utter another word, the old Indian breezes right past him. Peale reaches out to stop him and grabs his arm, but he feels nothing but a burst of cool misty air. The Indian looks bemused as he slides on by.

Peale is aghast. The gall of this Indian makes him seethe. "You must be one of those sneaky heathens hiding in the hills. Well I'm going to lock you up like I did with that crafty friend of yours… who just left. All he is is a younger version of you… minus the bird feathers." Unwilling to let some old geezer scare him, he bellows, "Get out of my house right now, or, I swear to God… I'll shoot!"

Broken Feather doesn't budge. Then Otis watches incredulously, as the Indian sits down in his chair, completely at ease, *like I invited him over for Sunday dinner*, he thinks, questioning his own sanity. Furious at the Indian's audacity, Otis brandishes his gun in the air, threatening him once more. "If you don't leave right now, I'm gonna blow a hole right through you."

The Indian simply smiles, and crosses his legs.

"Well, if my threats don't work, this just might," Otis says under his breath. He points the gun, closes his eyes, and fires. A loud bang explodes, sending Peale flying backwards against the wall, and causing Mrs. Stover to scream out in disbelief.

Otis slowly opens his eyes, wondering if he shot the man. He secretly hopes he did as he sees smoke emitting from the chair, which now sports a gaping hole. But, *no!* That blasted Indian doesn't have a scratch. *How can that be?* he wonders as the Indian stands up and smiles, and hands him the bullet.

"That was a nice chair. Looks like the bullet went right through and did a bit of damage."

Otis is stunned. He blew a hole right where that Indian had been sitting. He eyes the pistol and then the Indian. He is so angry he can barely speak. So, he hisses. "What kind of witchcraft are you people using, anyhow?"

The old Indian simply ignores him, and makes his way to the other side of the room, where he sits on the floor, and crosses his legs. Peale's mouth hangs open and he watches, fuming — incredulous at the gall of that Indian.

Broken Feather takes out his long ornate pipe, fills it with fragrant tobacco, leans back against the wall, and inhales. He seems unperturbed by Otis Peale or his damaged chair.

Peale's face turns ashen. He tries to get a grip on his senses, but he can't think clearly. Utterly frazzled, he wonders how that savage got into his house so mysteriously. And now, it seems clear that the old man has no intentions of leaving. Throwing his hands up in the air, he stomps over, clenches his teeth, and asks, "What do you heathens want from me?"

Broken Feather sits back and blows a smoke ring that circles lazily above Peale's head. Angrily brushing the smoke away, Peale crosses his arms and stands firm. He glares at the old man, who stares back, seemingly unperturbed, and tries to figure a way to get rid of him. *I tried shooting the old geezer, but that didn't work. A bribe might do the trick. I've got some cash upstairs,* he thinks, and, with a twisted smile, he turns to leave... but is halted by the old Indian, who motions him to the floor.

"Please, sit. Let us talk," says Broken Feather.

Otis can't believe the gall of this Indian. He states vehemently. "I will not sit next to the likes of you," as a muscle twitches angrily in his jaw. "Not now, or any other time." Defiantly he watches the old man, who seems at ease watching him. He finds his gaze unsettling and he finally gives in with a resigned sigh. He sits down, and says, "Just get to the point of what you want so you may hurry up and leave."

"I will be brief, but first I must tell you that I have seen your wife, Esther. She wanted me to bring you a message. She has…"

Otis abruptly cuts him off, slamming his fist on the floor. "How dare you insult me and th-the memory of my wife with your lies? You know nothing of her! If I could, I would kill you with my bare hands. You are evil to the core!"

Broken Feather sits unperturbed, listening to Otis rant while continuing to smoke his pipe and silently blows smoke rings. The smoke has a sweet, cloying smell, and the bluish haze floats lazily in circles, making its way to the ceiling. One of the larger smoke rings drifts languidly about, forming a curiously strange shape. The hazy silhouette drifts over to Otis, and lingers in place. He thinks he hears a faint wheeze, but is too distracted by the Indian to pay much attention.

Something gleams within the wispy smoke. It looks like two ghostly eyes staring at Peale… his heart races wildly. He slumps against the wall, eyes filled with terror. "Who are you? And why, oh why, is this happening to me? I have tried my best in this horrid place, and this is my thanks. I've heard how you Indians conjure up spirits, you know. I went to Yale. I am an educated man, and I will not fall for any of this hocus-pocus malarkey!"

Suddenly and from out of nowhere, Otis receives a sound slap to his face. His eyes fly open in shock. He is certain it was the old heathen who struck him, and he glares at him. But… the Indian hasn't moved an inch… still sitting in the same spot, smoking his pipe.

Then, a crisp voice arises from the smoke. "For once in your life, why don't you shut up?"

Otis is speechless. His mind reels. The voice is vaguely familiar. In fact, it sounds just like Esther. He scrunches his eyes, and peers into the smoky haze. His skin prickles. He whispers incredulously, "Is that you… Esther?" Hardly believing it could be.

"Yes, Otis. It is me."

"For the love of God, what are you doing, consorting with the Indians? They are most wicked…"

"Wicked, you say?" she says, swirling through a frothy wave of smoke. "You miserable wretch. You with your pompous and arrogant ways." Then she slaps him again. "I have waited to do that for a very long time. But of course it wouldn't have been proper for the subservient Mrs. Otis Peale. Oh, how I loathed being married to you! I cooked and cleaned and tended to your every need. But you treated me little better than you do Mrs. Stover, a servant. I wish I had been strong enough to tell you that when I was still alive, but I wasn't. I am now."

Otis can't believe this is really happening. He has to pinch himself to make certain. How can she possibly say such things? *That old goat has put a… uh… some sort of spell on me. No, wait… he must have put one on Esther… to keep her from entering the pearly gates of Heaven.*

"This kind man… Broken Feather… the one you regard as inferior, has helped me return to this world… to see you, to talk to you. But now that I'm here, all I can see is a pitiful man, who complains of hardships. What are your hardships, Otis… that is, besides a late supper? Ask the Indians about *their* hardships. Ask what they have suffered at the hands of people like you! But no, you sit here in comfort, and remain smug in your judgments.

Meanwhile, you have destroyed the lives of all those children you sent away. They are miserable at that place, and their families are despondent without them and worry about their safety."

Otis can't figure out if he is more shocked by the apparition in front of him or by the presence of the Indian. He half-whispers, "I wish I'd been a better shot earlier, and killed the evil savage." He scowls as the smoke circling his head. "Don't trust that heathen... Esther, please, I beg you..."

He hears a faint whisper. "I have heard whisperings from the Great Ones in the ethers. You might do well to rethink your ways." Without another word, the hazy form blends into the smoke, and vanishes.

Otis crumples in a heap, and bangs his head on the floor, sobbing, "Esther, my dear Esther, why would you say such cruel things? I loved you... and I thought you loved me." His mind is reeling from her accusations. Slowly, Otis stands and paces back and forth. A slight hint of smoke floats toward him, and stops within an inch of his face. He cringes at the bluish smoke and covers his face in fright.

Esther's voice is barely audible now. "I tell you, the Indians are very wise. You could learn a thing or two from them. They may dress differently from you, but that does not make them heathens. Just like your having attended Yale does not make you a smart man. You may have book knowledge, but you are missing the most essential knowledge of all... wisdom."

Otis stares at the bluish haze as it slowly evaporates, leaving behind a faint trail of smoke. He sits unmoving, staring at the wall. Slowly he looks over and sees the Indian still smoking his pipe, watching him intently.

Broken Feather nods his head, and offers Otis his pipe.

As exhausted and rattled as Otis is, he realizes that smoking a peace pipe is no crazier than anything else that has happened this evening. So he joins the Indian on the floor, looks dubiously at the pipe for a moment, and takes the long stem to his lips. Tentatively, at first, he inhales. But he likes the taste of the pungent smoke so he takes a deeper puff. Much to his surprise he finds the aroma relaxing, and leans back against the wall, taking another draw. He even finds himself enjoying the company of the Indian, whom a short while ago he wanted to shoot. Now, here he is, smoking a peace pipe with him. *Unbelievable.* He inhales the fragrant tobacco once again, and sighs — wondering what those Indians put in their tobacco that is so intoxicating. Enjoying himself immensely, he tilts his head and blows a perfectly formed smoke ring that rises high in the air. His anger seems to have evaporated along with the smoke, and he continues puffing contentedly. "This is certainly a beautiful pipe you have, uh... what did you say your name was? You might have mentioned it to me when you first arrived, but I was in no mood to listen. Your arrival was... most unusual. You caught me off guard." Curious, he asks, "Exactly... uh... how do you know my wife?" His face turns pale and his lips twitch nervously at the recent memory of her floating in the smoke. He stares at Broken Feather with mixed emotions and rubs his chin in wonderment. "I haven't seen you around these parts before."

"No," Broken Feather says softly, "you haven't."

A puzzled look sweeps across Otis's face. The words are not quite sinking in. "You must have come from a far-off reservation," he says in bewilderment.

"Well," Broken Feather says, looking up, "I would say the location is a bit elusive... hard to describe. Quite far from here, I would imagine." The Indian continues to smoke, eyes twinkling, as he watches the confused Otis Peale try to reason it out.

"Well," Otis states with authority. "You can't just up and leave a reservation. You might get yourself killed."

"Your concern is quite touching," Broken Feather says, as a melancholy frown settles across his face. "Let's start with your concern over Hidden Spirit, the young boy that was here earlier. You threw him into a stockade, charging him with a false crime. You let the guilty go free, and you want to hang the innocent. So, tell me what your real concerns are. Food for our people? Their welfare?"

Otis sits stiff as a stone, his mind reeling at the accusations. Then, slowly, the words begin to penetrate and he contemplates all that has been said. He shakes his head. He has no answers.

Broken Feather speaks in a soft tone. "Mother Earth is part of our spiritual soul. We have loved and nurtured her for eons. It has been foretold that the white man's greed for her riches will also be the white man's demise."

Otis frowns, listening to Broken Feather's words, as they float in front of him. His breath catches. *I'm actually seeing his words, seep into my brain… and in the most peculiar manner.*

"I see you have brought missionaries to convert our people to the white man's beliefs. Our religion, your people so eagerly spurn, has inspired us for centuries. You call us savages and worse, but you do not explain how your ways are superior. Please tell me! You people destroy the Creator's gifts, and then call yourselves civilized. It is a great mystery to me how that can be."

A tremendous realization dawns upon Otis — that Broken Feather speaks the truth. He slumps over and feels remorse, even sadness, then sits back again, lost in thought — all the while inhaling the aromatic smoke from the beautiful pipe.

Time seems to no longer matter as strange sensations flutter throughout Peale's body. Suddenly his eyes brighten and he straightens up. For the first time since he can recall, he feels light and free. He isn't certain why, but something has changed. He is in such high spirits he could twirl around the room, but feels silly even contemplating such a thing. And, yet, what a bizarre and wonderful sensation he is experiencing. He smiles over at the Indian, who looks so calm and peaceful, and briefly considers hugging him. But he lets go of that impulse. A wave of weightlessness overtakes him. He is so happy he could sing. Then he thinks about Esther, and he looks around the room to check for any lingering smoke. Hoping she might still be near, he calls out softly. "Esther. If you can hear me, please forgive me. I have been such a fool."

Glancing at the Indian, he swears he sees the slightest flicker of light dancing over his head — in jubilation. Then his stomach let off a loud rumble, which startles him. He is brought back to the moment, realizing he is hungry. Looking toward the kitchen, he wonders where Mrs. Stover has gone. When he notices Broken Feather staring at him, he generously states. "If you would care to dine with me, I could rustle us up something from the kitchen. Mrs. Stover made a tasty roast earlier, and I am sure there is plenty left."

Broken Feather stands up. "Thank you, but no. I must be going."

"Where to? I fear you may be captured, and I would hate to see anything happen to you. Won't you please reconsider, and stay?"

Broken Feather responds lightly. "I'll be fine, but thank you for your concern. I would ask that you give thought to our conversation."

"Yes, yes… of course. But please tell me, I am still a little confused about seeing Esther… how you talk to her, and… well, maybe you could come back again another time, and explain it all to me. Bring that pipe with you, too. Very pleasant, indeed." As he walks beside Broken Feather, he notices the Indian seems to glide along, and he feels a power emanate from his nearness. Just as he opens the door for the Indian to leave, he realizes he has already disappeared. Otis flies outside. He wants to say goodbye and to tell him how sorry he is — but it's too late. He stands for a few moments, waiting in vain. Then he goes back inside and closes the door.

*

Meanwhile in the kitchen, Mrs. Stover sets the pot of water on the stove for a cup of tea to soothe her nerves as her mind reels with confusion. She has just witnessed the most amazing happening in the next room, and holds her chest to capture the image of what she saw in vivid detail. It was Esther, Mr. Peale's late wife, floating in the smoke. Secretly hoping that the woman was still floating nearby, she looks up and whispers to her, shyly. "I heard what you told your husband, and I couldn't agree with you more. He is a miserable wretch. I hope you don't think I'm mad, but I have no one else to confide in. I am miserable here too, like you were, so I hope you don't mind my talking to you and telling you how I feel. I also saw an Indian sitting on the floor with Mr. Peale. It was most remarkable, and it takes my breath away to think of the happenings here at the house tonight. I wanted to quit, to tell Mr. Peale I'm leaving... but I have nowhere to go. Now, after hearing you, I have decided to be brave. I will find employment elsewhere. I'm not going to put up with his behavior anymore..." Mrs. Stover stops mid-sentence when she feels a blast of cool air, making her hair flutter about, and causing her to shiver. She wonders where the draft came from, and thinks for a moment it could be Esther. Then, suddenly, she clasps her hand over her mouth to stifle a scream. The old Indian is standing right next to her — so close she could touch his arm. She shivers again and feels a shock run through her body as her eyes lock with his.

Mrs. Stover starts to ask how he entered, when the realization comes flooding back of how he had entered Peale's house — seemingly out of nowhere. She trembles, not out of fear but awe, at the exceptional looking Indian. Feeling a bit embarrassed, she wonders if he had overheard her talking to Esther and she looks at him quizzically — breathless. His gaze is so intense it makes the blood pound in her temples. *He knew!* She looks down mortified, but he draws her gaze up to meet his and smiles into her eyes, brilliantly. Goosebumps start to crawl up her neck. She is so thrilled to see him up close she can only marvel at his presence. *How elegant he is,* she thinks wistfully. His beautiful clothes that seem to sway ever so slightly as he moves make the intricate patterns of beadwork twinkle in the soft light. She knows it's rude to stare at his splendid attire, but she can't seem to help herself. *How on earth did that garment ever get made*, she wonders. It's magnificent and it greatly accentuates his strong physique.

Unable to contain herself any longer, Mrs. Stover blurts out, "I must say, your arrival and Esther's was quite exciting... more like a fresh breeze drifting through the door... shining a light. Extraordinary! And, for some odd reason, it has changed my life. I cannot explain why it has done so, but it has, and profoundly. I thank you from the bottom of my heart. You have made a dejected woman feel alive... for the first time in her life. I don't know what it was... maybe the pleasant aroma from your pipe tobacco, or maybe it was seeing you and Esther..." Mrs. Stover stops. "I feel I've said too much. Forgive me for my bad manners. I have rambled on so, being engrossed, I guess, in all the goings-on. Anyway, I forgot myself. Here," she says, nearly tripping over her feet to pull out a chair. "Please sit. May I offer you something to eat? I have a stew simmering on the stove. It's a couple days old, but I think it is still edible. Mr. Peale lets me eat the leftovers." Mrs. Stover blushes as she continues, "I would be most flattered to have you dine with me," she says, feeling a bit silly about her invitation. "It would only take a couple of minutes to dish up, and I would..."

Broken Feather puts his fingers to her lips to silence her. "You are most kind, Mrs. Stover. Food is not what I require at this time, but I thank you. I have come to say farewell and to tell you that things will be quite different for you in the days ahead."

Some powerful spirits above must have sent this fine Indian to this house, Mrs. Stover thinks, as she sets the pot down with a clatter. She looks over in the direction of Broken Feather, but, to her disappointment, he is gone. She will surely miss this fine man, who only came into her life for the briefest of moments… to brighten her life. "Bless him and bless his people." Mrs. Stover peers out the window and sees a flash of light, so she hurries outside, hoping to say goodbye, not wanting to miss any excitement that might arise. As Mrs. Stover walks down the path, she gasps and stops in her tracks. There she sees a white buffalo with golden horns and she hears Broken Feather talking to the animal in his language. Even more amazing is that the buffalo seems to understand what is being said.

Mrs. Stover hesitates for a moment, not wanting to intrude on this fantastical sight. So she stays hidden behind the shrub and waits, holding her breath, wondering what in the world might happen next. Suddenly a bright light passes overhead, blinding her. She catches a glimpse, for the briefest moment, at what can only be *another realm of life* as the Indian and the buffalo go down an unusual path. She blinks her eyes. And the vision has disappeared as suddenly as it had appeared. Strange, tingling chills spread throughout her body and run up and down her spine. She wants to say something or, at least, reach out to him — but she is unable to move. Tears wells up in her eyes. She tries to blink them back, knowing the man will be gone — most likely forever. She then hears a silvery voice, tinkling on the night breeze. "My dear Mrs. Stover. Please do not be saddened by my departure. Perhaps we shall see each other again, somewhere other than here."

Mrs. Stover puts her hand to her face and feels his warmth on her cheek. She has to see him, and runs down the path. She wants to shout, "Please wait," but she can only manage a hoarse whisper. She sees Broken Feather looking regal in his ornate attire, riding atop the white buffalo... ambling down the road. He stops at the gate and waves back at her. She is so excited to see him one last time that she hurries even faster and trips and falls, bruising her knee and tearing her best dress. "Oh dear, how clumsy I am," she exclaims, rubbing her knee, disappointed she didn't get to say goodbye to the man with the magic. Suddenly she feels someone lift her up with ease. Startled by the magnanimous gesture, she is caught off-guard by the sight of him. This time it's a young and dazzling Indian wearing the same attire. He hops back onto the buffalo and ambles down the road as before. The sight of him makes her giddy, like a school girl. *He is like an ever-changing mystery*, she thinks as she hugs herself tightly, and takes in a deep breath, glad to be alive. Lowering herself to the ground, she sits on the grass, eyes full of wonder. Then she hears someone singing in the distance. She tilts her head toward the faint sounds, which are mournful and yet uplifting... all at the same time. Without thinking, she stands and finds herself beginning to move to the rhythm of the song — slowly at first, uncertain about what to do. Dancing was something she always dreamed of doing, but never dared. Now she *will* dance... she didn't care if it was by herself, or for that matter, if anyone might notice. She gasps as an eclectic array of light bursts in the distance, displaying the faint outline of the buffalo and the Indian as they continue on their journey down the road. Behind them, a kaleidoscope of colors is illuminating the night sky. Strobes of emerald green lights flash across the sky, turning to indigo blue, and whirling into azures that meld into crimson gold. Mrs. Stover wonders if she has somehow entered into another realm, where such enchanting occurrences are the norm. She is so caught up in the brilliance of the night that she starts to spin in circles, laughing in delight at the glorious feeling.

It's as if invisible shackles have been stripped away from her body and she kicks off her shoes, closes her eyes and lets the music and the night completely envelope her. As she relaxes into the bliss, her movements become more fluid and graceful. Suddenly amidst all this wonder, she feels a pair of arms holding her lightly about her waist. She sighs, thinking, *maybe this is a glimpse of heaven while being engulfed in the sublime. I feel so light and free... as if my feet are lifting off the ground... twirling higher and higher into the air.* She suddenly opens her eyes and sees the fine-looking Indian smiling at her. Then she closes them again, wishing this enchanting night would never end. Her head starts to reel, as they twirl at an electrifying speed. She is certain they must be dancing close to the stars now. Finally the music starts to subside and she can feel herself floating, ever so gently... lightly toward the ground, where she slowly opens her eyes and finds no one around. She wants to laugh, cry, and dance all at the same time as she thinks of the remarkable Indian with the magnificent face — simultaneously young and yet so old. He is not of this world — of that she is certain. She calls out to him, "Farewell, my friend. You have taken me places that I never before imagined." She blows him a silent kiss, looks up at the sky, and kicks up her heels before reluctantly walking back into the house.

*

Unable to eat, Otis looks out the window. To his delight and amazement, he sees a faint green light bobbing in the distance. He hurries outside hoping to say goodbye to the enigmatic Indian who, a short while ago, sat with him in earnest conversation. A wisp of smoke floats back, and he inhales the pleasant smell. A melancholic smile etches his face.

Sitting down on the worn steps, he stares blankly, trying to make sense of the evening's events. Deep in thought, he almost falls off the porch when he hears a woman's shrill voice echoing down the path. The voice sounds caustic against the stillness of the evening and grates on his nerves. "Oh, blast it!" he moans, irritated at the intrusion.

"Mr. Peale!" Mrs. Comford shrieks and comes running up the steps, out of breath. "Did you witness anything unusual a moment ago? I heard some kind of commotion and ran outside to make certain everything was all right. I must say my eyes are not as sharp as they once were, but I tell you I saw a heathen!" She fervently clutches his hands. "What I witnessed was ever so frightful," she says, with flushed face. "I saw an Indian. A wild one dressed in an even wilder get-up, covered in feathers head to toe, and… riding a white buffalo. I hid behind a tree to watch. He passed so close to me, I could have reached out and touched him. I thought it was the demon in disguise, and almost jumped out of my skin. I swear to you on all that is holy… that savage looked right at me. He seemed to know I was standing there, watching. And then he waved at me. It was unbelievable. I would put my hand on the Bible and give you my oath… I swear on all that is holy."

Otis pulls his hands away, and cringes at her closeness. He finds the woman irritating. All he wants to do is think — in peace. He certainly wouldn't mention his own encounter with the Indian. He sighs, trying to figure a way to placate the woman. "Now, now, Mrs. Comford. I think maybe your eyes were playing tricks on you. I know this place has been a source of distress for you — causing you to image all sorts of things."

"Mr. Peale," Mrs. Comford interrupts angrily, pursing her lips. "I am not imagining things around here. I feel the Devil is lurking nearby. He comes in many disguises and we cannot be caught off-guard. I insist we pray… right this instant. We shall pray to rid this place of its demons."

Otis recoils at her words. Beads of sweat break out on his

face. He's not certain he can take any more unusual happenings tonight, and he snaps in frustration.

"Not now, Mrs. Comford. I ask that you please control yourself. I have other pressing matters on my mind at the moment."

"Well, good heavens," she says, exasperated. "I am only trying to warn you of the demons who skulk around in the night. Besides, that's why the good Lord sent me here... to this place of sin... to save the godless souls... to pray for their salvation." Taking Peale's hands, she insists, "I beseech you... let's get on our knees right now, so I can pray mightily for your safety." She swiftly pulls him next to her.

Otis lands on the ground, too stunned to speak, and pulls his hand away. *That woman scares me,* he thinks, miserably. *I should have never invited her over for Sunday dinners. She has gotten the wrong impression, I fear. Plus she is too bossy for my liking.* His face pales as she leans close, looks into his eyes, and squeezes his fingers.

"I must say you don't look well. Why... you're trembling, poor dear. Let me take you inside and tend to you. Soothe you of your worries. I am most capable, dear Mr. Peale. I would bet it's most likely the food you eat. Your housekeeper can't cook for a hill-of-beans. Pardon me for being so blunt, but it's true. I know you're just too kind to say anything."

Otis is uncomfortable and wants to run... he feels his mind is unraveling.

"God also sent me here... to be with you," Mrs. Comford says — eyes blazing with intensity. "Because I am a missionary doesn't mean I lack... uh... feelings... feelings that I have kept buried deep inside, but cannot any longer." Before the man can react, she pulls him close, and hugs him tightly.

Shocked at her bold behavior, he tumbles backwards... his thoughts running wild. What am I to do now? Peale frets. *Oh, blast it,* he moans. *Women! They're so unpredictable. Just look at Esther, coming back from who-knows-where with an Indian who walks through doors… and riding a white buffalo.* He rubs his chin nervously, uncertain what to do. He wishes the Indian would have taken him with him… as far away as possible. This situation has gotten out of control. He looks warily at Mrs. Comford, and sees her determination as she prattles on.

"I am not immune to those sly looks you give me at supper table," she continues, with a smile, insinuating it to be their secret. "I must say that your interest in me has not gone unnoticed either. Mrs. Green, I believe is quite put out. I'm quite flattered by your intentions, so you do not have to be coy any longer. Let's put our faith in the Lord to see us through. I have prayed mightily for Him to bless this union." She moves in close, moistens her lips, and juts out her jaw — waiting.

Otis's head reels. *How the devil do I get out of this predicament,* he thinks, looking around, panicked. *Maybe I should call for help. That Indian might come to my aid if he sees the predicament I'm in.* Suddenly he hears words buzz around his head. "Help the people!" Panic overtakes him. "Did you hear someone call out? A voice perhaps telling me to…" He stops, looking up to the sky.

A puzzled Mrs. Comford says, "Well, I can't say that I heard anything." And then she makes a connection. "Was it the Lord talking to you… answering my call for our marriage vows?"

"Oh, for pity sake, Mrs. Comford, I can assure you it wasn't the Lord. And what marriage vows are you speaking of? I have never made that declaration to you."

Mrs. Comford is most annoyed. She does not like his brusque manner… and to speak in that tone of Our Heavenly Father is simply unacceptable. She moves away, thinking. *His manner is lacking… to say the least. Most certainly he is not the self-assured man I see on Sundays. Maybe I was a little hasty in my decision to tell him of my affections… and his behavior is to say the least… is odd.* Her passion has now cooled considerably.

Otis looks down the road, then back at Mrs. Comford. "I'm sorry to give you the wrong impression. Very sorry that you misunderstood my friendship," he says, and scrambles further away from the woman before she can try another move on him. "I have been besieged with many new revelations tonight. I realize I have been lacking in my duties at the reservation and my treatment of the Indians... who are wonderfully strange and gifted. I can see I was wrong to have you come out and declare them savages and in need of religious conversion. They are most wise, Mrs. Comford. I must say, I have come to my senses and after my new revelations... your services are no longer required. I know you believe they would perish if not for your teachings of the Bible. But I feel quite certain they have their own special place after death. I see now that it has been an intrusion on these good people. I will see to making the accommodations for your departure forthwith, Mrs. Comford." He follows with a curt, "Goodnight." Just to be sure she wouldn't follow, he hurries inside his house and slams the door behind him. He falls into a chair in relief.

At this surprising turn of events, a flabbergasted Mrs. Comford stands at the door in shock before gathering her wits about her and huffing down the path. "How dare he treat me in such an uncharitable manner! Telling me my services are no longer needed. This is the last straw." *I'm glad to be leaving this wretched place,* she thinks furiously. If they all go to Hell, it will not be her fault. She tried her best. *I'm quite certain Mr. Peale will join the heathens down there, as well. He's no prize, anyway, with his rotund belly and balding head. I surely was mistaken to think that man was worthy of me.* "Oh, dear Lord," she prays. "Please forgive my unkind thoughts. I have been put-up-under with the weight of this place and the wickedness that resides here. I would pray for all the lost souls, but I fear it is too late for any of them... the poor wretches."

SO GLAD YOU'RE HERE

MORNING STAR SNEAKS into town and arrives at Hidden Spirit's house just as dusk is settling in on this overcast, cold and gloomy day. Morning Star taps lightly on the front door, hearing voices inside. The door opens a crack, a face peers out, and an arm quickly pulls Morning Star inside to welcome her. White Tail hugs the girl tightly — with worry filling her face. The lantern casts orange shadows on the wall as White Cloud hurries over to the young girl, pulls over a chair for her to sit on, and asks about Little Moon and grandfather Plenty Feathers.

"They are both well, but I could no longer stay in the hills. I had to come to town to see Hidden Spirit. Is he here?"

White Tail's face fills with pain, as she sits at the table with a worried look, unable to answer.

"I fear for Hidden Spirit's safety," White Cloud says softly. "I heard he is being held in the cellar beneath the storage house, for stealing. Wigley has him under watch, day and night. They want to hang him... set an example. Wigley says he was stealing our supplies to trade for whiskey..." His voice cracks, and can say no more.

Morning Star can hardly believe his words, and cries out. "No. We must do something to stop this. Wigley hates Hidden Spirit and has been after him for a long time. He will do anything to destroy him... even lie about him."

"Let me see what I can find out tomorrow. Maybe I can speak with our son," White Cloud says, holding his wife's hand. "I don't know how I will survive if they hang my son. We have lost our beloved Chasing Rabbit and so many of our relatives and… White Tail bursts into tears as White Cloud puts his arms around his wife, saying, "We will not let this happen. Let's get some rest so we can think with a clear head in the morning. It has been a trying day for us all. Morning Star will spend the night here with us."

Everyone was up early the next morning. Morning Star got no sleep, anxious for the outcome, trying to figure out what to do.

White Cloud had left early to see what he could find out about Hidden Spirit and was back within the hour, sporting a black eye and a swollen lip. "I had no luck with Wigley," White Clouds states, solemnly. "I was told not to come back again, for if I did, he would charge me with interfering in his duties. But what I did have luck with, is this." He opens the door further as Ellie and Homer come walking into the room.

Morning Star's face beams with joy and runs to hug Ellie. "How did you… I don't know what to say besides, th-thank you for coming… we need your help. When did you arrive at the res- ervation, and h-how did you ever find us?" Morning Star is talking so fast, she is stumbling over her words. She says solemnly, "Hidden Spirit is… something dreadful has happened to him."

Ellie takes Morning Star's hand, and squeezes it. "Hidden Spirit has helped me in more ways than I can say. I am grateful to have met him and Little Moon and Chasing Rabbit. I… that is, we couldn't leave without doing something. I had a feeling that we must find you. My father, and others have inflicted so much damage well… I'm just glad to be here. I will do whatever I can to help."

White Tail is busily heating some coffee, grateful for the company.

White Cloud asks everyone to sit as they huddle together to devise a plan. As they talk, a feeling of hope fills the room.

SURPRISE FOR WILL

A BANG AT THE door about sets Will's head reeling. He stumbles out of bed and staggers toward the door, wondering who could be calling so early in the day. As he swings the door open, his jaw drops at the sight of the prettiest creature he has ever seen. He blinks twice, unable to believe his good fortune. He tries to let out a low whistle, but nothing comes out. So he says, "Howdy-do, ma'am. How can I help ya?" A lopsided grin crosses his face.

"Is this the home of Mr. Wigley?" the girl inquires, politely. "Mr. Will Wigley?"

"Sure the heck is," Will says proudly, scratching the stubble on his chin, wondering how this lovely angel appeared on his doorstep. And before he knows what's happening, she pushes the door open. *The little angel invites herself in.* Will stumbles back in surprise. His smile dims when he notices a young man with her. *Well now, that ain't nearly as appetizing,* he thinks, and he goes to slam the door shut. But to Will's amazement the boy sticks his foot in the door before he can get it closed, and slides his way inside. Will looks him up and down, irritated at the gumption of this kid. *Best to be polite, until I can figure what they're up to,* Will thinks. He ignores the kid and turns back to Ellie. "What can I do for ya, miss? Would ya like some coffee?" Will asks politely and brings her a chair.

Just then, a loud snore goes off behind a tattered curtain. "Excuse the noise, miss. That's just my stupid partner sleepin' off a little too much drink last night. Pay him no mind." He pulls a chair next to Ellie's and widens his grin. "Now, how can I be of help to a fine filly like yerself?" Will catches a glimpse of her big blue eyes, and clutches his heart.

"I work for the *Times Chronicle* newspaper, and I've traveled from New York to do a story about the Indians living on the reservation," she says. "My name is Ella Blossom, and this is my, uh, my colleague, Frank Burns."

Will turns and gives Homer a nasty stare before turning his eyes back to Ellie, admiringly.

"I think you've come to the right place, if you're looking for Injuns," Will hoots waving his hands, motioning outside. "We gotta whole bunch of 'em right here. Just take a look around." Will pulls up his suspenders and starts to scratch, but catches himself. "Me and my partner caught us a wild Injun last night, and we're gonna have us a hangin'." He inches closer to Ellie, saying importantly, "The savage was stealing supplies."

Ellie feels a sharp jolt to her chest at the mention of a hanging, and she starts to swoon. Fear trickles in her veins at the thought of Hidden Spirit. She looks at Homer, whose face pales in shock.

Will puffs up his chest, and offers his hand to Ellie. "No need ta be frightened, little miss. Nasty business, hanging is, but I'll see ya don't get too close to the perch." He studies the girl carefully, eyes roaming over her pleasing figure, and he ratchets up his grin. "Uh, like I was saying, miss, the neck gets snapped real quick like — ain't hardly nothin' to it. I'll even hold your hand, if you get scared. And if ya like, you can watch while I put the noose around his neck."

Ellie's eyes widen in alarm, and she fidgets. "Why… uh… thank you, Mr. Wigley. That's… uh… quite an offer." She looks away, fighting back tears and swinging her foot up and down, nervously.

"I'll tell ya what. You could write me up in your paper and tell 'em Mr. Will Wigley caught a crazy Injun an' rescued a damsel in distress just in the nick of time… 'fore she got herself scalped. How does that sound for yer paper?"

Ellie is at a loss for words. She takes a deep breath and adjusts her smile. "Well, I'm sure that would make you quite famous, Mr. Wigley, but…"

"I like the sound of that 'cause I likes women… an' women likes me," Will says, getting excited. "An' I'll be famous, ta boot." Will can't believe his change of fortune. Just a couple days ago, he thought he was going to die… and, on top of that, he almost lost his goods. And now… this! "Ya know," Will says, scooting his chair closer and lowering his voice, while eyeing Homer. "I'm gonna open me a fancy whorehouse down in Texas, so if ya wanna write about that, as well, that'd be fine with me. I'd even be willin' ta bring ya along." Will's getting so caught up with his plans about Ellie he absent-mindedly lifts up his behind and slips out a squeaker.

Will's face turns a light shade of red as he realizes the pretty girl is staring at him in amusement. She smiles as she puts a kerchief to her nose, real ladylike-like.

"Pardon me, ma'am," Will says, slightly embarrassed. "Not used to such fine company as yourself 'round here."

Not trusting her voice, Ellie holds back a giggle and manages to say, "Of course. But tell me… how are the Indians adjusting to their new way of life, Mr. Wigley? Are they treated fair? Is it difficult for them being confined to the reservation?"

"Well, now," Will says, leaning back in his chair, "I'd say

they're treated real fair an' adjustin' real good. Gettin' free handouts an' not having ta do a lick of work. Give 'em plenty of food,
too. I see to that, myself." Leaning further back in his chair, he
almost topples over, but quickly catches himself. "So I'd say, life
is pretty doggone good fer the savages."

Ellie is quiet, picking at her collar, trying to figure what to
say next. Seeing Will looking at her, she taps her pad as if to show
she's thinking about what he just said. Then she clears her throat.
"That was quite enlightening, Mr. Wigley. Thank you."

"Glad I could educate ya on the Injuns an' what it's like living
'round them, miss."

"Educate me you did… so you handle all of that?" Ellie says
sweetly, trying to conceal her disgust of the ogling Will. "My,
that's a lot of responsibility for a brave man like yourself."

In the corner Homer stifles a laugh upon hearing Ellie fawn
all over Will. "I heard you were in the military. I adore a man
who wears a uniform and carries a big gun. I bet you can shoot
real good, too."

Will's face is boiling hot, and he can't help but crow, proudly.
"Well, now, I can see yer a smart gal. Matter o' fact, I can shoot
a tooth off a rattler." He puffs up a bit more, and says, "I like a
little filly who speaks real s'phisticated-like." He scoots his chair
even closer until his nose is right next to hers, and he whispers,
"Why don't ya tell ole Frank here ta leave us alone fer a spell? I
could educate ya on some other matters… if ya get my drift." He
gives Ellie a wink, but his mouth drops open in surprise as she
knocks his chair back, and stands up indignantly. "Mr. Wigley, I
am surprised at your forward inclination."

Will cocks his head and wonders what the dickens is wrong
with her. *She was acting real sweet a moment ago, and now… well,
maybe she wants a little courtin' first, or some 'inclination,' whatever
that means.* He figures it must be something real impressive. He

continues to stare at the blond-haired angel and wonders, *should I knock ole Frank out so I can be alone with her.* But he returns to his senses when he hears her say, "Frank came with me to draw pictures for the paper. He could draw a picture of you and maybe some of the reservation. People are very curious about what life is like out here in the West." He frowns at the prospect of having Frank around, and gives him a glare.

Ellie continues. "I'll tell you what… why don't you pose for Frank, and he'll draw a nice picture of you for the newspaper? People from miles around will see you and be awed by your, uh… courage."

Will squirms at that idea. *I'm not too keen on that Frank fellow and I don't want him drawing my mug for nothing. Someone might get a load of me an' do some squealing.* He squints his eyes, looking for the kid, and sees him peeking around the curtain, being real quiet. Will jumps off his chair and hollers. "Hey, kid, whaddaya doing snooping around my business?"

Homer jumps about a mile in the air, his face turns bright red. "Pardon me, Mr. Wigley. I wasn't meaning to snoop. I w-was just f-figuring what I could draw for the paper, and…"

Will snarls, "I ain't interested in your drawin's or nothing else. I just don't like fellas snoopin' 'round my business. Especially nosey ones." Will is getting ready to shove Homer out the door, but Ellie comes rushing over, and intervenes.

"Oh, don't pay Frank any mind, Will," Ellie says, trying to sound calm while a quiver of fear rushes through her veins. Hesitantly, she pats his arm. "I've never seen an Indian before," she says, trying to control her emotions. "I'm simply dying to meet one, Mr. Wigley, and I would be very grateful if I could see the one you captured." She sighs, flashing a charming smile. "Almost single-handed, you say? How very impressive!"

Will is amazed and forgets about Homer. *Word sure gets around quick*, he thinks, and twirls his gun for show.

Ellie wants to laugh, but restrains herself. "It would make my article so much richer if I could ask him a few questions."

"Will grunts and puts his gun back in his holster. "Well, just fer a short time is all. You need to be careful around the savage and not get too close to 'im. He might try some underhanded stuff and hurt ya. He's got some potent spells, I seen for my own self. Hate to see what he might do to a real pretty woman."

Determined, Ellie continues. "Now, Will," she cajoles sweetly. "I'm sure I'll be just fine. I'm very… um… grateful… for your help." She forces a smile, as her hands tremble and tries not to flinch as she rubs Will's arm.

It makes Will a bit giddy being near her. *That beats all. This little lady's grateful, an' I'm gonna cash in.* "Well now, just how grateful ya gonna be, miss? What ya got in mind?" He gives her a real big smile, and bends close, licking his lips. "I'd take a big ole kiss for starters." Will puckers up, inching his face right next to hers. He sees her eyes get real wide, like she's seen a badger. Then, before Will knows what's happening, she pecks him on the cheek and backs away, quick as lightning.

"Whoa there, missy. Barely gotta taste of yer sweet lips. Let's give that another try," he says, pulling her close.

"I gave you your kiss, Mr. Wigley," she says, shoving him back. "I must say it was a bit forward, but I did what you asked. Now, you must keep your word."

Will frowns, fiddling with his moustache, thinking she's pretty sneaky.

"Now, you wouldn't go back on your promise, would you, Will?" Ellie asks, getting anxious.

"Oh, I don't know. He's real cagey-like, and mean. Best you

stand near me an' don't get too close to him. Like I said, he might try somethin' underhanded and hurt ya."

Will's not sure about any of this, and scratches his whiskers. But thinking he might get another kiss for his effort, he walks over and grabs the keys hanging on the wall. "Yer only gonna get a short time down there," he says, walking out the door. "Don't wanna get him all riled up, with ya bein' such a looker an' all."

Will walks down the path to the weather-beaten door, reaches for the rusty padlock, and sticks the key inside. It grinds and takes a few tries before he can get the lock to open. "Watch your step, little filly," he chortles, and gives Ellie's arm a squeeze. "The stairs are a bit rickety, and it's dark as Hell down there." Will lights a lantern hanging by the door, looks down into the cellar, and hollers. "Any Injuns home?" He gives a loud snort, laughing at his remark. "Hold it, sweet one. I'll help ya down there." But Ellie takes the lantern from his hand and before he can reply, she says sweetly, "I can manage."

Will spits on the ground, turns to Homer, and hisses. "Why don't you stay on up here, Frank? No need fer you to follow her an' me down there…" But before Will can get another word out, Homer marches right past him, and runs down the stairs.

"I hope you fall flat on yer face," Will mutters, irritated, then yanks up his britches and scurries right behind, itching to give Homer a shove.

Ellie walks down the dimly lit stairwell trembling as she holds the lantern high — not knowing what to expect or what to do… afraid for what might be coming next. Eyes adjusting to the darkness, she approaches Hidden Spirit and can see the unmistakable outline of his handsome face… she wants to reach out and touch him. Walking closer, she notices he appears totally at ease, even though his arms and feet are tightly bound around a chair. A slight smile creases the corners of his mouth, as he looks up at the girl.

Ellie is momentarily taken aback by the intensity of his gaze… *They seem fearless…like a warrior's eyes, full of pride.* A crackle of energy snaps. Ellie feels the hair on her arms start to rise. A wave of mystery surrounds the room, and she shivers. It doesn't make sense, but she knows that, somehow, Hidden Spirit will be protected.

Homer approaches, and glances curiously at the young Indian, who seems strangely preoccupied. As he walks around the room, he stops mid-stride and feels a whoosh of air float by… like a caress. For several surprised seconds, he stood and stared. *There is someone or something in this room, he thinks. It feels rather soothing, peaceful.* He looks over at Hidden Spirit and wonders if he feels the presence too. He seems so calm. *I can see why Ellie calls him a hero… not someone like me who can't get a word out without feeling foolish.* His jealousy he had once felt for the boy, is no more… now it's only admiration. Just as he gathers the courage to speak to Hidden Spirit, Will struts over and elbows him out of the way. "Move it, Frank," then elbows him again for good measure.

Will struts over to Hidden Spirit and chortles out. "This here little filly's come all the way from the East ta write about your connivin' ways." He grins wickedly. "So listen up. Yer gonna be real polite to her, ya hear?" Will grabs hold of his hair and gives it a tug. "And none of yer funny business, neither," he hisses. "Yer useless life's gonna be over real soon. Now, let's see yer feathers get ya outta *this* mess!"

Will pulls up a chair for Ellie and gives it a shake, then motions her over. "It's a bit wobbly, but I think it'll do, long as you don't wiggle too much," Will says with a grin. As Ellie walks past Will, it takes all of his restraint to keep from taking her in his arms and giving her a real big squeeze. He wipes his mustache, thinking, *my business would boom if I could talk her into goin' with me to Texas. She's gotta real sweet smell.* Then, before he knows it, Homer sidles up next to her with his paper and pencil. Will gives him a dirty look and says, "This here fella is gonna draw your ugly mug, so they got something ta remember ya by… after your neck gets snapped sideways."

Ignoring his threat, Ellie begins to question Hidden Spirit. Then, for some reason she can't explain, she turns to Will and asks sweetly, "Do you think you could open the window, Mr. Wigley? It's very stuffy down here, and I could breathe much easier if you did."

"Well, I don't know. Might be someone tryin' to get him outta here."

"That window is so small, I really don't think you have to worry," Ellie insists, wide eyed.

"Ya gonna be grateful ta me again if I do?"

Ellie gives a buttery smile and says, "Now, Mr. Wigley. I am, of course, grateful. I've told you before, so please. I'm not the kind of girl to be so forward, without a…"

Holy shits on fire! I wonder if the little angel wants ta get hitched. He hustles over to the window. "Let me open it for ya, little miss. Wouldn't want ya ta be short o' breath down here," he says, shoving the window open. "Now, where were we…" Will stops talking, as he hears a woman's voice call out from the doorway. "Who the blazes is it? I'm a might busy now."

"Mr. Wigley, are you down there?"

"Who wants ta know?" Will hollers out, thoroughly agitated.

"It's me, Mrs. Stover," she says, as she walks down the stairs, carrying a tray full of food.

Blast it all. It's that nosey cook of Peale's, he groans. "Well whadda ya want. Like I told ya, I'm a might busy right now."

"You remember me, don't you, Mr. Wigley?" she says, ignoring him. "I'm Mr. Peale's housekeeper. He asked me to bring the boy some food. Can't starve him, now, can we?" She sniffs, as she walks past Will without waiting for an answer.

"Now, hold on a darn minute. I know who you work for, an all, but you shoulda asked me first."

"Mr. Peale told me that you wouldn't mind. Besides, there's no need to ask your permission, since he is in charge of the reservation. So, please move out of my way," she says.

"I got a young miss out here from the paper back east. Gonna write about the Injuns."

"About time someone did."

Will grumbles. "I'd save you the trouble of walkin' all the way over here, but now that ya brought it, I see I'm mighty hungry, myself. Tell ole' Peale it was real good of him to think of me." With that he lifts up the cloth and gives the food a good sniff. His stomach starts rumbling in anticipation. As he grabs for a biscuit, Mrs. Stover slaps it out of his hand.

"Hands off, Mr. Wigley. I'm feeding that young man, whether you like it or not."

"This here Injun's a killer," Will says, getting riled, "among other things, too." But Mrs. Stover is undeterred as she walks over to the boy. "Oh, all right then. Just hurry on up," says Will, irritated at the pushy lady.

"You should be ashamed of yourself. Now untie this young man so he can eat proper-like," Mrs. Stover demands.

"I ain't gonna untie him for nothin', and you ain't gonna make me." Will glares at her as she glowers back. "I hate bossy women," he hisses.

Mrs. Stover ignores Will, and sets her tray next to Hidden Spirit. "I brought some leftover pork and fresh biscuits I made just this morning," she says warmly, offering the boy a slice of the tender meat. Mrs. Stover almost drops the food as she looks into his wild eyes. She thinks, this young man is not only splendid looking, but he's very unusual. Just like that Indian, Broken Feather. She smiles, remembering her encounter with the incredible man.

It was like a beautiful dream... as we danced into the night sky and soared into the *heavens*. Her hands tremble slightly... and, for a fleeting moment, she sees Broken Feather's reflection in the boy's eyes, smiling at her. She gasps and, at the sound of Will's loud voice, is startled back to reality.

"Say, whaddaya think he is — a baby, fer crying-out-loud? He's nothin' but a savage. I ain't got all day, ya know, so hurry up."

Mrs. Stover flinches at Will's abrasive tone, and quickly picks up the biscuit and meat off the floor. Then she turns to him with the biscuit in hand. "Would you care for one, Mr. Wigley?"

Will snatches it away before she can blink. "That's more like it," he grumbles, and he gobbles it down in one bite.

Ellie holds back a laugh as she watches Mrs. Stover slather some jam on a biscuit and put it into Hidden Spirit's mouth and wipes the crumbs away.

Will about comes unglued as he sees Ellie standing there, helping and cuddling up close to the Indian, while that old bat is feeding him and whispering in his ear, while Homer is drawing his picture. Fuming, Will jerks his hands in the air, shouting. "Now I've had 'bout enough of everyone cozyin' up to that killer. He may look real nice, but he's vicious."

"Oh, nonsense," says Mrs. Stover. "Let me feed him without you going on so." She slips another bite into Hidden Spirit's mouth, and Ellie wipes away the crumbs.

Will is enraged. "Yer time's up, lady. Gather up yer dishes and get on outta here. You, too, Frank! I don't like y'all gettin' so sweet on the Injun." He stomps over to Homer and yanks the drawing out of his hand. "Now, get. You and the old bitty," Then he shoves them toward the stairs.

Mrs. Stover huffs, "You need to learn some manners, Mr. Wigley... about how to treat a lady."

"Well, old lady, here's one fer ya." Will bends over and lets off a loud toot. Then, he slaps his knee, laughing. "So get on out the door. I'll be stayin' with the little miss down here. Gotta protect her while she's talkin' to the Injun." He slips his arm around her shoulder and pulls her close.

Ellie slides away from Will, looks at Hidden Spirit, and yanks out a pad of paper.

"Excuse me, Mr. Wigley, I have work to do." Ellie turns her back to Wigley, slides her chair closer to Hidden Spirit, and whispers. "We have come to help you get…" Suddenly she feels her chair being jerked backwards.

"You can't get that close, miss. Never know what he'll do. Stay near me. I need ta keep my eyeballs on him." Will places his hand on his gun. "Gotta hear what *yer* sayin', too."

Ellie's voice cracks as she asks, "You… uh… how did you… I mean, what did you do, to end up here?"

"I told you, miss, he's a thief," Will growls. "I'll give you all the answers ya want 'bout him. He stole a wagon full of supplies ta sell for whiskey."

Ellie shuffles her papers and taps her foot. She feels Will's eyes burrow into hers. "No need to be nervous, little miss. Just get yer question out." He turns to Hidden Spirit and gives him a glare, squeezing Ellie's arm, possessively. "Better be on yer best behavior for this sweet creature."

Shoving her shoulders back, Ellie sucks in a deep breath. "I've heard stories about your life on the plains before the white man came. Can you tell me what your life was like back then?"

Hidden Spirit ponders the question as his eyes drift off to another time. His voice is deep and mesmerizing as he calmly tells Ellie about his first buffalo hunt, when he was seven, and the thrill of it, and how he was celebrated by his elders at the time of his birth.

Will is disgusted by what he hears, and lets out a loud snort.

This is not at all what he had envisioned earlier. *I can't believe how she's talkin' real nice to that Injun...like they're old buddies.* His blood is beginning to boil as he sees Ellie smile at the Indian. *That's the same way she did to me. Something's not right here.*

Enthralled by what she hears, Ellie leans closer to Hidden Spirit, and scribbles on her pad, furiously. Ellie looks into his eyes... a lump clogs her throat and she hoarsely asks. "Do you feel your people are being fairly treated here?" He looks at the girl who is questioning him, with her intense look.

"No! We are not."

Will is beside himself with fury, and smacks Hidden Spirit upside his head. "I told ya we give the Injuns plenty of food. I dole it out to 'em myself. The whole lot of 'em are lazy buggers. This is gonna be the end of yer interview, little missy. Now you go on and gather up your paper, and scoot on up them stairs. I gotta 'spicion yer an Injun lover, an' I don't cotton much ta that. So, that's all the time yer gonna get with him. Mighty disappointed in ya, though. Had some big plans fer you and me."

"I didn't mean to make you upset, Mr. Wigley. I was trying to find out how he feels about the reservation life, that's all," she says, in a placating voice.

"I ain't playin' any more games with ya. You might be a looker, but ya ain't gonna trick me into fallin' for that malarkey again. So you take ole Frank here and skedaddle on outta town. I got a lotta work ta do and I don't wanna be bothered no more."

Ellie looks back at Hidden Spirit, not trusting her voice to speak. Her eyes fill with tears as she heads out the basement door.

Will slaps Hidden Spirit on the side of his face, this time with greater force. He sees the stubbornness in his eyes, and says, "You ain't gonna make it past the next sundown, skin. I'd hang the whole bunch of ya, if I could." He checks to see if the coast is clear, then races up the stairs and locks the door behind. Storming into the house he shakes Jeb out of bed. "Get up, ya lazy coot. We gotta getta movin'. There's trouble brewin' on the herizon."

*

A distraught Ellie sees Homer and Mrs. Stover waiting for her behind the house. She runs over, and smiles weakly. "Oh how foolish you must think we are," she says, wringing her hands. "Trying to convince Wigley that I was from the *Times Chronicle* and that Homer works for the paper as an artist. I'm not sure he believed any of it." Then she realizes she hasn't introduced herself, and half-heartedly explains. "Sorry for going on so. My name is Ellie, or rather, Ella, and…"

"Yes, my dear, nice to meet you. This young man has filled me in on your travels. I must say… you both seem so brave and adventurous. Not foolish at all. That boy downstairs is not one bit afraid, either. I saw him at Mr. Peale's house the other night. What a commotion it was, too. I thought he was going to send Mr. Peale flying against the wall. Then, something else happened… it was amazing to say the least and…" She stops and looks at the two of them. "I tell you what… why don't you come over to the house for some refreshments. Mr. Peale's gone for the day. Let's see if we can figure something out to help that fine young man."

"Are you certain, Mrs. Stover? I would hate to…"

"Nonsense. It would be my pleasure to help. First, I'll fix some breakfast. We'll be able to think better on full stomachs."

"Oh, that would be lovely," Ellie says, her eyes fill with relief.

"We… um… have another request, Mrs. Stover," Homer says, sheepishly. "Our friend, Morning Star, who escaped from the boarding school, is at Hidden Spirit's parents' house."

Ellie adds, "She and her sister, Little Moon, have been hiding out in the hills with his grandfather. She snuck into town a couple days ago. Would you mind if she comes over?"

"Oh, my goodness! Why, she is more than welcome. Escaped you say? I can't wait to hear."

Thrilled, Ellie says, "Everyone is frantic with worry, especially Morning Star. Hidden Spirit is all she can talk about... is all everyone can talk about. We are all so scared. We have to find a way to help."

"Yes, I agree we must help, but we must be careful."

"I will shoot Wigley, if I have to," Ellie says, feeling desperate.

"I'm not a very good shot, but I will go with you," Homer adds, shyly.

"Now, let's not get ahead of ourselves. Let's go to the house and discuss a plan, rationally."

"You're right, Mrs. Stover. It's just that Hidden Spirit is... well, unique. Their people would be devastated if anything happens to him."

"That's true. I saw the parents' sad faces after the children left. Broke my heart, it did, and no one cared a lick," Mrs. Stover says with a trace of anger. "I'm so glad that Morning Star got away from that awful place. I can hardly wait to meet her."

Shyly, Homer interrupts. "I-I could go get her, if you like. Then I could bring her with me to your house."

Ellie looks at him with a hint of admiration, and he blushes — like he does whenever he looks at her. "Good idea, Homer. Thank you."

"Now, let me tell you where to go. The house is at the end of this road... less than a mile on the right-hand side. It has a weathered fence, with a broken hinge. You can't miss it. Bring the girl in the back way through town, so no one sees you. We have no time to waste."

*

Hidden Spirit's arms and legs are numb as he shifts in the chair.

He was quite surprised to see the girl with the sunshine hair and the other boy. He can't believe those two made it all the way out here. The thought of the white girl makes him smile. *She would have made a good brave*, he thinks, *and that boy, he has a good heart. He would be good helping the women.* He wonders what they're up to, and thinks. *I can feel her desire to help. She is sincere.* As he sits alone in the darkness, contemplating their arrival a sudden breeze wafts through the window, sending his hair whipping high into the air and around his face. A chill pierces his body, penetrating deep inside, whispering… rumbling like thunder. *Wawoptetusni.* His teeth begin to chatter as the icy chill penetrates all the way to his bones. Then a sweet scent of tobacco follows, arousing his senses, recalling vivid memories of Broken Feather. His eyes tear, and, for a brief moment, the images of his regal face, haunt him. He can feel his power fill him as he sits alone… his feelings of revenge blow out the window along with the smoke. He feels an incredible surge of power course through his body… like a jolt of lightning. Then, there is a tap-tap-tap at the window and a shallow whisper. "Your powers are coming." He squints his eyes, looking for the source of the voice. A flock of feathers sweeps through the room, glowing silver in the dark, and his grandfather's face emerges within a whirl of clouds and smoke. Broken Feather's eyes look like bright green flecks — sparkling in the darkness. Every cell in Hidden Spirit's body tingles with energy.

"Grandson, I see you have learned many lessons on your journey. The lessons you have endured will make you stronger in the face of our future. Your ancestors have cheered you on through your difficult times. You are ready, Mi-thakoza. Your spirit is now wise." Broken Feather's eyes penetrate deep into his soul, setting off a flurry of emotions. "The ones that have taken the journey to the otherworld tell me they are pleased with you. They say you will make a fine leader. Tell our people we must keep our language…

our words have meanings that the white words cannot capture. If we lose that, we will be lost for generations to come."

Hidden Spirit feels his heart expanding with each word spoken.

"Remember, Mi-thakoza... we come from our dances and prayers and songs. They must never be forgotten, for this is who we are... a nation of Sioux Indians, with connections to the Great Spirit. That, they cannot kill."

The haze begins to shift and turn — and Broken Feather is gone. Hidden Spirit sits, contemplating Broken Feather's words when he hears the wind begin to sing... soothing, comforting sounds. It is hypnotic. It was music of a time long past, of another century, and it makes his heart yearn with longing as he hums, softly. A whisper of movement at the window catches his attention. He sees a flash of light, and then a faint tinkling of bells. He hears the door slowly creak open and watches in amazement as four withered ancients dance down the stairs... music flowing ethereally. Ghost Dancer clops down behind. The ancients swirl around the room, chanting sounds that rumble like thunder. Ghost Dancer whinnies. The four ancients look like golden orbs, floating and bobbing in the darkened room. Cool blasts of silky mist surrounds Hidden Spirit... like a kiss. He feels the rope slide to the floor. A sudden warmth spread throughout his arms as blood flows back into his veins. He squeezes his fingers and feels a prickling sensation, and he slowly stands. Ghost Dancer nibbles his cheek, his eyes piercing the darkness, and nudges the young man. The ancients glide in the night as a silken thread of light weaves throughout the room and weaves its way up the stairs... dancing like fireflies. Low silvery voices emit from the ancients... beckoning the young man to follow. He hops upon the back of Ghost Dancer and silently follows the mysterious beings out the door.

*

"We are so grateful for your kindness, Mrs. Stover," Ellie says, taking the woman's hand.

"Oh, nonsense, dear. It's my pleasure to help you. It's just awful to imagine what those children must have endured while they were away. "

Mrs. Stover tucks Ellie's arm in hers as they walk down the road and chat like they have known each other for years. Ellie tells her about the boarding school and her parents and her close call with Frae Beadle. She shivers, thinking about him and what he might do if he were to find her. But she brushes that notion aside.

Mrs. Stover is visibly moved by Ellie's story and of her miserable home life. "After Homer... helped me... well, it really was Hidden Spirit who helped get me out of my house. Then Homer and I ran away in the middle of the night and made our way to the train station. As frightened as I was about getting caught, I was far more terrified of staying. I had no choice but to run... it was worth the risk. So Homer led the way, and we walked all night. We decided we couldn't sit by and do nothing for the girls, whom I had grown so fond of, or for all the others at that miserable school. So we headed west and took the train to a town called Henderson, bought a horse, and rode out here... after asking folks numerous questions about the reservation. Some were hesitant to talk while others were more forthcoming."

"Good for you, child," Mrs. Stover says, giving Ellie a hug. "I can't believe you and Homer came all that way by yourselves. It makes my life seem so, well, unimportant. I wish I could do something more to help. But now that you're here, at least I get to be of more use than just cooking for Mr. Peale."

Ellie asks, "Tell me more about Wil Wigley."

"He's an awful creature. I never liked him... not from the moment I laid eyes on him. I tried to tell Mr. Peale about him, but he told me to mind my own affairs. He told me, 'Cooking is

the only thing you need to be concerned with around here.' So..."
Her words trail off. "I was desperate for work, and when this job
became available, I of course took it. I thought working for a nice
educated man like Mr. Peale might be a pleasant change, but," she
sighs, "no point going on about him. He's not going to change."

Soon they arrive at the house, and Mrs. Stover opens the back
door and welcomes Ellie inside. "Come in, and please sit down."
She pulls out a chair for her at the kitchen table. "Just give me
a few minutes while I get things ready." She throws on an apron
and gets to work. Ellie watches in amazement as the woman flies
about the room. She stokes the fire, puts a pot of coffee on the
stove, and pulls out a loaf of freshly baked bread, it seems all at
the same time. Then, she slices a big piece for Ellie.

Ellie watches as the steam rises from the crust, and inhales
the heavenly smell. She feels calm for the first time in weeks and
slumps back in her chair, letting out a sigh. This is nothing like
her house, she thinks, with a tinge of regret, as she looks around
at the homey kitchen.

Mrs. Stover holds up a jar of homemade gooseberry jam, and
smiles. "My secret recipe. I hope you like it." Setting it on the
table, she pops off the lid and says, "Help yourself, my dear."
Then she pulls out some bacon and begins slicing big chunks,
tossing them into the skillet while cracking eggs at the same time.
Her hair is tousled and her face flushed as she bustles to and fro,
talking all the while to Ellie and enjoying herself in the process.
"I haven't had company in a spell, so forgive me for prattling on.
It feels good to talk to another woman. Around here, it's just the
missionaries carrying on about their religion and the lack of mine.
It grows tiresome after a while. I suspect the ladies don't care
for me much... nor I for them. I'd like to box them right in the
ears." Brushing a stray piece of hair from her face, she continues.
"I suppose they mean well, but... not everybody has to believe

in another person's God to make them good people. Well that's enough carrying on, but still, I wish they would be nicer to the Indians. We should let the Indian people live their lives as they choose. But, rules, you know. Got 'em locked up here, telling them their ways are all wrong. Breaks my heart, it does. They're lovely people... but most around here don't care for them."

"We found that out," Ellie says, blue eyes widening as she speaks. "We stopped at a rancher's house for directions a few days back. His name was Jim Phillips. He said he owned the lands as far as we could see. When he found out we were sympathetic to the Indian people he proceeded to give us a lecture, and told us we have a lot to learn about life... and Indians!" When he finished, he sent us on our way with a final warning, "if you know what's good for you, you'll mind your own business."

A slight knock on the door sends Mrs. Stover scurrying over. Her eyes open in delight as she sees Morning Star standing there. She is tall and thin as a rail, with a determined look in her eyes. *She's lovely*, Mrs. Stover thinks. *The sweetest thing I have ever laid eyes on.*

Homer introduces her shyly. "Mrs. Stover, this is Morning Star." Mrs. Stover takes her hands, and speaks kindly. "I am very pleased to meet you. Welcome." She pulls the girl inside and walks her toward the kitchen where the inviting smells of frying bacon and eggs make the girl's stomach rumble.

Ellie gives Morning Star a big hug as chatter among the girls, fills the room. "Please sit down," Mrs. Stover says, clucking like a mother hen as she brings over a big platter of her bacon and eggs. "Hurry and eat before it gets cold," she says, looking pleased. "I have been thinking of a plan that might just work to free your intriguing friend. Now I'm going to cook up a big pot of stew for you to take over to Will. You'll tell him you're sorry for the mis-understanding. With his big ego, it shouldn't be hard to convince him that you're sorry… and that you want to set things right. Tell him you want to know about his life and the hardships *he* endures out here."

Excited at her suggestion, Ellie says, "that's a wonderful idea, Mrs. Stover. I think that could work. I'll do anything… even if I have kiss Wigley. I just hope it doesn't make me sick."

"Now, while you have his attention, I'll come a short while later, to really confuse him. Homer could leave early, and be on the lookout for anything suspicious his partner might be up to."

Everyone is nervous and excited at the dangerous plan to free Hidden Spirit. Then, the room quiets as everyone, deep in thought, eats their food and contemplates their role.

LIKE SOME STEW, MR. WIGLEY?

ELLIE TAKES A big breath as she sets out for Will Wigley's office. She walks up the steps, pot of stew in hand, hoping she can convince him of her sincerity about wanting to write about him. As she peers into the window, she gasps at the sight of huge crates full of food strewn in every direction. Bags of rice, beans, and coffee are piled high on the floor. Ellie is starting to get nervous... no longer the self-assured girl she was at Mrs. Stover's house. The longer she stands watching Will in the window, the more she questions her ability to carry out her plan. She hears Will grunt as he hoists a bag of flour from the back room. *Maybe we should come up with another plan,* Ellie thinks. Her brows draw together as she ponders her dilemma. It suddenly dawns on her... his friend isn't with him, and wonders where he is. *Maybe he's in the back room. I wonder what they're doing with all this food laid out. Morning Star said her people were going hungry.* She feels hackles rising up her neck. She doesn't know why, but the strangest of feelings creep into her mind... she wants to run... to change her mind about all this. She sees Will hauling another bag of flour across the floor, when she feels a tap on her shoulders.

She almost drops the pot of stew as she turns around, and looks into the snarling face of Jeb.

"Whattcha doing peekin' in the window. Lookin' ta squeal

on Will an me?" He grabs her by the arm and gives her a push, as Ellie stumbles through the door.

Busily counting all the bags, Will's mouth about drops open at all the commotion. His eyes practically bug out of their sockets when he sees Ellie fly into the room, with a furious Jeb trailing behind. Under his breath, he says, "She must be up to somethin' sneaky. I knew it." He drops the sack of flour he was holding, and yelps out. "Whaddaya doing here, Missy?"

"I'll tell ya what she's doin'. Spying on ya. I saw her eyeballing ya from the window," says a righteous Jeb as he grabs her arm. "I think she's a snooper... or why else would she be stickin' her nose in the window. This one's up to some funny business ... I can tell."

"I'd say ya got some gall showing up when I told ya to ske-daddle on outta here," Will says, getting riled.

"Excuse my intrusion, Mr. Wigley," Ellie finally manages to speak in her most sincere manner — all the while smoothing her hair, trying to hide her nervousness. "I know you said you're a busy man. Am I interrupting your work?" Without waiting for an answer, she walks up to Will and flashes her big blue eyes, catching him off guard as he stumbles back. Blazing a sweet smile, she holds up a steaming pot as a mouthwatering aroma drifts out. "I wanted to bring you a little surprise, a peace offering you might say, to ask that you forgive my actions earlier. I know it might have been... um... I think you misunderstood my interest in that Indian boy downstairs. I was nervous. I truly wanted to get a good story for the paper." Ellie lowers her head meekly. "I guess I just got carried away with all the excitement... Will." Then she inches her way closer to him. "I really am more interested in your fascinating life out here. And I would love to hear every little detail."

Will is befuddled by Ellie's charming manner. It was always hard for him to resist a handsome young lady. *Surely are my weak spot,* he thinks with a grin, *but whatever she's carrying smells as good as she looks… and I'm starving. Maybe I'll take her apology and her food…and then send her on her way. I ain't sure I can trust her with all the goods laid out here. She might suspect somethin'.*

When Ellie removes the cover and sticks the pot up to his nose, Will's stomach starts to roar, and he nearly faints from the heavenly smells. Unable to resist, Will sticks his fingers inside the pot and pulls out a big hunk of beef, which he immediately slides into his mouth. "Mighty good," he says, licking his fingers. "Well now, maybe I was a bit hasty, thinkin' about sendin' you away in such a big hurry like that." He chuckles with satisfaction. "Jeb, ya need ta get lost now. Me an' the little gal here have some business to attend at, an' you need ta get ta work." He turns and whispers to Ellie. "Jeb here is none too smart. He don't know a thing about women. O' course, I could teach him a thing or two." His eyes drift to her pretty face, and for a moment they get lost in her big blue eyes. He gives her a wink. *Maybe the little lady's had a change of heart,* Will is now pleased with the turn of events. Leaning back in his chair, he boasts, "Women can't seem to help themselves around me. Must be my manliness that 'tracts 'em. Got some real strong appeal, ya see. The ladies get a whiff of it an' I have ta fight 'em off… like a pack o' badgers."

Ellie turns her back to him, trying hard not to laugh. "I'll see if I can control myself around you," Ellie quips, then quickly changes the subject. "How about another taste of my stew, Will? It might even be better than the first." Ellie displays her pearly white teeth, trying not to cringe. She wonders how anyone can find this fool appealing. "Please call me Ella," she coos, "like my closest friends do."

Ellie picks up a big hunk of meat and slides it into his mouth. But before she can pull her fingers out, he takes a lick of them. "I'm not sure what's tastier, you or the beef," he says, smacking his lips." Then he reaches for her hand to give it a nibble, but she quickly pulls it away.

"Let's not get carried away," she says, not quite as sweet this time. Will frowns, watching her. *Something ain't quite right with the little lady*. Will's a real good poker player, and has a knack for sniffing out suspicious behavior. Still unsure of what Ellie is up to, he says suspiciously, "Reckon ya didn't poison me with yer tasty stew, did ya?"

Ellie bats her big blue eyes in alarm. "Why on earth would you ever think that, Will? I guess you must have a wicked sense of humor. Let me give you another taste to assure you." She takes the lid off the pot, and starts feeding him. Thoughts of poisoning him run through her mind, but she needs to stay focused on Hidden Spirit. She can't help but think... *It really sounds appealing... not a bad idea...*

"Never had a momma, miss, so this feels mighty fine." Ellie thoughts jerk back to reality. Will's tongue darts back and forth, as he keeps trying to get a hold of one of her fingers and finally manages to and bites down, making Ellie wince. Having had quite enough of this, she smacks him hard, leaving bright red imprints across his cheek.

Will recoils at the slap, and a rush of anger crosses his face.

"Don't be such a naughty boy, Will," Ellie says angrily. Then catching her tone, she quickly changes it, realizing she might have gone too far. "I do hope I didn't hurt you with my little bitty hands."

Will grunts out a reply. "Naw. Ya didn't hurt me none. Guess I can't help myself around ya, ma'am. Ya bring out the devil in me. Don't even mind ya smackin' my face," he says, with a frown, touching his cheek that still stings. Will stares at the girl and is starting to relax and enjoy himself once again until he remembers all the goods lying around and jumps up. "I'd better get back to work. I'm a mite busy right now, as ya can see. Look at all the food. Gotta real big load the other day and my back is killin' me from liftin' all the sacks. My work here ain't easy, miss... takin' care of the savages."

Ellie's eyes open wide. "That's just what I want to write about. How a fine gentleman like yourself is so caring about the Indians' welfare. I find that so admirable."

Will can't help himself, and lets out a real big snort. He thinks, *this one ain't so smart, after all... if she believes my malarkey.* He grabs her hand and says, "I'm real glad ya come around. Been itchin' for another one of them kisses." With that, Will slides up real close to Ellie, and grins. "So... how's about it?" he says, puckering up. But Ellie is quick, and gives him a shove so hard, he fall right off his seat and topples backwards onto the floor with a loud thump. Clinging to the side of the chair he rubs his head, and hollers. "I dang near busted my noggin. What's the matter with ya? One minute ya wanna be sweet as pie an' the next yer meaner'n a grizzly."

Forcing back a grin, Ellie speaks contritely. "Oopsy-daisy. Did you get hurt? Sometimes, I just don't know my own strength."

Still sputtering, Will says, "Just wanted ta show ya' a bit of affection, is all... 'sides, you're the one getting cozy-like with me. I was just obligin' ya..." Will stops mid-sentence as Jeb comes out of the back room, holding his belly he's laughing so hard. He fumes thinking, *my dang partner is laughing his fool head off while I'm tryin' to get myself off the floor. I oughtta shoot that smirk off his ugly mug.*

Jeb ignores the glare and hustles over and yanks him off the floor. He pulls Will aside, still snickering. "See what ya get for trustin' her? She's mighty handsome, but more trouble'n she's worth. 'Sides, it's time ta get to work. I need a little help back here. I'm sick and tired of bein' the pack mule, movin' all this crap around while yer out here yackin' away with the lady." Suddenly, his nose quivers and lifts involuntarily in the air toward the wondrous aroma. He sees the lid off the pot, rushes over and takes a real big sniff. "Oooh-wee. Smells mighty good," he says, hunkering down closer until the tip of his nose touches the stew.

Will whacks Jeb in the head. "Nothin'd better fall in there, so git yer snout outta the goods."

"You need to share some of that with me, partner," Jeb says, sticking his fingers in the pot, reaching for a tasty bite.

Will smacks his hands. "Show some manners. We got a real fine lady sitting here, so don't go embarrassin' me… an' get back ta work. I got some important stuff to discuss with the little lady."

"Well, it ain't fair, an' I'm awful hungry. So I'm helping myself, whether ya like it or not. Ya been out here stuffing yourself and having a high ol' time. Remember, we split fifty-fifty, right down the middle." He lifts the lid, licks his chops, grabs a big chunk of meat, and starts chomping. "Mighty good, little ma'am." He reaches for another bite, but Will slams the lid down. "Ya can have more when were finished. Now, git."

Jeb glares at Will, then backs off, scratching his head. "Look, I been thinkin'. This one's gotta wolf up her sleeve." He scoots closer and lowers his voice. "Besides, I thought ya told her to get her sweet ass on outta town 'cause she likes them Injuns better'n you. Plus, look at all this here food lying around. You can bet yer ass she 'spects something? Looks like we're having a big ol' Sunday picnic. What if she spills the beans on us? Then, what?"

"I told her this is for the Injuns. Not so sure she's a smart one. Besides, I mightta been a bit hasty before, that's all," Will says, boasting. He looks over at Ellie and gives her a big wink, and turns back to Jeb. "Looks to me like she's had a change of heart, and I'm gettin' ready ta ask her ta come along with me ta Waco."

"Ha! You're dreaming if you think she'll go with ya," Jeb

chokes. "You're not too swift when it comes to the ladies. 'Member that ole bitch, Joanne Risch, back down in Tucker? She cheated ya at poker and stole yer last sawbuck, then tried ta tell ya, it was just for fun."

"Shut up, now," Will shouts, fuming at Jeb. "Take these bags layin' here an' start haulin' 'em out the door."

Will sits down and scoots his chair close to Ellie. Rubbing his chin, he says, "How about it, sweet pie, ya wanna come along with me? I'm a helluva better catch than that ole sissy boy ya was with earlier. You can tell him ya found yerself a real man. Make ya sing like a lark, I will," he says puffing up his chest. "I'll take real good care of ya, too. I'm gonna buy a fancy whorehouse down in Texas with all the trimmings. I'll bring home the bacon and ya'll do the cooking — an everything else." Will gives her a little pinch on her cheeks. "Sounds like a plan," he whispers in her ear. Then he lets his gaze wander down her body.

Ellie's eyes narrow, barely able to contain her fury, and clamps her jaw shut.

Jeb comes back in the door, brushing the flour from his hair and looks over at Will, who's grinning from ear to ear. "See, Jeb. I told ya she'd be itchin' to go with me, didn't I. Yer always arguing with me 'bout the ladies. One o' these days, I'll show ya the ropes."

"I'd like to see that." Jeb says and cracks a laugh. "I'd like to see what kinda advice you'd be givin' me when this little gal up and leaves ya. Ha! I'd rather ya keep yer advice to yerself."

Irritated, Will says, "Shut your trap and git back to work. And leave me alone for a doggone minute." He turns back to Ellie. "He's got a jealous streak, that's all. Pay him no mind."

Tired of working, Jeb eyes the pot of stew, and edges over, ready to sneak another bite when his mouth flies open at the sight of Peale's housekeeper chugging through the door like a smoking freight train. "Damn it! What's *she* doing here?" Jeb chokes. "Will! Take a gander at who's at the door. You ain't gonna believe it."

"I thought you might like some homemade bread to go with Ellie's stew," Mrs. Stover says with a smile. "Made it special... added some extra lard to it. I wanted to bring it over while it's piping hot." She lays the basket on the table and takes a look around the room. Her eyes about pop, seeing all the food on the floor and slowly seethes. Holding back her fury, she smiles at Ellie. "I'd say I've come just in time. Looks like the Indian folks will finally get their rations."

He pulls Will over and lowers his voice. "That ole bat musta been snooping 'round here, too." He points to Ellie. "I think ya been tricked by the little lady, partner. She looks pretty shady ta me."

"Shut up, Jeb," Will says, irritably, as his eyes bulge out at the sight of that housekeeper. "She's barging in here like she owns the place. Wonder what's going 'round here?"

"I'd just bet my last plug nickel she's got something up her sleeve too." Then Will turns to Mrs. Stover, and hollers. "Leave them biscuits right here next to me and then skedaddle. We're a mite busy." He is agog as he watches Mrs. Stover ignore his demand, walks over to Ellie and starts chatting, like he wasn't even around. Will is getting hot under the collar, watching that old biddy out of the corner of his eye. "I know something ain't right. I can feel it in my bones," he says under his breath to Jeb. "I see her looking around the place, trying ta be cagey. I'm gonna see what's going on." He moves closer to Ellie, cocking his head, hoping to hear better.

Looking at Wigley with contempt, Mrs. Stover leans over and whispers to Ellie. "I see the keys on the wall. Do something to get Will's attention, and I'll slip them into my pocket." She squeezes Ellie's hand and slides across the room.

Ellie calls out to Will. "I was just telling Mrs. Stover how you were a crack shot in the military and quick as a whip with your big gun." Will perks up over the compliment, ready to remind Ellie he was a man not to be messed with. But his bravado was short lived as Jeb pokes him hard in the ribs. He points at Mrs. Stover, who spots the keys on the wall, ready to put them in her pocket. Will about trips over himself in his rush to snatch her hand before she can grab hold of the keys. "I've had enough of ya nosing around in my business, old lady. I think yer gonna go in the cellar with that Indian you like so dang much. You two can co-miserate about yer troubles."

A loud noise out back startles Will, and he jumps about a foot in the air. Then he sees a figure darting across the yard, and yanks out his gun. Will runs outside faster than a jackrabbit. He flies across the yard and tackles the girl to the ground. He pulls her hair back and looks into the eyes of the Indian squaw... the one from the hills that nearly shot his head off. She was a bit skinnier and her hair was cut off, but Will would recognize her anywhere. "Gotcha," he says triumphantly. For the moment he has forgotten about Mrs. Stover and Ellie — he is so caught up with the Indian girl. He had dreamed of the day he'd pay her back, but good and now that day has finally arrived. He pulls Morning Star up by her arm, and drags her inside, hollering like he had just won first prize at the fair, "Jeb, take a gander at what the ole fox drug in!"

Jeb runs over to Will. "Whatcha get?" He stops in his tracks, as Will pulls her into the room. "Hell's bells an' kick my balls! Whatcha doing with a squaw? We got enough trouble 'round here, an' last thing we need is more women traipsin' in here — 'specially a squaw, causin' trouble."

Will gloats victoriously. "Got business to attend to... squaw business, so never you mind. I can handle more'n one lady at a time."

Jeb's sputtering, trying to get a word out. Momentarily disconcerted, he scratches his jaw in confusion. Just then, Will whips around… jumps about a foot off the ground, and shouts. "Jeb! Go 'round the side of the house and see what's going on. I heard some glass break. I'm gonna hold on ta the squaw an' the little lady until we find out what's happenin'. I bet her sissy friend is up ta something." Will pulls out his gun, indicating for Morning Star and Ellie to stay put. He gives Mrs. Stover a shove, and says, "An' take this ole' battle-bag with you, an' throw her in the basement."

Mrs. Stover puts up a fuss as Jeb tries to hustle her out the door. She grabs a biscuit on her way and hurls it at him. It lands with a whack against the side of his face, and crumbles in his hair. She yells, "You leave me alone…" but Jeb clamps his hand over her mouth before she can finish her words and drags her out the door.

Will glares at Ellie. "You're gonna be mighty sorry if ya tricked me and I catch yer sissy friend sneaking around, trying ta git to that Injun. I'll plum shoot the whole bunch of ya, right on the spot. Changed my mind about takin' ya with me. That's 'cause I think yer nothin' but a snake in the grass." He looks at Morning Star. "I'm takin' the little squaw with me, instead. Do a might better business with her, anyhows." He grins at Morning Star, as he begins tying her wrists together. "Ya run away from the school, squaw? Yer gonna be in big trouble." He gives her a lick on her cheek, and says, "No need ta fret. They ain't gonna gitcha now. We're gonna have a good time… I'll show you all the ropes… 'bout pleasing a man. From now on, yer gonna be a'pleasing a whole passel o' them. Now this here Ellie… I was gonna be keeping her for my high f'luting customers. But she's too…"

Ellie quickly interrupts. "You're talking a great deal of nonsense, Mr. Wigley." Her heart's thumping painfully against her ribs as she fights off tremors and squeezes her hands together. Looking at Morning Star in alarm, she says, "I… I can't believe you would think I would spy on you... or anything like that. I'm telling you the truth."

Will stomps over and shakes her until her head all but snaps off. He hisses in her ear. "I think you're nothing but a fox all dolled up like one o' them hens. I wondered why ya'd be so nice ta me, cookin' up that grub... better not o' poisoned me, neither." He grabs her chin with a steely grasp, but stops when he hears a loud commotion going on outside as Jeb's yelling. "Ow-cch! Help!"

Momentarily stunned, Will hurries outside to investigate. Out of the corner of his eye he sees Ellie and the squaw take off running out the door. He goes flying after them until he hears Jeb by the side of the house hollering like a stuck pig for help. "Will! There's a flock of somethin' wild and mean trying to get at me," says a quivering Jeb. Will pulls out his gun and fires in the air, hoping to scare off whoever is out there. The horses are nervous and start to rear up and whinny, but before Will had hitched them to the wagon, they bolt and take off running.

Jeb scurries around the corner, limping and bleeding, and carrying on like a nitwit. Will walks over to him, cautious. "What's going on, Jeb? Someone shoot ya?"

"There were a bunch of Indians back there, surroundin' me, an' some little redskin brat 'bout bit the skin right off'n my arm."

"Well, why didn't ya shoot her?"

"I woulda, but I couldn't get at my gun. It's dark as hell back there. I couldn't see my own hand in front of my face, but I heard a lot of racket going on. They were hittin' an' a bitin'... one of 'em about broke my leg. I was lucky ta get outta there alive, I'll tell ya. If I ever getta holda that little squaw that called me a chicken-liver, I'm gonna beat the tar right outta her. She was a young'un, too. I could tell. I don't care what age they are... it's like tangling with a nest o' hornets. Then I heard someone in the bushes rustling around, and decided I'd better git outta there. I'm thinking someone's trying ta bust the Injun outta the cellar. I say, let them have him and that ol' bag. Who cares about them, anyhow? Looked ta me like there was a big ol' flock of buzzards back there, too!"

"Ya couldda shot at something," Will says, furious.

"I ain't gonna git shot over a lousy Injun. I don't give a bat's turd if he lives or dies, or the old lady, either… or any of 'em."

"I don't believe it. You're carrying on about some Injuns and here our horses done took off and left the wagon behind. Blast it, Jeb, you're plain worthless." Will stomps over to Jeb and raises his gun, threatening to shoot.

"Least we got the important stuff," Jeb cries out in alarm. "Let 'em have the food. I'm sick o' loading the crap on the wagon, anyhow, and my arms are bleeding. Let's get on outta this miserable hellhole. I ain't never coming back here neither, no matter what ya offer me. C'mon." He limps over to the wagon and says, "Okay. I'm ready."

"Hold up," Will shouts. "First, I'm gonna go downstairs and blast the Injun. Gonna make sure he's dead this time. Then, we're leaving."

Will runs down to the basement, lantern in hand, and sees a flock of feathers gather in a menacing cloud, with quills poised, ready to strike. He stops in his tracks, abruptly turns around, and, a moment later, he comes back up, looking like he had seen a ghost. "Git moving Jeb, fast, 'fore anyone else comes messing around."

Jeb obliges, and clicks the reins. They go flying down the road with a wagonload of whiskey, rattling and clinking. "Thanks be ta Jesus, Joseph, and Harry… we're outta that place. We're gonna be *rich*!"

Will's entire body is shaking, and reaches back for a bottle, and grips the side of the wagon. He would've toppled over, if he wasn't hanging on so tight. "Hold it up there partner… 'bout lost my whiskey. Slow it down."

Jeb ignores Will as he sways wildly on the buckboard. He isn't slowing down for nothing.

"Yer driving like a crazy man," Will hollers, as he clinks his tooth on the bottle, trying to take a drink. "Slow it down there, partner. Ya gonna kill us, driving like that. Besides, we gotta take it easy on our cargo. Don't wanna break the bottles an' have it all spillin' out."

"Well, if you don't like my driving, you take over, an' I'll have a drink. Need one, anyways, after that fiasco back there. You and yer ladies. They done took off. I told ya in the git-go they was too much work… an' I've had enough of them wild ones. That little looker you was carryin' on about was as bad as them Injuns. Come ta think about it… I thought you were gonna shoot that Injun in the basement. What'd ya do, chicken out? I'd 'a liked ta seen ya tangle with them renegades back there. See how ya'd git outta that tussle. Ha!"

Jeb is having a grand time making fun of Will, whose thoughts were elsewhere. *Just wait till I do the splitting with our loot. I'll be the one laughing then.*

His head was hurting from all the bouncing around, so Will takes another big swig of whiskey. "Oh, sweet Lordy, that hits the spot." Getting mad all over again, he says, "I shoulda lambasted her but good back there, making a fool outta me… an' I wouldda, too, if'n we weren't in such a big hurry. Shouldda shot that squaw too."

Then Jeb hits a great big pothole, and everything goes flying. Will hangs onto his bottle, and screams. "What the Hell…? You just hit a great big hole and knocked a wheel clean out from under us. I told ya ta slow down, but ya don't listen… and now look at the fix were in." Will is furious, and his head feels like it's going to explode. He climbs off the wagon and walks to the rear, where the wheel is lying on the ground, along with half of the whiskey bottles.

Will throws his hat on the ground. "I oughta shoot ya for yer in'continence."

Jeb comes skulking around the wagon. "Continence my ass. I need a drink, real bad. An' you ain't gonna be blaming me. Anyone couldda hit that ole big hole... so shut up 'bout calling me names. Ya tryin' to get fancy on me? What's it mean, anyhow... continence?"

"It means stupid," Will hollers. "Stupid, like you. How do ya like those shit-turds? How many times I gotta tell ya ta slow it down, but ya just kept on drivin' like a bat outta Hell."

"That's 'cause I had ta fight off a pack of Injuns back there... 'sides, you're making me jumpy all the damn time. Being your partner ain't no picnic, neither, ya know, so hand over the bottle."

They begin tussling and arguing over the bottle until Will sees a bright light flickering in the distance, with green orbs, that look like floating lanterns, bobbing down the road. Finally, a roaring flame shot above them, landing practically on top of them. "Damn," Will moans. "Who's it now?" He pulls out his gun, wondering, "What the devil?"

An Indian riding on top of a white buffalo, saunter over. "Have a little problem fellas?"

THE DEVIL IN THE LIGHT

P REACHER JIM IS barely able to sleep. He gets out of bed in the dark and hurries to his study where he paces back and forth, fretting about the school. *I'm surrounded by a bunch of heathens, who surely have put a curse on me. They must be in cahoots with the Devil. No wonder people think I'm going mad.* "Mad, mad, mad," he screeches in dismay. If I am, they're the reason. He stops pacing for a moment. *But what if it's true?* The preacher has been hearing whisperings and gossip about him in town... about his peculiar behavior. *They know nothing of what I have endured in this place*, he thinks angrily.

He ponders the idea of discussing his ills with Doc Brewer. Brewer is a gruff looking fellow who has never attended church — wasn't a believer. But what can you do if you're in need of help? Couldn't be picky. So when he summons Doc Brewer over to his house late one evening, something inexplicable came over him. To his very surprise, he swings the door wide open, jumps around the room, and starts to sing:

> *"Oh doctor, doctor, give me your views.*
>
> *I've got a case of nightmare blues.*
>
> *No remedy's gonna cure my nerves.*
>
> *Gotta case of need'n you."*

Doc Brewer's jaw drops, as he looks in dismay at this bizarre sight.

"So glad you came to see me, doc. My demands are many and my load is heavy. I've been seeing things in the middle of the night. I hear voices, shouting… demanding me to come visit the dark side."

Doc Brewer is immediately concerned as he pulls out his stethoscope, shoves the preacher into a chair, and listens to his heart rate, and then asks about his mental health. "Running the school is over-taxing your body. It's important you rest. If you don't heed my advice you may suffer a nervous collapse or worse. I ask you follow my instructions to the tee…" His words drift off, as he peers dubiously at the preacher.

I can see that Doc Brewer thinks I'm having some sort of mental lapse, he thinks, glaring at the man. Little does he know the cause! So, he bellows out, "It's the Devil haunting me day and night. I've had dreams about him… frightful dreams… dreams of him waiting for me… lurking around every corner. I'm becoming more paranoid by the day and wonder why God is persecuting me. I'm doing His work, preaching His gospel… and yet I feel terribly burdened. He asked me to help the heathens, knowing their evil is overpowering."

"The Devil, you say? How often does He come by?" Doc questions curiously.

"I told you! Every night!"

The doc wrinkles his brows, and says. "I think I have the solution to your problem. Laudanum. Knock you right out. You'll sleep like a log. Get rid of those dreams in a hurry. It so happens I have a bottle with me," he says as he begins to pour a tablespoonful.

Aghast, Preacher Jim knocks the bottle out of his hand, and demands. "What kind of doctor are you? A charlatan perhaps?"

Not waiting for an answer, he hastily shoves Doc Brewer out the door and bids him goodnight.

Good thing I was swift in my actions, he thinks with a crafty smile. *Trying to poison me, he was.*

The preacher continues to pace, cursing his fate, and begins to wail at the top of his lungs. "I can't take it anymore, oh Lord," he says, slamming his fist on the desk in despair. "I'm thinking about killing every last Indian at the school, and closing it for good. You know, dear Lord, I did my best. I truly did." Suddenly, as if a light has gone off in his head, he exclaims jubilantly. "That's it. I now know why you sent me here… to rid the earth of these savages. That's why I've been having these thoughts… so we can lead a better life. I'll tell Opal the good news."

Then another idea begins to take shape. "I know what… I'll meet up with the Devil… give him a few of the Indians. That should get him off my back. I'll tell the heathens they're going home. Ha! Give them a big surprise!" As he hurries home, he mumbles to himself. "These Indians are just as uncivilized now as when they first arrived… impossible to convert. I've tried my darndest to help them, but, like snakes, you can't change their nature. I have seen sinful behavior, dear Lord… squaws holding hands and such. Sinful! I should have ripped them apart. And my biggest regret is that wretched kid, Hidden Spirit… the one I tried to save from the depths of Hell. I've spent nights worrying about him… about his salvation. I even believed he was akin to Job, but, instead, he chose the Devil and eternal damnation. I was so certain it was just a matter of time before he saw the light… but then the ungrateful wretch ran away… made a fool of me!" The preacher screeches, in outrage. "I was so distraught I took my strap and whacked my body, while I prayed for redemption… but all I got for my troubles was pain and bloody gashes." The preacher trembles with rage at the memory, touching the scar on his shoulder.

Then, his mood shifts, as a feeling of excitement overcomes him at the thought of leaving this wretched place behind... for good!

He smiles at the notion — feeling excited for the first time in ages. "Yes, that's it. I'll tell Opal we're moving to a rural community where we can set up a small church... where no heathens will be allowed. I don't want to set my eyes on another one of them... ever again. Then, I'll continue doing God's work. My new church will be a shining beacon on a hill. I'll build it straight up to the sky... closer to the Lord, that He may better hear my sermons. I'll be like Jesus, on the Mount."

As Preacher Jim goes over his plans, he starts to sing, "One little, two little, three little Indians... deedle-dee, deedle-dum. Feeling better by the minute... maybe now my nightmares will end."

He hurries to his house and shakes Opal out of bed. "We're moving," he shouts. "I'm ready for a new start, so get packing. We'll leave in a couple of days. The gossip in town has become unbearable. I can see my work here has been for NOTHING!"

Opal is too stunned to speak, and can only stare at her wild-eyed husband in disbelief as he hustles back out the door, and runs to the school in his slippers and pajamas — hair standing straight up.

Ready to retire for the evening, Mrs. Trimble stumbles down the hallway looking flustered as she hears her name being called. She turns and sees Preacher Jim standing beside a confused Mrs. Burns, who is shouting for her to come. "The preacher has some dastardly news to tell you."

Mrs. Trimble looks at the peaked face of the preacher, wondering if he is ill. "Are you all right, Preacher Jim? Has there been some horrid event that has brought you here so late in the evening? Please tell me how I can help," she gushes in alarm.

"I am here to announce that the school will be closing forthwith… immediately," Preacher Jim states, twisting his hands together. "I've heard from the Lord and I know He has other plans for me. I will send the heathens back home, where they can be reunited with their people and their wanton, shameful behavior. They can commune with the Devil and do their evil dance… hips grinding and churning. I don't give a damn!"

Mrs. Trimble's stomach churns at the news. "I don't believe this!" she manages to say. "What will everyone say? I have devoted my entire being to this work… to turn the children into decent, God-fearing citizens." She puts her hands to her throat, tightening like a vise. "And at your behest, preacher."

"You have done well, Mrs. Trimble. Would've made a good soldier, I'd say, with the highest of praise. But your work here is now finished."

"I could run the school. I know the bones of this place. The children are still wild and… I have… uh… *we* have made such progress. Given a little more time, the children would be just like us. Civilized. Good Christians, who would go out into the world and proclaim victory in the name of the Lord."

Preacher Jim interrupts. "That will do, Mrs. Trimble. My mind is made up. You and Mrs. Burns can commiserate together and discuss your future plans." He looks at the stunned ladies and lets off a snicker. Under his breath he says, "Go fry a fish."

Mrs. Trimble looks at the man with a glint of contempt in her eyes. "You make a mockery of my… *our* work."

Composing himself, he straightens. "How could you say such a thing? God will reward you for your work, I'm certain," he manages to say with a straight face. "Now go back to bed, ladies. Goodnight."

Preacher Jim practically skips out the door. *Feeling better as each minute passes.* He thinks… *this might be a good time to go over my plans."* He hurries over to the barn and readies the horses and wagon.

With that finished, he scurries to his office and waits until all is quiet at the school. A surge of happiness rages through him. He remembers the gift he had been given by Otis Peale, before he left the reservation. Smiling, he opens the closet, drags out the dusty chest he has kept hidden and pulls out a huge war bonnet adorned with eagle feathers that falls to the floor. "Compliments of Chief Bonehead," he hollers. He straps the cumbersome bonnet around his head… prances around the room, while admiring himself, letting off a couple of war whoops, and stifles a laugh. "Wait till they get a load of me," he snickers. Feeling the moment is perfect, he starts to walk out the door, and, remembers the tomahawk in the bottom of the chest, and he turns back, quickly grabs it, and leaves. As he looks up at the moonlight, he says, "Perfect night. Thank you, Lord." Then he hurries over to the girl's dorm, rushes inside, and shimmies down the hallway to the girl's room. He stands at the door for a moment, and listens for any sounds of Mrs. Trimble and Mrs. Burns. Hearing nothing, he tiptoes into the room and plucks the first three girls he encounters from their beds.

"Time to get up, girls. No need to dress. We must hurry. I've got a great big surprise for you," he says, feigning politeness. "Follow me."

The sleepy girls are startled as they are yanked from their beds, and even more so by the sight of the preacher standing inside their room, in the middle of the night. Afraid to question the man, the girls do as they are told and follow him outside, where he hustles them over to the wagon. "We're going to take a little trip, so hop into the wagon, and sit back and enjoy the ride." He jumps into the driver's seat and cracks the whip. The horses take off in a flurry, and race down the road — the sound of hooves pounding, echoing in the night. The girls hang on tightly, faces filled with fear as they bump along inside the wagon.

Preacher Jim lifts his face to the sky, and lets off a howling yip as his war bonnet flutters like a banner, ready for surrender.

The preacher is relentless as he clicks the reins, shouting to the horses, "faster, faster."

A few miles further down the road, the girls look up at the sky, and stare open-mouthed at something resembling a falling star as it barrels down toward the ground. It looks as if the sky is on fire, with bright red streaks trailing behind and something that looks like a searing orange-ish tail. The girls scream in fright and duck down, as the horses screech to a halt. *I fear my nightmare has come true*, Preacher Jim thinks, as his eyes follow the bizarre sight.

The preacher snaps the reins and shouts for the horses to run, beating them with his whip. But they are exhausted and refuse to budge. The more he urges them on, the more they resist. Suddenly, a huge flaring light explodes close by, sending splinters of wood flying in the air. Then, something lands beside him with a tremendous thud and a searing crackle. Preacher Jim is afraid to look in its direction to see who it is. He feels a scorching flame singe his cheeks, his stomach lurches and his teeth chatter uncontrollably. He jumps off the wagon, and cowers — his eyes shut tight, afraid of what or who's out there as he starts to wail. Now he feels something sticky and foul smelling that oozes near his feet. He tries to back away, but a scalding hand grabs his wrist.

"Greetings, Jimmy. You seem a little nervous," the Devil says with a wicked grin. As his eyes assess the preacher, he plucks a feather from his war bonnet. "Well, lookie, what we got here... a white man dressed up as an Indian. Do tell," the Devil says with a smirk. "Are you going on the warpath in that wild get-up?" He flashes his jagged teeth, and grinds them together.

Preacher Jim is too stunned to reply.

"Say, did I catch you at a bad time?"

"Well... uh... no. Actually, I came looking for you. I... uh...

I have a-a g-gift for you." He reaches into the wagon and pulls the three scared girls out. "I brought you a few heathens. You can take them where they belong... with *you*... to the pits of Hell." He shoves them forward. "T-take th-them... instead of me. I don't belong down there," he whines. "I have other plans."

The Devil snarls, sending a huge flame snapping into the air.

Preacher Jim shakes at the sight. "L-look, Mr. D... I did your bidding. I brought you some worthless souls. Just what you're looking for I hear."

The Devil slinks over to the preacher. "Worthless souls, did you say? Whom are you talking about? Not these little Indians, are you? They haven't done anything wrong... they're innocents... but you, my wicked friend... you are far from innocent."

Preacher Jim feels the swish of his tail as it burns his leg. The Devil leans in close. "Where do you think you're gonna end up, preacher man? *The pearly gates of Heaven*? Ha! Up there," he says, pointing with a sharp talon, "are a bunch of fairies... flying all around. Do-gooders. I can't stand them little sissies." All worked up, the Devil stomps his feet and hacks up some spittle. "Hmmm. Sounds like you, Jimmy... thinking you're a do-gooder... hoping that's where you'll end up. Ha!" he snorts. "When Hell freezes over, Jimmy boy. And, I don't see that happening anytime soon. Do you?"

"Do you mean Hell freezing over or me going to ..." Preacher Jim gets on his knees and starts to beg, but the Devil ignores him and continues on. "Some sniveling idiots have the nerve to plead their case. Can you believe it... asking ME for help? It makes me madder than a sex-crazed bandit, and I'd really get fired up. I send my tail swishing and whirling... red-hot sparks flying every which way. Scares the Hell out of them, every time," He shouts with glee. Then He bends his head closer to Preacher Jim, and whispers maliciously. "Then those whiny little bitches would really squeal when I pull out my bullwhip. I'd give those whiny suckers a taste of what's to come. *'No! Please! Oow-wee! That hurts.'* I just holler out, 'SHUT THE CRAP UP!' Works like a charm, every time," the Devil hisses, as drool runs down his chin and his red-hot lips slurps it up, sending a trail of steam into the air. "I must say, preacher man, there's nothing I love more than a cowardly sinner… except… a whole *bunch* of cowardly sinners." He snorts out a ball of slimy snot, which rolls down his face, causing him to convulse with laughter. He swishes his fiery tail back and forth. "But I am disappointed in you. All you do is whine and moan, telling me I made a mistake. I assure you, I don't make mistakes, Jimmy," he says, shoving his fingers into the preacher's chest, leaving searing imprints.

The preacher coerces and tries to bargain. "I beg you to listen to me, Mr. Devil. I've tried to help you… and maybe I could again, if only you'd give me another chance…" He suddenly bursts into tears, sobbing.

The Devil can't stand it anymore. He swings his whip and smacks the preacher across his head. "SHUT THE CRAP UP!"

Preacher Jim moans, his lips trembling. "But I don't want to go with you. I must stay here. They need me…"

"Oh, stop your blubbering. You'll LOVE IT down there. It's summer, all year long… Hot as Hell! Hey, got something to cheer you up. A song just for you… made it up on my way here. So, how's about a dance, preacher man?" Not waiting for an answer, the Devil's hips start to gyrate, pulsing and pushing with bizarre, jerky movements, wheezing as he belts out.

> *"Sold my soul for riches and greed,*
> *Took a little extra to fill my need,*
> *I stuffed all the loot inside my heart,*
> *I twisted and shoved, till it fell apart,*

*Ooooohhhhh! I lost my soul,
In the big black hole."*

"Do you like it, preacher man? Made this song for the greedy bastards hoping to bring their loot with them. They just can't let it go. I tell 'em I've got the perfect place to stash it. You can stash yours there, too, Jimmy boy. I'll keep it safe."

Preacher Jim recoils.

The Devil grins wickedly. "I've got all kinds of fools down there... murderers, liars, and cheaters by the loads... but what I really need is someone crafty, who lies his fool head off... who thinks like me."

Inching his way over, the Devil sniggers and hocks so hard the preacher crosses his fingers, hoping the Devil would keel over... but, no. The Devil clears his throat, sending a chunk of sizzling phlegm flying overhead, landing on the preacher's arm. The preacher squeals out in pain. "That burned a hole right through my sleeve."

The Devil grins. "Don't mean to brag, but they do say, 'I'm a Red-Hot Devil.' You know preacher man, I loooove the stories you tell your holy-rollers. I bet you could tell 'em, the moon's made of cheese and they'd fall to their knees... *'I believe, I believe'...*" He mocks the preacher and waves his hands and swoons. "*Dunk me in the water, and I'll be saved.*" The Devil laughs and starts to wheeze again, but this time nothing comes out. "Quite a scheme you've got going, my friend. I see you got your coffers filled with all that malarkey you give them."

Preacher Jim swears he must be dreaming. In the dim light, he thinks he sees that Indian kid, and shouts out crazily to the Devil. "Get him! That's the lousy Indian that's caused me all this trouble."

The Devil turns, and sees a flash of light, but quickly turns back. A slight tremble echoes in his voice. "It's you that I want,

Jimmy, not him. So, hurry up…" The Devil grabs his arm, and scalds it with His touch.

"This cannot be happening," says Preacher Jim, shaking.

"We'll all go to the land of smoke and fire," the Devil grins, shooting a hot flame into the air.

From out of nowhere a loud noise erupts in the sky, followed by a dazzling light.

Preacher Jim looks up and sees a massive storm brewing as huge plumes of smoke rise in the distance. Every part of his body shakes. He looks around for the Devil, who is nowhere in sight, so he jumps onto the wagon and hurriedly cracks the whip. Wild with fear, the horses refuses to budge as the bright red glow hisses and sizzles as it edges ever closer and smashes into the ground, knocking Preacher Jim off balance and hurls him into the dirt. He crawls as fast as he can under the wagon, and hides beneath.

As the deafening noise grows louder, the preacher screams in fright. He covers his ears and shuts his eyes — too afraid to look up. "My life is doomed," he moans, petrified, and starts to pray. "Help me Lord. I'm going to die." Panting in ragged gulps, sweat drips from his face, as he pulls off the war bonnet and struggles to be free, but the feathers are tangled with his sweat and hair. "I'm going to die right here amongst the Devil and the heathens," he sobs. He slithers further under the wagon as the whirling noise starts to go crazy with high-pitched groans and screeching wails. Then, poof — the whirling stops. He sees a dim light begin to glow from the center, pulsing like a heartbeat. Preacher Jim crawls out from under the wagon and clears the fog from his eyes and blinks. As his eyes open wider, he jumps back at the sight before him. *It's the face of Jesus.* Nearly fainting as he clutches his head-dress, he staggers backwards. "Save me, sweet Jesus, save me," he cries out. "I have seen the Devil! He was going to take me to Hell. Help me!"

A thunderous voice booms out. "What have you done to the children?"

"I tried my best to save the wretched souls, dear Lord. I wanted them to believe. I truly did, but…" The preacher falters, falls to his knees, and looks toward the sky.

The vision vanishes in a whirling cloud and darkness descends around him like a heavy blanket.

Preacher Jim is in utter shock, and cries out. "Please don't blame me." He climbs inside the wagon and sits, holding his head in his hand, weeping. "I truly tried my best, dear Lord, but I can see that I have failed the ones I was sent to help. Can you ever forgive the wrongs that I have done?" He closes his eyes, and starts to wail, "Oh, dear God, why are you doing this to me? I wanted the children to be saved in your name. I almost drowned one of them to get her to submit," he shouts, drenched in tears of self-pity. Then he smacks himself with the reins — hard, on his shoulder, and startles the horses. They rear up, and take off in a gallop toward the school. "Maybe my methods were too harsh… but I meant well," he yells, running his hands through his hair.

Arriving at the school, he hops off the wagon, panting, and stands staring at the building, ideas swirling in his head. Slowly, he bends down on his knees, lights a piece of kindling, and waits for it to catch. Then, he begins to pray. "I can no longer bear my guilt, dear Lord. I am off to the land of tomorrow!" Once he hears the wood begin to sizzle, he tosses it through the window, shattering the glass, and waits a moment. Coming from somewhere, he isn't sure where, he hears a low voice.

"HOT-DIGGETY-DOG! Burning the skins. A man after my own heart! COME ON, JIMMY, LET'S GO…" The preacher's heart stops. He covers his ears to drown out the voice, and slowly looks around. The Devil is nowhere to be seen.

He looks back at the flames, which are starting to sputter and crackle, licking the wood. The fire is ablaze now, with dark smoke curling up through the haze. The preacher begins to howl like a wolf and dance an awkward war dance around in a circle, feathered headdress fluttering in the shadows. He chants, "kawewe, kawewe," as he hops on one foot, then the other, while the distant beat of drums pounds in his ears. "I now know it was about my vanity. Vanity, vanity, vanity. All of this was about my vanity… about *me*. What can I do?" he shrieks, raising his hands with increasing frenzy. "Father, forgive me, for the sin I have committed in your name against the Indians. The injustices I did caused great harm. I can see that now. The children will be set free… and, for my sins, I will burn in Hell. BURN BABY, BURN!" he screams, dancing in unrestrained lunacy. Then through the smoke, he sees something unusual and covers his eyes from the glaring fire. "Unbelievable," he shrieks as a white buffalo ambles out of the smoldering fire — its nostrils flaring. The buffalo stops at the edge of the flames, and snorts. The sight of an Indian riding atop the buffalo wearing a war bonnet is too much, and he falls backwards in shock. Clutching his tomahawk, the preacher lets off another war-whoop, and raises his hands to the sky. He shouts out in the language of the Sioux, "nablu, nablu," then starts dancing again, wildly. With his hands raised to the sky, he proclaims:

"I'm going to the promised land,

Promised land, promised land.

And here's what I have to say…" His words dwindle off.

A tattered Mrs. Trimble and Mrs. Burns come running out of the burning building, screaming. Their faces are blackened with smoke as they gather the children close. Everyone holds firmly onto one another as they watch the unbelievable spectacle.

They shout in alarm, "No… *No!*" But Preacher Jim ignores them as he dances faster, flames licking hungrily at his legs. He seems not to notice as he dances further into the flames. His words begin to fade out as he disappears into the roaring fire, which is now burning out of control. A brilliant display of fire sends sparks high into the night sky, scorching the air. The flames fizzle into a misty vapor with a dying hiss. The children stifle a scream. Mrs. Trimble and Mrs. Burns fall to the ground, praying for the preacher's soul.

*

White Cloud awakens with a start, and sits up. A low rumbling noise is heard overhead, shaking the house. Sensing the urgency, he jumps out of bed and shakes White Tail awake. "My dear, something is about to happen. I can feel it in my bones. You must get up and waken the others. It is in the wind — and it is power-ful. I can hear the words drifting around me, like a warm breeze, lifting the heaviness from our people. It says we must hurry."

As White Cloud and White Tail race to arouse the neighbors, a jagged bolt of lightning shoots from the sky — illuminating each house along the way. "Hurry, you must get up," they cry. "Something is about to happen." Then, another bolt of lightning flickers in the darkness. The families scramble from their beds... some still in their nightshirts, run to tell the others. Soon, a large crowd begins to gather as more and more people, some still half-asleep, hurry down the road. Shouts of wonder and confusion fill the night air. "What is it?" a few question. "What's going on?" a few more ask. Throngs of people from every direction are heading toward town, looking at the inexplicable vision in the sky. One woman asks White Cloud, "Why are we being summoned from our beds in the middle of the night?"

"Something unexplainable is about to happen. I can hear it in the wind. I feel it is wonderful," White Cloud says, speaking in an orderly manner, trying to control his joy, but his heart is beating wildly.

A steady buzz filters among the gathering crowd. The people are filled with a mixture of fear and excitement.

In the distance the large crowd sees a bright circular cloud in the sky overhead. Everyone stands transfixed as it floats around in dizzying circles. After a while, the undulating shape stops whirling, and softly sinks to the ground. A misty veil unfolds and a shimmering crescent-shaped staircase emerges from the clouds, gleaming as bright as the stars leading upwards and beyond the clouds.

The people stop talking as they look up in wonder. You could hear a feather drop, as the people stare at the night sky. Breaking the silence, the faint sound of neighing horses echoes from off in the distance and high above... seemingly through the thread of stars. Then the distinct sound of whinnying reverberates from the haze. A moment later, a herd of wild mustangs appear on the shimmering staircase, hooves clacking... their eyes as bright as Venus. As if to announce their arrival, they stop, paw at the air, and let off a shrill, hair-raising whinny. Then they begin to prance, delicately. Like prima ballerinas, they lift their legs gracefully, up and down in rhythm, as they slowly descend the crescent-shaped stairs. Each step glistens and glitters, flashing a surreal light from their hooves — as their scruffy manes flow like petals in the mist. The air is charged with electricity, and the people can feel the hair rise at the back of their necks. Mystical energy abounds as silvery-toned laughter echoes in the darkness. Like tinkling bells, it wafts through the crowd on the soft night breeze — filling the nocturnal sky. As they look on in awe, a few women pinch one another to make certain they are not dreaming. Holding their breath, they wait to see what will happen next. But the mist thickens and blurs their vision.

From out of the haze, a roaring light explodes, shooting celestial showers of azure sparks and crystalline flecks into the air. Everyone gasps, then cry out in disbelief. "Is it our children? Please, Great Spirit, please let it be true." They all stand reverently, watching, as the outline of faces start to take shape and glow in the shroud of light. They see children — their children, clinging to the manes of the prancing horses. One by one, they nobly descend the glittering steps as a hush falls over the crowd… silent as a shadow. They hold their breath, too afraid to speak, lest the vision will vanish. Like a royal warrior, Hidden Spirit sits proudly atop Ghost Dancer. The crowd goes wild with exultation at the triumphant return of their young hero.

The people run in circles, crying, "Our children have come home!" Overwhelmed and delirious with joy the people race to find their loved ones. The children wave excitedly as they scramble off the prancing horses and rush to their families, calling, "Momma! Papa!"

A fresh breath of life flows into the gathering crowd, bringing with it a most precious gift, their children — their hope for the future.

"We rode the horses through the air," one of the girls says to her parents, giggling. "It was like I had wings… it was magical, and now to be home is all we dreamed of."

The mustangs stamp their hooves, as if signaling to one another it is time to go. Within seconds, they form a single line, and in unison, begin to prance their way back up the mystical steps, whinnying as they go. Their tails flung high, swishing in harmony, they fade into the light, and into the mist, and into the enchantment of the unknown.

Mothers and fathers, aunts and uncles, all fall to their knees and give thanks to the Great Spirit. "Our most precious gift you gave us… is back." Their hearts beat with joy, grateful for this reunion.

*

A glimmer of light sparkles among the trees, setting the pines and cottonwoods ablaze with vibrant colors.

Hidden Spirit sees a golden orb with fragile yellow wings drifting along in the tips of the trees. He runs as fast as he can into the cottonwoods, following the yellow orb. It lands in a tree high above, where he sees two eyes beaming from the center. His attention is averted and his breath catches in his throat as he watches a small black crow fly overhead and land on a spindly branch of a nearby tree — a sparkly blue stone held tight in its beak. The crow seems to wink at him. He looks at the bird and smiles, noticing its silver wing. *This is the crow I shot when I was young*, he recalls, wincing. At first uncertain of what to think, or do, he says to the bird, "I was so foolish long ago. I pray you realize my ignorance. I'm sorry, little crow, for causing you pain." The silver winged crow lightly pecks his hand and drops the sparkly blue stone into his palm. "This is Chasing Rabbit's," he cries out in delight. "How did you find her? Did you see my sister?" Just then he feels a gentle whoosh of wings brush against his cheek. It's the golden orb... fluttering so close, it's within inches of his nose. He looks into the center— and into eyes that sparkle as brightly as the blue stone. "Chasing Rabbit, my beautiful sister. You are full of mischief in the otherworld as well, I see." Looking at her causes his heart to expand so wide it could encompass her entire being. Her wings flutter furiously as she hovers near. "My brother. You are the light of our people. I love you. Please give this stone to Little Moon. Tell her to keep it with her always."

The little black crow with the silver wing, flies down from the branch, and lands nearby. The golden orb zips over, fluttering its wings and slips onto the back of the crow. Amidst caws and goodbyes, he hears, "toksa akhe," as they zoom off into the night.

"I will see you again, my sister," Hidden Spirit says, waving at the fading light. He looks up at the stars, engrossed in the wonders of all, before setting off in search of Broken Feather. "I know he must be near," he says to himself with a smile. Thinking he sees something in the distance, he hurries his steps. As he approaches the edge of town, he sees a silky silhouette, lingering. "Broken Feather? Is it you?"

"Yes, Mi-thakoza. I have come back for just a short time. You have become what I have always hoped for… a symbol for our people… a symbol of strength and bravery. You are not only a fierce warrior, you are far more than that… you have the wakhan magic. You will lead our people far and you will help them survive. They now must live beside the whites, but they must not lose the Lakota way. Tell our people to stay away from the firewater the white eyes have brought to our lands. It is poison… a slow death."

Hidden Spirit nods his head as he looks with pride at his grandfather. He, who has mastered the mystery that he has long sought to find, is near. It's as if the world has shifted beneath his feet, as he sways ever so slightly—filling him with the sacredness of life.

Hidden Spirit is jolted back to reality, as he hears the nearby sound of a muffled cry and notice Brown Hare is sitting alone among the trees, weeping for her daughter that did not make it home.

Broken Feather glides over to her, as Hidden Spirit follows. "My dear one," Broken Feather says in his deep baritone voice. "Come sit. I can see your heart is troubled with pain. Let me help you see your daughter, who is waiting near." Broken Feather holds out his hands. "Please look inside."

Brown Hare wipes her eyes and looks at the outline of the magnificent warrior before her. She glances over at Hidden Spirit, who smiles and encourages her to peer inside his palms. "Look into the vast beyond," he whispers. Her eyes widen in shock. It is her beloved Otter, standing in front of her. Before she can stop herself, she reaches out to touch the wispy form and cries out, "Otter!"

"Mama, oh, Mama." Otter's form floats overs and drapes her arms around her mother's neck. "I hear your weeping throughout the heavens, Mama. Your cries make me sad and fill my heart with pain."

Brown Hare wipes her tears, and reaches out again, running her fingers across the form that wavers and sways to her touch. "Otter, my dear sweet daughter," she says, choked with emotion. "I miss you so much I can barely stand it. My body aches when I remember the day you left to that school. When they took you away, I thought I would die, and now... I wish I *would* die... so I could be with you. I grieve so for your death. I want to hold you in my arms, and give you your favorite treat, like I always used to do. But, now... it's too late." Her cries grow ever more mournful.

"Oh, Mama, I miss you, too," Otter whispers as she blows a misty kiss onto her forehead. "I love you more than the stars in the sky. But your tears hold me back. Please don't cry so. For I have seen the dancing flowers and watched the clouds that soar high in the sky. I have glimpsed into another world that awaits my arrival. It looks wonderful. My heart is filled with love for you, but I belong elsewhere now. It is time. Shil nzhoo, Mama." Another kiss floats over and lights on Brown Hare's cheek. "Bye, bye," whispers Otter. Then, in a blink, she disappears into the night sky, leaving a scarlet trail in her wake.

"I will take care of your Otter," Broken Feather says to the forlorn woman. "She will be with the ancients, who will help guide her in the afterlife. She will always be with you, but in a different place other than here."

Brown Hare nods her head and a faint smile appears on her face as she bows to the enigmatic warrior. "I thank you for coming back."

Broken Feather touches her face then glides along the shimmering currents and stops near the crowd of excited people, where everyone is talking all at the same time about the young one's unexpected return. Heart singing, Broken Feather moves through the crowd and stands next to his son, White Cloud, whose eyes are filled with tears. *I see he is thinking of his beloved Chasing Rabbit. I want to comfort him and tell him that all will be as it once was, but that will not be.* White Cloud strokes the silky feathers of his old war bonnet... remembering the time he wore the headdress to Washington, to talk to the Great White Father about stopping the roaring boxes from cutting through their lands. But men with forked tongues came with big lies and put an end to our talks. *I see now it was only for show.*

The elders are now gathering, talking in hushed tones. A large bonfire is burning and the drums begin to play. Broken Feather drifts closer to listen. *It has been too long since there has been joy among our people. To see our people dance and celebrate is a welcoming sight,* thinks Broken Feather. *How I miss the music.* He hovers near the drummers as the deep rhythmic sounds flood his soul with visions of his youth. As the enchanting sounds flow through him, he sways to the rhythmic beat.

Hidden Spirit looks over and sees Otis Peale walking through the crowd holding hands with Mrs. Stover. He looks years younger. *Not at all like the same man I encountered just a short time ago.* Peale is smiling and appears humble as he talks to the people, apologizing to the mothers and fathers whose children he had sent away. *I imagine he will be at that quite a while.* Peale waves at him among the crowd. Hidden Spirit waves back and walks over to thank Mrs. Stover for her help. "You are a very brave woman." Mrs. Stover beams at the compliment from the handsome young man.

Hidden Spirit is looking for Broken Feather, who is somewhere in the crowd. Hurrying so he wouldn't miss him, he finds him standing near the elders, who are assembled around a fire. He can see that Broken Feather's form is fading. *Soon he will be a mere wisp of smoke, he thinks as he notices one of the elders bring out* a beautifully carved pipe. Plenty Feathers lights the pipe and then passes it around the fire to the other men, who are talking solemnly as they inhale the musty fragrance with pleasure. Bending down, Broken Feather puts his arms around Plenty Feathers, whose eyes light up to see his dear old friend. "I will soon join you in the otherworld, mi-thakhola," Plenty Feathers says, eyes brimming with tears. "My time is nearing the end. The pain and suffering of our people has been hard to witness. My bones are weary from the strain."

"When your time comes, I will be waiting for you. Leaves Dancing will be delighted to see you again."

Plenty Feathers nods… grateful for his friend that lingers near.

Broken Feather observes another scene from behind the elders. They are the ancients from the otherworld who are lured down by the music… warriors and holy men of long ago. They silently look on and begin to chant in their ancient language. Broken Feather recognizes the famous leaders, hailed by the Lakota people for their bravery and wisdom. He spots Red Cloud, Sitting Bull, Crazy Horse, and Black Elk. These braves fought valiantly to protect the people of the plains, their lands and their way of life. They will need more like them in the future. Hidden Spirit will be among them.

Broken Feather looks over to the edge of the gathering, and smiles. He sees, Geronimo, Chief Joseph, and Black Kettle from other tribes, and he glides over to welcome them. He hugs his friend, Chief Joseph, the man whose famous words, "*From where the sun now stands, I will fight no more forever,*" echo in the universe and stirs my heart whenever I hear it… it stings my eyes with tears. He had a big heart for his people. Then the sound of the drums intensify… beating and pulsating, enticing the ancient warriors to dance, as the hypnotic music celebrates their lives.

Broken Feather smiles sadly, remembering Wounded Knee. *It wasn't just a war… it was a blood bath for our people, who were peacefully gathered to pray. The ancients have said that the white man shall not inhabit the earth for long. Their greed for Mother Earth's riches will be their undoing. I cannot understand how the wasicus would willingly destroy that which gives life. I grieve for our Mother Earth.*

When Hidden Spirit catches up with Broken Feather, they walk away from the group of people. Broken Feather asks him to come near. "Mi-thakoza. I have words that must be told. You tell the wasicus, the white eyes… for thousands of years we have roamed upon the earth, hunting the buffalo, living contentedly, keeping to our traditions… but no more. Our sacred Black Hills and lands being are being destroyed."

"Some of the wacisus might ask, 'why is this old fool, who is dead, lecturing us about our land?' Many know nothing of what I speak, or have any interest in our plight. They think it's just about a bunch of Indians who lost a war long ago. You must set them straight, mi-thakoza. They may not believe you if you tell them, but you must try."

"I will do as you ask, Grandfather."

"The ancients have said, that if you bond with nature, she will teach you much. Trust the silent voices when you walk through the forests. Your inner spirit will guide you. And remember… when you gaze upon her beauty, your dreams will flourish and your worries will vanish. Mother Earth, Giver of Life. That is how we connect with our Creator. The Great Mystery sees all. If you need any comfort or are troubled, look between the darkness and among the shadows, and know the Creator is near. As you sit in solitude, whisper what is in your heart. When your mind is quiet, the answer comes. We call our God, Great Spirit. You can call your God whatever you choose."

"You must tell the white man my words, Mi-thakoza. It is important."

And in a blink, Broken Feather disappears into the misty shadows.

"I will see you in the next story…" Broken Feather's words float down from the ethers.

Wakan takan kici un… May the Great Spirit bless you.

About the Author

Patricia Reynolds lives in Washington State with her partner of many years, along with their adopted family of dogs and cats. She has a passion for nature and the environment, and a soft spot for animals of all kinds. Patricia's primary goal in writing this book was to lend a voice to the forgotten. Her young adult fantasy series: *Keeper of the Souls*, is based on a few actual events.